CHRIS GRABENSTEIN

A YEARLING BOOK

Text copyright © 2013 by Chris Grabenstein
Nickelodeon and all related titles and logos are trademarks of Viacom International Inc.
Escape from Mr. Lemoncello's Library cover art by Arsonal Design/Nickelodeon
Brand and Design · Photography by Art Streiber
Logo design by Luciana Feldchtein/Nickelodeon Brand and Design

Visit us on the Web! rhcbooks.com

Educators and librarians, for a variety of teaching tools, visit us at RHTeachersLibrarians.com

Library of Congress Cataloging-in-Publication Data is available upon request.

ISBN 978-0-525-58037-9 (MTI pbk.)

Printed in the United States of America

10 9 8 7 6 5 4 3 2 1

First Yearling Edition 2014

For the late Jeanette P. Myers,
and all the other librarians who help us find
whatever we're looking for

This is how Kyle Keeley got grounded for a week.

First he took a shortcut through his mother's favorite rosebush.

Yes, the thorns hurt, but having crashed through the brambles and trampled a few petunias, he had a five-second jump on his oldest brother, Mike.

Both Kyle and his big brother knew exactly where to find what they needed to win the game: inside the house!

Kyle had already found the pinecone to complete his "outdoors" round. And he was pretty sure Mike had snagged his "yellow flower." Hey, it was June. Dandelions were everywhere.

"Give it up, Kyle!" shouted Mike as the brothers dashed up the driveway. "You don't stand a chance."

Mike zoomed past Kyle and headed for the front door, wiping out Kyle's temporary lead.

Of course he did.

Seventeen-year-old Mike Keeley was a total jock, a high school superstar. Football, basketball, baseball. If it had a ball, Mike Keeley was good at it.

Kyle, who was twelve, wasn't the star of anything.

Kyle's other brother, Curtis, who was fifteen, was still trapped over in the neighbor's yard, dealing with their dog. Curtis was the smartest Keeley. But for *his* "outdoors" round, he had pulled the always unfortunate Your Neighbor's Dog's Toy card. Any "dog" card was basically the same as a Lose a Turn.

As for why the three Keeley brothers were running around their neighborhood on a Sunday afternoon like crazed lunatics, grabbing all sorts of wacky stuff, well, it was their mother's fault.

She was the one who had suggested, "If you boys are bored, play a board game!"

So Kyle had gone down into the basement and dug up one of his all-time favorites: Mr. Lemoncello's Indoor-Outdoor Scavenger Hunt. It had been a huge hit for Mr. Lemoncello, the master game maker. Kyle and his brothers had played it so much when they were younger, Mrs. Keeley wrote to Mr. Lemoncello's company for a refresher pack of clue cards. The new cards listed all sorts of different bizarro stuff you needed to find, like "an adult's droopy underpants," "one dirty dish," and "a rotten banana peel."

(At the end of the game, the losers had to put everything back exactly where the items had been found. It was an official rule, printed inside the top of the box, and made winning the game that much more important!)

While Curtis was stranded next door, trying to talk the neighbor's Doberman, Twinky, out of his favorite tug toy, Kyle and Mike were both searching for the same two items, because for the final round, all the players were given the same Riddle Card.

That day's riddle, even though it was a card Kyle had never seen before, had been extra easy.

FIND TWO COINS FROM 1982 THAT ADD UP TO THIRTY CENTS AND ONE OF THEM CANNOT BE A NICKEL.

Duh. The answer was a quarter and a nickel because the riddle said only *one* of them couldn't be a nickel.

So to win, Kyle had to find a 1982 quarter *and* a 1982 nickel.

Also easy.

Their dad kept an apple cider jug filled with loose change down in his basement workshop.

That's why Kyle and Mike were racing to get there first.

Mike bolted through the front door.

Kyle grinned.

He loved playing games against his big brothers. As the youngest, it was just about the only chance he ever got to beat them fair and square. Board games leveled the playing field. You needed a good roll of the dice, a lucky draw of the cards, and some smarts, but if things went your way and you gave it your all, anyone could win.

Especially today, since Mike had blown his lead by choosing the standard route down to the basement. He'd go through the front door, tear to the back of the house, bound down the steps, and then run to their dad's workshop.

Kyle, on the other hand, would take a shortcut.

He hopped over a couple of boxy shrubs and kicked open the low-to-the-ground casement window. He heard something crackle when his tennis shoe hit the windowpane, but he couldn't worry about it. He had to beat his big brother.

He crawled through the narrow opening, dropped to the floor, and scrabbled over to the workbench, where he found the jug, dumped out the coins, and started sifting through the sea of pennies, nickels, dimes, and quarters.

Score!

Kyle quickly uncovered a 1982 nickel. He tucked it into his shirt pocket and sent pennies, nickels, and dimes skidding across the floor as he concentrated on quarters. 2010. 2003. 1986.

"Come on, come on," he muttered.

The workshop door swung open.

"What the . . . ?" Mike was surprised to see that Kyle had beaten him to the coin jar.

Mike fell to his knees and started searching for his own

coins just as Kyle shouted, "Got it!" and plucked a 1982 quarter out of the pile.

"What about the nickel?" demanded Mike.

Kyle pulled it out of his shirt pocket.

"You went through the window?" said a voice from outside.

It was Curtis. Kneeling in the flower beds.

"Yeah," said Kyle.

"I was going to do that. The shortest distance between two points is a straight line."

"I can't believe you won!" moaned Mike, who wasn't used to losing *anything*.

"Well," said Kyle, standing up and strutting a little, "believe it, brother. Because now you two *losers* have to put all the junk back."

"I am *not* taking this back to Twinky!" said Curtis. He held up a very slimy, knotted rope.

"Oh, yes you are," said Kyle. "Because you *lost*. Oh sure, you *thought* about using the window. . . ."

"Um, Kyle?" mumbled Curtis. "You might want to shut up. . . ."

"What? C'mon, Curtis. Don't be such a sore loser. Just because I was the one who took the shortcut and kicked open the window and—"

"You did this, Kyle?"

A new face appeared in the window.

Their dad's.

"Heh, heh, heh," chuckled Mike behind Kyle.

"You broke the glass?" Their father sounded ticked off. "Well, guess who's going to pay to have this window replaced."

That's why Kyle Keeley had fifty cents deducted from his allowance for the rest of the year.

And got grounded for a week.

2

Halfway across town, Dr. Yanina Zinchenko, the world-famous librarian, was walking briskly through the cavernous building that was only days away from its gala grand opening.

Alexandriaville's new public library had been under construction for five years. All work had been done with the utmost secrecy under the tightest possible security. One crew did the exterior renovations on what had once been the small Ohio city's most magnificent building, the Gold Leaf Bank. Other crews—carpenters, masons, electricians, and plumbers—worked on the interior.

No single construction crew stayed on the job longer than six weeks.

No crew knew what any of the other crews had done (or would be doing).

And when all those crews were finished, several

super-secret covert crews (highly paid workers who would deny ever having been near the library, Alexandriaville, *or* the state of Ohio) stealthily applied the final touches.

Dr. Zinchenko had supervised the construction project for her employer—a very eccentric (some would say loony) billionaire. Only she knew all the marvels and wonders the incredible new library would hold (and hide) within its walls.

Dr. Zinchenko was a tall woman with blazing-red hair. She wore an expensive, custom-tailored business suit, jazzy high-heeled shoes, a Bluetooth earpiece, and glasses with thick red frames.

Heels clicking on the marble floor, fingers tapping on the glass of her very advanced tablet computer, Dr. Zinchenko strode past the control center's red door, under an arch, and into the breathtakingly large circular reading room beneath the library's three-story-tall rotunda.

The bank building, which provided the shell for the new library, had been built in 1931. With towering Corinthian columns, an arched entryway, lots of fancy trim, and a mammoth shimmering gold dome, the building looked like it belonged next door to the triumphant memorials in Washington, D.C.—not on this small Ohio town's quaint streets.

Dr. Zinchenko paused to stare up at the library's most stunning visual effect: the Wonder Dome. Ten wedge-shaped, high-definition video screens—as brilliant as those in Times Square—lined the underbelly of the dome like so many orange slices. Each screen could operate independently or as part of a spectacular whole. The Wonder Dome could become the constellations of the night sky; a flight through the clouds that made viewers below sense that the whole building had somehow lifted off the ground; or, in Dewey decimal mode, ten sections depicting vibrant and constantly changing images associated with each category in the library cataloging system.

"I have the final numbers for the fourth sector of the Wonder Dome in Dewey mode," Dr. Zinchenko said into her Bluetooth earpiece. "364 point 1092." She carefully over-enunciated each word to make certain the video artist knew what specific numbers should occasionally drift across the fourth wedge amid the swirling social-sciences montage featuring a floating judge's gavel, a tumbling teacher's apple, and a gentle snowfall of holiday icons. "The numbers, however, should not appear until eleven a.m. Sunday. Is that clear?"

"Yes, Dr. Zinchenko," replied the tinny voice in her ear.

Next Dr. Zinchenko studied the holographic statues projected into black crepe-lined recesses cut into the massive stone piers that supported the arched windows from which the Wonder Dome rose.

"Why are Shakespeare and Dickens still here? They're not on the list for opening night."

"Sorry," replied the library's director of holographic imagery, who was also on the conference call. "I'll fix it."

"Thank you."

Exiting the rotunda, the librarian entered the Children's Room.

It was dim, with only a few work lights glowing, but Dr. Zinchenko had memorized the layout of the miniature tables and was able to march, without bumping her shins, to the Story Corner for a final check on her recently installed geese.

The flock of six audio-animatronic goslings—fluffy robots with ping-pongish eyeballs (created for the new library by imagineers who used to work at Disney World)—stood perched atop an angled bookcase in the corner. Mother Goose, in her bonnet and granny glasses, was frozen in the center.

"This is librarian One," said Dr. Zinchenko, loud enough for the microphones hidden in the ceiling to pick up her voice. "Initiate story-time sequence."

The geese sprang to mechanical life.

"Nursery rhyme."

The geese honked out "Baa-Baa Black Sheep" in six-part harmony.

"Treasure Island?"

The birds yo-ho-ho'ed their way through "Fifteen Men on a Dead Man's Chest."

Dr. Zinchenko clapped her hands. The rollicking geese stopped singing and swaying.

"One more," she said. Squinting, she saw a book sitting on a nearby table. *"Walter the Farting Dog."*

The six geese spun around and farted, their tail feathers flipping up in sync with the noisy blasts.

"Excellent. End story time."

The geese slumped back into their sleep mode. Dr. Zinchenko made one more tick on her computer tablet. Her final punch list was growing shorter and shorter, which was a very good thing. The library's grand opening was set for Friday night. Dr. Z and her army of associates had only a few days left to smooth out any kinks in the library's complex operating system.

Suddenly, Dr. Zinchenko heard a low, rumbling growl.

Turning around, she was eyeball to icy-blue eyeball with a very rare white tiger.

Dr. Zinchenko sighed and touched her Bluetooth earpiece.

"Ms. G? This is Dr. Z. What is our white Bengal tiger doing in the children's department? . . . I see. Apparently, there was a slight misunderstanding. We do not want him permanently positioned near *The Jungle Book*. Check the call number. 599 point 757. . . . Right. He should be in Zoology. . . . Yes, please. Right away. Thank you, Ms. G."

And like a vanishing mirage, the tiger disappeared.

3

Of course, even though he was grounded, Kyle Keeley still had to go to school.

"Mike, Curtis, Kyle, time to wake up!" his mother called from down in the kitchen.

Kyle plopped his feet on the floor, rubbed his eyes, and sleepily looked around his room.

The computer handed down from his brother Curtis was sitting on the desk that used to belong to his other brother, Mike. The rug on the floor, with its Cincinnati Reds logo, had also been Mike's when *he* was twelve years old. The books lined up in his bookcase had been lined up on Mike's and Curtis's shelves, except for the ones Kyle got each year for Christmas from his grandmother. He still hadn't read last year's addition.

Kyle wasn't big on books.

Unless they were the instruction manual or hint guide to a video game. He had a Sony PlayStation set up in the family room. It wasn't the high-def, Blu-ray PS3. It was the one Santa had brought Mike maybe four years earlier. (Mike kept the brand-new Blu-ray model locked up in his bedroom.)

But still, clunker that it was, the four-year-old gaming console in the family room worked.

Except this week.

Well, it *worked,* but Kyle's dad had taken away his TV and computer privileges, so unless he just wanted to hear the hard drive hum, there was really no point in firing up the PlayStation until the next Sunday, when his sentence ended.

"When you're grounded in this house," his father had said, "you're *grounded.*"

If Kyle needed a computer for homework during this last week of school, he could use his mom's, the one in the kitchen.

His mom had no games on her computer.

Okay, she had Diner Dash, but that didn't really count.

Being grounded in the Keeley household meant you couldn't do anything except, as his dad put it, "think about what you did that caused you to be grounded."

Kyle knew what he had done: He'd broken a window.

But hey—I also beat my big brothers!

*   *   *

"Good morning, Kyle," his mom said when he hit the kitchen. She was sitting at her computer desk, sipping coffee and tapping keys. "Grab a Toaster Tart for breakfast."

Curtis and Mike were already in the kitchen, chowing down on the last of the good Toaster Tarts—the frosted cupcake swirls. They'd left Kyle the unfrosted brown sugar cinnamon. The ones that tasted like the box they came in.

"New library opens Friday, just in time for summer vacation," Kyle's mom mumbled, reading her computer screen. "Been twelve years since they tore down the old one. Listen to this, boys: Dr. Yanina Zinchenko, the new public library's head librarian, promises that 'patrons will be surprised' by what they find inside."

"Really?" said Kyle, who always liked a good surprise. "I wonder what they'll have in there."

"Um, books maybe?" said Mike. "It's a *library*, Kyle."

"Still," said Curtis, "I can't wait to get my new library card!"

"Because you're a nerd," said Mike.

"I prefer the term 'geek,'" said Curtis.

"Well, I gotta go," said Kyle, grabbing his backpack. "Don't want to miss the bus."

He hurried out the door. What Kyle really didn't want to miss were his friends. A lot of them had Sony PSPs and Nintendo 3DSs.

Loaded with lots and lots of games!

* * *

Kyle fist-bumped and knuckle-knocked his way up the bus aisle to his usual seat. Almost everybody wanted to say "Hey" to him, except, of course, Sierra Russell.

Like always, Sierra, who was also a seventh grader, was sitting in the back of the bus, her nose buried in a book—probably one of those about girls who lived in tiny homes on the prairie or something.

Ever since her parents divorced and her dad moved out of town, Sierra Russell had been incredibly quiet and spent all her free time reading.

"Nice shirt," said Akimi Hughes as Kyle slid into the seat beside her.

"Thanks. It used to be Mike's."

"Doesn't matter. It's still cool."

Akimi's mother was Asian, her dad Irish. She had very long jet-black hair, extremely blue eyes, and a ton of freckles.

"What're you playing?" Kyle asked, because Akimi was frantically working the controls on her PSP 3000.

"Squirrel Squad," said Akimi.

"One of Mr. Lemoncello's best," said Kyle, who had the same game on his PlayStation.

The one he couldn't play with for a week.

"You need a hand?"

"Nah."

"Watch out for the beehives. . . ."

"I know about the beehives, Kyle."

"I'm just saying . . ."

15

"Yes!"

"What?"

"I cleared level six! Finally."

"Awesome." Kyle did not mention that he was up to level twenty-seven. Akimi was his best friend. Friends don't gloat to friends.

"When I shot the squirrels at the falcons," said Akimi, "the pilots parachuted. If a squirrel bit the pilot in the butt, I got a fifty-point bonus."

Yes, in Mr. Lemoncello's catapulting critters game, there were all sorts of wacky jokes. The falcons weren't birds; they were F-16 Falcon Fighter Jets. And the squirrels? They were nuts. Totally bonkers. With swirly whirlpool eyes. They flew through the air jabbering gibberish. They bit butts.

This was one of the main reasons why Kyle thought everything that came out of Mr. Lemoncello's Imagination Factory—board games, puzzles, video games—was amazingly awesome. For Mr. Lemoncello, a game just wasn't a game if it wasn't a little goofy around the edges.

"So, did you pick up the bonus code?" asked Kyle.

"Huh?"

"In the freeze-frame there."

Akimi studied the screen.

"Turn it over."

Akimi did.

"See that number tucked into the corner? Type that in the next time the home screen asks you for your password."

"Why? What happens?"

"You'll see."

Akimi slugged him in the arm. "What?"

"Well, don't be surprised if you start flinging *flaming* squirrels on level seven."

"Get. Out!"

"Try it. You'll see."

"I will. This afternoon. So, did you write your extra-credit essay?"

"Huh? What essay?"

"Um, the one that's due today. About the new public library?"

"Refresh my memory."

Akimi sighed. "Because the old library was torn down twelve years ago, the twelve twelve-year-olds who write the best essays on 'Why I'm Excited About the New Public Library' will get to go to the library lock-in this Friday night."

"Huh?"

"The winners will spend the night in the new library before anybody else even gets to see the place!"

"Is this like that movie *Night at the Museum*? Will the books come alive and chase people around and junk?"

"No. But there will probably be free movies, and food, and prizes, and *games*."

All of a sudden, Kyle was interested.

4

"So, exactly what kind of games are we talking about?"

"I don't know," said Akimi. "Fun book stuff, I guess."

"And do you think this new library will have equally new computers?"

"Definitely."

"Wi-Fi?"

"Probably."

Kyle nodded slowly. "And this all takes place Friday night?"

"Yep."

"Akimi, I think you just discovered a way for me to shorten my most recent groundation."

"Your what?"

"My game-deprived parental punishment."

Kyle figured being locked in a library with computers

on Friday night would be better than being stuck at home without any gaming gear at all.

"Can I borrow a pen and a sheet of paper?"

"What? You're going to write your essay now? On the bus?"

"Better late than never."

"They're due in homeroom, Kyle. First thing."

"Fine. I'll keep it brief."

Akimi shook her head and handed Kyle a notebook and a pen. The bus bounced over a speed bump into the school driveway.

He would need to make his essay really, really short.

He was hoping the twelve winners would be randomly pulled out of a hat or something and, like the lottery people always said in their TV commercials, you just had to "be in it to win it."

Meanwhile, in another part of town, Charles Chiltington was sitting in his father's library, working with the college student who'd been hired to help him polish up his extra-credit essay.

He was dressed in his typical school uniform: khaki slacks, blue blazer, button-down shirt, and tastefully striped tie. He was the only student at Alexandriaville Middle School who dressed that way.

"What's a big word for 'library'?" Charles asked his tutor. "Teachers love big words."

" 'Book repository.' "

"Bigger, please."

"Um, 'athenaeum.' "

"Perfect! It's such a weird word, they'll have to look it up."

Charles made the change, saved the file, and sent the document off to the printer.

"Your dad sure reads a lot," said his ELA tutor, admiring the leather-bound books lining the walls of Mr. Chiltington's home library.

"Knowledge is power," said Charles. "It's one of our fundamental family philosophies."

Another was *We eat losers for breakfast.*

Kyle and Akimi climbed off the bus and headed into the school.

"You know," said Akimi, "my dad told me the library people had like a bazillion different architects doing drawings and blueprints that they couldn't share with each other."

"How come?"

"To keep everything super secret. My dad and his firm did the front door and that was it."

The second they stepped into Mrs. Cameron's classroom for homeroom period, Miguel Fernandez shouted, "Hey, Kyle! Check it out, bro." He held up a clear plastic binder maybe two inches thick. "I totally aced my essay, man!"

"The library dealio?"

"Yeah! I put in pictures and charts, plus a whole section about the Ancient Library of Alexandria, Egypt, since this is *Alexandria*ville, Ohio!"

"Cool," said Kyle.

Miguel Fernandez was super enthusiastic about everything. He was also president of the school's Library Aide Society. "Hey, Kyle—you know what they say about libraries?"

"Uh, not really."

"They have something for every chapter of your life!"

While Kyle groaned, the second bell rang.

"All right, everybody," said Mrs. Dana Cameron, Kyle's homeroom teacher. "Time to turn in your extra-credit essays." She started walking up and down the rows of desks. "The judges will be meeting in the faculty lounge this morning to make the preliminary cut. . . ."

Crap, thought Kyle. There were *judges.* This was not going to be a bingo-ball drawing like the lottery.

"Mr. Keeley?" The teacher hovered over his desk. "Did you write an essay?"

"Yeah. Sort of."

"I'm sorry. I don't understand. Either you wrote an essay or you didn't."

Kyle halfheartedly handed her his hastily scribbled sheet of paper.

And unfortunately, Mrs. Cameron read it. Out loud.

" 'Balloons. There might be balloons.' "

The classroom erupted with laughter.

Until Mrs. Cameron did that tilt-down-her-glasses-and-glare-over-them thing she did to terrify everybody into total silence.

"This is your essay, Kyle?"

"Yes, ma'am. We were supposed to write why we're excited about the grand opening and, well, balloons are always my favorite part."

"I see," said Mrs. Cameron. "You know, Kyle, your brother Curtis wrote excellent essays when he was in my class."

"Yes, Mrs. Cameron," mumbled Kyle.

Mrs. Cameron sighed contentedly. "Please give him my regards."

"Yes, ma'am."

Mrs. Cameron moved on to the next desk. Miguel eagerly handed her his thick booklet.

"Very well done, Miguel."

"Thank you, Mrs. Cameron!"

Kyle heard an odd noise out in the parking lot. A puttering, clunking, clanking sound.

"Oh, my," said Mrs. Cameron, "I wonder if that's *him*!"

She hurried to the window and pulled up the blinds. All the kids in the classroom followed her.

And then they saw it.

Out in the visitor parking lot. A car that looked like a giant red boot on wheels. It had a strip of notched black boot sole for its bumper. Thick shoelaces crisscrossed their way up from the windshield to the top of a ten-foot-tall boot collar.

"It looks just like the red boot from that game," said Miguel. "Family Frenzy."

Kyle nodded. Family Frenzy was Mr. Lemoncello's first and probably most famous game. The red boot was one of ten tokens you could pick to move around the board.

A tall, gangly man stepped out of the boot car.

"It's Mr. Lemoncello!" gasped Kyle, his heart racing. "What's *he* doing here?"

"It was just announced," said Mrs. Cameron. "This evening, Mr. Luigi Lemoncello himself will be the final judge."

"Of what?"

"Your library essays."

5

Eating lunch in the cafeteria, Kyle stared at his wilted fish sticks, wishing he could pull a magic Take Another Turn card out of thin air.

"I blew it," he mumbled.

"Yep," Akimi agreed. "You basically did."

"Can you imagine how awesome that new library's gonna be if Mr. Lemoncello and his Imagination Factory guys had anything to do with it?"

"Yes. I can. And I'm kind of hoping I get to see it, too. After all, I wrote a real essay, not one sentence about balloons."

"Thanks. Rub it in."

Akimi eased up a little. "Hey, Kyle—when you're playing a game like Sorry and you get bumped back three spaces, do you usually quit?"

"No. If I get bumped, I play harder because I know I

need to find a way to get back those three spaces *and* pull ahead of the pack."

"Hey, guys!" Miguel Fernandez carried his tray over to join Kyle and Akimi.

He was being followed by a kid with spiky hair and glasses the size of welders' goggles.

"You two know Andrew Peckleman, right?"

"Hey," said Kyle and Akimi.

"Hello."

"Andrew is one of my top library aides," said Miguel.

"Cool," said Akimi.

"Mrs. Yunghans, the librarian, just confirmed that Mr. Lemoncello is the top-secret benefactor who donated all the money to build the new public library. Five hundred million dollars!"

"She heard it on NPR," added Peckleman, who more or less talked through his nose. "So we did some primary source research on Mr. Lemoncello and his connection to Alexandriaville."

"What'd you find out?" asked Kyle.

"First off," said Miguel, "he was born here."

"He had nine brothers and sisters," added Andrew.

"All of 'em crammed into a tiny apartment with only one bathroom over in Little Italy," said Miguel.

"And," said Peckleman, sounding like he wanted to one-up Miguel, "he *loved* the old public library down on Market Street. He used to go there when he was a kid and needed a quiet place to think and doodle his ideas."

"And get this," said Miguel eagerly. "Mrs. Tobin, the librarian back then, took an interest in little Luigi, even though he was just, you know, a kid like us. She kept the library open late some nights and let him borrow junk from her desk or her purse—thimbles and thumbtacks and glue bottles, even red Barbie doll boots—stuff he used for game pieces so he could map out his first ideas on a library table. Then . . ."

Andrew jumped in. "Then Mrs. Tobin took Mr. Lemoncello's sketch for Family Frenzy home to her husband, who ran a print shop. They signed some papers, created a company, and within a couple of years they were all millionaires."

But Miguel had the last word: "Now, of course, Mr. Lemoncello is a bazillionaire!"

"What are you four nerds so excited about?" said Haley Daley as she waltzed past with the gaggle of popular girls in her royal court. Haley was the princess of the seventh grade. Blond hair, blue eyes, blazingly bright smile. She looked like a walking toothpaste commercial.

"We're pumped about Mr. Lemoncello!" said Miguel.

"And the new library!" said Andrew.

"And," said Kyle melodramatically, "just seeing you, Haley."

"You are *so* immature. Come on, girls." Haley and her friends flounced away to the "cool kids" table.

"Check it out," said Akimi, gesturing toward the

cafeteria's food line, where Charles Chiltington was balancing two trays: his own and one for Mrs. Cameron.

"I'm so glad you have lunchroom duty today, Mrs. Cameron," Kyle heard Chiltington say. "If you don't mind, I have a few questions about how conventions within genres—such as poetry, drama, or essays—can affect meaning."

"Well, Charles, I'd be happy to discuss that with you."

"Thank you, Mrs. Cameron. And, may I say, that sweater certainly complements your eye color."

"What a suck-up," mumbled Akimi. "Chiltington's trying to use his weaselly charm to make sure Mrs. C sends his essay up the line to Mr. Lemoncello."

"Don't worry," said Kyle. "Mrs. Cameron isn't the final judge. Mr. Lemoncello is. And since he's a genius, he will definitely pick the essays you guys all wrote."

"Undoubtedly," said Peckleman.

"Thanks, Kyle," said Miguel.

"I just wish you could win with us," said Akimi.

"Well, maybe I can. Like you said, this is just a Move Back Three Spaces card. A Take a Walk on the Boardwalk when someone else owns it. It's a chute in Chutes and Ladders. A detour to the Molasses Swamp in Candy Land!"

"Yo, Kyle," said Miguel. "Exactly how many board games have you played?"

"Enough to know that you don't ever quit until

27

somebody else actually wins." He picked up his lunch and headed for the dirty-tray window.

Akimi called after him. "Where are you going?"

"I have the rest of lunch and all of study hall to work on a new essay."

"But Mrs. Cameron won't take it."

"Maybe. But I've got to roll the dice one more time. Maybe I'll get lucky."

"I hope so," said Akimi.

"Me too! See you guys on the bus!"

6

Working on his library essay like he'd never worked on any essay in his whole essay-writing life, Kyle crafted a killer thesis sentence that compared libraries to his favorite games.

"Using a library can make learning about anything (and everything) fun," he wrote. "When you're in a library, researching a topic, you're on a scavenger hunt, looking for clues and prizes in books instead of your attic or back-yard."

He put in points and sub-points.

He wrapped everything up with a tidy conclusion.

He even checked his spelling (twice).

But Akimi had been right.

"I'm sorry, Kyle," Mrs. Cameron said when he handed her his new paper at the end of the day. "This is very good and I am impressed by your extra effort. However, the deadline was this morning. Rules are rules. The same as they are in all the board games you mentioned in your essay."

She'd basically handed Kyle a Go Back Five Hundred Spaces card.

But Kyle refused to give up.

He remembered how his mother had written to Mr. Lemoncello's Imagination Factory when he and his brothers needed a fresh set of clue cards for the Indoor-Outdoor Scavenger Hunt.

Maybe he could send his essay directly to Mr. Lemoncello via email.

Maybe, if the game maker wasn't judging the essays until later that night, Kyle still had a shot. A long shot, but, hey, sometimes the long ones were the only shots you got.

The second he hit home he sat down at his mother's kitchen computer. He attached his essay file to a "high priority" email addressed to Mr. Lemoncello at the Imagination Factory.

"What are you doing, Kyle?" his mom asked when she came into the room and found him typing on her computer.

"Some extra-credit homework."

"Extra credit? School's out at the end of the week."

"So?"

"You're not playing my Diner Dash game, are you?"

"No, Mom. It's an essay. About Mr. Lemoncello's amazing new library downtown."

30

"Oh. Sounds interesting. I heard on the radio that there's going to be a gala grand opening reception this Friday night at the Parker House Hotel, right across the street from the old bank building. I mean, the *new* library."

Kyle typed in a P.S. to his email: "I hope at the party on Friday you have balloons."

He hit send.

"Who did you send your essay to?" his mother asked. "Your teacher?"

"No. Mr. Lemoncello himself. It took some digging, but I found his email address on his game company's website."

"Really? I'm impressed." His mom rubbed his hair. "You know, this morning, I said to your dad: 'Kyle can be just as smart as Curtis and just as focused as Mike—*when* he puts his mind to it.'"

Kyle smiled. "Thanks, Mom."

But his smile quickly disappeared when a *BONG!* alerted him to an incoming email.

From Mr. Lemoncello.

It was an auto-response form letter.

Dear Lemoncello Game Lover:

This is a no-reply mailbox. Your message did not go through. Do not try to resend it or you'll just hear another *BONG!* But thank you for playing our games.

7

Heading back to school on Tuesday, Kyle knew he had to put on a brave face.

He smiled as he walked with his class toward the auditorium for a special early-morning assembly. The one where Mr. Luigi L. Lemoncello himself would announce the winners of the Library Lock-In Essay Contest.

"I hope he picked yours," Kyle whispered to Akimi.

"Thanks. I do, too. But the lock-in won't be as much fun without you."

"Well, when it's over, and the library is officially open, you can take me on a tour."

"That's exactly what I'm going to do! *If* I win."

"If you don't, I'm sending a flaming squirrel after Mrs. Cameron."

For this assembly, the seventh graders, most of whom were twelve years old, were told to sit in the front rows, close to the stage. That made Kyle feel a little better. At least he'd get a chance to see Mr. Lemoncello up close and personal.

But his hero wasn't even onstage.

Just the principal; the school librarian, Mrs. Yunghans; and a redheaded woman in high-heeled shoes who Kyle didn't recognize. She sat up straight, like someone had slipped a yardstick down the back of her bright red business suit. Her glasses were bright red, too.

"That's Dr. Yanina Zinchenko!" gushed Miguel Fernandez, who was sitting on Kyle's right.

"Who's she?" asked Akimi, seated to Kyle's left.

"Just the most famous librarian in the whole wide world!"

"All right, boys and girls," said the principal at the podium. "Settle down. Quiet, please. It is my great honor to introduce the head librarian for the new Alexandriaville public library, Dr. Yanina Zinchenko."

Everybody clapped. The tall lady in the red outfit strode to the microphone.

"Good morning."

Her voice was breathy with just a hint of a Russian accent.

"Twelve years ago, this town lost its one and only public library when it was torn down to make room for an elevated parking garage. Back then, many said the Internet had rendered the 'old-fashioned' library obsolete, that a new parking garage would attract shoppers to the boutiques and dress shops near the old bank building. But the library's demolition also meant that those of you who are now twelve years old have lived your entire lives *without* a public library."

She looked down at the front rows.

"This is why, to kick off our summer reading program, twelve twelve-year-olds will be selected to be the very first to explore the wonders awaiting inside Mr. Lemoncello's extraordinary new library. You will, of course, need your parents' permission. We have slips for you to take home. You will also need a sleeping bag, a toothbrush, and, if you please, a change of clothes."

She smiled mysteriously.

"You might consider packing *two* pairs of underwear."

Oh-kay, thought Kyle. *That's bizarre.* Did the librarian really think seventh graders weren't toilet trained?

"There will be movies, food, fun, games, and prizes. Also, each of our twelve winners will receive a five-hundred-dollar gift card good toward the purchase of Lemoncello games and gizmos."

Oh, man. Five hundred bucks' worth of free games and gear? Kyle sank a little lower in his seat. The next time someone gave him an extra-credit essay assignment, he'd turn it in *early*!

"And now, here to announce our winners, the man behind the new library, the master gamester himself—Mr. Luigi Lemoncello!"

Dr. Zinchenko gestured to her left.

The whole auditorium swung their heads.

People were clapping and whistling and cheering.

But nobody came onstage.

The applause petered out.

And then, on the opposite side of the stage, Kyle heard a very peculiar sound.

It was a cross between a burp and the squeak from a squeeze toy.

8

Over on the side of the stage, a shoe that looked like a peeled-open banana appeared from behind a curtain.

When it landed, the shoe burp-squeaked.

As a second banana shoe burp-squeaked onto the floor, Kyle looked up and there he was—Mr. Lemoncello! He had loose and floppy limbs and was dressed in a three-piece black suit with a bright red tie. His black broad-brimmed hat was cocked at a crooked angle atop his curly white hair. Kyle was so close he could see a sly twinkle sparkling in Mr. Lemoncello's coal-black eyes.

Treading very carefully, Mr. Lemoncello walked toward the podium. The burp-squeaks in his shoes seemed to change pitch depending on how hard he landed on his heels. He added a couple of little jig steps, a quick hop and a stutter-step skip, and yes—his shoes were squeaking out a song.

"Pop Goes the Weasel."

On the *Pop!* Mr. Lemoncello popped behind the podium.

The crowd went wild.

Mr. Lemoncello politely bowed and said, very softly, "Tank you. Tank you. *Grazie. Grazie.*"

He bent forward so his mouth was maybe an inch away from the microphone.

"*Buon giorno,* boise and-uh girls-a." He spoke very timidly, very slowly. "Tees ees how my-uh momma and my-uh poppa teach-uh me to speak-eh de English."

He wiggled his ears. Straightened his back.

"But then," he said in a crisp, clear voice, "I went to the Alexandriaville Public Library, where a wonderful librarian named Mrs. Gail Tobin helped me learn how to speak like this: 'If two witches were watching two watches, which witch would watch which watch?' I can also speak while upside down and underwater, but not today because I just had this suit dry-cleaned and do *not* want to get it wet."

Mr. Lemoncello bounced across the stage like a happy grasshopper.

"Now then, children, if I may call you that—which I must because I have not yet memorized all of your names, even though I *am* working on it—what do you think is the most amazingly incredible thing you'll find inside your wondrous new library, besides, of course, all the knowledge you need to do anything and everything you ever want or need to do?"

No one said anything. They were too mesmerized by Mr. Lemoncello's rat-a-tat words.

"Would it be: A) robots silently whizzing their way through the library, restocking the shelves, B) the Electronic Learning Center, with three dozen plasma-screen TVs all connected to flight simulators and educational video games, or C) the Wonder Dome? Lined with ten giant video screens, it can make the whole building feel like a rocket ship blasting off into outer space!"

"The game room!" someone shouted.

"The robots!"

"The video dome!"

Mr. Lemoncello raced back to the podium and made a buzzing noise into the microphone.

"Sorry. The correct answer is—and not just because of Winn-Dixie—D) all of the above!"

The crowd went wild.

Mr. Lemoncello whirled around to face his head librarian.

"Dr. Zinchenko? Will you kindly help me pass out our first twelve library cards?"

It was time to announce the essay contest winners.

Dr. Zinchenko placed a stack of twelve shiny cards on the podium in front of Mr. Lemoncello.

"Please," he said, "as I call your name, come join me onstage. Miguel Fernandez."

"Yes!" Miguel jumped up out of his seat.

"Akimi Hughes."

"Whoo-hoo."

Kyle was thrilled to see his two friends be the first ones called to the stage.

"Andrew Peckleman, Bridgette Wadge, Sierra Russell, Yasmeen Smith-Snyder."

Yasmeen squealed when her name was called.

"Sean Keegan, Haley Daley, Rose Vermette, and Kayla Corson."

Ten kids, all the same age as Kyle, were up onstage with his idol, Mr. Lemoncello. He was not. Only two more chances.

As if reading his mind, Mr. Lemoncello said, "Only two more," and tapped a pair of library cards on the podium. "Charles Chiltington."

"Gosh, really?" He dashed up to the podium and started pumping Mr. Lemoncello's hand. "Thank you, sir. This is such an honor. Truly. I mean that."

"Thank you, Charles. May I have my hand back? I need it to flip over this final card."

"Of course, sir. But I cannot wait to spend the night in your library, or, as I like to call it, your athenaeum. Because, as I said in my essay, when you open a book, you open your mind!"

Finally, Charles the brownnoser let go of Mr. Lemoncello's hand and went over to line up with the other winners.

"And last but not least," said Mr. Lemoncello, "Kyle Keeley."

Kyle could not believe his ears. He thought he was dreaming.

But then Akimi started waving for him to come on up!

Dazed, Kyle made his way up the steps to join the others onstage. Mr. Lemoncello handed Kyle a library card. His name and the number twelve were printed on the front. Two book covers—*I Love You, Stinky Face* and *The Napping House*—were on the back.

"Let's all pose for a picture, please," said the principal.

When everybody moved into position for the photographer, Kyle found himself standing *right next to* Mr. Lemoncello.

He swallowed hard. "I'm a big fan, sir," he said, his voice kind of shaky.

"Why, thank you. And remind me—you are?"

"I'm Kyle, sir. Kyle Keeley."

"Ah, yes. The boy who proved what I've always known to be true: The game is never over till it's over. *BONG!*"

9

Kyle couldn't wait to tell his family the good news.

"I won the essay contest!" He showed them his shiny new library card.

"Congratulations!" said his mom.

"Way to go!" said his dad.

His brothers, Curtis and Mike, were more interested in Kyle's other card: his five-hundred-dollar Lemoncello gift card.

"It's good for twelve months," said Kyle.

"But you need to use it *now*," said Mike. "We need to go to the store tonight so you can buy me Mr. Lemoncello's Kooky-Wacky Hockey."

"I can't."

"Why not?"

"I have to show my library card at the store to cash it in."

"And?"

"Um, I'm grounded, remember?"

"You know, Kyle," said his dad, looking at his mother, who nodded, "since you worked extra hard and did such a bang-up job on your essay, I think we might consider suspending your punishment."

"Really?"

"Really."

Kyle's mom and dad smiled at him.

The way they smiled whenever Mike won a football game or Curtis won the science fair.

After supper, all five Keeleys piled into the family van and headed off to the local toy store.

"Lemoncello's hockey game is awesome," said Mike as they drove to the store. "Especially when the penguins play the polar bears."

"I'm hoping to find a classic board game," mused Curtis. "Mr. Lemoncello's Bewilderingly Baffling Bibliomania."

"Is that about the Bible?" asked their dad from behind the wheel.

"Not exactly," said Curtis, "although the Bible, especially a rare Gutenberg edition, may be one of the treasures you must find and collect, because the object of the game is to collect rare and valuable books by—"

"The penguins in Kooky-Wacky Hockey aren't from Pittsburgh like in the NHL," said Mike, cutting off Curtis.

"They're from Antarctica. And the polar bears? They're from Alaska."

Kyle had decided to divvy up his gift card five ways. To give everybody—including his mom and dad—one hundred dollars to play with.

As soon as they entered the toy store, the family split up, cruising the aisles with their own shopping carts. His mom was going to upgrade to Mr. Lemoncello's Restaurant Rush. His dad was looking for one of Mr. Lemoncello's complicated What If? historical games: What If the Romans Had Won the American Civil War?

Kyle hung with Curtis and Mike for a while. Being the one with the gift card made him feel like he was suddenly *their* big brother.

Mike quickly found his PlayStation hockey game and Curtis was in geek heaven when he finally found Bibliomania.

"They only have one left!" he gushed, tearing off the cellophane shrink-wrap and prying open the lid. He sat down right in the middle of the store and unfolded the game board on his lap. "You see, you start under the rotunda in this circular reading room. Then you go upstairs and enter each of these ten chambers, where you have to answer a question about a book. . . ."

"Um, I think I hear Mom calling me," said Kyle. "She must need the gift card. Enjoy!"

And Kyle took off.

"The store will close in fifteen minutes," announced a voice from the ceiling speakers.

Kyle flew up and down the aisles and grabbed a couple of board games he didn't own yet, including Mr. Lemoncello's Absolutely Incredible Iron Horse—a game where you build your own transcontinental railroad, complete with locomotive game pieces that actually puff steam.

As Kyle was doing some quick math to see if he'd spent his one hundred dollars, Charles Chiltington rolled up the aisle with a cart crammed full with *five* hundred dollars' worth of loot. Games stacked on top of games were practically spilling over the sides. Mr. Lemoncello's Phenomenal Picture Word Puzzler, one of Kyle's favorites, was teetering on the top.

"Hello, Keeley," said Chiltington with a smirk. He looked down at the three games sitting in the bottom of Kyle's shopping cart. "Just getting started?"

"No. I shared my gift card with my family."

"Really? Well, that was a mistake, wasn't it?"

Kyle was about to answer when Chiltington said, "So long. See you on Friday." Kyle wasn't 100 percent sure but Charles might've also muttered, "Loser."

Since the store was about to close, Kyle headed toward the checkout lanes. When he passed the customer service department, he saw Haley Daley.

"No," Kyle heard Haley say in a hushed tone to the clerk working the Returns window. "I do not want to return these items for *store credit*. I would prefer cash."

Kyle finally found his family, showed the cashier his library card, and paid for everything with a single swipe of his gift card.

"You know, Kyle," said his dad as the family walked across the parking lot, "your mother and I are extremely proud of you. Writing a good essay isn't easy."

"Maybe you'll be an author someday," added his mom. "Then you could write books that'll be on the shelves of the new library."

"Thanks, little brother," said Curtis, practically hugging his Bibliomania box.

"Yeah," said Mike. "This was awesome. Way to win one for the team!"

"Best 'family game night' ever," joked their dad.

Kyle was enjoying his rare moment of glory, playing Santa Claus for his whole family. As the week dragged on, Friday night and the library lock-in started to remind Kyle of Christmas, too: It felt like they would never come.

Then, finally, they did.

10

"Now this is what I call a party," said Kyle's mother as she helped herself to a bacon-wrapped shrimp from a tray being carried by a waiter in a tuxedo.

Kyle and his parents were in the crowded ballroom of the Parker House Hotel for the Lemoncello Library's Gala Grand Opening Reception. The Parker House was located right across the street from the old Gold Leaf Bank building and the cluster of office buildings, craft shops, clothing stores, and restaurants called Old Town.

"I'm going to see if I can find Akimi," Kyle said to his mom and dad.

"Give her our congratulations!" said his mom.

"We're proud of *her,* too," added his dad.

Kyle made his way through the glittering sea of dressed-up adults.

Even though his parents had put on fancy clothes for

the reception, Kyle was wearing "something comfortable to go exploring in," as instructed by the Lock-In Guide he'd received on Wednesday. He'd packed a sleeping bag and a small suitcase with a change of clothes, toiletries, and yes, as requested, an extra pair of underpants.

Kyle saw Sierra Russell all alone in a corner near a clump of curtains. It didn't look like her mother had come to the party with her. Sierra, of course, had her nose buried in a book. Kyle shook his head. The girl was about to spend the night in a building filled with books and she was skipping all the free food and pop so she could read? That was just nutty.

Haley Daley, wearing a sparkly blouse, was posing for a wall of photographers who wanted to snap her picture. Her mother was at the party, too. While the cameras were focused on Haley's smile, Mrs. Daley wrapped up a couple of chicken kebabs in a napkin and slipped them inside her purse.

Now Kyle saw Charles Chiltington. Poor guy must not have read the memo about comfortable clothes. He was still wearing his khakis and blazer, just like his dad. Kyle figured the Chiltington family must own like three hundred pairs of pleated tan pants.

"Hey, Kyle!" Akimi waved at him from near a fake shrub curled to look like a Silly Straw.

"Hey," said Kyle.

"Did you remember to bring your library card?"

"Yep." Kyle pulled it out of his pocket.

"Huh," said Akimi. "I got different books on the back of mine. *One Fish Two Fish Red Fish Blue Fish* by Dr. Seuss and *Nine Stories* by J. D. Salinger."

"Guess they're like baseball cards," said Kyle. "They're all different."

"Hey, you guys!" Miguel Fernandez, more excited than usual (which was saying something), pushed through the mob to join them. "Did you try these puffy cheesy things?"

"Nah," said Kyle. "I'm sticking to food I recognize."

"The 'puffy cheesy things' are called fromage tartlets," said Andrew Peckleman, coming over to join the group.

"Huh," said Kyle. "Good to know."

A waiter passed by with a tray loaded down with small boxes of Mr. Lemoncello's Anagraham Cracker cookies.

"Oh, I love these," said Kyle, taking a box off the platter and opening it. "The cookies are in the shapes of letters. You have to see how many words you can spell."

"Cool," said Miguel, snagging a fistful of cookies out of Kyle's box. "Taste good, too!"

"Yep," said Kyle. "But the more you eat, the harder the game gets."

"Why?" asked Andrew Peckleman.

"Less letters," said Akimi, snatching two "B's" and a "Q" and wolfing them down. "Mmm. Barbecue-flavored."

Kyle spread out the remaining cookies in his palm: U N F E H A V. He grinned as he deciphered an easy anagram. "HAVE FUN. Sweet."

"Ladies and gentlemen? Boys and girls?" Dr. Zinchenko,

dressed in a bright red suit, strode to the center of the ball-room. "May I have your attention, please? Mr. Lemoncello will be arriving shortly to say a few brief words. After that, I will escort the twelve essay contest winners across the street to the library. Therefore, children, might I suggest that you eat up? Food and drink are not permitted any-where in the library except in the Book Nook Café, conve-niently located on the first floor."

Miguel grabbed a few more puffy cheesy things.

When she thought no one was looking, Mrs. Daley shoved a napkined bundle of bacon-wrapped shrimp into her purse.

Akimi nibbled a couple of chocolate-dipped pretzel sticks.

"Aren't you gonna grab some more grub?" she said to Kyle.

"No thanks. I only like food I can play with."

"One last thing," announced Dr. Zinchenko. "We, of course, want our winners to have fun tonight. However, I must insist that each of you respect my number one rule: Be gentle. With each other and, most especially, the library's books and exhibits. Can you do that for me?"

"Yes!" shouted all the winners except Charles Chil-tington. He said, "Indubitably."

"Good thing the library has dictionaries," muttered Akimi. "Half the time, it's the only way to figure out what Chiltington's saying."

Suddenly, all the adults in the ballroom started clapping.

Mr. Lemoncello, looking like a beanpole wearing a tail-coat and a tiny birthday-party fireman's hat, strode into the room through a side door.

"Thank you, thank you," he said, stretching the elastic band to raise his kid-sized hat and tipping it toward the crowd. "You are too kind."

When he let go of the hat, it snapped back with a sharp *THWACK!*

"As Dr. Zinchenko informed you, I'd like to say a few brief words. Here they are: 'short,' 'memorandum,' and 'underpants.' And let us pause to remember the immortal words of Dr. Seuss: 'The more that you read, the more things you will know. The more that you learn, the more places you'll go.' Children? . . ."

Mr. Lemoncello flourished his arm toward the ball-room doors.

"It's time to go across the street. Your amazingly spectacular new public library awaits!"

11

Eager to see what was inside the new library, the twelve essay contest winners quickly gathered behind Dr. Zinchenko.

"This way, children," said the head librarian. "Follow me."

The crowd cheered as they marched out of the ballroom, all toting their sleeping bags and suitcases. There was more cheering (plus some hooting and hollering) when they reached the hotel lobby and went out the revolving doors into the street.

The new public library, with its glistening gold dome, took up half a downtown block, its back butting up against an old-fashioned office tower. The building was a boxy fortress, three stories tall, with stately columns that acted like bookends, because the windowless walls had been painted to resemble a row of giant books lined up on a shelf.

"It's like a majestic Greek temple," gushed Miguel.

"And the world's biggest bookcase," added Sierra Russell, who had finally put away her paperback.

Velvet ropes lined a path across Main Street that led to a red carpet leading up a flight of steps to the arched entryway and seriously steel (not to mention *round*) front door.

Kyle had to smile when he saw what was tethered to the railings on either side of the steps: balloons!

A big bruiser—maybe six four, 250 pounds—in sunglasses and a black sports coat stood in front of the library's circular door, which had several large valve wheels like you'd see on a submarine hatch. The burly guard wore his hair in long, ropy dreadlocks.

"What's with that door?" asked Haley Daley, who, of course, had pushed her way to the front. "It looks like it came from a bank vault or something."

"It is the door from the old Gold Leaf Bank's walk-in vault," said Dr. Zinchenko. "It weighs twenty tons."

Akimi turned around and whispered, "My dad designed the support structure for that thing. Check out the hinges."

Kyle nodded. He was impressed.

"Why a vault door?" asked Kayla Corson.

"Because," said Dr. Zinchenko, "one sleepy Saturday, when Mr. Lemoncello was your age, he was working in the old public library over on Market Street. He was so lost in his thoughts, he did not hear the sirens as police cars raced past the library to the bank, where a burglar alarm had just been activated. This door serves as a reminder to us all: Our thoughts are safe when they are inside a library. Not even a bank robbery can disturb them."

Miguel was nodding like crazy. He could relate.

"It also helps us keep our most valuable treasures secure."

"There aren't any windows," observed Andrew Peckleman. "Probably to stop bank robbers from busting in. But shouldn't you people have added windows when you turned it into a library?"

"A library doesn't need windows, Andrew. We have books, which are windows into worlds we never even dreamed possible."

"An open book is an open mind," added Charles Chiltington. "That's what I always say."

Dr. Zinchenko pulled out a bright red note card. "Before we enter, please listen very carefully. 'Your library cards are the keys to everything you will need,'" she read. "'The library staff is here to help you find whatever it is you are looking for.'"

She smiled slightly, tucked the card back into her pocket, turned to the security guard, and said, "Clarence? Will you do the honors?"

"With pleasure, Dr. Z."

Clarence turned one giant wheel, spun another, and cranked a third.

Noiselessly, the twenty-ton door swung open.

* * *

53

The first thing Kyle could see inside was a trickling fountain in a grand foyer of brilliant white marble. The fountain featured a life-size statue of Mr. Lemoncello standing on a lily pad in the middle of a shallow reflecting pool ten feet wide. His head was tilted back so water could spurt up from his mouth in an arc.

Kyle noticed a quote chiseled into the statue's pedestal: KNOWLEDGE NOT SHARED REMAINS UNKNOWN. —LUIGI L. LEMONCELLO

Beyond the fountain, through an arched walkway, was a huge room filled with desks.

When everybody had shuffled into the entrance hall, Dr. Zinchenko turned to the security guard.

"Clarence?"

Clarence hauled the heavy steel door shut. Kyle heard the whir of spinning wheels, the clink of grinding gears, and a reverberating clunk.

"Wow!" said Miguel. "Talk about a lock-in!"

"I'll be in the control center, Dr. Z," said the security guard.

"Very well, Clarence."

Clarence disappeared behind a red door.

"Now then, children," said the librarian, "if you will all follow me into the Rotunda Reading Room."

As the rest of the group started filing into the gigantic circular room, Kyle checked out a display case beside the red door. A sign over it read "Staff Picks: Our Most

Memorable Reads." A dozen books were lined up on four shelves.

One cover in the middle of the bottom row caught Kyle's eye. It showed a football player wearing a number nineteen jersey dropping back to hurl a pass. Kyle made a mental note of the title: *In the Pocket: Johnny Unitas and Me*. Tomorrow morning, when the lock-in was over, he might use his library card to check it out for his big brother, Mike.

"Wow!"

Everybody gasped as they stepped into the Rotunda Reading Room and looked up. The entire underside of the dome looked like space as seen from the Hubble telescope: A dusty spiral nebula billowed up, a galaxy of stars twinkled, and meteorites whizzed across the ceiling.

"Ooh!"

The space imagery on the ceiling dissolved into ten distinct panels, each one becoming a display of swirling graphics.

"Those are the ten categories of the Dewey decimal system," whispered Miguel, sounding awestruck. "See the panel with Cleopatra, the guy mountain climbing, and the Viking ship sailing across it? That's for 900 to 999. History and Geography."

"Cool," said Kyle.

Tucked beneath the ten screens in arched niches were incredible 3-D statues glowing a ghostly green.

"I believe those are holographic projections," said Andrew Peckleman, waving up at a statue that was waving down at him.

The room under the dome was huge. It was circular, with a round desk at the center that was surrounded by four rings of reading desks.

Kyle saw that half of the rotunda was filled with floor-to-ceiling bookshelves. The other half had balconies on the second and third floors that reminded him of the open atrium of a hotel he and his family had stayed at once.

While everybody was gawking at the architecture, Dr. Zinchenko said the words Kyle had been waiting to hear all day:

"Now then, who's ready for our first game?"

12

"Will everybody please line up behind that far desk in front of the Children's Room?" said Dr. Zinchenko, gesturing toward one of the wooden tables in the outermost ring of the room.

"How many of you are familiar with Mr. Lemoncello's classic board game Hurry to the Top of the Heap?"

Twelve hands shot up.

"Very good," said Dr. Zinchenko.

Overhead, the Wonder Dome dissolved into a gigantic, curved Heap box top.

"This will be a live, three-dimensional version of that game. Each of you will be asked a trivia question. If you are able to answer it correctly, you will roll the dice and advance the equivalent number of desks. When you return to the starting point, you will move into the next concentric circle of desks. When you complete that ring, you will move into the next, and so on. If one of you makes it all the way to my desk at the center, you will be declared the winner."

"But we don't have any dice," said Yasmeen Smith-Snyder.

"Yes you do. See that smoky glass panel in the center of the desk? It is actually a touch-screen computer, currently running Mr. Lemoncello's dice-rolling app. Simply swipe and flick your fingers across the glass to toss and tumble the animated dice."

Dr. Zinchenko placed a stack of red cards on her desk. She looked like the host of a TV game show. "Before we begin, are there any other questions?"

Charles Chiltington raised his hand.

"Yes, Mr. Chiltington?"

"What will the winner win? After all, the prize is the most important part of any game."

Kyle didn't totally agree, but he was too excited about playing the game to say anything.

"Tonight's first prize," said Dr. Zinchenko, "is this golden key granting the winner access to Mr. Lemoncello's private and very posh bedroom suite up on the library's third floor. Instead of spending the night on the floor in a sleeping bag, you will be relaxing in luxury with a feather bed, a seventy-two-inch television screen and a state-of-the-art gaming console."

Okay. Kyle was definitely interested in this particular prize.

Judging from the wide-open eyes and chorus of "oohs" and "wows" all around him, so was everybody else.

Dr. Zinchenko flipped over the first question card.

"What major-league pitcher was the last to win at least thirty games in one season?"

Six players got it wrong before Kyle got it right.

"Denny McLain."

"Correct."

He swiped the glass panel, rolled a ten, and advanced ten desks around the room.

"What United States Navy ship was once captured by the North Koreans?"

Miguel nailed that one: "The USS *Pueblo*." He flew twelve spaces around the room.

"What did *Apollo 8* accomplish that had never been done before?"

Akimi, Andrew Peckleman, and Kayla Corson struck out on that one.

But Charles Chiltington knew the answer: "It was the first spacecraft to orbit the moon."

"Correct."

Chiltington rolled a five, landing him in last place.

Kyle's next question was tougher:

"Who was famous for saying, 'Book 'em, Danno'?"

"Um, that guy on *Hawaii Five-0*?"

"Please be more specific."

"Uh, the one with the shiny hair. Jack Lord?"

"That is correct."

Kyle breathed a sigh of relief. Thank goodness he and his dad sometimes watched reruns of old TV shows from the 1960s.

But when he flicked the computerized dice, his luck hit a brick wall. He rolled snake eyes and moved up two measly desks.

Meanwhile, Miguel went down with a question about Barbra Streisand. (Kyle wasn't exactly sure who she was.)

And Charles Chiltington surged ahead with a correct answer about the Beatles' "Hey Jude" and a double-sixes roll.

As the game went on, Kyle and Chiltington, the only players still standing, kept answering correctly and moving around the room, until they were both seated at a desk in the innermost ring—only six spaces away from Dr. Zinchenko's desk and victory. Kyle was seriously glad he and his mom had played so many games of Trivial Pursuit—with the original, extremely *old* cards.

"Kyle, here is your next question: What song in the movie *Doctor Dolittle* won an Academy Award?"

Kyle squinted. He had that movie. An old VHS cassette tape that his mom had bought at a garage sale. Too bad they didn't have a VCR to watch it on. But even though he'd never seen the movie, he had read the front and back of the box a couple of times.

"Um, 'Talk to the Animals'?"

"Correct."

He started breathing again.

"Roll the dice, please, Mr. Keeley."

Kyle did.

Another pair of ones. He moved up two spaces. Now he was only four desks away from winning.

"Mr. Chiltington, here is your next question: Who was elected president in 1968?"

"I believe that was Richard Milhous Nixon."

"You are also correct."

Chiltington didn't wait for the librarian to tell him to roll the dice. He flicked his fingers across the glass pad.

"Yes! Double sixes. Again." He moved around the last ring of desks, tapping their tops, counting them off even though everybody knew his twelve was more than good enough to carry him to the finish line.

"Congratulations, Mr. Chiltington," Dr. Zinchenko said as she handed him the key to the private suite. "You are this evening's first winner."

"Thank you, Dr. Zinchenko. I am truly and sincerely honored."

"Congratulations, Charles," said Kyle. "Way to win."

"Get used to it, Keeley," he answered in a voice only the other kids could hear. "I'm a Chiltington. We never lose."

13

What happened next was extremely cool.

A holographic image of a second librarian appeared beside Dr. Zinchenko at the center desk. She looked a little like Princess Leia being beamed out of R2-D2 in *Star Wars*. Except she had an old-fashioned bubble-top hairdo, cat's-eye glasses, and a tweed jacket with patches on the elbows.

"Here to present our official library lock-in rules," said Dr. Zinchenko, "is Mrs. Gail Tobin, head librarian of the Alexandriaville Public Library back in the 1960s, when Mr. Lemoncello was your age."

Overhead, the Wonder Dome had shifted back to its ten Dewey decimal displays.

"How old is she?" asked Sean Keegan.

"She'd be a hundred and ten if she were still alive."

"But she's dead and working here?"

"Let's just say her spirit lives on in this hologram."

"Mrs. Tobin's the one who helped Mr. Lemoncello so much," Kyle whispered to Akimi. "When he was a kid."

"I know. Her hair looks like a beehive."

Kyle shrugged. "From what I've seen on TV, the 1960s were generally weird."

"Welcome, children, to the library of the future," said the flickering projection. "Dr. Zinchenko will now pass out Lemoncello Library floor plans—your map and guide to all that this extraordinary building has to offer. Your new library cards will grant you access to all rooms except the master control center—the red door you passed on your way in—and, of course, Mr. Lemoncello's private suite on the third floor."

Charles Chiltington dangled his golden key in front of his face. "I believe you need *this* to enter that."

Mrs. Tobin ignored him. She was a hologram. That made it easier.

"Security personnel are on duty twenty-four hours a day," she continued. "During your stay, all of your actions will be recorded by video cameras, as outlined in the consent agreements you and your parents signed earlier."

"Are we going to be on a reality TV show?" asked Haley, smiling up at a tiny camera with a blinking red light.

"It is a distinct possibility," said Dr. Zinchenko.

"I like television," said the ghostly image of Mrs. Tobin. "*Rowan and Martin's Laugh-In* is my favorite program. Returning to the rules. The use of personal electronic devices is strictly prohibited at all times during the lock-in."

63

The security guard, Clarence, and a guy who looked like his identical twin brother entered the rotunda, each of them carrying an aluminum attaché case.

"Kindly deposit all cell phones, iPods, and iPads in the receptacles provided by our security guards, Clarence and Clement. Your devices will be safely stored for the duration of your stay and will be returned to you at the conclusion of our activities. Also, you may use the desktop pad computers in this room to comb through our card catalog and conduct Internet research. However, these devices cannot send or receive email or text messages—whatever those might be. Remember, I retired in 1973. We still used carbon paper. And now Dr. Zinchenko will walk you through the floor plan."

Everybody unfolded their map pamphlets.

"As you can see," said Dr. Zinchenko, "fiction titles are located here in the reading room. The Children's Enrichment Room, with soundproof walls, is over there. Two fully equipped community meeting rooms as well as the Book Nook Café—behind those windows where the curtains are drawn—are also located on this floor. Upstairs on two, you will find ten numbered doors, each leading into a chamber filled with books, information, and, well, *displays* related to its corresponding Dewey decimal category."

Kyle raised his hand.

"Yes?"

"Where's the Electronic Learning Center?"

Dr. Zinchenko grinned. "Upstairs on the third floor, where you will also find the Board Room, the Art and Artifacts Room, the IMAX theater, the Lemoncello-abilia Room, the—"

"Can we go upstairs and play?" asked Bridgette Wadge. "I want to try out the space shuttle simulator."

"I want to learn how to drive a car!" said Sean Keegan. "A race car!"

"I want to conquer the world with Alexander the Great!" said Yasmeen Smith-Snyder.

Apparently, everybody was doing what Kyle had already done: checking out the "Available Educational Gameware" listed on the back of the floor plan.

"Early access to the Electronic Learning Center will be tonight's second prize," said Dr. Zinchenko. "To win it, you must use the library's resources to find dessert, which we have hidden somewhere in the building. Whoever does the research and locates the goodies first will also be the first one allowed into the Electronic Learning Center. So use your wits and use your library. Go find dessert!"

Everybody raced around the room and sat down at separate desks to start tapping on the glass computer pads.

Well, everybody except Sierra Russell. She spent like two seconds swiping her fingers across a screen, wrote something down with a stubby pencil on a slip of paper, then wandered off to inspect the three-story-tall curved bookcases lining the walls at the back half of the rotunda. Kyle watched as she stepped onto a slightly elevated platform with handles like you'd see on your grandmother's walker. It even had a basket attached to the front.

"Dr. Zinchenko?"

"Yes, Ms. Russell?"

"Is this safe? Because the book I want is all the way up at the top."

"Yes. Just make sure your feet are securely locked in."

Sierra wiggled her leg. Kyle heard a metallic snap.

"It's like a ski boot," said Sierra.

"That's right. Now use the keypad to tell the hover ladder the call number for the book you are interested in and hang on tight."

Sierra consulted the slip of paper and tapped some keys.

"The bottom of that platform you are standing on is a magnet," said Dr. Zinchenko. "There are ribbons of electromagnetic material in the lining of the bookcases. The strength of those magnets will be modulated by our maglev computer based on the call number you input."

Two seconds later, Sierra Russell was floating in the air, drifting up and to the left. It was absolutely awesome.

"The hover ladder must use advanced magnetic levitation technology," said Miguel, seated at the desk to Kyle's right. "Just like the maglev bullet trains in Japan."

"Cool," mumbled Kyle.

And for the first time in his life, Kyle Keeley wanted to check out a library book more than anything in the world.

14

"How about we work together?" said Akimi when she sat down at Kyle's table.

"Hmmm?"

Kyle couldn't take his eyes off Sierra Russell. She had drifted up about twenty-five feet and was leaning against the railings of her floating platform, completely lost in a new book.

"Hello? Earth to Kyle? Do you want somebody else to get first dibs on the Electronic Learning Center?"

"No."

"Then focus."

"Okay. So how do we use our wits and the library to find dessert?"

Akimi nodded toward Miguel, whose fingers were dancing across the screen of his desktop's tablet computer.

"I think he's doing a search in the card catalog," whispered Akimi.

"Why?"

"It's how you find stuff in a library, Kyle."

"I know that. But we're not looking for *books* about dessert. We need to find actual food."

Andrew Peckleman stood up from his desk and sprinted up a wrought-iron spiral staircase leading to the second floor. Two seconds later, Charles Chiltington was sprinting up the staircase behind him.

All the other players soon followed. Everybody was headed to the second floor and the Dewey decimal rooms. Miguel finally popped up from his desk and made a mad dash for the nearest staircase.

"It's got to be up in the six hundreds, you guys," he called out to Kyle and Akimi.

"Thanks," said Kyle. But he still didn't budge from his seat.

"I guess the six hundreds is the Dewey decimal category where you find books about desserts," said Akimi. "Maybe we should . . ."

"Wait a second," said Kyle.

"Um, Kyle, in case you haven't noticed, you, me, and glider girl Sierra are the only ones still on this floor, and Sierra isn't really *on* the floor because she's floating."

"Hang on, Akimi. I have an idea." Kyle pulled out his floor plan. "Dessert is probably hiding in plain sight. Just like the bonus codes in Squirrel Squad. Follow me."

"Where to?"

"The Book Nook Café. The one room in the library where, according to what Dr. Zinchenko told us back at the hotel, food and drinks are actually allowed."

They strolled into the cozy café.

"Whoo-hoo!" shouted Akimi.

The walls were decorated with shelves of cookbooks but several tables were loaded down with trays of cookies, cakes, ice cream, and fruit!

"That's why the curtains were closed behind the windows into the rotunda," said Akimi. "So we couldn't see all this food. Way to go, Kyle."

Kyle did his best imitation of Charles Chiltington: "I'm a Keeley, Akimi. We never lose. Except, of course, when we don't win."

After everyone had dessert, Kyle and Akimi were the first ones allowed to enter the Electronic Learning Center.

Kyle flew the space shuttle, making an excellent landing on Mars before crashing into one of Saturn's moons. Akimi rode a horse with Paul Revere. Then Kyle learned how to drive a stick-shift stock car on the Talladega racetrack while Akimi climbed into a tiny submarine to swim with sharks, dolphins, and sea turtles—all of which were projected on the glass walls of her undersea simulator.

All the educational video games had 3-D visuals, digital surround sound, and something new that Mr. Lemoncello was developing for his video games: smell-a-vision. When you sacked Rome with the Visigoths, you could smell the smoky scent of the burning city as well as the barbarians' b.o.

After an hour, Dr. Zinchenko ushered everybody else into the Electronic Learning Center. They'd been watching George Washington debate George W. Bush (both were audio-animatronic dummies) in the "town square" at the center of the 900s room.

At ten p.m. they all tromped into the IMAX theater, also on the third floor, to see a jukebox concert. 3-D images of the world's best musicians (living and dead) performed their hits "live." The best part was Mozart jamming with Metallica.

Finally, around three in the morning, Clarence and his twin brother, Clement, came to escort the kids to their sleeping quarters. The boys would roll out their sleeping bags in the Children's Room, just off the rotunda; the girls would be upstairs on the third floor in the Board Room. Charles Chiltington would be luxuriating all alone in Mr. Lemoncello's private suite.

Exhausted from the excitement of the day—and crashing after eating way too much sugar—Kyle slept like a baby.

He only woke up because he heard music.

Loud, blaring music.

The theme song from that boxing movie *Rocky,* his brother Mike's favorite.

"Whazzat?" he mumbled, crawling out of his sleeping bag.

Kyle glanced at his watch. It was eleven a.m. He figured the library lock-in was officially over and this was the group's wake-up call.

The music kept blaring.

"This is how they wake up astronauts," groaned Miguel.

"Turn it off!" moaned Andrew Peckleman.

Kyle slipped on his jeans and sneakers and staggered out into the giant reading room.

"Dr. Zinchenko?"

His voice echoed off the dome. No answer.

"Clarence? Clement?"

Nothing.

The *Rocky* music got louder.

Akimi leaned in from the third-floor balcony.

"What's going on down there?"

"I think they're trying to wake up astronauts," said Kyle. "On the moon."

He made his way to the front door and reached for the handle.

It wouldn't budge.

He jiggled it.

Nothing.

He jiggled harder.

Still nothing.

Kyle realized that the library lock-in might be over but they were still locked in the library.

15

"Everybody, please take your seats," Dr. Zinchenko said to the parents gathered in a conference room at the Parker House Hotel.

"When do our kids come home?" asked one of the mothers.

"Rose has soccer at two," said another.

The librarian nodded. "Mr. Lemoncello will—"

Just then, an accordion-panel door at the far end of the room flew open, revealing the eccentric billionaire dressed in a bright purple tracksuit and a plumed pirate hat. He was eating a slice of seven-layer birthday cake.

"Good morning or, as they're currently saying in Reykjavik, *gott síðdegi*, which means 'good afternoon,' because there is a four-hour time difference between Ohio and Iceland, a fact I first learned spinning a globe in my local library."

Mr. Lemoncello, his banana shoes burp-squeaking, stepped out of a room filled with dozens of black-and-white television monitors—the kind security guards watch at their workstations.

"Ladies and gentlemen, thank you for joining us on this grand and auspicious day. Today I am pleased to announce the most marvelously stupendous game ever created: Escape from Mr. Lemoncello's Library! The entire library will be the game board. Your children will be the game pieces. The winner will become famous all over the world."

"How?" asked one of the fathers.

"By starring in all of my commercials this holiday season. TV. Radio. Print. Billboards. Cardboard cutouts in toy stores. His or her face will be everywhere."

Mrs. Daley raised her hand. "Will they get paid?"

"Oh, yes. In fact, you'll probably want to call me The Giver."

"And what exactly does Haley have to do to win?"

"Escape! From the library. I thought the game's title more or less gave that bit away." Mr. Lemoncello tapped a button in his pirate hat and an animated version of the library's floor plan was instantly displayed on the conference room's plasma-screen TVs.

"Whoever is the first to use what they find *in* the library to find their way *out* of the library will be crowned the winner. Now then, the children cannot use the front door or the fire exits or set off any alarms. They cannot go out the way they went in. They can only use their wits, cunning, and intelligence to decipher clues and solve riddles that will eventually lead them to the location of the library's super-secret alternate exit. And, ladies and gentlemen, I assure you, such an alternate exit does indeed exist."

The parents around the table started buzzing with excitement.

"Participation, of course, will be purely optional and voluntary," said Mr. Lemoncello, clasping his hands behind his back and stalking around the room.

Several parents pulled out cell phones.

"And please—do *not* attempt to phone, email, text, fax, or send smoke signals to your children, encouraging them to enter the competition. We have blocked all communication into and out of the library. Only those who truly wish to stay and play shall stay and play. Anyone who chooses to leave the library will go home with lovely parting gifts and a souvenir pirate hat very similar to mine. They'll also be invited to my birthday party tomorrow afternoon." He held up his crumb-filled plate. "I've been sampling potential cake candidates for breakfast."

Mrs. Keegan crossed her arms over her chest. "Will this game be dangerous?"

"No," said Mr. Lemoncello. "Your children will be under constant video surveillance by security personnel in the library's control center. Dr. Zinchenko and I will also be monitoring their progress here in my private video-viewing suite. Should anything go wrong, we have paramedics, firefighters, and a team of former Navy SEALs—each with the heart of a samurai—standing by to swoop in and rescue your children. It'll be like *The Hunger Games* but with lots of food and no bows or arrows."

"Why not just have the kids play one of your other games?" a parent suggested. "Why all this fuss?"

"Because, my dear friends, these twelve children have lived their entire lives without a public library. As a result, they have no idea how extraordinarily useful, helpful, and funful—a word I recently invented—a library can be. This is their chance to discover that a library is more than a collection of dusty old books. It is a place to learn, explore, and grow!"

"Mr. Lemoncello, I think what you're doing is fantastic," said one of the mothers.

"Thank you," said Mr. Lemoncello, bowing and clicking his heels (which made them *bruck* like a chicken).

"If any of you would like to check up on your children," announced Dr. Zinchenko, "please join us in the adjoining room."

"Oh, they're a lot of fun to watch," said Mr. Lemoncello. "However, Mr. and Mrs. Keeley, I'm afraid your son Kyle does not enjoy the theme song from *Rocky* quite as much as I do!"

16

Rocky had done its job.

Kyle—and everybody else locked inside the library—was definitely awake.

Even Charles Chiltington had come down to the Rotunda Reading Room from Mr. Lemoncello's private suite. The only essay writer not with the group was Sierra Russell, who, Kyle figured, was off looking for another book to read.

"We're still locked in?" squealed Haley Daley.

"This is so lame," added Sean Keegan. "It's like eleven-thirty. I've got things to do. Places to be."

"Look, you guys," said Kyle, "they'll probably open the front door right after we eat or something."

"Well, where's that ridiculous librarian?" said Charles Chiltington, who was never very nice when there weren't any adults in the room.

"Yeah," said Rose Vermette. "I can't stay in here all day. I have a soccer game at two."

"And, dudes," said Sean Keegan, "*I* have a life."

"Do you children require assistance?" said a soft, motherly voice.

It was the semi-transparent holographic image of Mrs. Tobin, the librarian from the 1960s. She was hovering a few inches off the ground in front of the center desk.

"Yes," said Kayla Corson. "How do we get out of here?"

The librarian blinked, the way a secondhand calculator (the one your oldest brother dropped on the floor a billion times) does when it's figuring out a square root.

"I'm sorry," said the robotic librarian. "I have not been provided with the answer to that question."

"Will we be doing brunch here this morning?" Chiltington asked politely. "I'm not hungry, but some of my chums sure are. After all, it is eleven-thirty."

"The kitchen staff recently placed fresh food in the Book Nook Café."

"Thank you, Mrs. Tobin," said Chiltington. "Would you like anything? A bowl of oatmeal, perhaps."

"No. Thank you, CHARLES. I am a hologram. I do not eat food."

"I guess that's how you stay so super skinny."

Kyle shook his head. The smarmy guy was oilier than a soggy sack of fries. He was even sucking up to a hologram.

Chiltington and the others traipsed off to have

breakfast, but Kyle and Akimi stayed with the holographic librarian.

"Um, I have a question," said Kyle.

"I'm listening."

"Is the library lock-in over? Are we supposed to go home now?"

"Mr. Lemoncello will be addressing that issue shortly."

"Okay. Thanks, Mrs. Tobin."

"You are welcome, KYLE."

After the librarian faded to a flicker, Akimi said, "By the way, Kyle, before we leave, you need to check out that room I slept in last night."

"The Board Room?"

"Yeah. They call it that because, guess what? It's filled with board games!"

"All Lemoncellos?"

"Nuh-uh. Stuff from other companies. Some of it goes way back to the 1890s. I think it's Mr. Lemoncello's personal collection. It's like a museum up there."

Kyle's eyes went wide. "You hungry?" he asked.

"Not really. We ate so much last night."

"You think we have time to check out this game museum?"

"Follow me."

The two friends bounded up a spiral staircase to the second floor, where they found another set of steps to take them up to the third.

When he entered the Board Room, Kyle was blown away. "Wow!"

The walls were lined with bookcases filled with antique games, tin toys, and card games.

"This is incredible."

"I guess," said Akimi. "If, you know, you like games."

Kyle smiled. "Which, you know, I do."

They spent several quiet minutes wandering around the room, taking in all the wacky games that people used to play. There was one display case featuring eight games with amazingly illustrated box tops. A tiny spotlight illuminated each one.

"Wonder what's so special about these games," said Kyle.

"Maybe those were Mr. Lemoncello's favorites when he was a kid."

"Maybe." But the slogan etched into the glass case confused Kyle: "Luigi Lemoncello: the first and last word in games."

"But these aren't Lemoncello games," he mumbled.

The first spotlighted game in the case was Howdy Doody's TV Game. After that came Hüsker Dü?, You Don't Say!, Like Minds, Fun City, Big 6 Sports Games, Get the Message, and Ruff and Reddy.

"It's a puzzle," Kyle said with a grin.

"I thought they were games."

"They are. But if you string together the first or last

word of each game title . . ." He tapped the glass in front of the first box on the bottom shelf. "You *get the message*."

"Really?" said Akimi, sounding extremely skeptical. "You're sure it's not just a bunch of junk somebody picked up for like fifty cents at a yard sale?"

"Positive." Kyle pointed to each box top as he cracked the code. "Howdy. Dü you like fun games? Get Reddy."

Miguel Fernandez barged into the Board Room.

"Here you are! We need you guys in the Electronic Learning Center. Now."

"Why?"

"Charles Chiltington wolfed down his breakfast, then raced up here to finish the game he started last night so he can enter his name as the first high scorer."

"So?"

"The game he's playing is all about medieval castles and dungeons!"

This time Akimi said it: "So?"

"He's escaping through the sewers. The game has smell-a-vision. You ever smell a medieval sewer? Trust me, it is foul *and* disgusting."

The three of them dashed up the hall and entered the stinky room where Charles was sitting in a vibrating pedestal chair, thumbing his controller. As his avatar sloshed through a sewer pipe, the subwoofers built into his seat made every *SQUISH!* and *SPLAT!* rumble across the floor.

"Whoa!" said Kyle. "Knock it off, Charles. You're pumping out total tear gas."

"Because I'm in the sewers underneath the horse stables. It's the secret way out of the castle. I'm going to win another game. That's two for me, Keeley. How many for you?"

"Yo," said Miguel. "This room is two stories above the café. The ductwork is connected."

"What's your point?"

"You're making everybody's food downstairs smell like horse manure!"

"Who cares? I'm winning."

Charles's chair went *FLUMP!* again.

But this time, Kyle smelled . . . pine trees?

Like one of those evergreen air fresheners people hang inside their cars.

"Aw, this stupid thing is broken." Charles jumped out of the chair and reared back to kick it.

"Um, I wouldn't do that if I were you," said Kyle.

"Why not?"

"Because there's a security camera over there and it's aimed right at you."

"What? Where?"

"See the blinking red light?"

Suddenly, an image of Kyle pointing up at the camera lens appeared on every video screen in the Electronic Learning Center.

Until he was replaced by Mr. Lemoncello.

17

"Excellent escape plan, Charles," said Mr. Lemoncello on the video screens.

"Thank you, sir," said Chiltington, smoothing out his khaki pants. "And just so you know, I saw an ant crawling up the side of this seat. That's why I almost kicked it."

"How very thoughtful of you, Charles."

"Mr. Lemoncello?" said Akimi.

"Yes?"

"How come the sewer started smelling like a pine tree?"

"Because I enjoy the odor of pine trees much more than the stench of horse poop. How about you?"

"Definitely."

"Now then, will everybody else please join us upstairs in the Electronic Learning Center? I have a very important announcement to make."

Kyle heard feet clomping up the stairs and soon Andrew, Bridgette, Yasmeen, Sean, Haley, Rose, and Kayla hurried into the room.

"Are we all here?" said Mr. Lemoncello.

"Everybody except Sierra Russell," said Kyle.

"Ah, yes. I saw her downstairs reading *When You Reach Me* by Rebecca Stead. We'll reach her later. It's nearly noon and I'm eager to move on to the next round of our competition."

"What competition?" asked Yasmeen Smith-Snyder.

"The one we are about to begin."

"Sir?" said Sean Keegan. "I have stuff to do today."

"That's fine, Sean. You are, of course, free to leave. If any of the rest of you do not wish to stay and play, kindly deposit your library cards in the discard pile."

A tile in the floor popped open and an empty goldfish bowl atop an ornate column rose up about three feet.

"Just drop it in the bowl there, Sean. Attaboy. Follow the flashing red arrows in the floor to the nearest exit, where you will receive a lovely parting gift along with my everlasting admiration for your essay-writing abilities."

Bright red arrows danced across the floor. Sean followed them.

"What happens if we decide to stay?" asked Akimi.

"You will be given the chance to play a brand-new, exciting game!"

"Is there a prize for the winner?" demanded Haley Daley.

"Oh, yes."

Now Miguel shot up his hand. "Mr. Lemoncello? What do we have to do to win?"

"Simple: Find your way *out* of the library using only what's *in* the library."

"Awesome!"

"Lame," mumbled Kayla Corson. "I'm outta here."

She plunked her library card into the fishbowl and followed the blinking arrows out the door.

"Does anyone else want or need to leave?"

"Sorry, sir. I have soccer at two," said Rose Vermette. "See you guys later." She dropped her card into the discard bowl.

The instant she did, bells rang, confetti fell from the ceiling, and every electronic console in the game room started *ding-ding-ding*ing.

"Congratulations, Rose!" cried Mr. Lemoncello, who had put on a pointy party hat. "For sticking to your prior commitments, you will receive our special Prior Commitment Sticker prize: a complete set of Lemoncello Sticker Picture Games and a laptop computer to play them on! Enjoy."

Charles Chiltington stepped a little closer to the security camera as Rose Vermette skipped out of the room.

"Sir, might we assume that the prize for winning your brand-new game will be even better than a laptop computer?"

"Yes," said Mr. Lemoncello, taking off his party hat. "You may so assume."

"I'm in," said Chiltington.

"Me too," said Kyle.

"Me too," added Akimi, Miguel, Andrew, Bridgette, Yasmeen, and Haley.

Sierra Russell wandered into the room. Her nose was buried so deep in her book she didn't even notice Mr. Lemoncello's gigantic face on all the video screens.

"Is something going on?" she said, mostly to her book pages.

"You bet!" boomed Mr. Lemoncello.

Sierra's head snapped up.

"Oh. Hello, sir."

"Greetings, Sierra. Sorry to interrupt your reading. Just have a quick question: Will you be staying or leaving?"

"Well, sir, I'd like to stay. If that's okay?"

"Okay? It is *wondermous,* another word I just made up. Now then, to read you the rules of the game—because every game needs rules—here is your friend and mine, Dr. Yanina Zinchenko!"

The video screens switched to a close-up of the librarian with the red hair and glasses.

"Your exit from the library must be completed between noon today and noon tomorrow," said Dr. Zinchenko.

Mr. Lemoncello's head popped into a corner of her screen.

"Tomorrow's my birthday, by the way. Mark your calendars."

And he ducked back out of the frame.

"Our security guards will continue holding your cell phones," said Dr. Zinchenko. "You may not use the library computers to contact anyone outside the building. You may, however, use them to conduct research.

"You may also request three different types of outside assistance: one 'Ask an Expert,' one 'Librarian Consultation,' and one 'Extreme Challenge.' Please be advised: The Extreme Challenges are, as the name implies, extremely difficult. If you pass the challenge, your reward will be great. However, if you fail, you will be eliminated from the competition."

Kyle figured he'd avoid asking for one of those—unless he extremely needed to.

"To use any of these 'lifelines,'" Dr. Zinchenko continued, "simply summon Mrs. Tobin."

Chiltington raised his hand.

"Yes, Charles?"

"Would you mind telling us what the prize will be for the winner?"

The video screen switched to an image of Mr. Lemoncello, who had done some sort of quick change. Now he was wearing sunglasses and had a silk ascot tucked into his shirt collar. He looked like a flashy Hollywood movie star. From 1939.

"Fame and glory! The winner will become my new spokesperson and will star in all of my holiday promotions."

"We'll be famous?" gushed Yasmeen, fluffing up her hair and smiling at the security camera.

Haley stepped in front of Yasmeen. "I've done some modeling work. For Sherman's Shoes in Old Town."

Yasmeen stepped in front of Haley. "I was an extra in a hot dog commercial once. . . ."

"Well, I'm a cheerleader; Yasmeen isn't. . . ."

While the two girls continued primping and posing for the camera, Dr. Zinchenko came back on-screen to quickly rattle off some final words.

"Your library cards are the keys to everything you will need. The library staff is here to help you find whatever it is you are looking for. The way out is not the way you came in. You may *not* use any of the fire exits. If you do, an alarm will sound and you will be immediately eliminated from the game. For safety purposes, you will be under constant video surveillance and you will be recorded. In the unlikely event of an emergency, you will be evacuated from the building. Creating an incident that requires evacuation will not count as having discovered a way to exit the library. Any questions?"

"Just one," said Andrew Peckleman, adjusting his goggle-sized glasses with his fingertip. "When exactly will the game begin?"

Mr. Lemoncello's face reappeared on the screens.

"Good question, Andrew! Oh, my. It's noon! How about . . . let's say . . . oh, I don't know . . . *now*!"

18

The contestants raced down the stairs to the Rotunda Reading Room.

Kyle saw Haley Daley dash down another set of steps into the basement, to what the floor plan called the Stacks.

Miguel and Andrew, the two library experts, grabbed separate tables and started working the touch-screen computers. Bridgette Wadge did the same thing.

Charles Chiltington strolled out the arched doorway and into the foyer with the fountain.

Yasmeen Smith-Snyder was running around the circular room with her floor plan in front of her face, like someone frantically checking their text messages while racing down a crowded sidewalk.

Sierra Russell found a comfy chair and sat down.

To finish her book.

The girl definitely wasn't into the whole spirit of The Game.

"So, Kyle," said Akimi, "you want to form an alliance?"

"What do you mean?"

"It's what people do on reality shows like *Survivor*. We help each other until, you know, everybody else is eliminated and we have to stab each other in the back."

"Um, I don't remember hearing anything about 'eliminations.'"

"Oh. Right."

"But, hey, there was nothing in the rules that said we couldn't share the top prize. I just want to *win*!"

"Cool. So, we're a team?"

"Sure."

"Great," said Akimi. "I nominate you to be our captain. All in favor raise their hands."

Kyle and Akimi both raised their hands.

"It's unanimous," said Akimi. "Okay. Let's go ask that antique librarian a question."

"What?"

"We both get to ask one question, right?"

"Right."

"Okay, here's mine: 'Hey, lady—how do we get out of here?'"

"And you think she'll tell you?"

"No. Not really. So, what's your plan?"

"Well, I was thinking—"

Suddenly, Yasmeen shouted, "I win!"

The rest of them stopped whatever they were doing.

"It's just like last night when Kyle found dessert in the most obvious place. To get out of the library, all we have to do is use one of the fire exits. Duh."

She headed toward a hallway between the Book Nook Café and Community Meeting Room A.

Kyle stood up. "Um, Yasmeen? I think maybe you missed some of what . . ."

Charles Chiltington dashed into the room and shouted, "You're not going to win, Yasmeen. Not unless you beat me to that fire exit!"

He bolted toward the corridor.

Yasmeen bolted toward it, too.

"You guys?" said Kyle.

Kyle could see a red Exit light glowing at the far end of the hallway Charles and Yasmeen were sprinting down. Charles stumbled and fell. Yasmeen kept running. Harder. Faster. She slammed into the exit bar on the metal door.

Alarms sounded. Flashing red lights swirled. Somewhere, a tiger roared. Mr. Lemoncello's voice rang out of the overhead speakers. "Sorry, Yasmeen. That's where your sidewalk ends. You broke the rules. You are out of the game. Your library card will be placed in the discard bowl and you will be going home."

As the fire exit door slowly swung shut and Yasmeen disappeared into the bright sunshine outside the library,

Kyle checked out Charles Chiltington, who would've been sent home if he hadn't stumbled and had reached the exit first.

The guy was smirking.

That was when it hit Kyle: Chiltington had faked Yasmeen out. He knew she couldn't win by going out a fire exit. But he ran down the hall to fool her into thinking she was doing the right thing.

Oh, yeah. Chiltington was definitely in it to win it.

No matter who he had to trample.

Whistling casually, Charles strolled back to the lobby.

"What's Chiltington doing out in the entrance hall?" said Akimi. "They told us the way out isn't the way in."

Before Kyle could answer, Andrew Peckleman started shouting at Miguel, who had wandered over to Peckleman's table.

"Get away! You're trying to steal my idea!"

"No, man," said Miguel. "I just happened to see your screen and I don't think that particular periodical—"

"You know what, Miguel? I don't really care what you think! This isn't school. This is the *public* library and you're not the boss in here, so just leave me alone!"

Miguel tossed up his hands. "No problem, bro. I was just trying to help."

"Ha! You mean help me lose." Andrew stormed up the closest spiral staircase to the second floor and the Dewey decimal rooms. Miguel, looking sort of sad, headed up a separate spiral staircase. Bridgette Wadge trailed after them.

"Want to follow those guys like Bridgette did?" whispered Akimi. "I'll take Peckleman, you take Miguel."

"No thanks," said Kyle, looking up at the domed ceiling. "I'm much more interested in the windows up there."

Three stories above the rotunda floor, just below the Wonder Dome, there was a series of ten arched windows set between the recessed statue nooks. The windows acted like skylights at the base of the dome, allowing sunshine to flood into the room below.

"Do you think those windows open?" asked Akimi.

"Maybe. Maybe not. But I've never let a closed or locked window stand between me and winning a game. Just ask my dad."

"What?"

"Never mind. Come on." Kyle trotted over to the cushy chair where Sierra Russell was peacefully reading her book.

"Um, excuse me, hate to interrupt . . ."

Sierra raised her head. She had a very dreamy look in her eyes.

"I need a book."

"Really?" said Sierra. "What kind?"

"Like the one you found. Up there." He gestured to the curving bookcases climbing up the back half of the rotunda.

"Fiction," said Sierra.

"Right," said Kyle. "Love me some fiction."

"Well, what sort of story do you like?"

"Something way up high," said Kyle. "The higher the better."

"Really?"

"Yep."

"Well, that's an interesting way to put together a reading list, basing it on bookcase elevation. . . ."

"I'd like something on the top shelf. Maybe right under the hologram statue of that guy hanging out with the Cat in the Hat."

"That's Dr. Seuss," said Sierra. "He wrote *The Cat in the Hat*."

"Sweet," said Kyle. "But I just like how close he is to that window."

19

"Oh, Mrs. Tobin?" Akimi called out. "I need to use my Librarian Consultation."

"You sure about this?" said Kyle.

"That's the beauty of being a team. After we burn through mine, we'll still have yours."

The hologram librarian appeared and advised Akimi that *Huckleberry Finn* by Mark Twain was the book located right underneath the holographic image of Dr. Seuss and the Cat in the Hat.

After Mrs. Tobin vanished, Kyle and Akimi used their desktop computer to find the call number for *Huckleberry Finn*. Kyle grabbed a pen and scribbled it down on his palm.

"Are you going to do what I think you're going to do?" said Akimi.

"Yep. I'm going to float up there, hoist myself into that nook where the hologram is, reach over to the window, push it open, and stick out my hand. Technically, I will have found my way *out* of the library. Nothing in the rules said anything about how *far* outside we had to go to win."

"You could fall."

"I don't think so. I'm wiry, like a monkey."

"Seriously, Kyle. It isn't worth it."

"Um, yes it is. Did I mention I want to *win*?"

"You should improvise a safety harness," suggested Sierra Russell.

"Huh?"

"Well, in this adventure book I read once, the hero was in a very similar predicament. So he removed the curled handset wires from several telephones, bundled them together, and made a safety rope."

Ten minutes later, Kyle, Akimi, and Sierra had stripped the sproingy wires off a couple of telephone handsets. Kyle looped the cables around his waist and tied the other end to the handrail of the hover ladder. When fully extended, the safety rope would stretch out to a little more than twenty feet.

It should work.

"Be careful up there," said Akimi.

"Yes," said Sierra, who wasn't reading her book anymore. Apparently, watching a real live person risk his real live life by doing something really, really scary was one thing more exciting than reading.

Kyle locked his feet into the hover ladder's ski boot brackets. "Here we go."

Serious adrenaline raced through his body as he tapped the call number for *Huckleberry Finn* into the hover ladder's book locator keypad.

"When you open the window," said Akimi, "just shout, 'I found the way out!' and we win."

"Right," said Kyle. "All three of us."

"Huh?"

"Hey, Sierra came up with the safety rope idea. She's on our team now, too."

"Fine. Whatever. Just don't break your neck."

"Not part of the plan."

Kyle pressed the enter button on the control panel. The platform floated up off the ground and drifted slightly to the right.

"Be careful!" said Akimi. "Watch it!"

"I'm not doing anything," said Kyle. "This thingama-jiggy is doing all the work. I'm just along for the ride."

Kyle gripped the handles as the platform rose higher and higher. He sailed past books by Tolstoy and Thackeray. Tilting back his head, he looked up at the semi-transparent statues projected into the curved niches next to the arched windows.

They were a weird mix. A thoughtful African American man in a three-piece suit and a bow tie. A guy with long curly hair, old-fashioned clothes, and a looking glass. A long-haired dude in a scruffy shirt hiding behind cutouts of the letters "P" and "B." A bald guy with a beard.

Since the statues were really holographic projections, they had chisel-type labels floating in front of their pedestals identifying who the famous people were. The ones closest to Kyle were George Orwell, Lewis Carroll, Dr. Seuss, and Maya Angelou.

As he continued to climb, Kyle could hear the soft whir of the electromagnets invisibly lifting him toward the ceiling.

And then he heard something much louder.

"What a ridiculous idea!"

Charles Chiltington. He was standing on the second-floor balcony at the far side of the rotunda.

"You know, Keeley, I thought about doing the same thing. But then I noticed something you obviously overlooked: There's a wire mesh security screen on the other side of those windows."

The levitating platform stuttered to a stop.

"Enjoy staring at the ceiling, Keeley. I'm off to win yet another game!"

Kyle ignored Chiltington and grabbed hold of the ledge beneath Dr. Seuss's berth. He tried to haul himself up but his feet wouldn't budge.

They were locked in place by those ski boot clamps.

And this close to the skylights, Kyle could see that Chiltington was right—there was a security screen on the other side of the windows.

Kyle checked his wristwatch. It was one p.m. He and

his teammates had wasted an hour on the lame window idea. He sighed heavily and stared up at the quivering Seuss projection in the bowed niche above his head.

The Cat in the Hat's mouth started to move.

" 'Think left and think right and think low and think high.' "

Kyle recognized the voice.

It was Mr. Lemoncello.

" 'Oh, the thinks you can think up if only you try!' "

In other words, Kyle was back to square one. He needed to think up a whole new escape plan.

The ladder began a slow and steady descent to the floor—even though Kyle hadn't pushed a button.

"Don't listen to smarmypants Charles," Akimi coached as Kyle coasted toward the floor. "It was worth a shot."

"I agree," said Sierra.

A bloodcurdling scream came ringing up the staircase from the basement.

"That's Haley!" said Akimi. "I saw her go downstairs."

"That's where the Stacks are," added Sierra.

"Come on," said Kyle. "She could be in serious trouble."

"You should never help your competition, Keeley," scoffed Charles as he casually strolled down a spiral staircase. "Unless, of course, you *always* play to lose!"

20

Losers.

That's what Charles Chiltington thought about sentimental saps like Kyle Keeley. A damsel in distress starts
screaming and he forgets all about winning the game to go
rescue her?

What a pathetic loser.

Unless, of course, Haley Daley was screaming because
she had already found the alternate exit.

That made Charles laugh.

Impossible.

Although quite pretty, Haley Daley, the princess of the
seventh grade, was a total airhead. There was no way a
dumb girl like her could've outsmarted Charles Chiltington.

It was time to play his hunch.

Twice already, the head librarian, Dr. Zinchenko, had
said, "The library staff is here to help you find whatever it

is you are looking for." She said it once when they were just about to enter the library, again when she was reading the laundry list of rules.

Well, what Charles was looking for was a way out of the building that wasn't the front door and wouldn't set off any alarms.

That was why he kept coming back to the lobby with the gurgling fountain. Why he kept studying the display case labeled "Staff Picks: Our Most Memorable Reads."

"The staff is here to help," he muttered. "These are staff picks. Ipso facto, this has to be some sort of enormous clue."

Inside the sealed bookcase, Charles saw twelve book covers.

One for each of the twelve twelve-year-old players? he wondered.

The display items weren't actual books. They were cover art mounted on book-sized foam core. Three covers were lined up on each of the case's four shelves. Since they weren't actual books with spines, none of the covers included their call numbers.

Charles focused on the three books lined up on the bottom row.

Hoosier Hospitality was on the left. *In the Pocket: Johnny Unitas and Me* was in the middle. *The Dinner Party* was on the right.

Charles decided to concentrate on the Johnny Unitas

title. He moved into the rotunda and did a quick card catalog search on one of the desktop computers. When he typed *"In the Pocket,"* a matching cover image popped up.

But still no call number.

In the spot where the identifier should have been, there were instead a censor's thick black box and the words "I.D. Temporarily Removed from System."

Scrolling further down the screen, Charles came across a rather unusual annotation: "You didn't really think we'd make it that easy, did you?"

Charles grinned.

The computer was telling him he was on the right track.

He glanced up from the desk. The Children's Room was directly in front of him. The book about Johnny Unitas, with its cartoony cover depicting a football player wearing a number nineteen jersey and dropping back to launch a pass, was most likely a children's book.

Of course, it was also a sports biography.

So would it be shelved with sports books, biographies, or children's books?

Charles went back to the computerized card catalog. He read the book's description: "Billy wants to be a great quarterback like his hero, Johnny Unitas, but his coach is worried he'll get hurt."

It sounded like fiction. A made-up story. It had to be in the Children's Room.

As Charles crossed the slick marble floor, something else struck him.

This was like Hüsker Dü?, a memory game he had played when he was in kindergarten. He was on a hunt to find a hidden match for the football book cover he had just memorized. This was, in short, another memory game—that was why the Staff Picks display had been subtitled "Our Most *Memorable* Reads."

"Clever, Lemoncello," he mumbled. "Very clever indeed."

Charles entered the children's department. It didn't take him very long to find the book, because *In the Pocket* was propped up on a miniature stand on top of a shelf.

"Found it!" Charles proclaimed. Then, savoring the moment, he picked up the book and read the title out loud: *"In the Pocket: Johnny Unitas and Me."*

All of a sudden, a row of animatronic geese tucked into a corner of the room started honking and singing.

"They call him Mr. Touchdown, yes, they call him Mr. T."

The squawking birds startled Charles so much he dropped the book.

When he did, a four-by-four card fluttered out from behind its cover.

Charles bent down to pick it up.

Printed on the card was a black-and-white silhouette. A quarterback, wearing a number nineteen jersey (just like Johnny Unitas), was arching back his arm to throw a pass.

Charles grinned.

He was definitely on the right track.

He tucked the silhouette card into his pocket and hurried back to the lobby to memorize more book covers.

21

"Ouch! I'm stuck! Help!"

Haley Daley's cries sailed up the staircase as Kyle led the charge down the steps into the Stacks.

"So, what exactly are the Stacks?" asked Akimi, three steps behind Kyle.

"It's where the library stores its collection of research material," said Sierra, who was two stairs behind Akimi.

The three of them reached the basement. It was filled with tidy rows of floor-to-ceiling shelving units.

"Help!"

Haley sounded like she was on the far side of the room, behind the walls of metal storage racks crowded with boxes, books, and bins.

"What is all this stuff?" said Kyle, looking for a passageway, trying to figure out how to get to wherever Haley was.

"Mostly rare books and documents you can't check out," said Sierra. "But if you fill out a call slip, you can use this material up in the reading room."

With a whir and whoosh of its electric motor, a shiny robot the color of the storm troopers in *Star Wars* scooted across an intersection between bookshelves. It moved on tank treads and had what looked like a shopping cart attached to its front.

"Let's follow that robot!" said Kyle. "It might know the fastest way to reach Haley."

The trio dashed up a narrow pathway to where they saw the robot extending its quadruple-jointed mechanical arm to pluck a flat metal box out of a slide-in compartment. The box had been stored in a section of shelving with a flashing LCD that read "Magazines & Periodicals. 1930s."

"Somebody upstairs wants an old magazine?" said Akimi.

"They're probably researching the Gold Leaf Bank building," said Sierra. "I think it was built in the 1930s."

"Help!" screamed Haley. "I'm stuck."

"Hang on!" shouted Kyle. "We're coming."

"Well, hurry up already!"

"This way," said Kyle.

They scampered up another aisle, turned right, and saw Haley, her hand jammed through a horizontal slot near the top of the basement wall. To reach it, she'd had to stand on an elevated treadmill maybe thirty feet long. Since the thing was rolling, Haley was jogging in place so she wouldn't fall on her face. The high-tech conveyor belt was actually a series of rollers. Ten robot carts—staggered so no two were directly across from each other—were lined up on either side.

"I think it's an automatic book sorter," said Sierra. "That laser beam near Haley's ankles probably scans a book's tag and tells the conveyor belt which of the ten sorting trays to shove it into."

"You guys?" screamed Haley. "Hurry up and rescue me!"

Kyle stepped back. Tried to assess the situation.

"What is that slot you're hanging on to?"

"The bottom of the stupid book drop," said Haley, trotting on the treadmill. "I saw it on the floor plan. People can walk up to it on the sidewalk and return their books. I figured it had to lead down here."

"Smart move," said Kyle. "You could crawl through the slot and escape."

"*If* you were the size of a book," Akimi said sarcastically.

"I never got that far," said Haley. "The minute I stepped onto this belt thing, it started moving."

Kyle nodded. "Probably a weight-activated switch."

"A book falls in," said Akimi. "The sorter starts up."

"Clever," said Kyle. "Plus, it gives our game its first booby trap."

"Well, the game is no fun if you're the booby stuck in the trap!" said Haley.

Kyle turned to Sierra. "We need to stop the belt so Haley can yank her hand out of that slot without falling on her butt or cracking open her skull. Have you ever read a book where the hero outwits an escalator or a rolling checkout belt in the grocery store or something?"

"No," said Sierra. "Not really."

"How about one where the hero just flips an emergency shutoff switch?" asked Akimi. "Because that's what I'd do if, you know, I found one."

Akimi was standing next to a wall-mounted switch box. She flicked it down. The conveyor belt slowed to a stop.

"Ta-da! Another chapter for my amazingly awesome autobiography—if I ever write one."

Haley yanked her hand out of the book return slot. It sort of popped when it finally sprang free. She collapsed to her knees on the frozen treadmill.

"My hand feels flatter than a pancake," she moaned.

"Are you hurt?" asked Kyle. "Maybe we should tell the security guys that . . ."

"What? That I have a boo-boo and need to go home? Forget it, Kyle Keeley. You're not going to beat me that easily."

"I'm not trying to—"

Haley showed him the palm of her hand. "Save it, Keeley." She crawled off the conveyor belt. "One way or another, I'm going to win this game. I just hope starring in Mr. Lemon-cello's commercials earns me some decent money."

She hobbled around the bookshelves toward the stair-case up to the reading room.

When she was gone, Akimi raised her hand. "Question?"

"Yeah?" said Kyle.

"How come the guys inside the control room didn't flip a switch to shut down the book sorter when they saw Haley doing her cardio cha-cha-cha on it?"

Kyle shrugged. "Maybe they weren't watching."

"Actually," said Sierra, pointing to a square tile on the floor near the book sorter, "I think they were."

Kyle looked down. The tile was glowing like one of the tablet computer screens upstairs in the rotunda. Kyle read the words zipping across the illuminated square.

"'Congratulations,'" he read out loud. "'For helping Haley and being a sport, you've earned much more than a good report.'"

The tile popped open.

Inside a small compartment was a rolled-up tube of paper with a yellow card clipped to its end.

"Huh," said Akimi. "I guess somebody *was* watching."

Kyle pulled the yellow card off the paper tube. It smelled like lemons.

"What's it say?" asked Sierra.

Kyle flipped the card over so Sierra and Akimi could see what was printed on it:

SUPER-DOOPER BONUS CLUE.

22

"Oh, man, that was so dumb!"

Haley could not believe how idiotic she had been.

"Trying to crawl out of a book return slot? Chya. Like that was going to work."

She was giving herself a good talking-to as she trudged up the steps to the first floor.

When she entered the rotunda, she saw Charles Chiltington slipping out into the lobby again.

Chiltington was a snake. Worse. A garden slug. Maybe a leech. Something oily and slimy that left a greasy trail and liked to mooch off other people's ideas. That was why Chiltington had tailed the twin library nerds, Peckleman and Fernandez, upstairs during last night's dessert hunt. Haley was smart enough to know that Chiltington was hoping to steal the book geeks' ideas.

Actually, Haley was a lot smarter than anybody (except

her teachers and whoever scored her IQ tests) knew. With certain people, mainly grown-ups and silly boys, pretending to be a ditzy princess made getting what she wanted a whole lot easier.

And what she wanted right now was money. Lots of money. Her dad had been out of work for nearly a year. They'd run through all their rainy-day savings. They'd had to borrow from relatives and in-laws.

If Haley could win this competition and become Mr. Lemoncello's spokesmodel, her family's money woes would be over and they wouldn't have to sell their home. And once other people saw her on TV for Lemoncello games, they'd want her for their commercials, too. And movies. Maybe her own sitcom. Something on the Disney Channel.

But for all that to happen, Haley needed a winning idea—and fast. Something better than "crawl through a slot that's barely wide enough for your wrist." Maybe she should flush herself down the toilet and escape through the sewers like Charles did in that video game.

She headed over to the Book Nook Café so she could sit down and think.

She stepped into the room and checked out the snack table. There were trays of cookies, strawberries, bananas, and brownies. Sitting down to nibble on a macaroon, she studied the row of cookbooks displayed on the bookshelves lining the wall.

One in particular caught her eye: *Cupcakes, Cookies & Pie, Oh, My!*

Because the cover looked extremely familiar: two googly-eyed sheep made out of chocolate-frosted cakes with gobs of mini marshmallows for fleece. Haley had seen the cover before.

In the lobby!

It was in that glass case of memorable reads selected by the library staff.

She went over to the shelf and picked up the book. When she opened the cover, she discovered two cards.

One was a four-by-four piece of white cardboard with the black silhouette of a sheep on it.

The second card was yellow and about the same size as a Community Chest card in Monopoly. Haley sniffed the card. It smelled like lemons.

She grinned. "For *Lemon*cello!"

On one side of the yellow card was printed:

SUPER-DOOPER BONUS CLUE

On the other was the clue:

YOUR MARVELOUS MEMORY HAS EARNED YOU EVEN MORE MEMORIES. PROCEED TO THE LEMONCELLO-ABILIA ROOM.

LOOK FOR ITEM #12.

Haley slid both cards into the back pocket of her jeans,

pulled out her library floor plan, and found the Lemoncello-abilia Room. It was up on the third floor.

Making certain nobody (i.e., Charles Chiltington) was following her, Haley quietly dashed up a spiral staircase to the second floor. Checking for Chiltington one more time, she tiptoed up to the third floor, where she found the room labeled "Lemoncello-abilia: Mini-Museum of Personally Interesting and Somewhat Quirky Junk."

Haley opened the door and stepped inside.

The front room was like a storage warehouse. Cardboard boxes were stacked on top of wooden crates sitting on plastic bins stuffed with papers. All the boxes, bins, and crates were numbered. She saw one labeled "#576."

"Guess Mr. Lemoncello never throws anything away," Haley remarked as she scanned the heaps, looking for the #12 mentioned on her bonus card.

Weaving her way through the stacks and columns, Haley finally found her Super-Dooper Bonus. Item #12 was an old boot box from an Alexandriaville shoe store Haley had never heard of. Someone had taped a label on the lid: "Paraphernalia, Accoutrements, and Doodads from Mr. Lemoncello's 12th Year."

Haley lifted the lid. The box was filled with all sorts of confusing knickknacks: hand-whittled prototypes for game pieces; a star-spangled, red-white-and-blue "H-H-H Humphrey" button; a battered clasp envelope sealed up with tons of tape.

Someone had scribbled "First and Worst Idea Ever" on the front of the envelope with a Magic Marker.

There were also a felt pennant from Disneyland and a rubber-banded stack of cartoony cards for something called Wacky Packages. (The card on top was Weakies, Breakfast of Chumps.)

Haley knew this memory box had to be an important clue.

Why? She had absolutely no idea.

23

Kyle flipped over his lemon-scented Super-Dooper Bonus card and read what was written on the other side.

YOU WILL FIND THE ULTIMATE VERSION OF THIS BOARD GAME ON THE SECOND-FLOOR BALCONY CIRCLING THE ROTUNDA.

"Huh?" said Akimi. "What's that mean?"

"I don't know. Let's roll out the paper and see."

Akimi and Sierra helped Kyle anchor the edges of the scroll on the tiled floor.

"Okay," said Kyle. "It looks like the early sketch for a board game. See the circle in the center of the other circle? That's probably where you place the spinner. You move your pieces around the ten rooms. . . ."

He stopped.

"Wait a second."

"What?" said Akimi.

"Do you recognize the game?" asked Sierra.

"Yep," said Kyle. "I played it this week with my brother Curtis. It's Mr. Lemoncello's Bewilderingly Baffling Bibliomania. It takes place in a make-believe *library*."

"What about finding the 'ultimate version' up on the second-floor balcony?" asked Sierra.

Kyle grinned. "You'll see."

Coming up from the basement, Kyle saw Andrew Peckleman in the middle of the Rotunda Reading Room, opening a long metal box sitting on top of the center desk.

The holographic image of Mrs. Tobin was there, smiling patiently, as Peckleman pulled some kind of magazine out of the box. Miguel was also near the librarian's desk, apparently waiting his turn for a consultation.

"That's the box we saw the robot pluck off the shelf," whispered Akimi.

Kyle nodded. He motioned for the others to follow him and slipped around the circumference of the rotunda. Akimi and Sierra slunk after him.

In the shadows on the far side of the room, they saw Haley Daley heading for the staircase they'd just come up: steps that would take her back to the basement.

Kyle wondered if she'd found something else to crawl through. If so, he hoped it was bigger than a mailbox.

"Is this the *real* magazine?" he heard Peckleman shout at the hologram.

"Yes, ANDREW. This concludes your Librarian Consultation. Next? How may I help you, MIGUEL?"

"Not so fast," snapped Andrew. "I'm not done."

"Um, your consultation just concluded," said Miguel.

"Says who?"

"The librarian."

"MIGUEL?" said the hologram of Mrs. Tobin. "What is *your* question?"

"Sorry, bro. I told you."

"She's just like Mrs. Yunghans at school," snapped Peckleman. "All the librarians like you better than me!"

"Yo. Ease up."

"You'll see, Mrs. Tobin! You'll all see. I'm gonna beat Miguel Fernandez, big-time! And when I win, I'm gonna tell Mr. Lemoncello to fire you!"

"She's a hologram," said Miguel with a laugh. "You can't fire somebody who doesn't actually exist."

"Then I'll tell Lemoncello to pull her plug." Peckleman grabbed his magazine and stormed out of the rotunda into the lobby.

"I guess Andrew's planning on doing something with the front door," Kyle whispered to Akimi.

"Well, that's totally dumb. They already told us the way out isn't the way we came in."

"Maybe Andrew doesn't think Dr. Zinchenko was telling us the truth," suggested Sierra.

116

"Come on," said Kyle, leading his team toward the closest staircase up to the second floor. Glancing over his shoulder, he watched Miguel place a slip of paper on the table in front of the semi-translucent librarian.

"This item has been temporarily removed from the Stacks, MIGUEL," said Mrs. Tobin. "You will find it in a display case next to the original Winkle and Grimble scale model. Let me give you that location."

There was a grinding sound, like when movie tickets shoot up through the slot at the box office. Miguel snatched the small square of paper that popped up from the librarian's desk and spun around.

He froze the instant he saw Kyle, Akimi, and Sierra sneaking around the room behind him.

24

"Hey," said Miguel, hiding the tiny square of paper behind his back. "Yo."

"Yo," said Kyle. "Whazzup?"

"Nothin'. Just, you know, workin' the puzzle."

"Yeah. Us too."

"Okay. Later."

"Later."

Both boys thumped their fists on their chests like baseball players do. Miguel turned and ran for a staircase winding up to the second floor.

"Come on, you guys," said Kyle as he took off running for a different set of steps.

When Kyle, Akimi, and Sierra made it up to the balcony, they watched Miguel run up to the third floor. As soon as he disappeared into a room up there, Kyle unrolled the game sketch.

"Look at the drawing, then look down at the floor," said Kyle.

"They're the same!" said Sierra.

"Exactly. A circular room with a round desk at the center of that circle."

"Awesome," said Akimi. "And there are ten doors ringed around the balcony up here on the second floor, just like on the game board."

Kyle tapped the rendering of the spinner in the right-hand corner of the game plans. "See how the spinner is divided into ten different-colored sections numbered zero to nine?"

"It looks like the Wonder Dome," said Akimi, "when it's not doing its kaleidoscope thing or running a video that makes you think the building is hang gliding across Alaska, which totally made me airsick."

"Well, in the game, you have to go into all ten Dewey decimal book rooms and answer a trivia question about a book. If you answer correctly, you slip a book into your bookshelf and move on to another part of the library. When you have ten books, one from each room, it's basically a race to see who can exit the library first."

"Okay," said Akimi, sounding pumped. "This is good. This is major."

"Except one thing's missing," said Kyle.

"What?" asked Sierra.

"Mr. Lemoncello always works a clever back-door shortcut into his games. For instance, in Family Frenzy . . ."

119

"You can use the coal chute to slide into the million-aire's mansion at the end," said Akimi.

"Exactly. And in that castle game, Charles snuck out through the sewers. Anyway, when my brother Curtis beat me at Bibliomania . . ."

"You lost?" Akimi acted surprised.

"It happens. Occasionally. But only because Curtis used this shortcut." Kyle tapped a black square on the game diagram. "It took him straight out to the street. He beat me by one spin of the spinner."

"I don't see any black squares in the floor of our rotunda," said Akimi.

"Maybe," said Sierra, "for this new game, Mr. Lemon-cello put the secret square someplace besides the main room."

Kyle nodded. "And maybe to win this *new* game we need to play the *old* one."

"You're a genius!" said Akimi.

"No. My brother Curtis is the genius. I just like to play games. So, do libraries even have board games?"

"Sure," said Sierra. "I think. I mean, the library in my dad's town has them."

"Which department?" asked Akimi, pulling out her floor plan.

"Young adult."

Akimi tapped her map. "Third floor. Stairs over there."

"Let's go!" said Kyle.

But before they could take off, they heard Mr. Lemon-cello's voice echoing in the rotunda.

"Are you ready for your Extreme Challenge, Bridgette?"

Kyle and his teammates peered over the ledge of the balcony. Bridgette Wadge was alone in front of the librarian's desk, staring up at the ceiling.

"Yes, sir," she said.

"Are you sure?" Mr. Lemoncello's voice boomed out of hidden speakers. "You still have twenty-two hours to find the exit."

"I want to go for it now, sir. Get a jump on everybody else."

"Very well. Dr. Zinchenko? Reset the statues."

The ten holographic statues in their recessed nooks flickered off, leaving black and empty spaces.

"This Extreme Challenge is based on the classic Game of Authors card game," said Mr. Lemoncello. "Here are the authors in your deck."

Magically, new holographic statues appeared as Mr. Lemoncello rattled off the authors' names. "Charles Dickens, Raymond Chandler, Edgar Allan Poe, Agatha Christie, Patricia Highsmith, Mario Puzo, Frederick Forsyth, John Le Carré, Dashiell Hammett, and Fyodor Dostoyevsky."

"He wrote *Crime and Punishment*," said Bridgette excitedly.

"Indeed he did."

"In fact," said Bridgette, "all those authors wrote crime novels."

"Correct again. However, that's the easy part. Dr. Z?

121

How do we make this authors game ridiculously difficult enough to qualify as an Extreme Challenge?"

"Simple," the librarian's voice echoed under the dome. "You will have two minutes, Bridgette, to name four books written by each of our authors."

Kyle gulped. "That's impossible," he whispered.

"Not really," said Sierra. She was about to start rattling off titles when Mr. Lemoncello said, "Go!" The sound of a ticking clock reverberated around the room.

"Um, okay," said Bridgette down on the main floor. "Agatha Christie. *Murder on the Orient Express, Ten Little Indians, Death on the Nile, The Mousetrap.*"

Somewhere, a bell dinged, and the British lady in the sensible shoes disappeared.

"Poe. *The Murders in the Rue Morgue, The Masque of the Red Death, The Purloined Letter, The Cask of Amontillado.*"

Another ding. Another statue vanished.

Bridgette kept going.

"Man," whispered Kyle, "what grade is she in? College?"

"Seventh," said Akimi, "just like us."

Bridgette Wadge kept tearing through the authors. The bell kept dinging.

But the clock kept ticking, too.

"Ten seconds," said Mr. Lemoncello.

Bridgette had saved the worst for last.

"Fyodor Dostoyevsky. *Crime and Punishment.* Um,

Crime and Punishment . . . The one about the brothers . . . *The Brothers* . . ."

And then she stalled.

She'd run out of gas.

A buzzer sounded.

"I'm sorry, Bridgette," said Dr. Zinchenko. "But, as we advised you, the Extreme Challenges are extremely difficult. You will be going home with lovely parting gifts. Kindly hand your library card to Clarence and thank you for playing Escape from Mr. Lemoncello's Library."

"That settles it," muttered Kyle. "I am *never, ever* asking for one of those Extreme Challenge dealios."

"Me neither," said Akimi.

"I might," said Sierra. "Maybe."

And then she showed Kyle and Akimi the rumpled sheet of paper where she had written down *five* book titles for all ten authors.

25

Akimi grabbed the door handle to the Young Adult Room. "It's locked."

"Here," said Sierra. "Use my library card."

"Huh," said Akimi. "Your books on the back are different, too."

"I think they all are. I got *The Egypt Game* and *The Westing Game*."

"Two books about games?" said Kyle. "Sweet."

Akimi slipped Sierra's card into a reader slot above the doorknob. The door clicked. Kyle pushed it open.

The walls of the Young Adult Room were painted purple and yellow. There were swirly zebra-print rugs on the floor and a lumpy cluster of beanbag chairs. A couple of sofas were designed to look like Scrabble trays, with letter-square pillows.

Akimi nudged Kyle in the ribs. "Check it out."

In the far corner stood a carnival ticket booth with a mechanical dummy seated inside. A "Fun & Games" banner hung off the booth's striped roof. The dummy inside the glass booth?

He looked like Mr. Lemoncello.

He wasn't wearing a turban, but the Mr. Lemoncello mannequin reminded Kyle of the Zoltar Speaks fortune-teller booths he'd seen in video game arcades.

"That's not really him, is it?" said Akimi, who was right behind Kyle.

"No. It's a mechanical doll."

The frozen automaton was dressed in a black top hat and a bright red ringmaster jacket. Since the booth had the "Fun & Games" banner, Kyle figured you might have to talk to the dummy to get a game.

"Um, hello," he said. "We'd like to play a board game."

Bells rang, whistles whistled, and chaser lights blinked. The mechanical Mr. Lemoncello jostled to life.

"If you want a game, just say its name." The life-size puppet's blocky jaw flapped open and shut—almost in sync with the words.

"Do you have Mr. Lemoncello's Bewilderingly Baffling Bibliomania?"

"Did Joey Pigza lose control? Was Ella enchanted?"

"Huh?"

"Just say yes," suggested Sierra.

125

"Yes," said Kyle.

"Well, great Gilly Hopkins," said the Lemoncello dummy, "here you go!"

Kyle heard some mechanical noises and some whirring. Then, with a clunk, a wide slot popped open in the front of the booth and a game box slid out.

"Enjoy!" said the dummy. "And remember, it's not whether you win or lose, it's how you play the game. So be sure to read the instructions—so you'll know how to *play the game*."

Kyle took the box to a table.

"Okay," he said, raising the lid, "let's set it up and—"

There was a beep and the door opened. . . .

"Where is he?"

Andrew Peckleman barged into the room waving his antique magazine—something called *Popular Science Monthly*.

"Who're you looking for?" said Kyle.

"Mr. Lemoncello. I heard him. Is he in here?"

Kyle pointed toward the frozen Lemoncello doll sitting in the carnie booth. "It's a dummy."

Peckleman whipped his head around from side to side. "Is there a camera in here?"

"Right over the door."

Peckleman spun around to face it. Kyle, Akimi, and Sierra formed a human shield to hide their Bibliomania box.

"I want to use a second lifeline!" Peckleman shouted at the camera. "I want to talk to an expert!"

"Very well," said a calm voice Kyle immediately recognized as belonging to Dr. Zinchenko. "With whom do you wish to speak?"

"The guy who wrote this stupid magazine article about cracking open bank vaults in the 1930s!"

"I'm afraid we cannot arrange that for you, Andrew."

"Why not? The guy's a moron. He didn't tell me anything about how to open the front door, which is what my Google search said this magazine would do!"

"We told you the way out isn't the way in."

"That was just a red herring! A trick, to throw us off course."

"No, Andrew. It was not. What is the title of the article?"

" 'Newest Bank Vaults Defy the Cracksman.' "

"Ah. Well, that should have been a hint. Apparently, the reporter concluded that thieves could *not* break open the vault doors. When doing Internet research, it is important to—"

"Let me talk to the stupid idiot!"

"I am sorry. That magazine was published in 1936. The reporter is dead."

"Well, then, I want to talk to Mr. Lemoncello!"

"Excuse me?"

"I want to talk to Mr. Lemoncello!"

"This is highly irregular. . . ."

"And so's this game. You people have it rigged so

Miguel Fernandez will win. I know you do! That's why Mr. Lemoncello is afraid to talk to me."

Kyle heard the carnival booth dummy clatter back to life.

"Hello, Andrew. How may I help you?"

This Lemoncello didn't sound prerecorded. Apparently, the real deal was using the dummy to do his talking.

"Your library stinks!" shouted Peckleman.

"Oh, dear. Have you boys been playing that castle sewer game again?"

"No! But this stupid article should've given me the stupid answer but the stupid writer didn't write what he should've written."

"I see. And can you rephrase that in the form of a question?"

"How many can I ask you?"

"Just one. And then we're done."

"Okay. You're the expert on this stupid new library game. So where's your favorite contestant? Where's Miguel?"

"Is that your final question?"

"Yes!"

"Assuming our video monitors are correct, Mr. Fernandez is on the other side of the third floor, doing research in the Art and Artifacts Room."

"Thanks!"

Andrew bolted out the door.

The Lemoncello puppet bucked and drooped into its "off" mode.

Kyle sprang up from the table. "Come on," he said to Akimi and Sierra.

Akimi sighed. "*Now* where are we going?"

"To make sure Peckleman doesn't do something stupid that gets Miguel kicked out of the game."

"And why would we do that?"

"Because Miguel's our friend."

Akimi glanced at her floor plan. "The Art and Artifacts Room is on the other side of the circle."

"Sierra—stay here and guard the game box. Come on, Akimi."

Kyle and Akimi looped around the third-floor balcony to the other side. Kyle glanced at his watch. It was almost three p.m. They really needed to start focusing on The Game and not all this other monkey junk.

As they neared the Art & Artifacts Room, there was a shout, and the door flew open. Andrew Peckleman came running out.

Behind him were a woman with the head and tail of a lioness, and a Pharaoh in a cobra headpiece.

The Pharaoh stopped. "May onions grow in your earwax!" And a series of holographic hieroglyphics danced across the air.

Andrew Peckleman raced to a staircase, grabbed both handrails, and hurried down to the second floor. The Egyptians vanished.

Kyle and Akimi entered the Art & Artifacts Room and found Miguel seated at a desk with what looked like blueprints.

"You okay?" asked Kyle.

"Yeah, man. I'm fine. Thanks."

"Those guys chasing Andrew. Where'd they come from?"

"Holograms from the giant Lego Sphinx and Pyramid exhibit."

"So why'd they turn on Andrew?" asked Akimi.

"I don't know. One minute he's yelling at me. The next, the Pharaoh and Sekhmet are yelling at him."

"Sek-who?" said Kyle.

"Sekhmet," said Akimi. "The Egyptian lion goddess and warrior. Haven't you read *The Red Pyramid* by Rick Riordan?"

"It's on my list," said Kyle. Or it would be. He definitely needed to start a reading list soon so he could catch up with everybody else.

"I bet the security guards in the control room fired up the Egyptian holograms when they saw Andrew going berserk in here," said Akimi.

"Good," said Miguel. "A library is supposed to be a place for peaceful contemplation."

That was when Sierra Russell rushed into the room.

"You guys! Right after you left! The Mr. Lemoncello dummy spit out a bonus card!"

26

"Very clever," said Charles, pulling another silhouette card out of a book.

This cover had been easy to find. It was the third book on the top shelf of the Staff Picks display. The image on the front was a bright yellow yield sign. The title? *Universal Road Signs* by "renowned trafficologist" Abigail Rose Painter. Charles had found the matching book in the 300s room on the second floor. The 300s were all about social sciences, including things like commerce, communications, and—ta-da!—transportation.

The image also fit nicely with the pictogram he had found in the 700s room in a book called *The Umpire Strikes Back*. That baseball book was the first cover on the *second* shelf in the display case and had given Charles a card with the classic pose of an umpire calling an out.

Reading the images from left to right, then down—just like you'd read a book—Charles knew he was on the right track. The traffic sign book gave him "walk" and the umpire book gave him "out."

Put the two picture words together and he had "walk out."

Clearly, if he could find all twelve silhouettes, the Staff Picks display would tell him how to "walk out" of the library (although he had absolutely no idea what the first image he had found, the quarterback tossing a pass, had to do with escaping the library—not yet, anyway).

"Three down, nine to go," said Charles, winking up at the closest security camera. "And, Mr. Lemoncello, if you're watching, may I just say that you are an extremely brilliant man?"

Charles had never sucked up to a video camera before. He figured it was worth a shot. Maybe Mr. Lemoncello would send him a bonus clue or something.

Instead, when Charles stepped out of the 300s room, somebody sent him Andrew Peckleman. The goggle-eyed library geek was sputtering mad as he rushed down the steps and stomped around the second-floor balcony.

"Stupid library. Stupid Lemoncello. Stupid sphinx and Sekhmet."

"Why so glum, Andrew?" Charles called out.

"Because this game stinks. Mr. Lemoncello just sent a bunch of holograms hurling hieroglyphics after me. He could put somebody's eye out with those things."

"Really? With a hologram?"

"Hey, they're made with lasers, aren't they?"

"Indeed. Say, speaking of hieroglyphics, where might I find a book about picture languages?"

"Ha! Why should I help you?"

"Because Kyle Keeley is working with Akimi Hughes *and* Sierra Russell. I imagine it is only a matter of time before your friend Miguel Fernandez joins their team, too."

"Miguel isn't my friend! Besides, I'm better at navigating my way through a library than he'll ever be."

"I know. That's why I want you on my team."

"Really?"

Charles smiled. Kids like Andrew Peckleman were so easy to manipulate.

"Oh, yes. Work with me and I guarantee you the

133

world will know that *you* should be the head library aide at Alexandriaville Middle School."

"The four hundreds!" blurted Peckleman.

"Pardon?"

"That's where you'll find books on hieroglyphics and all kinds of languages. If you want secret codes, those are in the six hundreds room. The six-fifties, to be exact."

Charles shot out his hand. "Welcome to Team Charles, Andrew."

The new teammates stepped into the 400s room. For some reason, it was pitch dark and smelled like pine trees.

"*Bienvenida! Bienvenue! Witamy! Kuwakaribisha!* Welcome!" boomed a voice from the ceiling speakers. "This is the four hundreds room, home of foreign languages. Here, CHARLES and ANDREW, you can learn all about your American heritage."

A bank of spotlights thumped on.

Charles and Andrew were face-to-blank-face with a row of four featureless mannequins. An overhead projector beamed a movie onto dummy number two, turning it into a perky woman who looked like a flight attendant.

"Hello, and welcome to *your* American heritage. I'm Debbie. Let's begin your voyage!"

"That's okay," said Charles. "We're rather busy."

"Let's begin your voyage," the mannequin repeated.

Charles sighed. Obviously, there was no way to turn

this silly display off. He might as well speed things along by telling the dummy what it wanted to hear.

"Fine. But can we go with the abridged version? We're in a bit of a rush."

"Yeah," added Andrew, "we have to escape before noon tomorrow."

The woman, whose body remained frozen while a movie made her face and costume spring to life, reminded Charles of the graveyard statues from the Haunted Mansion ride at Disney World.

"While we research your family trees," she said, "please enjoy this short and informative film."

"Is this part of the game?" Andrew whispered to Charles.

"Possibly. Pay attention for any bonus clues."

"Okay. What do they look like?"

"Who can ever say?"

A screen behind the life-size dummies leapt to life with all sorts of scratchy images of people huddled together on the deck of a boat near the Statue of Liberty.

"For decades," narrated the ceiling voice, "public libraries have proudly served America's newest citizens—the immigrants who flock to these shores yearning for the freedom to build their own American dreams."

Charles really wasn't interested in this kind of stuff. His ancestors were all *Americans;* the only language they spoke was English.

"Yes, the library is where many new arrivals journey

first. To learn their new homeland's language. To keep in touch with the world they left behind. To search for the gainful employment that will make them productive residents of their newly adopted home!"

The movie dissolved into blackness.

"Thank you for your kind attention," chirped the cheerful Debbie. "We have completed your American family tree. Let's meet your first American ancestors!"

Two mannequins sprang to illuminated life, both of them dressed in traditional Thanksgiving pilgrim costumes.

"I know who they are already," said Charles. "That's John Chiltington and his wife, Elinor. They came to Plymouth Colony on the *Mayflower*. Can we move on to Andrew's family? Please?"

"Of course," said Debbie.

The mannequins quickly went through Andrew Peckleman's ancestry. Apparently, the family name had originally been Pickleman, because they made pickles. After a prolonged parade of pickle people, the dummies took on the guise of Andrew's most famous ancestor, a guy in horn-rimmed glasses and a tweed sports coat named Peter Paul Peckleman.

"I appeared on the TV game show *Concentration* in 1968," he announced, "and won a roomful of furniture and wood paneling for my rumpus room."

Charles smiled. He knew the TV game show *Concentration* was very similar to Mr. Lemoncello's Phenomenal

Picture Word Puzzler, one of the games he had picked up at the toy store. Peter Paul Peckleman's claim to fame was further confirmation that piecing together the picture puzzle would show Charles how to escape from the library.

He'd been right.

The dummies had just given him a bonus clue.

27

Excited by the sudden appearance of a second bonus card, Sierra read it out loud:

"'Two plus two can equal more than four. Put two and two together and you'll be closer than before.'"

Akimi raised her hand.

"Yes?" said Sierra.

"You do realize that Miguel here isn't on our team?"

"Oh. Right. Sorry."

Miguel turned to Kyle. "You guys are a team?"

"Yep. You want to join?"

"Maybe. Not sure. Check back with me later, man."

"No problem," said Kyle.

He fist-thumped his chest. Miguel fist-thumped his. They were flashing each other peace signs when Sierra said, "I think this means we should all play together as a team. Remember what it says on the fountain down in the lobby: 'Knowledge not shared remains unknown.' "

"Maybe," said Miguel. "Like I said—let me get back to you guys. I'm workin' on a few angles of my own. Flying solo."

"Sure. No problem." Kyle was about to do the whole fist-chest-bump-peace-sign thing again when he had a brainstorm. "Miguel? Quick question. What's on your library card?"

Miguel shrugged. "My name and the number one."

"Anything else? Like on the back?"

"Nothing really. Couple of books."

"Two?"

"Yeah."

"What're their titles?"

Miguel bit his lip. "Don't want to say."

"Because you think they might be clues?"

"Not saying what I might or might not be thinking, bro."

Kyle nodded.

"There are two different books on the back of everybody's library cards," said Akimi, thinking out loud. " 'Put two and two together and you'll be closer than before.' The book titles *are* some sort of clue. My books are *One*—"

"Um, Akimi?" Kyle shook his head. Nodded toward Miguel.

"Right. Sorry. My bad."

139

"Oh-kay, Miguel," said Kyle. "If and when you decide to team up with us, you can show us the two books on the back of your card; we'll all show you ours. We'll also split the prize four ways. Deal?"

"Deal."

"Come on, guys." Kyle gestured toward the exit.

"Where are we going?" asked Sierra.

Kyle dropped his voice. "The Electronic Learning Center."

"You want to play video games?" said Akimi. "Now? Seriously, Kyle, we may need to rethink your status as team captain."

"I don't want to play video games. I want to check out the discard pile."

"Huh?"

"The cards the players who went home early dumped into that goldfish bowl!"

"I'm comin' with you guys," said Miguel. "I've been thinking about those extra cards, too."

"Fine," said Kyle. "Whatever."

When they entered the game room, they saw Clarence, his arms folded across his chest genie-style. He was standing guard in front of the discard pile.

"May I help you?" he asked.

"Um, yeah," said Kyle. "We want to check out the cards in the bowl."

"Sorry," said Clarence. "You can't have them."

"But," said Mr. Lemoncello, his face suddenly appearing on every video screen in the room, "you can win them!"

Dressed in a polka-dotted bow tie and snazzy jacket like a game show host, Mr. Lemoncello had one arm resting on a slender Plexiglas podium. Behind him, Dr. Zinchenko—all decked out in a sparkly red minidress—looked like the models that point at prizes on TV.

"Are the four of you ready to play Let's Do a Deal?" When Mr. Lemoncello said that, he pushed a big red button in his podium. A prerecorded studio audience whistled, cheered, and applauded.

"Um, what's Let's Do a Deal?" asked Kyle.

"My first game to ever be turned into a TV show. Brought to you by lemon Pledge!"

Dr. Zinchenko started singing: *"Lemon Pledge, very pretty. Put the shine down, lemon good . . ."*

"Thank you, Dr. Z!" said Mr. Lemoncello, bopping the button to make the audience cheer again. "Now then, kids, here's the deal: Solve one simple picture puzzle and you four win the five library cards in the bowl."

"And if we lose?"

"Simple. Each of you loses his or her library card and adds it to the discard bowl for our next lucky contestants to try and win."

He banged the red button again. The audience cheered exactly the same way they cheered before.

Kyle turned to the others. "What do you say, guys?"

"Let's go for it," said Akimi.

Sierra nodded.

"Miguel?"

"I'm in, bro."

"You're joining our team?"

"Absolutely." They knocked knuckles to seal the deal.

Mr. Lemoncello must've whacked his button again, because the canned studio audience started cheering.

Kyle wondered what the sound effects would be if he and his friends lost their library cards playing Let's Do a Deal.

Probably groans.

And weeping. Lots and lots of weeping.

28

"Now then," said Mr. Lemoncello, "are you ready to play Risking Everything for Five Little Library Cards?"

Kyle swallowed hard. Then he nodded.

"All right, you Maniac Magees, here is your picture puzzle. The category is Famous Quotes. You have sixty seconds to solve this rebus."

"Wait a second," said Akimi. "What's a rebus?"

"You figure out the words in a phrase by looking at pictures and symbols," said Kyle.

"For instance," added Miguel, "the letters 'R' and 'E' plus a picture of a school bus would equal 'rebus.'"

"Oh. Okay," said Akimi. "If you guys say so."

"Are you ready to play?" asked Mr. Lemoncello.

Kyle looked at his teammates, who nodded.

"Yes, sir."

"Then on your mark . . . get set . . . go, dog, go!"

Mr. Lemoncello's image disappeared. Ticktock clock music started playing. The video screens all projected the same picture:

let=side

-g
-l

A

A

-d
-k

-wo

+'s

-an

+t

s=nd

+ide
-p

-g
-l

A

-w
ch='s

-ls

sh=d

2

-b

gr +

+ o

le=rx

"We're officially dead," said Akimi.

"Fifty-five seconds," said Mr. Lemoncello.

"Okay, we break it up four ways," said Kyle. "The first and third rows are similar, I'll do them."

"I'll do the last one," said Akimi.

"I'll take the second row," said Miguel.

"I'm four," said Sierra.

"Fifty seconds," said Mr. Lemoncello.

Everyone went to work.

"Mine is some guy hitting himself in the thumb but with a 'gr' and an 'o'?" muttered Akimi. "Then the male symbol where the 'le' equals 'rx'? 'Marx'? Does that make sense? Hello? Kyle? Is my second half 'Marx'?"

Kyle didn't answer. He was too busy deciphering his own clue lines. "'Outlet,' change the 'let' to 'side,'" he mumbled. "'Golf' minus the 'g' and the 'l.' The letter 'A.'"

"Forty seconds."

"'Dog.'" He dropped to the third line. He just needed the first word. "'Bowling *pins*' without the 'p' but add an 'ide.'"

"Thirty seconds."

Kyle glanced at Miguel. He was moving his lips, mouthing out his part of the quote. Sierra, too.

"You guys ready?" Kyle whispered.

"Hang on," said Miguel.

"Twenty seconds."

"Okay. Go."

Kyle read the first line: "'Outside of a dog . . .'"

145

Miguel picked up the thread: "'. . . a book is man's best friend.'"

Kyle continued. "'Inside of a dog . . .'"

Sierra took over. "'. . . it's too dark to read.'"

Akimi brought them home: "'Groucho Marx!'"

"Is that your final answer?" asked Mr. Lemoncello.

"Yes," said Kyle, and then he repeated the entire quote: "'Outside of a dog, a book is man's best friend. Inside of a dog, it's too dark to read.'—Groucho Marx."

Bells rang. Chaser lights flashed. The audience went wild. Akimi and Sierra actually squealed and hugged each other.

"You are correct!" shouted Mr. Lemoncello. "There's no dead end in Norvelt, not today! Take those five library cards, Team Kyle! You won them fair and square!"

Charles and Andrew heard a commotion on the third floor. Bells ringing. An audience whooping it up. Girls squealing.

"Come on," said Charles.

They raced up the stairs and peeked into the Electronic Learning Center. Kyle Keeley and his teammates were all hugging each other and slapping high fives. On every video screen in the game room, Charles could see a pictogram puzzle.

"What's going on in there?" whispered Andrew.

"They might be gaining on us," Charles whispered back. "We need to pick up our pace. Quick—where would I find a book called *Hoosier Hospitality* written by Eve Healy Aresty?"

"The nine hundreds room."

"Let's go."

Charles and Andrew scurried back to the second floor and the 900s room.

Where they found Haley Daley holding *Hoosier Hospitality* by Eve Healy Aresty.

"Oh, hello, you guys," she said, slamming the book shut.

Charles moved toward her. Slowly.

"Find anything interesting in that book, Haley?"

"Not really." She giggled. "Just a bunch of dumb junk about Indiana."

Charles knew she was hiding something.

"I wonder, Haley, if you and I might share a quiet word?" He turned to Andrew. "In private."

"Does that mean I'm supposed to leave?"

"Yes, Andrew. It's for the good of the team. Trust me."

"Okay. But I'll be right outside that door if you decide to double-cross me or something."

"Thank you, Andrew. This will only take a quick minute."

Peckleman left the room.

Smiling, Charles moved even closer to Haley. So close he could smell her bubble gum. Or shampoo. Maybe both.

"Let's step over here," he said, taking Haley by the elbow. "I found another fascinating book that I think you'll just love." He guided her to a spot behind a bookcase where their conversation couldn't be observed by the security camera blinking up in the ceiling.

Haley went with Charles.

If he had been looking for the same book she'd just found, that meant he was playing the library escape game along a similar path. Charles Chiltington might have clues Haley could use. Clues she needed.

"Rumor has it," Charles whispered, "that your parents wrote your library essay for you."

Inside, Haley was grinning. Obviously, Charles would try to bully her into joining his team. Fine. She'd pretend to be frightened.

"What?" she whispered back, pretending to be terrified. "That's a lie. My dad just helped me with some of the spelling."

"Aha! So you admit it. All the spelling in your essay wasn't your own?"

Okay. This was going to take more acting skill than usual. Having someone check your spelling wasn't against anybody's rules for anything.

She widened her eyes. Made her lips quiver. "What do you want, Charles?"

"For you to join my team."

"Why should I do that?"

"Two reasons. One, if you're on my side, your flagrant plagiarism remains our dirty little secret. Two, I know what to do with that silhouette card you just found in the *Hoosier Hospitality* book."

"You do?"

"Oh, yes. If we share our clues, the pictures will create a phrase telling us how to find the alternate exit."

Haley smiled. For real. This was working out perfectly. She'd get all their clues, and even if they all won together, Mr. Lemoncello would definitely make her the real star of his TV commercials. She had "zazz." Charles and Andrew did not.

"Okay," she said. "Deal. I'm on your team."

Then she handed Charles the clue she had found in the *Hoosier* book:

"Of course!" said Charles. "After all, Indiana is the Hoosier State."

29

"Oh, man," said Kyle, leading his team around the balcony, back to the Young Adult Room. "Nine library cards. This is fantastic!"

They gathered around a table.

"Okay, guys. Time for everybody to put their cards on the table. Literally."

The teammates set down their cards. Kyle spread out the five from the discard bowl. Akimi pulled out a pad and wrote all the information on one master list:

BOOKS/AUTHORS ON THE BACKS OF
LIBRARY CARDS

#1 Miguel Fernandez
Incident at Hawk's Hill by Allan W. Eckert/
No, David! by David Shannon

#2 Akimi Hughes
One Fish Two Fish Red Fish Blue Fish
by Dr. Seuss/Nine Stories by J. D. Salinger

#3 UNKNOWN

#4 Bridgette Wadge
Tales of a Fourth Grade Nothing
by Judy Blume/Harry Potter and the
Sorcerer's Stone by J. K. Rowling

#5 Sierra Russell
The Egypt Game by Zilpha Keatley Snyder/
The Westing Game by Ellen Raskin

#6 Yasmeen Smith-Snyder
Around the World in Eighty Days
by Jules Verne/The Yak Who Yelled Yuck
by Carol Pugliano-Martin

#7 Sean Keegan
Olivia by Ian Falconer/Unreal! by Paul Jennings

#8 UNKNOWN

#9 Rose Vermette
All-of-a-Kind Family by Sydney Taylor/
Scat by Carl Hiaasen

#10 Kayla Corson
Anna to the Infinite Power
by Mildred Ames/Where the Sidewalk
Ends by Shel Silverstein

#11 UNKNOWN

#12 Kyle Keeley
I Love You, Stinky Face by Lisa McCourt/
The Napping House by Audrey Wood

"Wow," said Sierra. "That's a lot of good books. But what do all those authors and titles mean?"

"It means we need Charles's, Andrew's, and Haley's cards," said Kyle.

"Really?" said Akimi. "Because if you ask me, we already have way too much information."

"Well," said Kyle, "maybe later we'll find a clue that'll tell us how to read *this* clue."

"And how are we going to do that?" asked Miguel.

"Have you ever played this?" Kyle pointed to the Bibliomania box.

"Nope. Always wanted to."

"We were just about to get up a game."

"Does this have anything to do with finding our way out of the library?"

"We sure hope so," said Akimi.

"Awesome."

"By the way," Kyle said to Miguel, "what'd you find in the Art and Artifacts Room?"

"Yeah," said Akimi. "All those papers you kept trying to hide from us."

Miguel grinned. "The original blueprints for the Gold Leaf Bank building."

"Clever," said Kyle. "That way you could look for old exits that might still exist behind new walls."

"Exactly."

"Find any extra exits?" asked Akimi.

"Nope. No hidden windows, either."

"Yeah, what's up with that? How come they built this place with so few windows?"

"To discourage bank robbers, I guess," said Kyle.

"Yep," said Miguel. "The only way in was through the front door. The fire exits could only be opened from the inside, like at a movie theater. The vault itself was all the way down in the basement."

"Mr. Lemoncello kept all that security," said Kyle, "and added his own."

"So it would seem."

"Well, hopefully Bibliomania will lead us to some kind of alternate exit."

"And fast," said Akimi. "Don't forget, we're not the only ones playing this game. One of those other guys is probably halfway out the door already."

"Okay," said Kyle, "game play is pretty simple. You spin the spinner and advance your piece the number of spaces the needle points to. You move around the library and go into each of the ten Dewey decimal rooms, where you can pick up a book by answering a clue card. If you guess wrong, you get a new clue card in the same room on your next turn. The first person to fill the ten slots in their 'bookshelf' and spin their way out of the library wins."

"It's sort of like Trivial Pursuit," said Sierra. "And the questions aren't all that hard because they're mostly multiple-choice."

"Let's hear one!" said Miguel eagerly.

The cards were separated into ten multicolored ministacks, one for each room. Kyle grabbed a green card.

"Okay, this is for the eight hundreds room. Literature. 'Deathly ill and pursued by the Ringwraiths, Frodo Baggins was carried safely across the River Bruinen on the gleaming white elf-horse of Glorfindel named: A) Asphodel, B) Asfaloth, C) Almarian, D) Anglachel.' "

Akimi shook her head like she was having a brain freeze. "Wha-huh?"

"I think the answer might be 'A,' " said Miguel.

"They're all 'A's,' " said Kyle. "Asphodel, Asfaloth, Al—"

"It's 'B) Asfaloth,' " said Sierra. "It's from J. R. R. Tolkien's *Lord of the Rings*."

Kyle flipped the card over and read the answer. " 'You are correct. You get a copy of *Lord of the Rings* to put in your bookshelf.' "

"So, Kyle," said Akimi, "how exactly is knowing the name of an elf-horse going to help us get out of the library?"

"Maybe it's like a secret code," suggested Miguel. "And the ten book titles will form a sentence telling us how to get out."

"Possibly," said Kyle. "But I see one problem."

"What's that?"

"It's too random. Mr. Lemoncello would have no idea which ten cards we might pick."

"Well," said Sierra, "maybe there are only *ten* questions. One for each room."

Akimi grabbed the card stacks, fanned them out. "Nope. They're all different."

"Hang on," said Kyle.

He was remembering something about another game: Mr. Lemoncello's Indoor-Outdoor Scavenger Hunt.

How his mother had been able to write to the company and request a fresh set of cards.

He turned to the video camera mounted in a corner. "I'd like my Librarian Consultation, please."

"What's up, Kyle?" asked Miguel.

"I'm playing a hunch."

The holographic Mrs. Tobin appeared behind the young adult librarian's desk.

"How may I help you, KYLE?"

"My friends and I want to play Bibliomania but we were wondering: Is there a new set of cards?"

"Yes, KYLE. There is."

And a fresh deck of cards popped up through a slot in the desk.

30

"We'll just play one bookshelf," said Kyle.

"Because we're a team now, right, bro?" said Miguel.

"Right. Plus, we don't have all day."

"Well," said Akimi, "technically we do. In fact, we have the rest of today and tomorrow till noon."

"We've got like nineteen hours left," said Miguel.

"But Charles and the others," said Sierra. "They could beat us."

"Right," said Kyle. "After all, he *is* a Chiltington. And according to Sir Charles, they never lose. Miguel, you're the newest member of the team. You spin first."

Miguel rubbed his hands together. Limbered up his fingers. Practiced flicking his index finger off his thumb. Made sure he had a good snap and follow-through.

"Would you hurry up and spin before my brain explodes?" pleaded Akimi.

"No problem." Miguel flicked the plastic pointer. It whirled around the cardboard square decorated with a sunburst of ten colorful triangles.

"Boo-yah! The triple zeros. General Knowledge."

"Um, that's not so great," said Kyle.

"How come?"

"You get to move zero spaces."

"Oh. Bummer."

Akimi shot up her hand.

"Yes?" said Kyle.

"Do we really have to spin and count spaces and all that junk? We have a deadline. Clocks everywhere are ticking against us."

"Maybe we can just pull a pink card," suggested Sierra.

"It's really not how you play the game," said Kyle.

"Um, we're not really playing this game, Kyle," said Akimi. "We're playing the other one. The Big Game. The one with the ginormous prize."

"I have to agree with Akimi," said Miguel.

"Fine," said Kyle. "It's against the rules, but pull a pink card."

"You sure, bro?"

"Just pull a pink!"

Miguel quickly sorted the new deck into ten stacks of different colors. He pulled the pink on the top of its pile.

"Hmmm. These are different from the regular cards."

He turned it over and showed it to the group.

$0 + 27 + 0.4 = ????$

"Easy-peasy," said Akimi. "The answer is twenty-seven-point-four, because the zero doesn't change the sum."

"Not in math," said Miguel. "But this isn't math. This is the Dewey decimal system and there's always three numbers to the left of the decimal point."

"We need to find a book with the call number 027.4," added Sierra.

"Fine," said Akimi. "But I guarantee you it isn't a math book!"

The team made their way around the balcony circling the Dewey decimal doors.

"Here we go," said Miguel. He slid his library card into a reader on a door labeled "000s."

"Okay," said Miguel, "in here we're gonna find General Knowledge. Almanacs, encyclopedias, bibliographies, books about library science . . ."

"It's a science?" said Akimi. "Where do they keep the chemicals?"

"In the library paste," joked Sierra, who was loosening up. She hadn't read one page of a book in hours.

"Found it," said Miguel, reaching up to pull a book off a shelf. "027.4. Man, it's old. Look how yellow the pages are."

"So what's the antique's title?" asked Akimi.

"*Get to Know Your Local Library* by Amy Alessio and Erin Downey."

Miguel held the book so everybody could see the cover. It was illustrated with a cartoony-looking detective in a checkered hat who was holding up a magnifying glass to examine books on a shelf.

"Looks like a library guide for kids," said Miguel, opening the cover to read one of the inside pages. "First publication was way back in 1952." He flipped through a few pages. "It explains the Dewey decimal system. Contains a glossary of library terms. A brief history of libraries . . ."

He reached the back of the book.

"Awesome."

"What?" asked Kyle as he and the others moved closer to see what Miguel had found.

"It's an old-fashioned book slip. From the Alexandria-ville Public Library."

"The one they tore down?"

"Yep. And this card, tucked into a sleeve glued to the back cover, comes from the olden days when they used to stamp the date the book was due on a grid and you had to fill in your name under 'issued to.'"

"And?"

"Look who checked this book out on 26 May '64!"

Kyle and the others looked.

"Luigi Lemoncello!"

* * *

Down on the first floor, Charles used his library card to open the door to Community Meeting Room A.

"Who is to have access to this room?" cooed a soothing voice from the ceiling.

"Me and my teammates," said Charles. "Andrew Peckleman and Haley Daley."

"Thank you. Please have ANDREW PECKLEMAN and HALEY DALEY swipe their cards through the reader now."

Both of them did.

"Thank you. Entrance to Community Meeting Room A will be limited to those approved by the host, CHARLES CHILTINGTON. Have a good meeting."

Charles and his team entered the sleek, ultramodern, white-on-white conference room. There were twelve comfy chairs set up around a glass-topped table and a cabinet filled with top-of-the-line audiovisual equipment.

"You can write on the walls," said Andrew. "They're like the Smart Boards at school."

"Excellent," said Charles, clasping his hands behind his back and pacing around the room. "Now, when we find all twelve pictograms and lay them out according to their position in the Staff Picks display case, they will create a rebus for a phrase that, I am quite certain, will tell us exactly how to exit this library without triggering any alarms. Therefore, it is time for all of us to lay our cards on the table."

Haley nodded. And pulled two more silhouettes out of the back pocket of her jeans.

"I found one of these in a cookbook," she said. "The other was in juvenile fiction. *Nancy Drew: The Mystery at Lilac Inn*."

"There are blank note cards in this drawer," announced Andrew. "We should use them as placeholders for the books we still need to find."

They laid out a three-by-four grid of cards on the tabletop:

"What does it mean?" said Andrew.

"Simple," said Charles. "It means we need to find those other six books!"

31

"So, does anybody have a clue as to why we were supposed to find this book?" asked Kyle.

He and his teammates were back in the Young Adult Room staring at the cover of *Get to Know Your Local Library.*

"Too early to tell," said Miguel. "Let's keep playing. This book will probably make more sense once we go into the other rooms and pick up more clues."

"Whose turn is it?" asked Akimi.

"Yours," said Kyle. "Flick the spinner."

Akimi finger-kicked the plastic pointer.

"Purple!" she yelled when the arrow slid to a stop. "The eight hundreds."

"That means you move eight spaces," mumbled Kyle.

"Except today." Akimi reached for the card on top of

the purple stack. When she saw what was written on it, she frowned.

"What's the clue?" asked Kyle.

"Something about Literature, Rhetoric, or Criticism?" asked Miguel.

"Nope," said Akimi. "It's a wild card. With a riddle."

"Read it!" said Sierra.

"'I rhyme with dart and crackerjacks. Visit me and find a rhyme for Andy.'"

"Peckleman?" said Kyle. "How'd he get his name on a game card?"

"Bro," said Miguel, "nobody calls Andrew Peckleman 'Andy.' Of course, it could mean Andrew Jackson. The seventh president of the United States."

"Or Andy Panda," said Akimi.

"Or Andrew Carnegie," said Sierra. "He was a generous supporter of libraries."

"Okay," said Kyle. "Let's concentrate on the first part of the riddle. What rhymes with 'dart and crackerjacks'?"

"Smart and heart attacks?" suggested Miguel.

"Art and bric-a-bracs?" said Sierra.

"Art and *Artifacts*!" said Akimi, nailing it.

They hurried over to the Art & Artifacts Room.

"Everybody—check out the display cases," said Kyle. "See if anything rhymes with the word 'Andy.'"

"Well, this model of the old bank building is certainly 'grandy,'" said Miguel. "And the Pharaoh's pyramid and sphinx would be *sandy* if they weren't made out of Legos."

"True," said Kyle, sounding unconvinced about both.

"Check it out, you guys," cried Akimi, who was studying a row of Styrofoam heads sporting hats. "This plaid fedora from 1968 was worn by a guy named Leopold Loblolly."

"So?" said Kyle.

"According to this plaque, Loblolly was 'one of the notorious *Dandy* Bandits.' 'Dandy' rhymes with 'Andy.'"

"That it does," said Miguel. "However, 'Loblolly' does not."

"Neither does 'Leopold,'" added Kyle.

"'Candy' rhymes with 'Andy'!" said Sierra. She was staring at the objects in a display case under a banner reading "Welcome to the Wonderful World of Willy Wonka."

"Awesome!" said Miguel, hurrying over to admire the collection of Everlasting Gobstoppers, Glumptious Globgobblers, Laffy Taffy, and Pixy Stix displayed under glass in a sea of purple velvet.

"Mr. Lemoncello is a lot like Willy Wonka," said Kyle.

"You mean crazy?" said Akimi.

"I prefer the term 'eccentric.'"

"And Dr. Zinchenko is his Oompa-Loompa," said Sierra. Everybody started giggling.

"Nah," Akimi joked, "she's too tall."

164

"And not nearly orange enough," added Miguel.

"The Willy Wonka book was written by Roald Dahl," said Sierra, who, Kyle figured, could name twelve other books the guy wrote, too. "In it, Mr. Wonka takes Charlie and Grandpa Joe home in a flying glass elevator that crashes through the roof of his chocolate factory."

Everybody thought about that for a second.

"So now we have to find a glass elevator?" said Akimi. "Because there isn't one on the floor plan."

"But Mr. Lemoncello is just wild enough to build one," said Kyle. "And if he did, he probably wouldn't put it on the floor plan."

"No way," said Miguel. "Everybody would want to ride on it."

"I know I would," said Sierra.

"So we're seriously searching for a secret glass elevator?" said Akimi.

"Maybe," said Kyle. "Maybe not. This is just another piece of a gigantic jigsaw puzzle. We won't see the whole picture until we collect all the pieces."

"Or someone shows us the box lid," cracked Akimi.

"Look, it's only six p.m.," said Kyle. "And we're collecting a ton of good information."

"You mean a ton of *random* information," said Akimi.

"Well," said Miguel, "once we have more clues, we can use Sherlock Holmes's famous 'deductive reasoning' method to make logical connections between all the random junk."

165

"Works for me," said Kyle. "But if we're going to play Sherlock Holmes, we need to go spin that spinner and dig up more clues."

"The game's afoot," said Sierra.

"Huh?" Kyle and Akimi said it together.

"Sorry. It's just something Sherlock says to Watson whenever he gets excited."

Sherlock Holmes. Kyle had just found another bunch of books to add to his reading list.

32

"Okay, Sierra," said Kyle, "your turn."

Sierra flicked the spinner. The pointy tip ended up in the yellow 200s zone, so she went ahead and pulled a yellow card.

"It's definitely for the two hundreds section," she said, showing her clue to Miguel before revealing it to Kyle and Akimi.

"Weird," said Miguel.

"What?" said Akimi before Kyle could.

"Well, the two hundreds are where they keep books on world religions."

"But there are *two* numbers on this card," said Sierra.

"Maybe this time we need to find *two* books?" suggested Kyle.

"I don't know," said Sierra, studying her card. " '220.5203' is obviously a call number."

"Obviously," said Akimi.

"But this other number isn't in the proper format. 'Two-twenty-fifteen.'"

"February twentieth, 2015!" said Akimi. "Quick—what happened on that date?"

"Um, nobody knows," said Kyle. "Because *it hasn't happened yet.*"

"Oh. Right. Okay—how about February twentieth, 1915?"

"That was the opening day of the Panama-Pacific International Exposition in San Francisco," said Sierra.

Jaws dropped.

"Sorry. I'm a big world's fair fan."

Everybody else just nodded.

Finally, Miguel spoke up. "Look, let's just go down to the two hundreds room and find 220.5203. We can figure out the second chunk later."

The team once again trooped down to the second floor and worked their way around the circular balcony.

"You guys?" said Sierra, looking across the atrium at the statues. "Remember how they switched all the hologram authors when Bridgette Wadge did her Extreme Challenge?"

"Yep," said Kyle. "She was doing good till she got to the Russian dude."

"What Russian dude?" asked Miguel, who hadn't witnessed Bridgette's elimination.

"Guy who wrote five or six books Sierra could tell you about."

"But look," said Sierra. "Now all the author statues are the same ones they were last night."

"So," said Kyle thoughtfully, "if they can switch 'em around . . ."

"These must be clues for our game!" blurted Akimi. She pulled out a pen and her notepad. "I'll write down their names."

"Start with the guy under the triple zeros wedge of the Wonder Dome," suggested Kyle.

"Right."

Akimi read the labeled pedestals and jotted down all the authors' names:

Thomas Wolfe, Booker T. Washington, Stephen Sondheim, George Orwell, Lewis Carroll, Dr. Seuss, Maya Angelou, Shel Silverstein, Pseudonymous Bosch, Todd Strasser.

"So," said Akimi when she'd finished writing, "do you think this game could get any more complicated?"

"Maybe," said Kyle. "It's possible that Mr. Lemoncello left a couple different paths to the same solution."

"Well, personally, I can only take one path at a time," said Akimi. "So let's go find two-twenty-point-whatever."

* * *

"Should be in the next row of bookcases," said Miguel. "Here we go. 220.5203. The King James Bible."

"*Ach der lieber!* An excellent choice," said a man with a thick German accent.

The four teammates spun around.

And were face to face with a semi-transparent guy in medieval garb with a fur-trimmed cap and a beard that looked like two raccoon tails sewn together under his nose and chin.

"I am Johannes Gensfleisch zur Laden zum Gutenberg," said the holographic image, who had ink stains all over his fingertips.

"You created the Gutenberg Bibles on your printing press!" gushed Sierra.

"Ja, ja, ja. Big bestseller. You need help with der Bible, I am at your service." He bowed.

"Oh-kay," said Akimi, turning to Miguel. "Take it away, Miguel."

"Herr Gutenberg, sir, we're looking for two-twenty-fifteen."

"*Das ist einfach.*"

"Huh?"

"That is easy. TWO, TWENTY, FIFTEEN is EXODUS, chapter TWENTY, verse FIFTEEN."

"Of course!" said Miguel. "Exodus is the second book of the Bible. Twenty and fifteen are the chapter and verse." He flipped through some pages. "Here we go. Exodus, chapter twenty, verse fifteen. It's one of the Ten Commandments: 'Thou shalt not steal.'"

33

"Let's put the two new cards on the table," said Charles.

He and his so-called teammates, Andrew and Haley (Charles planned on dumping them both right before he made his glorious solo exit from the library), had scoured the library together for hours looking for more book cover matches.

Peckleman wasn't nearly as good with the Dewey decimal system as he had claimed to be. And Charles needed someone to do that sort of thing for him. His father always hired tutors or research assistants for him whenever Charles had to do a major paper or report.

Finally, around six in, coincidentally, the 600s room, they scored twice, finding *Tea for You and Me* (641.3372) and *Why Wait to Lose Weight?* (613.2522).

Now their picture puzzle had only four blanks remaining:

"Okay," said Andrew, "I think it's pretty clear. 'Woolly BLANK walk up the skinny BLANK BLANK house Indian and nineteen BLANK.'"

Charles nodded and said, "Interesting," even though he knew Peckleman was way off.

"Uh, hello?" said Haley. "That doesn't make any sense."

"Sure it does," said Andrew.

"Uh, no it doesn't."

In his head, Charles had decoded the clues so far as

"Ewe (a female sheep) BLANK walk out the (t+h+e) way (weigh) BLANK BLANK Inn in passed (past) BLANK."

But out loud, he said, "I think we just need to tweak Andrew's translation a little."

"Fine. Go ahead. I don't care." Andrew slumped down in his seat to sulk.

"How about 'She BLANK walks out the skinny BLANK BLANK house five hundred and past BLANK.'"

"Where'd you get 'she'?" asked Haley.

"From 'sheep.' The card you gave us."

"Actually, I think the sheep is supposed to represent 'you.' Because a ewe is a female sheep."

"Fascinating," said Charles. "I didn't figure that out."

What he did figure out was that Haley Daley was much smarter than he had assumed. She could be a serious threat. And no way was Charles sharing his prize with anybody, especially her.

"And how did you get 'five hundred' from Indiana?" she asked.

"Simple. Indianapolis, the capital of Indiana, is home to a race known as the Indy 500."

"Okay. So how about 'You BLANK walk out the skinny BLANK BLANK in—because the Nancy Drew book was about an inn—five hundred pass, or *past*, BLANK."

Now Peckleman piped up. "That makes more sense than what you said, Charles."

"Indeed," said Charles, sounding magnanimous.

"Perhaps the clues are telling us to locate a secret skinny passageway five hundred paces past some landmark here in the library."

Andrew was excited. "This is like the pirate map from *Treasure Island*!"

"Or," said Haley, "maybe these clues are telling us we need to go out and find the four books we haven't found yet. We should split up. I'll go back to the four hundreds room."

"We've already been there," said Andrew.

"Well, you guys might've missed something."

"Good idea," said Charles. He figured if Haley Daley wasted time retracing steps he and Andrew had already taken, she would find nothing new and become less of a threat. "Let's meet back here at, say, seven."

"Fine."

Haley left the meeting room.

Charles went to the door and closed it.

"You know what we really need?" he said to Andrew.

"Chocolate milk and maybe some cookies?"

Charles shook his head. "No, Andrew. We need whatever clues Kyle Keeley and his team have found. Especially if they have our missing cards."

34

Veering left the instant she reached the second floor, Haley made her way toward the 400s room.

She figured that Charles and Andrew had probably missed something important in the foreign languages room because they'd spent too much time talking to "these awesome mannequins" that told them all about their "American heritage."

As she rounded the bend, Haley saw Kyle Keeley and his crew tumble out of the 200s room.

It looked like Miguel was carrying a Bible.

But a Bible wasn't one of the books on display in the Staff Picks case.

We're following separate paths to the same goal, Haley thought. *And somewhere, those two paths are going to collide.*

Haley slid her card key down the reader slot in the 400s door. The lock clicked and she pushed the door open.

The room was dimly lit.

"*Bienvenida! Bienvenue! Witamy! Kuwakaribisha!* Welcome!" boomed a voice from the ceiling speakers.

"Sorry," said Haley, blindly feeling her way forward and bumping into something hard and lumpy.

"This is the four hundreds room, home of foreign languages. Here, HALEY, you can learn all about your American heritage."

A bank of spotlights thumped on.

Haley was basically hugging a department store mannequin.

An overhead projector beamed a movie onto the dummy to her left, turning it into a perky woman who looked like Haley would probably look a couple of years after she graduated from college.

"Hello, HALEY. Welcome to *your* American heritage. Let's begin your voyage!"

"That's okay, I don't have time right now. I'm Haley Daley. My ancestors were Irish, okay? So can we skip the history lesson and . . ."

Suddenly, the two mannequins at the far end of the row turned into sepia-toned versions of her great-great-great-grandmother and great-great-great-grandfather. Haley knew it was them because her dad had a bunch of old photos hanging in their family room. The two dummies looked exactly like Patrick and Oona Daley did in their wedding portrait.

"No man ever wore a scarf as warm as his daughter's arm around his neck," said Patrick in his thick Irish brogue. "Yer da is proud of you, Haley."

"Thanks. But I really need to win this competition."

"Watch out for sneaky rascals," said Oona. "Them that would steal the sugar out of your punch."

Haley had to smile. It sounded like her ancestor had met Charles Chiltington.

"And always remember, Haley," said her great-great-great-grandfather, "every woman's mind is her kingdom. Rule it wisely, lassie."

"I'm trying!"

"This library can help," said her great-great-great-grandmother with a wink.

And when she did, a secret panel in the wall slid open.

"What's going on?" said Haley.

"You're our third visitor!" boomed the jolly announcer in the ceiling.

"So?"

"According to *The American Heritage Dictionary of Idioms*—available in our reference department, by the way—'the third time is a charm'! Therefore, as our third visitor, you have won this charming bonus."

Two bonuses in one day?

She was right! Mr. Lemoncello definitely wanted Haley Daley to win this game, because clearly he knew she'd be the perfect, best-looking spokesmodel for his holiday commercials.

"Don't worry, sir!" Haley said to the nearest TV camera. "I won't let you down."

She hurried through the open wall panel and into the 300s room on the other side.

Ta-da!

The first thing she saw was one of the books they'd been searching for all day long: *True Crime Ohio: The Buckeye State's Most Notorious Brigands, Burglars, and Bandits* by Clare Taylor-Winters.

She quickly opened the cover and found the hidden four-by-four card. It took her two seconds to decipher the clue:

"Bandits."

Haley remembered another bit of Irish wisdom, something her dad said all the time: "Never bolt your door with a boiled carrot!"

She decided to keep this new clue secret and secure. She wouldn't share it with Charles or Andrew.

Haley took off her left sneaker, folded the card in half, and slid the clue into her shoe for safekeeping. When her sneak was laced up tight again, she took the *True Crime Ohio* book off its display stand and tucked it into the bookshelf, making sure it was in the proper position: right between 364.1091 and 364.1093. That way, she'd know where to find it if, for whatever reason, she needed the book again.

Haley looked up at the nearest camera and flashed it her brightest toothpaste-commercial smile.

"Goooo, Le-moncell-ooooo! That's a cheer I just made up. We can use it in one of the commercials—after I win!"

35

"Entrance to Community Meeting Room B will only be granted to KYLE KEELEY, SIERRA RUSSELL, AKIMI HUGHES, and MIGUEL FERNANDEZ," said the soothing female voice in the ceiling after the four teammates had swiped their cards through the meeting room door's reader slot.

"This makes sense," said Akimi. "We needed a place to organize all this material, put it on the walls, and draw a chart like the FBI always does on TV when they're tailing the mob."

"Stole the meeting room idea from me, eh, Keeley?"

Charles Chiltington was standing in the doorway to Meeting Room A on the far side of the rotunda.

"No," said Kyle. "We just needed someplace to throw our victory party after we win."

"Not going to happen," Charles said smugly. "Must

I remind you? I'm a Chiltington. We never lose." And he disappeared back into Meeting Room A.

After Charles was gone, Kyle led his team into Meeting Room B.

Miguel posted the bank blueprints he had found up on the walls while Sierra set up the Bibliomania game board on the conference table.

"I'm glad this room won't let anybody else in," said Kyle.

"And by 'anybody' you mean Charles Chiltington, right?" said Akimi.

"Totally."

Akimi grabbed a marker and wrote a neat outline on the dry-erase walls:

CLUES SO FAR

DEFINITE CLUES

1) From the 000s room:
Get to Know Your Local Library book

2) From the Art & Artifacts Room:
Willy Wonka candy (rhymes with "Andy").
Find glass elevator?

3) From the 200s room:
Bible verse—"Thou shalt not steal."

181

PROBABLY CLUES

BOOKS/AUTHORS ON THE BACKS OF LIBRARY CARDS

#1 Miguel Fernandez
Incident at Hawk's Hill by Allan W. Eckert/
No, David! by David Shannon

#2 Akimi Hughes
One Fish Two Fish Red Fish Blue Fish
by Dr. Seuss/Nine Stories by J. D. Salinger

#3 UNKNOWN

#4 Bridgette Wadge
Tales of a Fourth Grade Nothing
by Judy Blume/Harry Potter and the
Sorcerer's Stone by J. K. Rowling

#5 Sierra Russell
The Egypt Game by Zilpha Keatley Snyder/
The Westing Game by Ellen Raskin

#6 Yasmeen Smith-Snyder
Around the World in Eighty Days
by Jules Verne/The Yak Who Yelled Yuck
by Carol Pugliano-Martin

#7 Sean Keegan
Olivia by Ian Falconer/Unreal! by Paul Jennings

#8 UNKNOWN

#9 Rose Vermette
All-of-a-Kind Family by Sydney Taylor/
Scat by Carl Hiaasen

#10 Kayla Corson
Anna to the Infinite Power
by Mildred Ames/Where the Sidewalk
Ends by Shel Silverstein

#11 UNKNOWN

#12 Kyle Keeley
I Love You, Stinky Face by Lisa McCourt/
The Napping House by Audrey Wood

MAYBE CLUES???

Statues ringed around the dome:

Thomas Wolfe, Booker T. Washington, Stephen
Sondheim, George Orwell, Lewis Carroll,
Dr. Seuss, Maya Angelou, Shel Silverstein,
Pseudonymous Bosch, Todd Strasser

"Wow," said Akimi, stepping back to study the walls. "What an incredible mess."

"Yeah," said Kyle. "Okay, guys—there are eight more book rooms to explore and who knows how many more wild cards. Whose turn is it?"

"Yours," said Sierra.

Kyle flicked the spinner. "Green. The five hundreds. Science."

He pulled the first green card from the deck.

" 'Four and twenty were once in a pie. 598.367 might tell you why.' "

"Blackbirds?" said Miguel.

"I guess."

"Well," sighed Akimi, "let's go check out *another* book. There's still like an inch or two left on our whiteboard."

The 500s room was like a miniature museum of natural history.

In addition to towering walls of books, there was a whole planetarium of stars and constellations projected on the ceiling. Models of planets whirled in their orbits. Sparkle-tailed comets shot around the corners of book-shelves.

Kyle and his teammates made their way back to the 590s—Zoology.

Shelving units were arranged in a square around an open area, maybe twenty feet by twenty feet wide. When the team entered the empty space, the lights dimmed and a guy with long wavy hair who looked like an artistic Daniel Boone faded into view. He was wearing some kind of bear-fur coat and toting a musket.

"*Bonjour,*" said the hologram.

"It's John James Audubon," said Sierra. "The famous ornithologist."

"He gives people braces?" said Kyle.

"No," Sierra said with a laugh. "He studied and painted birds."

A blackbird with a yellow beak flew into the open area and roosted on a tree branch. The bird and the tree were both holograms, too.

"This beautiful blackbird from Alexandriaville, Ohio," said the semi-transparent Audubon image, "can mimic in song the sounds it has heard."

And the bird started wailing.

"Wow," said Akimi. "That sounds exactly like a police siren!"

"Yo," said Miguel. "Freaky."

"To learn more," said Audubon, "be sure to read *Bird Songs, Warbles, and Whistles* written by Dr. Diana Victoria Garcia, with classic illustrations by *moi.*"

With that, Audubon sat down on a campstool. An easel appeared, the blackbird struck a pose, and the outdoorsy artist started painting the bird's portrait, while humming "Blackbird" by the Beatles.

"Okay," said Kyle. "This is the strangest clue yet."

185

"Well, here's the book at least," said Sierra, who had found 598.367 on the shelf.

"So what do a blackbird's wails and warbles have to do with finding our way out of the library?" said Akimi.

Just then, they heard a very different sound.

Behind one of the bookcases, something growled, then roared.

"Did you guys hear that?" said Sierra.

"Yeah," said Akimi. "I don't think it's a robin red-breast."

A very rare white Bengal tiger, with icy-blue eyeballs, crept out from behind a wall of bookshelves and stalked into the open area where Audubon sat painting his bird portrait.

"Uh, is that another hologram?" asked Miguel.

ROAR!

No one stuck around to find out.

36

Down on the first floor, Charles and Andrew were working their way around the semicircle of three-story-tall floor-to-dome bookcases filled with fiction.

It was nearly eight p.m.

"We need to find that blasted book," said Charles, craning his neck to study the shelves.

"I'm getting kind of hungry," mumbled Andrew.

"You had a snack this afternoon," snapped Charles.

"Well, now it's time for dinner."

"No. We need to find *Anne of Green Gables* first."

The classic by Lucy Maud Montgomery was the middle book on the top shelf in the Staff Picks display case. So far, Charles, Haley, and Andrew had not been able to find it anywhere in the library.

"Unfortunately," said Andrew, "they've temporarily erased the book's call number from the database."

"So we wouldn't know what to punch into the hover ladder's control panel," grumbled Charles.

"Actually," said Andrew, "they might've shelved it in the Children's Room. Or maybe the eight hundreds, with Literature. Could be in the four hundreds, too, because it was originally written in Canadian, which is, technically, a foreign language."

"So you have said, Andrew. Repeatedly. But we've already searched those other locations. Several times. It has to be here with the other fiction titles. You just need to fly up and find it."

"Well," said Andrew, "I'm kind of afraid of heights."

"Fine. Whatever. I'll go up and grab it. But you have to give me some kind of call number to enter into the hover ladder."

"Lucy Maud Montgomery wrote other Anne books. There's *Anne of Avonlea*. . . ."

Charles dashed over to the nearest library table and swiped his fingers across the glass face of its built-in computer pad.

"Here we go. *Anne of Avonlea* by Lucy Maud Montgomery. F-MON."

"Yes," said Andrew. "Fiction books are usually put on the shelf in alphabetical order by the author's last name. Nonfiction titles are classified according to the Dewey decimal system."

"How long have you known this?"

Andrew's nose twitched. "Since second grade."

"So all we ever needed was 'F-MON'? We could've found this book hours ago?"

Andrew gulped.

"You are such a disappointment." Shaking his head, Charles huffed over to one of the hover ladders. He quickly jabbed "F," "M," "O," and "N" into the keypad. The boot clamps locked into place around his ankles. "You owe me for wasting all this time, Andrew. You owe me big-time. If you let me down once more, I swear I will tell everybody you're a big blubbering baby. I'll Twitter it *and* post it on Facebook."

"Don't worry. I'll make you glad you picked me for your team, Charles! I promise."

The hover ladder lifted off the floor and gently glided up to the M section of the fiction wall. Shuttling sideways, it carried Charles over to a shelf displaying all the Anne books.

He grabbed a copy of *Anne of Green Gables*.

As soon as he did, the ladder started its slow descent to the floor.

"What'd you find?" asked Andrew when Charles landed.

"The clue we needed."

He showed Andrew the card that had been tucked inside the front cover.

"Okay," said Andrew. "It's 'C plus hat'! So the word is 'chat,' which, by the way, could also be *'chat,'* the French word for cat!"

"Well done, Andrew," said Charles, even though he knew the clue was really "C plus Anne," equaling "can," thereby making the puzzle "You *can* walk out the way BLANK BLANK inn in past BLANK."

The way what did what? he wondered. *And what does "inn in" mean?*

Charles desperately needed to find the three missing pictograms.

Suddenly, Mr. Lemoncello's voice boomed out of speakers ringing the rotunda.

"Hey, Charles! Hey, Andrew! Let's Do a Deal!"

Game show music blared. A canned crowd cheered.

Charles turned around and saw shafts of colored light illuminating three envelopes perched on top of the librarian's round desk. Clarence the security guard marched into the reading room and, folding his arms over his chest, took up a position near the three envelopes.

"We have a green envelope, a blue envelope, and a red envelope," said Mr. Lemoncello. "In two of those three envelopes are copies of two of the three pictogram clues you still need. In one, there is a Clunker Card. If you pick an envelope with a clue, you get to keep it—and you get to keep going. But once you pick the Clunker Card, you're done . . . and you must suffer the consequences."

Andrew raised his hand.

"Yes, Andrew?"

"What are the consequences?"

"Something bad," said Mr. Lemoncello. "In fact, something wicked this way will probably come. Do you want to do a deal?"

"Yes!" said Charles.

The canned audience cheered.

"All right, then! Charles, you roll first."

"Pardon?"

"Swipe your fingers across the nearest desktop computer panel. The dice tumbler app is up and running!"

Again, the prerecorded audience cheered. They sounded like they loved watching dice tumble more than anything in the world.

Charles slid his fingers across a glass pane. The animated dice rolled.

"Oooh!" cried Mr. Lemoncello. "Double sixes. That gives you a twelve."

"Is that good, sir?"

"Maybe. Maybe not. Okay, Andrew—your turn!"

Peckleman tapped the glass. The dice flipped over.

"Another set of doubles!" said Mr. Lemoncello.

"Yeah," muttered Charles. "Two ones. Snake eyes."

"Is that bad?" asked Andrew.

"Maybe," said Mr. Lemoncello. "Maybe not. Okay, guys—which envelope would you like to open?"

Charles thought about it while ticktock music played.

They were given this chance to play Let's Do a Deal

after they located the *Anne of Green Gables* clue. Coincidence? He didn't think so.

"We'll take the green envelope, sir."

Clarence presented the green envelope to Charles.

"Open it!" said Andrew. "Open it."

Charles undid the clasp. Pulled out a card.

A loud *ZONK!* rocked the room.

The card was black. With blocky white type.

"Uh-oh," mumbled Andrew. "What's it say on that card?"

" 'Sorry, kids, you're out of luck,' " read Charles. " 'So out of doors you're all now stuck.' "

Clarence picked up the blue and red envelopes and marched back toward the entrance hall.

"What's that mean?" said Andrew.

"Well," said Mr. Lemoncello, "Charles rolled a twelve and you rolled a two. What's twelve plus two?"

"Fourteen," said Charles eagerly, the way he always did in math when he wanted to remind the teacher that he was the smartest kid in the class.

"Oooh," said Mr. Lemoncello. "This is not good. In fact, I'd say it's stinkerrific."

"Stinkerrific?" said Andrew. "Is that even a word?"

"It is now," said Mr. Lemoncello. "J.J.? Tell them what they've lost."

An authoritative female voice boomed out of the ceiling speakers:

"Warning: Due to a Clunker Card, all ten Dewey decimal doors will lock in ten minutes, at exactly eight o'clock. If you are in one of those rooms, kindly leave immediately. The ten doors on the second floor will remain locked for fourteen hours."

Andrew panicked. "What? Fourteen hours?"

"I told you twelve plus two was bad," quipped Mr. Lemoncello. "Of course, it could've been good. If you had picked one of the other envelopes, you would've received a clue and a free fourteen-month subscription to *Library Journal*."

Charles did some quick math. "Sir? Does this mean we'll be locked out of the ten Dewey decimal rooms until ten o'clock tomorrow morning?"

"Bingo!" said Mr. Lemoncello. "It sure does!"

"This stinks," whined Andrew. "We need those stupid rooms to solve your stupid puzzle! Clunker Cards stink. This game stinks. Fourteen-hour penalties stink."

Charles did his best to block out Andrew's rant.

He needed to think.

And then it hit him: *Kyle Keeley's team had to be working on some other solution to the bigger puzzle of how to escape from the library.* Otherwise, Charles and his team would not have been able to find the nine clues they'd already picked up. Surely, if Keeley's team had been playing the same memory match game, they would've found at least one of the pictograms before Charles, Andrew, or Haley did.

They must be working a completely different angle.

Charles was certain that if he could use this downtime

to learn what Keeley and his team had in their meeting room, and combined it with his picture puzzle, he would emerge from the library victorious.

"Do not despair, Andrew," Charles said confidently. "We are still going to win."

"How?"

Charles leaned in and cupped a hand around his mouth so no security cameras could read his lips.

"Remember," he whispered, "you need to pay me back for wasting a ton of time in finding *Anne of Green Gables*."

"What? You're the one who picked the stupid green envelope with the stupid Clunker Card!"

Charles narrowed his eyes and chilled his hushed voice. "So?"

"Um, nothing," said Andrew nervously. "Just thought I'd, you know, point it out."

Charles turned his eyes into blue ice.

"So," whispered Andrew, swallowing hard, "what exactly do you want me to do?"

"Find a way to sneak into Community Meeting Room *B*."

Andrew wheezed in panic. "That's impossible."

"Don't worry. I have an idea."

"What is it?"

"Two words: Sierra Russell."

37

"Ever wonder if this could reek any worse?" said Akimi. "Because it couldn't."

"Yo, none of us pulled a Clunker Card," groused Miguel. "That means somebody on Charles's team did it."

"Akimi and Miguel are right, Kyle," said Sierra. "This really isn't fair."

"I know," was all Kyle could say. "But it's like in Mr. Lemoncello's Family Frenzy, where one player pulls the Orthodontist card and *everybody* has to move back seven spaces to buy their kids braces."

Kyle and his teammates were back in Community Meeting Room B. They'd been staring at the clue board, wondering what a wailing blackbird had to do with Willy Wonka and the Ten Commandments—not to mention that long list of books and all the statues—when the voice in the ceiling made its announcement about the Dewey decimal doors being locked for fourteen hours.

"Well, Mr. Lemoncello better have a *good* reason," said Akimi.

"Oh, I do," said Mr. Lemoncello.

His face appeared on one of the meeting room walls, which was really a giant plasma-screen video monitor.

"Team Kyle is not being penalized for Team Charles's blunder," he said. "Far from it. In fact, you are being rewarded."

Akimi arched her eyebrows in disbelief. "Really? How?"

"The other team's penalty gives you a wrinkle in time."

"A wrinkle in time?" said Kyle. "Is that a clue?"

"No. It's a book. And sometimes, Kyle, a book is just a book. But thanks to the Clunker Card, you have the gift of wrinkled time to seek clues *outside* the ten Dewey decimal rooms. Speaking of *Time*, a magazine available in our periodicals section, it's dinnertime!"

"So the game is basically suspended until ten o'clock tomorrow?" said Kyle.

"Well, Kyle, that's up to you. You can use this time as a bonus, to think, read, and explore. Or you can run upstairs and play video games all night long. The choice is yours."

"We want to win *this* game," said Kyle. His teammates nodded in agreement.

"Wondermous!" said Mr. Lemoncello. "Keep working the puzzle but try to avoid Mrs. Basil E. Frankweiler's files.

They're all mixed up. And before you turn in this evening, you might want to spend some time curled up with a good book."

"Um, they just said the book rooms are locked," said Akimi.

"The nice lady in the ceiling was only talking about the ten Dewey decimal rooms. There is plenty of first-class fiction in the Rotunda Reading Room. Dr. Zinchenko has even selected seven books specifically for our seven remaining contestants. After dinner, you'll find those books on her desk."

When he said that, Mr. Lemoncello started winking.

"I think you'll find the books to be very *enlightening*. Inspirational, even."

And then he winked some more.

"And now, I must return to my side of the mountain. See you in the morning, children! I have great expectations for you all!"

Mr. Lemoncello's image disappeared from the wall.

"Okay," said Akimi, "from the way Mr. Lemoncello was just winking, either somebody kicked a bucket of sand in his face or our recommended reading list is another clue."

On the other side of the rotunda, Charles huddled with Andrew in Meeting Room A.

"I don't trust Haley," he said.

"Why not?"

Charles placed his hand on Andrew's shoulder. "Well, my friend, I'm not sure if I should tell you this, but Haley told me she didn't think you were 'handsome enough' to appear in Mr. Lemoncello's holiday commercials with us when we win."

"Because of my glasses?"

Charles bit his lip. Nodded. "Of course, I totally disagree."

"I see," said Andrew, his ears burning bright red. "Then she doesn't get to see what we found in that *Anne of Green Gables* book."

"Very well, Andrew. If that's how you want to play it."

"You bet I do."

"Fine. Let's go see what's for dinner. I'm starving."

When Charles and Andrew entered the café, the Keeley team was already inside, filling their trays.

"Hey, way to go, Charles!" joked Miguel Fernandez. "You guys pulled a Clunker Card?"

"Indeed we did. However, not even that bit of bad luck can derail our juggernaut!"

"Huh?" said Akimi.

"He means we're still gonna win!" said Andrew.

Charles and Andrew crossed to the far side of the room to join Haley, who was sitting in a corner.

"You guys find any clues this afternoon?" she asked.

"Sadly, no," said Charles.

"All we found was that door-locking penalty," said Andrew, who could lie almost as well as Charles.

"How about you, Haley?" Charles asked. "Find anything interesting?"

"Nope. Nada." Then she yawned and finished her dinner. "I think I'll head upstairs and sack out."

"Really? It's only eight-forty-eight."

"I know. But I'm totally pooped." She yawned again. "Plus, I want to be up bright and early, before the Dewey decimal doors reopen. We have more clues to find. See you guys tomorrow. Unless we have more team business to discuss?"

"No. Nothing."

She walked out of the café.

38

"Very interesting," said Akimi, looking through the café's glass walls and into the Rotunda Reading Room.

"What?" said Miguel.

"I think Clarence just dropped off our books."

Kyle pushed back from the table. He could see the shadowy figure of the bulky security guard slinking away from the round desk at the center of the rotunda. He left behind a stack of books.

"Come on," he said. "Let's go see what sort of 'inspirational' reading Dr. Zinchenko has selected for us."

"What about those guys?" said Miguel, gesturing toward the table where Charles and Andrew were finishing their desserts.

Kyle was torn.

On one hand, he didn't want to give away the bonus his team had received thanks to the other team's penalty.

On the other hand, he didn't want people saying he and his friends won because Mr. Lemoncello had tossed them an extra clue.

He came up with a compromise.

"Hey, Charles? Andrew? We're all going to go grab some books to read to kill time till tomorrow morning. You two might want to do the same thing."

"No thanks." Charles stood up. "We pretty much have this thing figured out. In fact, I think Mr. Lemoncello steered us toward the Clunker Card so we wouldn't win too easily. I mean, how would it look if we escaped from his library in less than twenty-four hours?"

"Bad," said Andrew. "Real bad."

"Indeed," said Charles. "In fact, I suspect nobody would buy Lemoncello games anymore if we showed them how consistently easy they are to win. Anyway, we're going upstairs so I can give Andrew a tour of my private suite. Would any of you care to join us?"

"No thanks," said Akimi.

"Suit yourself. Oh, by the way, Mr. Lemoncello has a real video game console upstairs."

Kyle felt his mouth going dry.

"It's top-of-the-line equipment. And it plays real games. Not just educational stuff. Care to join us, Keeley?"

"Um . . ."

"We're going to play Squirrel Squad Six. The new edition. According to the game box, it won't be released to the general public until early December."

Kyle felt sweat beading on his forehead. His palms were moist. His fingers were twitching, itching to thumb-toggle a joystick.

But finally, after the inside of his mouth had turned to sandpaper, he said, "No thanks, Charles. We're just gonna, you know, read."

After Charles and Andrew headed up to the third floor to play what was probably the most awesome version ever of Mr. Lemoncello's most awesome video game ever (if Charles Chiltington was actually telling the truth), Kyle and his teammates hurried out to see what books were waiting for them on the librarian's table.

They found seven different versions of the same book: *The Complete Sherlock Holmes*. One was a leather-bound limited edition; another was a tattered paperback; three were hardcovers with different illustrations on their fronts; one was a bigger kind of paperback with lots of scholarly essays; and the seventh was an e-reader with only the one title loaded onto it.

"I think Mr. Lemoncello wants us to start a book club," said Sierra.

"What do you mean?" asked Kyle.

"You know—we all read the same book and then get together later to discuss it and share our opinions."

"It's fun," said Miguel. "We have a book group at school."

"Are you in it?" asked Sierra.

"Yeah. Maybe you'd like to join us sometime?"

"I would. Thank you, Miguel."

Akimi cleared her throat. "Now what?" she said to Kyle.

Kyle shrugged. "Like I told Charles. We read."

Everybody grabbed a copy of the Sherlock Holmes book.

Nobody went for the e-reader.

Upstairs on the third floor, Haley tiptoed around the Lemoncello-abilia Room.

When she had visited the mini-museum earlier, she hadn't really looked around. Now she hoped to find another book from the "memorable reads" display, a Little Golden Book called *Baby's Mother Goose: Pat-a-Cake*, which could've been something Mr. Lemoncello read (or had read to him) when he was a very young boy.

Haley made her way past the orderly stacks of boxes through a doorway and into what looked like a re-creation of Mr. Lemoncello's childhood bedroom—a cramped space crammed with two bunk beds that he had shared with his three brothers. Next to one of the lower bunks was a bookcase made out of plastic milk crates.

There it was, filed away with maybe three dozen other skinny, hardboard-covered picture books.

Haley pried open the cover.

Out plopped a four-by-four art card:

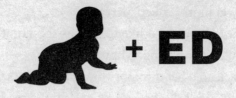 + ED

She quickly folded it in half and stuffed it inside her sneaker with her "BANDITS" clue.

Because now she was pretty certain that "bandits" had, at one time or another, "crawled in" to this building back when it was a bank.

The silhouette of Indiana didn't represent the Indianapolis 500 like Charles had insisted.

It stood for "IN," the official post office abbreviation for the Hoosier State.

First thing in the morning, when the doors reopened, she needed to search through the Dewey decimal rooms to find a clue that would tell her exactly how and where the bandits had crawled in.

A tunnel? An air vent? A secret passageway on the first, second, or third floor between the old bank and the office building behind it?

There was only one thing Haley was certain of: They hadn't crawled in through a book return slot.

39

Everyone in the reading room was quietly lost in the adventures of Sherlock Holmes.

Kyle had just finished a pretty cool story called "A Scandal in Bohemia," about a king who was going to get married to a royal heiress with maybe six names. But the king was being blackmailed by an old girlfriend, an opera singer from New Jersey named Irene Adler.

Something Sherlock Holmes said to Dr. Watson early in the story really stuck with Kyle: "You see, but you do not observe."

Kyle figured that was why Mr. Lemoncello wanted them all to take a break from chasing clues and read these classic mysteries. Not to find new clues but to become better puzzle solvers. Had they been seeing things without really observing them? Probably.

Reading the story was also kind of fun. Kyle could

totally see Holmes's apartment at 221b Baker Street and the snooty king and the horse-drawn carriages on the foggy London streets and the disguises Holmes wore and the smoke bomb Dr. Watson tossed through a window and everybody on the street screaming, "Fire!"

It was like he was watching a 3-D IMAX movie in his head. Kyle couldn't wait to start the second story in the book, "The Adventure of the Red-Headed League."

"How's it going?" whispered Akimi.

"This book is pretty cool. This Sir Arthur Conan Doyle guy knows how to keep his readers hooked."

"His characters leap off the pages," said Sierra.

"Yeah," said Miguel. "I dig the 'consulting detective.'"

"Huh?" said Kyle.

"That's what Holmes calls himself sometimes."

"Oh. I've only read one story so far and . . ."

Suddenly, something seemed odd to Kyle.

"Hey—how come Conan Doyle isn't one of those statues up there?"

"What do you mean?" said Akimi.

"He's a famous author, right? How come they're projecting a statue of a modern writer like Pseudonymous Bosch but not the author who created a classic like Sherlock Holmes?"

"Good question, bro," said Miguel.

"I need to *consult* with my brother Curtis."

"How come?"

"Curtis has read more books than anyone I know,

except maybe Sierra. He scored an 808 on his SAT Subject Test in Literature."

"Uh, Kyle?" said Akimi. "I think the top score for any SAT test is 800."

"Yep. Then Curtis took it. They had to raise it."

"So maybe he can help us figure out what's up with all the statues," said Miguel.

"Exactly. Why these ten? Why not ten other writers?"

"Why not the same ten Bridgette Wadge had for her Extreme Challenge?" added Sierra.

Kyle looked around the room.

"Mrs. Tobin? Hello? Mrs. Tobin?"

The hazy holographic image of the 1960s librarian flickered into view.

"How may I help you, KYLE?"

"I'd like to talk to an expert."

"And whom do you wish to speak to?"

"Mr. Curtis Keeley."

"Your brother?"

"And an SAT-certified expert on the subject of literature and authors and other literary-type junk."

Suddenly, the hologram vanished and Dr. Zinchenko's voice came over the ceiling speakers.

"This is a rather irregular request, Mr. Keeley."

"Hey," said Akimi, "this whole game is rather irregular, don't ya think?"

"We just need some more data," said Kyle. "Because,

like Sherlock says to Dr. Watson, 'it is a capital mistake to theorize before one has data.'"

"I take it you're enjoying your book?" said the librarian.

Kyle gave the closest security camera a big thumbs-up. "Boo-yeah. Can't wait to see what's up with that league of redheaded gentlemen."

"Ah, yes," said Dr. Zinchenko. "A fascinating story. I recently reread it myself. Very well, Kyle. We will contact your brother to determine if he does indeed qualify as a literary expert. It may take a while."

"No rush," said Kyle. "I've got a good book."

Kyle was busy helping Holmes figure out that the Red-Headed League was just a clever ploy pulled by some robbers to get a red-haired pawnbroker to leave his shop long enough for them to dig a tunnel from his basement to the bank next door when the librarian's voice jolted him out of London and brought him home to Ohio.

"My apologies for the interruption."

Akimi, Miguel, and Sierra closed their books, too. It was eleven-fifteen. Everyone had sleepy, dreamy looks in their eyes because they'd been kind of drifting off in their comfy reading chairs.

"What's up?" said Kyle.

"We have arranged for your expert consultation with Mr. Curtis Keeley."

"Awesome! How do we do it?"

"You and your expert may have a five-minute video chat on my computer terminal, which is located behind the main desk."

Kyle hurried over to the round desk in the center of the room. His three teammates hurried right behind him.

"Your consultation begins . . . now."

And there was Curtis. Sitting at his computer in his bedroom.

"Hey, Curtis!"

"Hi, Kyle. How's it going in there?"

"Great."

Kyle's oldest brother, Mike, popped into the doorway behind Curtis.

"Ky-le, Ky-le," Mike chanted. "Whoo-hoo!"

Kyle had never had his own cheerleader before.

"We need you to give us one hundred and ten percent in there, li'l brother!" Mike squinted at the screen over Curtis's shoulder. "Who are those other guys?"

"My teammates, Miguel, Sierra, and you know Akimi."

"You guys are a team? Smart move. Even I can't win football games without help from ten other guys."

"Um, Mike?" said Kyle. "Curtis and I only have five minutes to chat."

"Cool. I'm outta here. Win, baby, win!"

Mike backpedaled out of the bedroom, making double fist pumps the whole way.

"You have four minutes remaining," advised Dr. Zinchenko.

"Okay, Curtis, here's my question. What do these authors have in common?"

Kyle rattled off the list of the statues in order.

And Curtis stared blankly into his computer cam.

For a real long time.

Then he shook his head. "I'm sorry, Kyle. I have no earthly idea."

40

"Really?" Kyle was astonished. "You've got nothing?"

"Well," said Curtis, "the only connection I can see is Thomas Wolfe wrote *Look Homeward, Angel* and Lewis Carroll wrote *Through the Looking-Glass*. Both titles have the word 'look' in them. But the two books are otherwise completely different. The two authors as well."

Kyle and his whole team stood in stunned silence.

Until Sierra started jumping up and down.

"Of course!" she shouted.

"Your time is up," announced Dr. Zinchenko.

"Um, okay," Kyle said to the computer screen. "Thanks, Curtis. That was, uh, really helpful."

"It was!" said Sierra, daintily clapping her hands together like a very polite seal. The computer screen faded to black.

"What's up?" asked Miguel.

"I think I know how to crack the statue code."

"There's a code?" said Akimi. "Who knew?"

"It'll take time," said Sierra. "And I need a computer."

"Oh-kay," said Kyle, who was sort of shocked to see Sierra so completely jazzed. "We'll be in our meeting room, putting together a list of new Dewey decimal numbers from the Bibliomania cards so we're ready to hit the ground running when the doors reopen at ten tomorrow morning."

While Sierra settled in at a desktop computer pad, the rest of the team returned to the Bibliomania board game.

"We should just start flipping over cards and putting together a list of call numbers," Kyle suggested.

"Sounds like a plan," said Akimi.

She plucked a purple card out of the pile.

Lose a Turn was all that was printed on the other side.

"Try a different color," urged Miguel.

Akimi flipped up a blue card.

Take an Extra Turn was printed on it. So Akimi flipped over all the other blue cards while Miguel flipped over all the purples.

The purple cards all said **Lose a Turn**. The blue ones all said **Take an Extra Turn**.

Kyle had been checking out the red and maroon piles.

"The reds all say 'Pick a Yellow Card,'" he reported. "The maroons say 'Grab a Green.'"

"The grays do the same thing," said Miguel. "Only they say 'Pick a Pink.' The tan cards say 'Go Grab an Orange.'"

"So that leaves the colors we've already played." Kyle flipped over a yellow card. "'In the square root of 48,629.20271209 . . .'"

"What the . . . ?" said Akimi.

"Hang on," said Miguel. "There's a calculator app in this desktop computer."

Kyle read the rest of the card: ". . . 'find half of 4-40-30.'"

"Well, that's 2-20-15, again," said Sierra.

"And the square root of forty-eight thousand whatever is 220.5203," said Miguel. "The King James Bible we already found."

Akimi flipped through the rest of the yellow cards. "Same with these. They all send us into the Religion section to find that Bible verse."

"Ditto with the greens," reported Miguel. "All clues leading to *Bird Songs, Warbles, and Whistles*."

"And the pinks all lead back to 027.4," said Kyle. "I guess they really wanted to make sure we found *Get to Know Your Local Library*."

"Which leaves the wild cards," said Akimi. She examined the orange deck. "Find a rhyme for 'cart and paperbacks,' 'smart and zodiacs,' 'tart and potato sacks.'"

"The Art and Artifacts Room," said Miguel with a sigh.

"Where," Akimi continued, "we need to find a rhyme for 'Randy,' 'Sandy,' or 'Brandi.'"

"The Willy Wonka candy," said Miguel.

"So," said Kyle, "I'm guessing the Bibliomania game was only supposed to help us find the four clues we've already found."

"But we need to know more numbers," said Miguel. "Because a library should be a know-place for know-bodies."

When Miguel made his pun, Kyle and Akimi both groaned.

But then Kyle thought of something: "This is why Mr. Lemoncello called our time-out a bonus. He knew we'd need a ton of time to find a new source of numbers."

Just then Sierra burst into the meeting room.

"You guys! I found a whole bunch of new numbers!"

"What?" said Kyle, Akimi, and Miguel. "Where?"

"Up on the ceiling!"

41

"You need to look up at the Wonder Dome," said Sierra.

"Huh?" said Kyle.

Sierra and her whole team were standing together outside the door to Community Meeting Room B. She hadn't been this happy or excited in a long time.

"Um, Sierra?" said Akimi. "Why exactly are you suggesting we all give ourselves a crick in the neck by staring at the ceiling?"

"Okay. This is a game some of us play online called What's the Connection? I put up a list of authors and you have to figure out how they're linked by the titles of their books."

"Whoa," said Akimi, sort of sarcastically. "Sounds like fun."

"It is. But believe me, it's not easy."

"What'd you figure out?" asked Miguel.

"Well, like Curtis said, Thomas Wolfe wrote *Look Homeward, Angel* and Lewis Carroll wrote *Through the Looking-Glass*. That got me thinking. And running computer searches. Stephen Sondheim wrote a book called *Look, I Made a Hat*. Maya Angelou wrote *Even the Stars Look Lonesome*, and Pseudonymous Bosch wrote *This Isn't What It Looks Like*."

"They all have 'look' in the title," said Kyle.

"What about the other five authors?" asked Akimi. "Did they write 'look' books, too?"

"No, they're up there for a different word."

"Huh?"

"Booker T. Washington wrote *Up from Slavery* and Shel Silverstein wrote *Falling Up*."

"And Dr. Seuss?" said Kyle.

"*Great Day for Up*. George Orwell did *Coming Up for Air*, and Todd Strasser has a book called *If I Grow Up*."

"So the ten statues give us two words," said Miguel.

"Yep. 'Look' and 'up.' So I did. I looked up. At the Wonder Dome. There! Did you see it? That string of numbers that just drifted across the two hundreds screen under the Star of David?"

"220.5203," said Miguel.

Akimi knuckle-punched Kyle in the arm. "This is just like that bonus code thingie you showed me on the school bus!"

"Of course," said Kyle. "This is a Lemoncello game.

He always hides secret codes in screwy places. Way to go, Sierra!"

"Thanks," said Sierra, realizing how much more fun it was to play this kind of game with real friends instead of virtual ones on the Internet.

"But we already found that same two hundreds number playing Bibliomania," said Miguel.

"True," said Kyle. "Check out the sections for numbers the cards wouldn't give us."

Everybody craned their necks and focused on the graphics swimming across the ten panels overhead.

"Here comes another one!" said Sierra. "In the six hundreds. Right underneath the floating stethoscope."

"Got it!" said Kyle. "624.193."

"Whoo-hoo!" said Akimi.

"Sierra, you're my new hero," said Kyle. "You saved the day."

Sierra blushed. "Thanks."

"The spinner," said Akimi.

"Huh?" said Miguel.

"That was another clue. The Bibliomania game was pointing us to the ceiling, too. Because in Dewey decimal mode, the Wonder Dome looks like a giant 3-D version of the board game's spinner."

"Awesome, Sierra," said Miguel. "Absolutely awesome."

* * *

217

Sierra and her teammates stared up at the ceiling for over an hour. At 12:30, they finally lay down on the floor so they wouldn't cramp their neck muscles.

Because every fifteen minutes, the animated ceiling looped through call numbers for every Dewey decimal room in the library.

Except one.

And then the sequence repeated itself.

"How come there's no three hundreds number?" said Miguel.

"Probably because that's the one book we really, really, *really* need," said Kyle.

"That Lemoncello," said Akimi. "What a comedian."

42

Peering over the railing on the third-floor balcony at close to two a.m., Andrew Peckleman saw Sierra Russell sitting all alone in the Rotunda Reading Room.

Andrew had spent the night on the third floor losing video games to Charles.

And being reminded about how much he needed to break into Community Meeting Room B to "borrow" any clues Kyle Keeley's team had gathered, to pay Charles back for wasting so much of "the team's time" on the *Anne of Green Gables* clue due to his "foolish fear" of heights.

Andrew had promised Charles he'd do whatever it took.

"If anyone on Team Keeley is going to help us break into their headquarters," Charles had said, "it will be the shy girl who is constantly reading. Have you noticed what Sierra Russell uses for a bookmark?"

"No," Andrew had honestly answered.

"Her library card, which of course doubles as a key card for Meeting Room B. Find a way to borrow it."

"Isn't that illegal?"

"Of course not. This is a library. People borrow books, don't they?"

"Well, yeah . . ."

"Did I mention that I have three thousand Facebook friends? Two thousand Twitter followers? Each and every one of them will hear what a weenie and wimp you are if you don't do this thing to guarantee that our team wins."

So Andrew made his way down to the first floor.

Sierra, as usual, was reading a book.

As he moved closer, Andrew saw a flash of white.

Charles was right. Sierra was using her shiny white library card to mark her place in the book's pages.

He made his way to the cluster of overstuffed reading chairs.

"Good book?"

His voice startled her.

"Oh. Hello. Yes."

"Mind if I join you?" He slid into a crinkly leather seat opposite Sierra. "So, um, what're you reading?"

"*Charlie and the Great Glass Elevator* by Roald Dahl."

"Oh, yeah. I've heard about that book. Where's the rest of your team?"

"They went to bed. Want to get up bright and early. Before the doors on the second floor open again."

"Yeah. Haley and Charles conked out, too. Guess it's just us bookworms, huh?"

"Well, it is kind of late," said Sierra. "I'm going to go upstairs and . . ."

"May I take a look?"

"Hmmm?"

"At your book. I've never actually read it. I just tell people I have."

"Oh. Sure." Sierra handed it to him.

"Thank you."

Andrew flipped through the pages until he found the spot where Sierra had tucked in her library card. "Wouldn't it be cool if this library had a flying elevator like in that Willy Wonka movie? Especially if you could use it to crash through the roof like Charlie and Wonka did. That'd be a pretty cool way to escape from the library, huh?"

"Yeah. I guess."

That was when Andrew made the switch. He slipped his library card into Sierra's book and palmed hers.

Charles would be so proud of him!

"So," he said, closing the book, "did you ever read *The Elevator Family*?"

"No. I don't think so."

"It's all about this family that lives in the elevator of a San Francisco hotel. And let's just say, the book has its ups and its downs!"

Andrew laughed hysterically, because it was one of the

funniest jokes he knew. Sierra sort of chuckled. He handed back her book.

Overhead, the Wonder Dome dissolved out of its Dewey decimal mode and, with a swirl of colors, became a bright green bedroom with a pair of red-framed windows looking out on a blue night sky with a full moon and a blanket of twinkling stars. In the great green room, there was a telephone, and a red balloon, and a picture of a cow jumping over the moon.

The ceiling had become the bunny's bedroom from *Goodnight Moon.*

A quiet old lady bunny in a frumpy blue dress hopped into the Rotunda Reading Room. Two tiny cats followed her.

"Great," said Andrew. "Another stupid hologram."

"I think she's cute," said Sierra.

"Hush," said the bunny. "Goodnight clocks and goodnight socks. Goodnight, Sierra."

"Goodnight, Bunny." Sierra took her book and headed upstairs.

"Goodnight, Andrew," said the bunny.

"Right."

He pocketed the purloined library card. He couldn't do anything with it right away. Not while the holographic bunny's handlers were watching on the spy cameras.

But first thing in the morning . . .

"Goodnight old bunny saying hush," he called out.

And then, under his breath, he muttered, "In the morning, our competition we're gonna crush."

43

Up bright and early the next morning, Kyle made his way across the Rotunda Reading Room.

It was eight-fifteen. The Dewey decimal doors would open in one hour and forty-five minutes. The game would be over in less than four hours.

Kyle was totally pumped.

Sierra Russell, on the other hand, was sitting in a comfy chair reading a book.

"Hey," said Kyle.

"Hi," said Sierra, stifling a small yawn.

"Did you stay up all night reading?"

"No. I went upstairs around two. But there was a new stack of books on the librarian's desk when I came down."

"Oh, really? What'd you find?"

"Five copies of this."

She showed Kyle her book. It was *The Eleventh Hour: A Curious Mystery*.

"It's a rhyming picture book about Horace the Elephant's eleventh birthday party and the search to find out who ran off with all the food. There are hidden messages and cryptic codes all over the pages."

"Why's it called *The Eleventh Hour*?"

"The birthday feast was supposed to take place at eleven a.m. But since somebody stole all the food . . ."

Kyle laughed. "Eleven a.m."

"What?"

"The eleventh hour! The last possible moment." Kyle nudged his head up at the Wonder Dome. "How much do you want to bet that at eleven o'clock, on the dot, the clue we need most of all will pop up in the three hundreds section?"

Sierra smiled. "So this new book is a clue about our clue?"

"That's my guess. Did you eat breakfast?"

"Not yet."

"Well, what are you waiting for?" said Miguel as he strode into the room. "Today's the big day. We're gonna need our energy for the final sprint."

"He's right," said Akimi, climbing down the spiral staircase. "The doors open in less than two hours. Then we only have two more hours to figure everything out."

"But," said Kyle to his other teammates, "Sierra just figured out when we'll get the big three hundreds clue."

224

He gestured toward the picture book. "At the last possible minute."

"What?" said Akimi. "Eleven-fifty-nine?"

"Close. Eleven o'clock."

"Awesome," said Miguel. "It must be a very good clue."

Kyle and his team went into the café, where they found Haley Daley seated at a table, eating half a grapefruit and staring blankly through the glass walls into the rotunda.

"Hey, Haley," said Kyle. "How's it going?"

"Not bad. You?"

"Good. Win or lose, we're having a blast."

"We're the fun bunch," said Akimi.

"You guys really get along, huh?"

"Oh, yes," said Sierra. "I haven't had this much fun since I was six."

"Seriously?"

"What's the matter, Haley?" said Akimi. "Life not so good on Team Charles?"

"It's okay, I guess. I mean, we've pulled together some good clues and all. . . ."

"Well," said Miguel, "if you ever want to switch sides, we're always looking for new members."

"Can I do that? Just switch sides? Even though I know everything about what Team Charles did all day yesterday?"

"I think so," said Kyle. "I mean, there was nothing in the rules about teams."

"Huh," said Haley. "And Andrew's teamed up with you guys, too?"

"No," said Kyle.

Haley nodded toward the wall of windows behind Kyle. "Then why'd he just swipe his library card and go into your meeting room?"

44

Zipping across the slick marble floor, Kyle and his team, trailed by Haley, practically slid into Community Meeting Room B.

Where Andrew Peckleman stood with a notepad jotting down everything that was written on the whiteboard walls.

"Hey!" shouted Akimi. "That's cheating!"

Andrew spun around.

His eyes were the size of tennis balls behind his goggle glasses.

"Uh, uh, uh," he sputtered. "You guys left the door open!"

"No we did not," said Kyle extremely calmly, especially considering how much he wanted to throttle Peckleman. "It locks automatically; I checked."

"And I double-checked the door before we went to bed," said Miguel.

Kyle was surprised to hear it. "You did?"

"You bet, bro. It's what teammates do."

They knocked knuckles.

"Well, you don't have anything but a stupid list of stupid books and stupid authors and a stupid Bible verse. . . ."

"A verse which," boomed Mr. Lemoncello, whose face had just appeared on the video-screen wall, "you would do well to memorize, Mr. Peckleman. 'Thou shalt not steal.' "

Mr. Lemoncello was dressed in a curled white wig and a long black robe. He looked like a judge in England. He slammed down a rubber gavel on his desk. It made a noise like a whoopee cushion.

"Will everyone kindly join me in the Rotunda Reading Room? At once."

Everybody shuffled out of the meeting room and into the rotunda. They were shocked to see that Mr. Lemoncello himself was seated behind the librarian's desk at the center of the circular room. This was no hologram. This was the real deal.

Charles, all smiles, made a grand entrance, slowly descending one of the spiral staircases.

"Good morning, everybody," he called out cheerfully. "What's all the excitement? Did I miss something?"

"Just your man Andrew trying to cheat," said Miguel.

"What? Oh, good morning, Mr. Lemoncello. I didn't expect to find you here, inside the library. Isn't today your birthday, sir?"

"Yes, Charles. And there's no place I'd rather be on my

big day than inside a library, surrounded by books. Unless, of course, I could be on a bridge to Terabithia."

"Well, sir, I must say, you're certainly looking fit and trim. Have you been working out?"

"No, Charles, today I will be working *in*."

"I beg your pardon?"

"Today I will be working here, inside the library, supervising the final hours of this competition."

"Oh, I don't think it will take *hours,* sir," said Charles. "Not to brag, but I suspect some of us will be going home very soon."

"You are correct. For instance, Mr. Peckleman. He will be leaving right now."

"What?" whined Peckleman. "Why?"

"Because you cheated. You tried to steal the other team's hard-earned information."

Peckleman's eyes darted back and forth. "It wasn't my fault. It was Charles's idea." He whipped up his arm and waggled his finger. "Charles told me to do it. He *made* me do it!"

"Mr. Peckleman, please approach the bench, which, in this instance, is actually a desk. Let me see the library card you used to gain access to Community Meeting Room B."

Somewhat reluctantly, Andrew handed it over.

"Is your name Sierra Russell?"

"No, sir," Andrew said to his shoes.

"He stole my card?" said Sierra. She opened her latest book and pulled out the library card bookmark.

229

"Whose card do you have, Sierra?" asked Charles.

"Andrew Peckleman's."

"Aha," said Charles. "He pulled the old switcheroo, eh?"

"Because you told me to!" said Peckleman.

"Really?" Charles said, sniggering. "How dare you make such a scandalous accusation? Do you have any proof?"

"I don't need any stupid proof. You bullied me into stealing Sierra's card!"

Mr. Lemoncello banged his gavel again. "And thus ends the story of Andrew and the terrible, horrible, no good, very bad day. Mrs. Bunny?"

A hologram of the old lady bunny from *Goodnight Moon* hopped on top of the librarian's desk.

"Goodnight, Andrew," said the bunny. "Your time with us is all through."

Clarence and Clement, the security guards, appeared and escorted Peckleman out of the building.

"Sir?" said Sierra. "Would you like Andrew's library card for the discard pile?"

"No, thank you. That card is now property of Team Kyle."

Haley Daley raised her hand.

"Yes, Haley?"

Kyle saw her shoot a withering glance at Charles.

"How may I help you, dear?" asked Mr. Lemoncello.

"Well, sir, if it's okay with you, I'd like to switch sides. I want to join Kyle Keeley's team."

45

"*Zap!*" said Mr. Lemoncello, waving his arms like a magician. "*Zip!* You're now on Kyle Keeley's team!"

"Haley?" said Charles. "How can you desert me?"

"The same way you just deserted Andrew."

"Um, do we get *her* library card, too?" asked Kyle.

"Indeed you do. Plus any and all information she chooses to share with you. And so, Charles, I ask you: Would *you* like to quit your team and join Kyle's?"

"Excuse me?"

"You know, all for one and one for all?"

"Sir, with all due respect, that may have worked for those three musketeers in a trumped-up work of fiction, but I'm sorry, that is not how things work in the real world. Out here, it's every man for himself. What good is a prize if everyone wins it?"

"I see. But Haley knows all the clues you've collected."

"True, sir. But I doubt she realizes what any of them mean."

Kyle could see Mr. Lemoncello's nose twitch when Charles said that. And it wasn't a happy-bunny kind of twitch, either.

"It was a joke, sir." Charles must've seen the nose twitch, too.

"Oh. I see. Like the one about the boy named Charles. Hilarious. Remind me to tell it to you sometime. Anyway, be that as it may, I insist that you be given a few extra clues to compensate for the fact that all your teammates are either being kicked out of the game or abandoning your ship." Mr. Lemoncello reached under the desk and pulled out a white envelope. "This, Charles, is for your eyes only."

Charles stepped forward and took the envelope.

"Thank you, sir. That is very generous."

"I know. You may also ask me one question. But please, don't waste your question asking me, 'Where is the alternate exit?' because I do not know."

"You don't know?" Kyle said it before Charles could.

"Haven't a clue. This entire game was designed by my head librarian, Dr. Yanina Zinchenko, as my birthday present."

"But," said Akimi, "you could just ask Dr. Zinchenko how to get out, right?"

"Akimi Hughes? Are you one of those people who read the last chapter of a book first to see how it ends?"

"No, but . . ."

"Good. It's much more fun when the ending is a surprise. Dr. Zinchenko is the only one who knows how and where to exit this building without setting off all sorts of fire alarms. Any clues I personally delivered during the course of this game were completely scripted for me by Dr. Z."

"Okay," said Charles, "here's my question. . . ."

Mr. Lemoncello raised a hand. "Before you ask it, be advised: Your opponents will also hear my answer."

"Fine. Why is the book on the bedside table in your private suite *From the Mixed-Up Files of Mrs. Basil E. Frankweiler* by E. L. Konigsburg?"

"Because when I was your age, Mrs. Tobin, my local librarian, gave it to me."

Miguel raised his hand.

"Yes, Miguel?"

"Can we have one bonus question, too?" he asked politely.

"No," said Mr. Lemoncello. "However, I will give you one bonus answer, which Charles, of course, will also hear. Your bonus answer is 'lodgepole, loblolly, and Rocky Mountain white.' "

"What are three different kinds of pine trees?" said Charles, just to show off—and to let Kyle's team know their bonus answer didn't give them any kind of advantage.

"I am told that is correct," said Mr. Lemoncello, touching his ear.

He reached under the desk again and this time pulled up a three-foot-tall hourglass, a giant version of the red plastic timers that came as standard equipment in a lot of his games.

He turned it over.

"It's the jumbo, three-hour size," he said as the sand started trickling down. "Because it is now nine o'clock and you have only three more hours to find your way out of the library. Good luck. And may the best team—or, in Charles's case, the best solo effort—win!"

46

"Let's see what kind of *real* bonus clues Mr. Lemoncello is serving up today," Charles said to his empty conference room.

He really didn't mind flying solo. It meant he wouldn't have to share his prize when he won it.

Winner won all.

Losers lost all.

That was just the way the world rolled.

And Charles knew he would win.

After all, he was a Chiltington. They never lost.

Even if he had wasted his question about the *Mixed-Up Files* book. Turned out that Mr. Lemoncello was just a sentimental sap like Kyle Keeley. The book was there because his beloved librarian gave it to the old fool when he was the same age as all the library lock-in contestants. Boo-hoo. Big whoop.

And what was all that nonsense about pine trees?
Preposterous.

Unclasping the sealed envelope, Charles found two silhouette cards. Each of them was numbered, in case Charles couldn't figure out which books they would've been hidden in.

#8

Babied? Charles wondered. *No. Crawled!*
He examined the second free card.

#12

Three dinners? Three couples? A restaurant?
This one was difficult.

Charles decided to put the two new pieces into the puzzle, to see if their meanings would become clearer:

236

Charles was missing only one clue, but he had every-thing else.

"You can walk out the way BLANK crawled in in passed restaurant."

No. That didn't make sense.

In fact, all he was really certain about were the first two lines: "You can walk out the way."

The way what? Past the restaurant? The Book Nook Café?

And what about the image of the football player?

It came from the Johnny Unitas book. Maybe Johnny Unitas, who had played football back when Mr. Lemoncello was Charles's age, had owned a restaurant? Perhaps a popular national chain?

If so, there might've been one in Alexandriaville. Maybe right here in the old Gold Leaf Bank building.

Could the last bit be "In Johnny Unitas's Restaurant"?

Or what if Andrew Peckleman had been right all along and it was the NINETEEN that was the clue from the football player card? That would make the final line "In nineteen . . ." WHAT? *Diners? Couples?*

No.

Anniversaries!

The three couples in the bonus clue were obviously celebrating their anniversaries!

Nineteen anniversaries? Was today the nineteenth anniversary of some major event in Alexandriaville?

Charles shook his head. He knew the phrase would make sense only *after* he had completed the third line, the only one that still had a blank in it: "BLANK, CRAWLED, INN."

What if the missing image is an eyeball? Then the third line could be "I crawled *in*."

Hang on, Charles thought. The one book in the Staff Picks display case nobody had found yet was *True Crime Ohio: The Buckeye State's Most Notorious Brigands, Burglars, and Bandits* by Clare Taylor-Winters. The last image was going to be a criminal of some sort.

That one, single missing book might tell Charles who had crawled into the bank and, more importantly, *where* they had crawled in. Was this the nineteenth anniversary of a famous bank robbery?

Charles realized he needed help.

It was time to use his Ask an Expert.

That made him laugh.

Because Charles knew the top library expert in all of America, maybe the world. Someone much more important than Dr. Yanina Zinchenko.

Kyle Keeley and the rest of that bunch didn't stand a chance.

47

Eager to find out all he could in the final minutes before the Dewey decimal doors reopened on the second floor, Kyle listened as Haley Daley detailed everything she had learned on Team Charles.

Meanwhile, Akimi added Andrew's and Haley's library cards to the list on the whiteboards in Community Meeting Room B.

"We were piecing together a picture puzzle," said Haley. "It was like a memory match game, or that old TV show *Concentration*."

"We played one of those, too," said Miguel. "A rebus."

"Right. So far, I'm pretty sure it says something like 'You walk out the way bandits crawled in.' "

" 'Thou shalt not steal,' " said Kyle, tapping the Bible verse they had found in the 200s room. "That points to bandits, too."

"And the blackbird," said Sierra. "It wailed like a police siren."

"Chasing bandits!"

"Hang on," said Miguel. "What about Willy Wonka? Were there criminals in the chocolate factory?"

"No," said Sierra.

"And what about all this?" said Akimi, pointing at the list of library cards. "I added the new cards but it still doesn't make much sense."

BOOKS/AUTHORS ON THE BACKS OF LIBRARY CARDS

#1 Miguel Fernandez
Incident at Hawk's Hill by Allan W. Eckert/
No, David! by David Shannon

#2 Akimi Hughes
One Fish Two Fish Red Fish Blue Fish
by Dr. Seuss/Nine Stories by J. D. Salinger

#3 Andrew Peckleman
Six Days of the Condor by James Grady/
Eight Cousins by Louisa May Alcott

#4 Bridgette Wadge
Tales of a Fourth Grade Nothing
by Judy Blume/

Harry Potter and the
Sorcerer's Stone by J. K. Rowling

#5 Sierra Russell
The Egypt Game by Zilpha Keatley Snyder/
The Westing Game by Ellen Raskin

#6 Yasmeen Smith-Snyder
Around the World in Eighty Days
by Jules Verne/The Yak Who Yelled Yuck
by Carol Pugliano-Martin

#7 Sean Keegan
Olivia by Ian Falconer/Unreal! by Paul Jennings

#8 Haley Daley
Turtle in Paradise by Jennifer L. Holm/
A Wrinkle in Time by Madeleine L'Engle

#9 Rose Vermette
All-of-a-Kind Family by Sydney Taylor/
Scat by Carl Hiaasen

#10 Kayla Corson
Anna to the Infinite Power
by Mildred Ames/Where the Sidewalk
Ends by Shel Silverstein

#12 Kyle Keeley
I Love You, Stinky Face by Lisa McCourt/
The Napping House by Audrey Wood

"Wow," said Haley. "What a mess."

"Tell me about it," said Akimi.

"I don't think it's another author-title game," said Sierra, "like up on the Wonder Dome."

"Huh?" said Haley.

"Long story," said Miguel. "We'll save it for later."

"What we need," said Kyle, "is some kind of clue to show us how to unscramble this list. Remember what Dr. Zinchenko said when the game started: 'Your library cards are the keys to everything you will need.' This clue is the big one, guys. We need to crack it."

That's when Mr. Lemoncello popped his head in the door.

"Hello, hope I'm not interrupting. We have twenty minutes till the doors open upstairs. Anybody up for an Extreme Challenge?"

48

"In case you forgot," said Mr. Lemoncello, "Extreme Challenges are extremely challenging and sometimes extremely dangerous."

"Is Charles doing one?" asked Akimi.

"He might. I'm going to ask him if he'd like to next."

Mr. Lemoncello had changed out of his judge's costume into some kind of cat burglar outfit—black pants, ribbed black turtleneck, and sporty black beret.

"Is that costume a clue?" asked Haley. "Because it goes with the whole bandit theme."

"Don't know. But Dr. Zinchenko told me to wear it for the big finale. Is there going to be a finale?"

"Maybe with Charles," mumbled Kyle. "We're sort of stuck."

"At least till eleven," added Sierra. "That's when the most important clue will appear on the ceiling."

"Really?" said Mr. Lemoncello. "That Dr. Zinchenko. The woman knows how to build suspense."

"So let's do the Extreme Challenge," said Haley. "What do we have to lose?"

"Um, the whole game," said Akimi.

"Not for all of us," said Kyle. "I'll do the challenge. After all, I'm the team captain."

"You are?" said Haley.

"We had an election," said Akimi. "Yesterday."

"Oh. Cool."

"But, Kyle," said Miguel, "if you blow the Extreme Challenge, you lose, bro."

"Not if my team wins."

"No," said Mr. Lemoncello. "If you lose, Kyle, you *lose*. You will not be allowed to share in the big prize."

"Fine."

"I'm going with you," said Haley.

"No, you're not," said Mr. Lemoncello.

"I have to. Look, we both know I'd be a *fabulous* spokesmodel for your games and stuff, but I can't just glom on to everything Kyle and his team have already dug up. I have to earn my place on this team."

"Sorry, Haley. Extreme Challenges are, and always will be, solo efforts."

"But . . ."

Mr. Lemoncello held up his hand. "No buts. Kyle must face this challenge alone. However . . ."

"Yes?"

245

"The rest of you can watch his progress on the video screens and cheer him on over the intercom system. You are a cheerleader, aren't you, Haley?"

"Yep," said Kyle. "But she's never cheered for me."

"Well, I will this time. I promise."

"Excellent," said Mr. Lemoncello. "By the way, Kyle, there is no backing out once you commit to the challenge."

"Fine," said Kyle. "Let's do it."

"Go, Kyle, gooooo!" shouted Haley.

Akimi flinched. "Um, a warning next time . . . please?"

"Sorry."

Mr. Lemoncello touched his ear again. "Here is your Extreme Challenge. Dr. Zinchenko tells me:

"*'The answer you seek . . .'*"

He paused to listen.

"*' . . . the key to this code . . .*
is a memory box . . .
that holds the mother lode.'"

"What?"

Mr. Lemoncello shrugged. "Sorry. I don't write 'em. I only recite 'em. Wait. There's more:

"*'Forget the Industrial Revolution;*
my first idea is your certain solution.'"

The room was silent.

Mr. Lemoncello touched his ear once more and continued, "'And now, it's time for the addendum.'"

"Huh?"

"A last-minute addition:

"*'The box had been here*
but now it is there.
Poor Kyle. Your fate
is up in the air.'"

Mr. Lemoncello stood there grinning. For several seconds.

"Is that it?" said Kyle.

"Yes. Find what you're looking for before the second-floor doors open, and it is yours. Fail, and you, Kyle, will be eliminated from the game, and your team, due to that series of unfortunate events, will be forced to struggle on without you. Good luck. You have fifteen minutes."

And Mr. Lemoncello left the room.

"Dude," said Miguel, shaking his head. "You are so dead."

"Wait a second," said Haley. "I think I know how to find what Mr. Lemoncello was talking about!"

"You do?" said Kyle.

"I better. I'm the one who moved it from 'here' to 'there'!"

49

"Now then, Charles," said Mr. Lemoncello, "would you like to utilize any of your remaining lifelines? Perhaps an Extreme Challenge? An Ask an Expert?"

"Yes, sir," said Charles. "And may I just say, it's kind of you to come in here and ask me that question."

"Well, it's cloudy with a chance of meatballs and I had nothing better to do."

"Pardon?"

"Nothing. Just a brief flight of fancy, my mind sailing off past the phantom tollbooth. So, which lifeline would you like to use?"

"My Ask an Expert, sir."

"Fine. See Mrs. Tobin at the main desk. I must go to my office to monitor Kyle's Extreme Challenge."

"What's he doing?"

"Trying to beat you. Tootles!"

Mr. Lemoncello raised his beret by its stem, turned on his heel, and headed for one of the bookcases on the far side of the rotunda.

Charles watched him tilt back the head on a bust and press a red button in the middle of what would have been the man's neck. A door-sized section of the bookcase swung open. Mr. Lemoncello stepped into the darkness. The bookcase swung shut.

Charles hurried to the librarian's desk at the center of the Rotunda Reading Room.

"Mrs. Tobin?" He clapped his hands. "Mrs. Tobin? Chop-chop. I'm in a bit of a rush. The doors upstairs will be open in thirteen minutes. Mrs. Tobin?"

The holographic librarian finally appeared.

"Good morning, CHARLES. How may I help you?"

"I need to use my Ask an Expert."

"Very well. Whom do you wish to consult with?"

"Someone who knows his way around a library."

"If that is all you require, CHARLES, perhaps I can be of assistance."

"I need to talk to my uncle Jimmy."

"Your uncle Jimmy? Could you please be more specific?"

"Yes. Of course. James F. Willoughby the third."

"*The* James F. Willoughby the third?"

"Yes, ma'am."

"The *head librarian* of the *Library of Congress* in *Washington, D.C.,* is your uncle?"

"That's right. If my mother's brother, Uncle Jimmy, the top librarian in all of America, can't help me find the one book I'm looking for, nobody can!"

50

"The memory box is down in the Stacks," Haley told Kyle.

So he raced down to the basement. The very long, very wide cellar was just as he remembered it: filled with tidy rows of floor-to-ceiling shelving units.

Kyle looked up at the closest security camera.

"Where to next?"

"I hid it way over on the far side," said Haley through the ceiling speakers. "On a shelf near that horrible book-sorting machine."

Kyle hurried up the center aisle.

Suddenly, a heavy metal bookcase thundered in from the right, sliding like it was on roller skates.

"Watch it!" shouted Haley.

The bookcase skidded to a screeching halt, blocking Kyle's path forward.

"Go left," suggested Miguel.

The whole team was watching and cheering him on.

Kyle went left.

And another steel shelving unit shuffled in from the side.

"Jump back!" shouted Akimi.

The shelf slammed to a stop two inches in front of Kyle's feet.

"Kyle? You okay?"

"Yeah."

"This is like the hedge maze in the Triwizard Tournament," said Sierra.

"Huh?"

"Harry Potter. Book four. *Goblet of Fire*."

"Right. Need to read that one, too."

Kyle, of course, realized he'd just discovered the most "extreme" part of his Extreme Challenge. Each one of the sliding floor-to-ceiling bookcases was loaded down with heavy cardboard cartons, books, or metal storage bins. They probably weighed several tons each. If Kyle was in the wrong place when a shelving unit came shooting in from the side, he'd be flattened like a pancake under a steamroller.

"Warning," announced the official-sounding lady in the ceiling. "You have twelve minutes to complete this challenge."

He had to keep going. Like Mr. Lemoncello said, there was no turning back now. Unless, of course, he wanted to go home a loser.

Ha! Never!

Kyle jogged up an alleyway between two walls of bookshelves.

"Left turn!" Haley shouted. "Now!"

The wall on Kyle's right swung open, revealing six swiveling sections, each pivoting panel maybe twenty feet long, all skittering sideways and gliding backward to create new walls and reconfigured pathways.

"You've only got like ten more yards to go," coached Haley.

Kyle weaved his way around the randomly shuffling shelves.

But as soon as he was on any kind of straightaway, the walls started to rearrange themselves again.

Finally, Kyle scooted down a corridor so tight he had to turn sideways to squeeze through. The walls stuttered to a stop.

And the voice made another announcement. "Warning. You have eight minutes to complete this challenge."

"I'm trapped!" Kyle shouted. "There's no exit."

None of his teammates said anything for a real long time.

Finally, Sierra's voice rang out from the overhead speakers.

"Put your hand on the right wall," she said.

"What? Why?"

"When I was little, I played a lot of maze games. If the walls are connected, all you have to do is keep one hand in contact with one wall at all times and eventually you'll reach the exit or return to the entrance."

"Do it," coached Akimi.

"It'll work, bro," added Miguel.

So Kyle kept his right hand firmly planted on the right wall of shelves and started inching his way forward.

"Go, Kyle!" cheered Haley. "Hug that wall! Hug that wall!"

The passageway widened. Kyle kept his hand glued to the right wall and went around corners, through switch-backs, until finally, he stepped into an opening near the book return conveyor belt.

"You made it!" shouted Haley. "Whoo-hoo!"

All the shelves streamed back into their orderly church pew positions.

"Good," said Kyle. "Getting out should be easier than getting in. Where's the box, Haley?"

"I put it on the shelf."

"Which one?"

"That one."

"Warning," announced the calm female voice in the ceiling again. "You have THREE MINUTES to complete this challenge."

Kyle stared up at a nearby camera. "Um, Haley? What exactly am I looking for?"

"A cardboard box. In a drawer."

"Okay. There are like a billion of those. . . ."

"I flagged it with a piece of pink tissue."

Kyle raced to a shelf.

"TWO MINUTES," announced the calm lady.

"This one?" said Kyle.

"Yes! Look in the steel drawer."

"I thought you said it was cardboard. . . ."

"It is. Open the lid. Not that lid. The other one."

"This one?"

"No! The one under it!"

"ONE MINUTE."

"Hurry, Kyle!"

"I'm hurrying."

"Flip it open."

Kyle did as he was told. He flipped up the lid on a steel drawer and found a battered boot box.

Every member of Kyle's team shouted the same thing: "Grab it!"

"And run!" added Akimi.

Kyle did.

He tucked the boot box under his arm and ran like he had never run before.

He sprinted across the basement floor. He raced up the steps, two at a time.

When he hit the rotunda, his heart was pounding against his ribs.

"THIRTY SECONDS."

He speed-skated across the marble floor. It was so slippery he lost his balance.

He fell forward.

Dropped the box.

It flew out of his hands, hit the slick floor, and slid like a hockey puck across the threshold into Community Meeting Room B.

A buzzer sounded.

"Time is up," announced the calm voice.

"Yo," shouted Miguel, "you made it, bro!"

And Kyle started breathing again.

51

Having made his request, all Charles could do was wait.

"Apparently," said Mr. Lemoncello when he came back into the rotunda, "your uncle Jimmy is a very, *very* busy man. Reminds me of a spider I once knew. But it is a Sunday morning. We will attempt to track him down at home."

"Thank you, sir. I told Uncle Jimmy to stand by. That I might need him this weekend."

"And now—*WHOOSH!* He's as elusive as the wind in the willows. You'll have to discuss this with him the next time your family gets together for Thanksgiving dinner. Now, if you will excuse me, it is currently nine-fifty-eight a.m. Almost time to reopen the Dewey decimal chambers."

Mr. Lemoncello opened a filing cabinet and pulled out a megaphone.

"Is there some room you should be ready to run to? Isn't there some clue or book you need to go find?"

"Just one," said Charles. "And I need my uncle Jimmy to tell me which one it is. Will you keep looking for him? Please."

"Of course." Mr. Lemoncello pointed to a smudge on Charles's shirt. "If you like, I will also have Al Capone do your shirts."

All Charles could do was nod, smile, and wonder when Al Capone had opened a laundry.

52

"Everyone, please pay very close attention," cried Mr. Lemoncello through a squealing, screeching megaphone. "The Dewey decimal doors are now open and, unlike Tuck, this game will not be everlasting. Therefore, it is time to race upstairs like the rats of NIMH!"

Kyle and his teammates heard Mr. Lemoncello's announcement but stayed inside Community Meeting Room B so they could examine the dusty old boot box.

"It's from when Mr. Lemoncello was our age," said Haley. "Here. I'm pretty sure this is what we need." She handed Kyle a large manila envelope sealed up with tons of tape. "First and Worst Idea Ever" had been scribbled on the front.

"Awesome," said Kyle as he started undoing the tape. "The clue said his first idea might be our best solution."

Inside the envelope were a stack of cards, a bunch of rubber stamps, an ink pad, and a sheet of three-ring-binder paper filled with a fifth grader's sloppy handwriting.

Kyle read out loud what the young Luigi Lemoncello had written: " 'Presenting First Letters: the Amazingly Incredible Secret Code Game.' "

Haley held up some of the cards. Each one showed a cartoony drawing and a single letter: Apple = A, Bee = B, Carrot = C, and so on.

Kyle continued reading: " 'Want to send your friend a secret message to meet you after school? Just use your super-secret rubber stamps.' "

Miguel examined a couple of the wood-handled stamps. "The stamps match the cards."

"So how exactly do you use this junk to tell your friends to meet you after school?" asked Akimi.

"This is so bad," said Kyle. " 'Moon, Elephant, Elephant, Tiger. Moon, Elephant. Apple, Flamingo . . .' "

Akimi held up her hand. "Okay. Stop. I get it."

"Maybe it was for little kids," said Sierra.

"Definitely," said Kyle. "Because anybody over the age of six could crack this code in like ten seconds."

And then he froze.

"This is it!"

He went to the wall with the list of library cards. "What would happen if we played First Letters with these book titles?"

BOOKS/AUTHORS ON THE BACKS OF
LIBRARY CARDS

#1 Miguel Fernandez
Incident at Hawk's Hill by Allan W. Eckert/
No, David! by David Shannon

#2 Akimi Hughes
One Fish Two Fish Red Fish Blue Fish
by Dr. Seuss/Nine Stories by J. D. Salinger

#3 Andrew Peckleman
Six Days of the Condor by James Grady/
Eight Cousins by Louisa May Alcott

#4 Bridgette Wadge
Tales of a Fourth Grade Nothing
by Judy Blume/Harry Potter and the
Sorcerer's Stone by J. K. Rowling

#5 Sierra Russell
The Egypt Game by Zilpha Keatley Snyder/
The Westing Game by Ellen Raskin

#6 Yasmeen Smith-Snyder
Around the World in Eighty Days
by Jules Verne/The Yak Who Yelled Yuck
by Carol Pugliano-Martin

#7 Sean Keegan
Olivia by Ian Falconer/Unreal! by Paul Jennings

#8 Haley Daley
Turtle in Paradise by Jennifer L. Holm/
A Wrinkle in Time by Madeleine L'Engle

#9 Rose Vermette
All-of-a-Kind Family by Sydney Taylor/
Scat by Carl Hiaasen

#10 Kayla Corson
Anna to the Infinite Power
by Mildred Ames/Where the Sidewalk
Ends by Shel Silverstein

#11 UNKNOWN/CHARLES CHILTINGTON

#12 Kyle Keeley
I Love You, Stinky Face by Lisa McCourt/
The Napping House by Audrey Wood

"Okay," said Miguel, moving to a clean space on the wall. "Here are the first letters of all the titles."

INONSETHTTATOUTAASAW??IT

"It still makes no sense," said Akimi.

"Wait a second," said Sierra. "If the title starts with an article, drop that word, and use the letter from the second word."

"Got it," said Miguel.

INONSETHEWAYOUTWASAW??IN

"Okay," said Akimi. "It's making some sense."

She went to the board and broke Miguel's string of letters into words.

I/NON/SET/HE/WAY/OUT/WAS/A/W??/IN

"Hang on," said Kyle. "It could be . . ."

IN/ON/SE/THE/WAY/OUT/WAS/A/W??/IN

"What's 'In on se'?" said Akimi.

"Wait! Look!" said Miguel. "The books on the second and third library cards actually start with *numbers*!"

Kyle grabbed a marker:

IN/1968/THE/WAY/OUT/WAS/A/W??/IN

"Hang on," said Haley. "You know all those questions in the trivia contest Friday? I did so badly, I Googled a bunch of them later that night. They were all from 1968."

"You guys?" said Sierra. "I did some research, too.

263

Mr. Lemoncello was born in 1956. That means he turned twelve in 1968."

"Oh-kay," said Akimi. "Is this something besides a fun fact to know and tell?"

"You bet it is," said Kyle. "Nineteen sixty-eight is key. And we don't need Charles's library card to finish this phrase." He went to the whiteboard.

IN 1968, THE WAY OUT WAS A WAY IN.

"So what happened in 1968?" said Haley.

"Was that when *Charlie and the Chocolate Factory* came out?" asked Miguel.

"No," said Sierra. "Nineteen sixty-four."

"So what's up with the candy clue from the Art and Artifacts Room?"

"We messed up," said Akimi. "We need to go back and find a new rhyme for 'Andy'!"

"Really?" said Haley. "I thought he got kicked out for cheating."

"Another long story," said Miguel.

"For later," said Kyle. "Right now, we need to be on the third floor!"

53

Back in the Art & Artifacts Room, Kyle felt confident they were pretty close to figuring out, well, whatever it was they were supposed to figure out.

How it would help them escape from the library was still anybody's guess.

"It's ten-forty-four," said Akimi. "The last clue should pop up on the Wonder Dome in sixteen minutes."

"Okay, you guys," said Kyle. "Spread out. We need a new rhyme for 'Andy.'"

"This model of the bank building came in *handy*," added Miguel.

"The Dandy Bandits!" shouted Akimi, once again studying the display of hats.

"Yes!" said Haley, pulling off her shoe so she could show everybody her clue card.

+ ITS

"Bandits! I found this in the three hundreds room."

"That's the room clue we're waiting for," said Kyle.

"Because the Dewey decimal number for True Crime books always starts with the number three," said Miguel. "When we find that book, it'll tell us how and where the 'bandits crawled in in 1968.'"

"Listen to this, you guys," said Akimi. She read a placard in the display case: "'This plaid fedora from *1968* was worn by bank robber Leopold Loblolly, one of the notorious *Dandy* Bandits.'"

"Loblolly!" Miguel shouted.

"The smell-a-vision clue," said Kyle. "That's why everything kept smelling like pine trees."

"Loblolly was one of the pine trees in the answer Mr. Lemoncello gave you guys!" said Haley.

"Whoop-whoop-whoop," said Mr. Lemoncello as, banana shoes squeaking, he stepped into the room. "Well done, Miss Daley . . . and Miss Hughes."

"See?" said Akimi. "I was right the first time we came in here. I said 'dandy' and everybody else said, 'Noooo, *candy*. Willy Wonka . . .'"

"Yes, it's all coming back to me," said Mr. Lemoncello.

"Nineteen sixty-eight. I was pondering an idea for a game at the old public library."

"And," said Kyle, "you were so totally focused, you didn't hear the police sirens screaming past the library as they raced to the Gold Leaf Bank. . . ."

"The blackbird was from Alexandriaville," said Sierra. "The police siren wail was from that day."

Miguel finished that thought: "When the Dandy Bandits tried to crawl into the bank!"

"My goodness," said Mr. Lemoncello. "How could you kids know all that?"

"From the game clues," said Kyle, "and from the story Dr. Zinchenko told us on Friday night when somebody asked her why a library building needed a bank vault door."

"She was already feeding us clues!" said Akimi.

"The time is now ELEVEN a.m.," announced the ceiling lady. "This game will end in ONE hour."

"Come on," said Kyle, heading for the door. "It's the eleventh hour. We need to go check out the Wonder Dome again."

They raced to the balcony.

"There it is!" said Sierra.

"364 point 1092!" shouted Miguel.

"Whoo-hoo!" cried Akimi. "We're gonna win!"

54

On the first floor, Charles was at long last video chatting with his uncle, James Willoughby III, the librarian of Congress, who had finally shown up for the Ask an Expert call.

"Sorry for the delay, Charles."

"That's okay, Uncle Jimmy," Charles said, straining to smile and not scream.

"The time is now ELEVEN a.m.," announced the annoyingly placid lady in the ceiling. "This game will end in ONE hour."

Charles had to hustle.

"Sir, I know you're a very important, very busy man, so I just have one quick question: If I were a book on true crimes in the state of Ohio, where would you shelve me?"

"Library of Congress classification?"

"No, sir. Dewey decimal."

"Ah. Easy. 364 point 1. What comes after the one will depend, of course, on how many books a library . . ."

Charles didn't stick around to hear the rest of his uncle's answer.

He took off running for the closest spiral staircase up to the second floor. As he ascended the steps, two at a time, he saw Kyle Keeley and his entire entourage running down a staircase from the third floor.

Charles reached the second-floor balcony first.

He darted around the bend, past the door to the 500s room, the 400s.

Keeley and his crew were coming from the opposite direction, but Charles reached the door to the 300s room before them.

He swiped his library card, yanked on the handle, and dashed into the room.

He scanned the shelves and headed to his right.

He heard Keeley enter the room.

Glancing over his shoulder, Charles saw Keeley go left.

Charles dashed up an aisle between bookcases. He read the number at the end of each row of shelves.

310.

320.

330.

One of those robots with the book baskets came rumbling across his path, but Charles was able to dodge it.

340.

350.

Keeley's footsteps pounded up the passageway on the other side of the shelving units to his left.

In the middle of the 300s room, they entered an open space with a judge's bench and witness box.

Charles was getting closer to the True Crime section.

But so was Kyle.

Charles saw Keeley read something off his palm.

He had the whole call number!

It was time to change tactics.

Charles hung back and let Keeley take the lead.

Kyle rushed toward a bookcase.

Charles sprinted after him.

"Got it!" Kyle shouted as he reached for a book on the shelf.

But before he could completely pull it out, Charles grabbed hold of the book, too.

They both yanked it off the shelf.

Kyle had the spine; Charles had hold of the top.

They tugged it back and forth.

While they wrestled with the book, Keeley's teammates caught up to them.

"Careful, Kyle," cried Sierra Russell. "Don't hurt the book."

Charles grinned. Keeley, the sentimental sap, was listening to the silly, bookish girl and easing up on his grip.

Giving Charles his chance.

He body-checked Keeley. Slammed into him with his

shoulder. Sent him flying, the book tumbling. Charles snatched it off the floor.

He had the book. He quickly flipped through the table of contents. Saw chapter 11 was about a robbery at the Gold Leaf Bank in Alexandriaville.

He knew he'd won the game.

Charles used his free hand to slap an "L" on his forehead.

"Loser," he sneered at Keeley.

A tiger roared, a whistle blew, and Mr. Lemoncello entered the room, accompanied by Clarence, Clement, and what looked like a rare Bengal tiger.

"Mr. Chiltington?"

Charles smiled. He knew Mr. Lemoncello was about to congratulate him for defying the odds and winning the game. He had single-handedly defeated Kyle Keeley's entire team! "Yes, sir, Mr. Lemoncello?"

"Do you remember Dr. Zinchenko's number one rule?"

"You bet, sir. No food or drink except in the Book Nook Café."

"No," said Mr. Lemoncello, touching the tip of his nose and making a buzzer noise. "Dr. Z? Tell him what he should've said."

Dr. Zinchenko's voice purred out of the ceiling speakers. "Be gentle. With each other and, most especially, the library's books and exhibits."

"I know," said Charles. "That's why I had to stop Kyle

Keeley. He was ready to rip the cover off this poor book. Heck, sir, everybody at school knows that Kyle Keeley is a maniac. He'll do anything to win a game."

Mr. Lemoncello turned to Keeley.

"Is that true, Kyle? Would you actually destroy property if it stood between you and your prize?"

"W-well, sir . . ."

Keeley was stammering. The fool didn't know how to lie.

Charles quickly opened the book to chapter 11 and slipped in his library card to bookmark the location.

"You should ask Keeley about the window he broke, sir."

Mr. Lemoncello turned to face Charles again.

"The window?"

"Yes, sir. The whole school heard about it. See, Kyle Keeley and his two brothers were playing some sort of wild scavenger hunt game and . . ."

Mr. Lemoncello pointed at the book. "That's clever. You use your library card as a bookmark?"

"Yes, sir, I sure do," said Charles, turning on the charm. "Of course, I can't take full credit for such a clever idea. On Friday night, I saw Sierra Russell doing it and . . ."

"You told Andrew Peckleman to 'borrow' her card."

Charles blinked. Several times. "I beg your pardon?"

"You broke Dr. Zinchenko's number one rule. You

were not gentle with your teammate Andrew. In fact, you bullied him into stealing Miss Russell's library card, which you knew she always used as a bookmark."

"No, sir. I did not."

"Yes, Charles. You did." Mr. Lemoncello touched his right ear. "In fact, Dr. Zinchenko has spent the past few hours combing through security tapes, and guess what she just found?"

Charles heard his own voice ringing out of the ceiling speakers:

"*Have you noticed what Sierra Russell uses for a bookmark?*"

"*No.*"

"That was Andrew," said Mr. Lemoncello. "This is you again."

"*Her library card, which, of course, doubles as a key card for Meeting Room B. Find a way to borrow it.*"

"You told Andrew to steal Sierra's library card."

"How could you record that?" said Charles. "I was whispering!"

"And *I* have very good microphones. You're done, Charles. Dr. Zinchenko? Tell our departing guest what he has just won."

"Absolutely nothing," said the voice of the Russian librarian. "But please, Mr. L, tell Charles the correct answer to the final pictogram."

"Ah, yes!" Mr. Lemoncello reached into his back

pocket, pulled out a four-by-four card, and showed it to Charles.

Charles stood there fuming.

"Anyone care to help Charles out?"

"Hmmm," said Kyle. "Is it 'six eat'?"

"You are very close," said Mr. Lemoncello.

There was a pause and then Haley laughed. "Did it come after the football player?"

"Yeah," said Charles. "So?"

"Andrew was right all along," said Haley. "The football player clue wasn't 'past,' it was 'nineteen.'"

Mr. Lemoncello shifted into his game show voice. "So, Haley Daley, would you care to solve the puzzle?"

"Sure: 'You can walk out the way bandits crawled in in nineteen six ate.'"

"I don't get it," said Charles.

"Nineteen, six-ate," said Akimi. "You know: 1968."

"Ah, yes," said Mr. Lemoncello. "The year *From the Mixed-Up Files of Mrs. Basil E. Frankweiler* won the Newbery Medal for excellence in children's literature. Another clue you completely missed, Charles."

"Wow," said Miguel. "And I thought Chiltingtons never lose."

"There's a first time for everything," said Mr. Lemoncello. "Clarence? Clement? Kindly escort young Mr. Chiltington from the building."

"Buh-bye," said Akimi. "There goes this game's biggest loser."

55

"Open it!" Akimi said to Kyle. "We only have like forty minutes to figure out how Loblolly and the Dandy Bandits crawled into the bank back in 1968!"

Kyle flipped through *True Crime Ohio* to the place where Charles had slipped in his bookmark.

"Well?" said Miguel.

" 'Chapter Eleven. The Dandy Bandits Burrow into a Bank Vault.' "

"Even though thou should not steal," said Akimi.

"And I'll bet they crawled in, right?" said Haley.

" 'The clever thieves,' " Kyle read from the book, " 'took up residence in an abandoned dress factory next door to the Gold Leaf Bank and spent weeks tunneling from its basement into the bank vault.' "

"Which," said Miguel, "according to those old

blueprints I found, was down where the book-sorting machine is now."

"That explains the first clue," said Kyle. "The book title was *Get to Know Your Local Library*. Dr. Zinchenko meant we needed to get to know *this* library. This also explains why she wanted us to read those Sherlock Holmes stories."

"'The Adventure of the Red-Headed League,'" said Sierra. "The story about robbers tunneling into a bank from the building next door."

Kyle nodded. "Dr. Zinchenko told me *she* had just reread it. I'll bet that's where she got the idea for this whole game."

"Hey, Charles should've stuck with crawling through sewers like he did in that video game," joked Miguel. "He might've found the Dandy Bandits' tunnel before we did."

"Come on, you guys," said Haley. "We need to be back in the basement."

"I'm coming with you," said Mr. Lemoncello. "I just have to see how this story ends!"

Clutching the *True Crime* book against his chest, Kyle led the way down to the Stacks.

"Why are you bringing that book?" asked Akimi.

"We'll put it on that conveyor belt thing," Kyle explained. "Whatever basket the scanner sends it to, I'm guessing that's where we'll find our 'black square.'"

"Our shortcut out of the library!"

"Exactly."

As the team trooped down the steps to the basement, Mr. Lemoncello turned to Kyle and said, "So, Mr. Keeley, did you have fun this weekend?"

"Yeah."

"Good. Congratulations, Miss Hughes, it seems *you* have already won."

Akimi sort of blushed.

"What do you mean?" asked Kyle.

"In her essay, your extremely good friend wrote, and I quote: 'I want to see the new library so I can tell my friend Kyle Keeley how cool it is.'"

"You wrote your essay about me?"

"Maybe," mumbled Akimi.

"Wow," said Kyle. "No one's ever done that before."

"Well, no one's ever going to do it again if you blow our chance at winning this thing. So can we please stop yakking and find our way out of here?"

"Works for me."

"Warning," said the calm voice in the ceiling speakers. "This game will terminate in THIRTY minutes."

Everybody moved a little faster.

Fortunately, when the group reached the basement, the floor-to-ceiling bookshelves didn't start sliding into another maze formation.

"The automatic book sorter is straight up this path, near the far wall," said Kyle.

They made it to the conveyor belt.

"From what I remember from the old blueprints," said Miguel, "the vault was right here, in the same spot as this machine."

"Okay, you guys," said Kyle. "Whatever robo-basket this book ends up in is probably sitting right on top of the entrance to the tunnel."

"Here goes everything." Kyle placed *True Crime Ohio* into the array of crisscrossing beams.

Nothing happened.

"What's going on?" cried Miguel. "Why isn't it working?"

"Maybe this book isn't heavy enough." Kyle pushed down on the cover of the book a bit.

Still nothing.

They stared, dumbfounded, at the book sitting on the immobile belt.

"It wouldn't *stop* moving yesterday," muttered Haley.

"That's it!" cried Akimi. She hurried to the wall and flipped the emergency shutoff switch back to the "on" position.

Several red laser scanners sprang to life under the book drop slot.

The belt started moving. Slowly.

The single book worked its way down the line like a

candy bar on a wrapping machine. When it reached the third robo-basket from the end, a set of rollers popped up and shunted the book off to the side into the waiting wire basket.

The conveyor belt stopped rolling. The robo-cart rolled away.

Nothing else happened.

"That's it?"

"Warning," said the calm voice. "This game will terminate in TWENTY minutes."

"It didn't work," said Haley.

"We're toast," added Akimi.

"Wait," said Kyle, pointing to a square tile on the floor where the robo-basket had been. It was glowing, like one of the touch-screen computers in the desks upstairs. "It says 'Howdy. Dü you like fun games? Get Reddy.'"

"Excellent!" Akimi giggled. Then she and Kyle cracked up, remembering the box tops from their first puzzle in the Board Room on Saturday morning.

"Now it says we're going to get an anagram," said Kyle.

"My favorite kind of cookies," said Mr. Lemoncello.

"Okay, everybody," said Kyle. "Gather round. Get ready."

Kyle, Akimi, Sierra, Miguel, and Haley knelt on the floor in a circle around the square. Mr. Lemoncello hovered behind them.

"Here we go," said Kyle as game instructions scrolled across the screen.

A sixty-second clock popped up at the bottom of the
screen. And then a four-by-four Boggle jumble of letters:

L U I G
I L L E
M O N C
E L L O

"Luigi L. Lemoncello," mumbled Kyle.

The sixty-second clock started ticking down.

Sierra shouted out, "Lemon!" and a *ding* sounded from
the speaker above. The five teammates started shouting
out words:

"Cello!"

"Eon!"

"Elm!"

"Lion!"

"Mole!"

"Leg!"

"Oil!"

"Thirty seconds left," said Mr. Lemoncello.

"One!"

"Cell!"

"Cone!"

"Lone!"

"Glen!"

"Lime!"

"Eh, mole."

"We already said that."

"Melon."

"That's fifteen," said the voice in the ceiling.

"Um . . ."

"Ten seconds left."

"Anybody?"

"Five."

"Four."

"Colonel!" shouted Haley.

The computer screen flashed "Congratulations!" and "Winners!"

Somewhere, a game show audience cheered, fireworks rockets whistled through the air, and several geese honked out a "Hooray!"

"Please stand back," said the soothing voice in the ceiling.

Kyle and his teammates did as they were told.

"Warning," the voice continued. "This game will terminate in FIFTEEN minutes."

"We still need to get out, you guys!" said Akimi. "Hurry, floor. Do something!"

The eight tiles surrounding the glowing tablet also started to glow. First yellow, then orange, then purple.

"Our secret square," said Akimi.

There was a series of clicks, and the tiles began folding up on themselves and retracting into the floor, opening up like an origami trapdoor.

"Look," said Haley, "there's steps."

Mr. Lemoncello peered down into the hole at the well-lit staircase and tunnel. "My, my. Dr. Zinchenko has certainly cleaned things up since Mr. Loblolly was here."

"Of course she did," said Haley. "So we 'can walk out the way bandits crawled in in nineteen six-ate.'"

"Hurry, everybody!" said Mr. Lemoncello. "I don't want to be late to my own birthday party."

56

Kyle led the way up the tunnel and brought his team (plus Mr. Lemoncello) into an empty basement filled with mannequins and cardboard boxes.

"This must be the cellar of one of the clothing shops in Old Town," said Kyle.

"The Fitting Factory," said Haley, reading a tag on a shipping crate. "It's one of my faves."

"And," said Sierra, "back in 1968, it was the real dress factory that Leopold Loblolly and the Dandy Bandits used."

"There's some steps over here," said Miguel, climbing a wooden staircase. "And a door." He jiggled the knob. "Oh, man—it's locked."

Kyle looked up at the dingy casement windows, about ten feet above the cellar floor.

He couldn't help grinning.

It reminded him of another game he'd won once. This time, he'd just have to reverse things a little.

"Help me drag over a couple cartons," Kyle said to Miguel. "We can stack them on top of each other underneath this window."

After they built a step unit out of boxes, Kyle climbed up and examined the window latch.

"Great," he said.

"Don't tell me," said Akimi. "Another game?"

"Yep. There's a combination lock—the kind with four wheels of random letters."

"Warning," said the voice.

"What?" said Akimi. "Dr. Zinchenko put loudspeakers in this basement, too?"

"This game will terminate in FOUR minutes."

"Yo, open the lock, Kyle!" said Miguel.

"Hang on. It's some kind of word game."

"Is there a clue?" asked Haley.

"Of course." Kyle read the tiny slip of paper taped to the glass. " 'Once you learn how to do this, you will be forever free.' "

Everyone started laughing.

This last puzzle was ridiculously easy.

"Ready, children?" said Mr. Lemoncello. "All together now!"

And they all shouted it at the same time: "READ!"

Kyle thumbed the wheels to spell R-E-A-D. The lock clicked. The window opened.

And this time, he didn't need to shatter any glass to win the game.

Kyle and Mr. Lemoncello stood on top of the highest box and helped the others up and out of the basement.

When Haley crawled through the window frame, someone in the crowd that had gathered around the library for the game's big finale saw her and started screaming.

"Look! It's Haley Daley! She's the first one out. She won! With just two minutes to go!"

"Nuh-uh!" Kyle heard Haley shout in her perky cheerleader voice. "I'm just one member of a super-amazing team. We're all winners. Whoo-hoo!"

When Akimi climbed through the window, the crowd chanted her name.

"How do you people know my name?" Kyle heard her say. "Dad? Did you tell them?"

Sierra Russell was set to crawl out next.

"Mr. Lemoncello?"

"Yes, Sierra?"

"What time does the library open tomorrow?"

"For you, Sierra, nine a.m.!"

Smiling, she stepped into their hands and climbed out the window.

Kyle felt bad when Sierra stood up on the sidewalk. Who was out there to cheer for her?

But then he heard Haley shout, "Hey, you guys. You gotta meet our amazing new friend, Sierra Russell! She's so smart, she could tell you who wrote the phone book!"

The crowd went crazy. "Sierra! Sierra! Sierra!"

"Okay," said Kyle, "you're next, Miguel."

"And, Miguel," said Mr. Lemoncello, "if your summer schedule permits it, I'd love for you to head up my team of Lemoncello Library Aides."

"Thank you, sir. It'd be an honor."

"And please invite Mr. Peckleman to join you."

"But Andrew thinks this library is stupid."

"All the more reason for him to spend time getting to know us a little better. Now, off you go!"

They gave Miguel a boost up and out the window.

The chanting outside grew even louder.

"Miguel! Miguel! Miguel!"

"You guys?" Miguel shouted. "This library is like a good book. You just gotta check it out!"

The crowd laughed. Kyle groaned.

"You're next, Mr. Keeley," said Mr. Lemoncello.

"Okay. Can I ask one last question?"

"Certainly. And I hope it won't be the last."

"Are you really going to put all of us in your television commercials?"

"Oh, yes. You'll be quite famous."

"Cool."

"Indeed. Who knew spending time in your local library could be such a rewarding experience?"

Kyle smiled. "You did, Mr. Lemoncello."

"And now you do, too."

Kyle put his foot in Mr. Lemoncello's hands and grabbed hold of the window frame.

"See you at the birthday party, sir!"

"Oh, yes. And you know what, Kyle?"

"What?"

"There might be balloons!"

AUTHOR'S NOTE

Is the game really over?

Maybe not.

There is one more puzzle in the book that wasn't in the story. (Although a clue about how to find it was!)

If you figure out the solution, let me know. Send an email to author@ChrisGrabenstein.com.

THANK YOU . . .

To R. Schuyler Hooke, my longtime editor at Random House, for his incredible patience, faith, and input on this project.

To designer Nicole de las Heras and artist Gilbert Ford, who made the book look so darn good.

To my wife, J. J. Myers, who is a terrific first editor.

To Ms. Macrina, librarian, and all the folks at P.S. 10 in Brooklyn, whose library gave me the initial inspiration for this story.

To Darrell Robertson, Gail Tobin, Amy Alessio, Erin Downey, Yanna Zinchenko, Scot Smith, and all the other librarians and media specialists I have met in my travels as an author, at public libraries and in schools. When I see how you inspire the love of reading on a daily basis, I realize you are much more amazing and incredible than Mr. Lemoncello.

RANDOM CHATTER WITH
CHRIS GRABENSTEIN

What were you like as a kid?

Kind of chubby. Not very good at sports. But I liked to make my friends (and teachers) laugh. Sometimes I'd do this with comic books that I wrote and drew and passed around in class. I guess those were my first "published" books!

I also spent a lot of time making up imaginary stories. I could play basketball in our driveway all by myself and turn it into the most exciting championship game ever played—complete with sound effects—and do it all in my head. By the way, in those imaginary games, I was *excellent* at sports!

Did you want to be an author when you grew up?

You know, I vaguely remember reading a book in the backseat of the station wagon during my family's long and hot (it was August) car ride from Buffalo, New York, to the beaches of St. Petersburg, Florida (where my grandparents lived), and thinking, *I should write a book. About a boy. In the backseat of a station wagon. Dying of heat exhaustion and lack of cupcakes.*

Other than that, I don't really think I ever thought I could be an author when I grew up. I knew I could probably be a writer. But an *author*? I didn't own any tweed sport coats with patches on the elbows.

When I was a kid, I think I wanted to be a famous movie star. Or Johnny Carson. One of those.

Writing wasn't your first career, was it?
Well, I was always writing, but when I moved to New York City right after college (with nothing but seven suitcases and a typewriter I had received as a high school graduation gift), I spent five years doing improvisational comedy down in a basement theater in Greenwich Village and on the college tour circuit. A guy named Bruce Willis was in one of my comedy troupes. Robin Williams would drop by and hop onstage with us whenever he was in town doing a movie.

When you do improv, you make up scenes and songs right on the spot, based on audience suggestions. For instance, we'd ask the audience for a "personal problem" and then we'd make up an entire instant opera about "BO" or "acne" or whatever they shouted out.

While I was doing improv (and supporting myself with office work), I also had the great good fortune to write for Jim Henson and the Muppets. What an inspirational man. I think he named his company Henson Associates just so he could have "ha!" as a corporate logo.

I also cowrote a made-for-TV movie called *The Christmas Gift,* starring John Denver, which first aired on CBS way back in 1986. It's still on TV every year during the holiday season. Usually on the Hallmark Channel. At three a.m. I know this because my mother calls me up and tells me.

Then, in 1984, I landed a job on Madison Avenue, writing copy for the J. Walter Thompson advertising agency. I actually got the job by answering a writing aptitude test headlined "Write If You Want Work" that ran in the *New York Times*. It was full of fun questions like "How would you sell a telephone to a Trappist monk who had taken a strict vow of silence?" (I'd convince him he'd need the phone to connect to Monkmail, a new kind of email for silent monks only.)

The creative director of J. Walter Thompson, New York, wrote the test and questions. His name was James Patterson. Yes, *that* James Patterson. Before he became the world-record holder for the Most Number One *New York Times* Bestsellers Ever, he wrote commercials and ran the entire creative department at one of New York's biggest advertising agencies. I learned a lot about writing while working for Mr. Patterson, and I'm thrilled to be working with him again, coauthoring books like *I Funny* and *Treasure Hunters*.

What was your inspiration for *Escape from Mr. Lemoncello's Library?*

During an author visit to P.S. 10, a school in Brooklyn, New York, I marveled at their incredibly beautiful library. The librarian, Ms. Macrina, told me that it had been "donated by a very generous benefactor."

That got my mental wheels spinning. *What if . . . a generous benefactor, an eccentric bazillionaire, gave the town where he grew up the most amazingly awesome library ever built?*

By the way, most of my books start with a big *What if . . . ?*

And since, when I was a kid, I loved playing games like Monopoly, Sorry, and Risk, I decided to make my eccentric benefactor a wackier version of one of the Parker Brothers, the name behind many of my favorite games.

I think I named him Lemoncello and made him the son of Italian immigrants in honor of my Greek immigrant grandparents, whose last name was Lemonopoulos.

Recently, my mother told me that when she was a little girl growing up in Canton, Ohio, speaking and reading more English than her mom and dad, who were still speaking Greek, she was determined to read every book in the library. The library was where she could learn even more about her family's new home. That's one of the reasons I chose to celebrate the connection between libraries and immigrants in this book.

People have compared Mr. Lemoncello to Willy Wonka. Were you thinking of him when you wrote the book?

I was—but only to avoid making Mr. Lemoncello too much like Willy Wonka, particularly Gene Wilder's depiction of him in the old movie, which is one of my favorite films. But any time you have an eccentric bazillionaire in a fantastical setting and surround him with kids, it's hard not to be reminded of Willy Wonka. However, Mr. Lemoncello has no Oompa-Loompas to help him restock the shelves.

Kyle is very competitive with his brothers, Mike and Curtis. Do you have any brothers?

Yes! Four of them: Tom, Jeff, Steve, and Bill. Three of them are now doctors; the other is a lawyer. When we were kids, Tom, the oldest, wasn't a jock like Mike, but he was definitely the Big Brother, the guy we all looked up to, the one who did all the stuff we wished we could do. Jeff, my other older brother, was (and is) a genius like Curtis. I would get straight As at school, but it wasn't really all that impressive. Jeff, who had been in the same class the year before me, got straight A++s.

What's your favorite Dewey decimal number?

641.3373. I'm having some right now. Delicious.

Have you ever been to a library as amazing as Mr. Lemoncello's?

Actually, a lot of the libraries I visit are even more amazing. I see librarians making great suggestions about books they know kids will love. I see kids working together on school projects, and librarians helping them find the information they need, either online or in the stacks. In one of my favorite libraries, outside Chicago, they have even built Collaboration Stations in their new wing for young adults.

I like Mr. Lemoncello's motto: "Knowledge not shared remains unknown." A library is, and always has been, a place where we can come together and share what we know—as the whole human race and as individuals.

If you had as much money as Mr. Lemoncello, what would you build with it?

The world's largest and nicest animal rescue shelter with gourmet kibble and tuna for all! Fred, our rescue dog, and Parker, Tiger Lilly, and Phoebe Squeak, our rescue cats, had nothing to do with that answer.

BONUS CLUE

Have you solved the extra puzzle mentioned in the author's note? The one that was in the book but wasn't in the story? Here's a hint.

(Of course you have to solve this puzzle to get it!)

B = W
D = T

- C
R = D

R = H
- E

E = ST

- D
G = F

- T
- ER

I = PTE

W +

- S

W = YS

The Books, Stories, and Periodicals in
Mr. Lemoncello's Library
(How many have you read?)

- [ ] *All-of-a-Kind Family* by Sydney Taylor
- [ ] *The American Heritage Dictionary of Idioms*
- [ ] *Anna to the Infinite Power* by Mildred Ames
- [ ] *Anne of Avonlea* by Lucy Maud Montgomery
- [ ] *Anne of Green Gables* by Lucy Maud Montgomery
- [ ] *Around the World in Eighty Days* by Jules Verne
- [ ] *Baby's Mother Goose: Pat-A-Cake*
- [ ] *The Brothers Karamazov* by Fyodor Dostoyevsky
- [ ] "The Cask of Amontillado" by Edgar Allan Poe
- [ ] *The Cat in the Hat* by Dr. Seuss
- [ ] *Charlie and the Chocolate Factory* by Roald Dahl
- [ ] *Charlie and the Great Glass Elevator* by Roald Dahl
- [ ] *Coming Up for Air* by George Orwell
- [ ] *The Complete Sherlock Holmes* by Sir Arthur Conan Doyle
- [ ] *Crime and Punishment* by Fyodor Dostoyevsky
- [ ] *Cupcakes, Cookies & Pie, Oh, My!* by Karen Tack and Alan Richardson
- [ ] *Death on the Nile* by Agatha Christie
- [ ] *The Egypt Game* by Zilpha Keatley Snyder
- [ ] *Eight Cousins* by Louisa May Alcott
- [ ] *The Elevator Family* by Douglas Evans
- [ ] *The Eleventh Hour: A Curious Mystery* by Graeme Base
- [ ] *Even the Stars Look Lonesome* by Maya Angelou
- [ ] *Falling Up* by Shel Silverstein
- [ ] *From the Mixed-Up Files of Mrs. Basil E. Frankweiler* by E. L. Konigsburg
- [ ] *The Giver* by Lois Lowry
- [ ] *Goodnight Moon* by Margaret Wise Brown
- [ ] *Great Day for Up* by Dr. Seuss
- [ ] *Harry Potter and the Goblet of Fire* by J. K. Rowling
- [ ] *Harry Potter and the Sorcerer's Stone* by J. K. Rowling
- [ ] *Huckleberry Finn* by Mark Twain
- [ ] *The Hunger Games* by Suzanne Collins
- [ ] *If I Grow Up* by Todd Strasser
- [ ] *I Love You, Stinky Face* by Lisa McCourt
- [ ] *Incident at Hawk's Hill* by Allan W. Eckert

- [ ] *In the Pocket: Johnny Unitas and Me* by Mike Leonetti
- [ ] *The Jungle Book* by Rudyard Kipling
- [ ] The King James Bible
- [ ] *Little House on the Prairie* by Laura Ingalls Wilder
- [ ] *Look Homeward, Angel* by Thomas Wolfe
- [ ] *Look, I Made a Hat* by Stephen Sondheim
- [ ] *Lord of the Rings* by J. R. R. Tolkien
- [ ] "The Masque of the Red Death" by Edgar Allan Poe
- [ ] *The Mousetrap* by Agatha Christie
- [ ] *Murder on the Orient Express* by Agatha Christie
- [ ] "The Murders in the Rue Morgue" by Edgar Allan Poe
- [ ] Nancy Drew: *The Mystery at Lilac Inn* by Carolyn Keene
- [ ] *The Napping House* by Audrey Wood
- [ ] *Nine Stories* by J. D. Salinger
- [ ] *No, David!* by David Shannon
- [ ] *Olivia* by Ian Falconer
- [ ] *One Fish Two Fish Red Fish Blue Fish* by Dr. Seuss
- [ ] *Popular Science Monthly* magazine
- [ ] "The Purloined Letter" by Edgar Allan Poe
- [ ] *The Red Pyramid* by Rick Riordan
- [ ] *Scat* by Carl Hiaasen
- [ ] *Six Days of the Condor* by James Grady
- [ ] *Tales of a Fourth Grade Nothing* by Judy Blume
- [ ] *Ten Little Indians* by Agatha Christie
- [ ] *This Isn't What It Looks Like* by Pseudonymous Bosch
- [ ] *Through the Looking-Glass* by Lewis Carroll
- [ ] *Time* magazine
- [ ] *Treasure Island* by Robert Louis Stevenson
- [ ] *Turtle in Paradise* by Jennifer L. Holm
- [ ] *The Umpire Strikes Back* by Ron Luciano and David Fisher
- [ ] *Unreal!* by Paul Jennings
- [ ] *Up from Slavery* by Booker T. Washington
- [ ] *Walter the Farting Dog* by William Kotzwinkle and Glenn Murray
- [ ] *The Westing Game* by Ellen Raskin
- [ ] *When You Reach Me* by Rebecca Stead
- [ ] *Where the Sidewalk Ends* by Shel Silverstein
- [ ] *A Wrinkle in Time* by Madeleine L'Engle
- [ ] *The Yak Who Yelled Yuck* by Carol Pugliano-Martin

Books Sprinkled into Mr. Lemoncello's Dialogue

- *Al Capone Does My Shirts* by Gennifer Choldenko
- *Alexander and the Terrible, Horrible, No Good, Very Bad Day* by Judith Viorst
- *Because of Winn-Dixie* by Kate DiCamillo
- *Bridge to Terabithia* by Katherine Paterson
- *Cloudy with a Chance of Meatballs* by Judi Barrett
- *Dead End in Norvelt* by Jack Gantos
- *Ella Enchanted* by Gail Carson Levine
- *The Essential Groucho,* edited by Stefan Kanfer
- *For Your Eyes Only* (James Bond) by Ian Fleming
- *Go, Dog. Go!* by P. D. Eastman
- *Great Expectations* by Charles Dickens
- *The Great Gilly Hopkins* by Katherine Paterson
- *Heart of a Samurai* by Margi Preus
- *I Can Read with My Eyes Shut!* by Dr. Seuss
- *Joey Pigza Loses Control* by Jack Gantos
- *Maniac Magee* by Jerry Spinelli
- *Mrs. Frisby and the Rats of NIMH* by Robert C. O'Brien
- *My Side of the Mountain* by Jean Craighead George
- *Oh, the Thinks You Can Think!* by Dr. Seuss
- *The Phantom Tollbooth* by Norton Juster
- A Series of Unfortunate Events by Lemony Snicket
- *Something Wicked This Way Comes* by Ray Bradbury
- *Tuck Everlasting* by Natalie Babbitt
- *The Very Busy Spider* by Eric Carle
- *The Wind in the Willows* by Kenneth Grahame

BRING THE FUN AND EXCITEMENT OF MR. LEMONCELLO'S LIBRARY INTO YOUR LIBRARY!

Now you can host a Lemoncello-style scavenger hunt in YOUR library. Working with children's services librarians from the Carroll County Public Library in Finksburg, Maryland, Chris Grabenstein has created Mr. Lemoncello's Great Library Escape Game for libraries everywhere!

To access the downloadable PDFs, go to:
chrisgrabenstein.com/kids/
escape-from-mr-lemoncellos-library-game.php

To get all the game pieces, you will need a user name and a password. If you are a librarian or the person organizing the game, just send an email to author@ ChrisGrabenstein.com, and Mr. Lemoncello himself will send you the two secret codes.

IF YOU LIKED
ESCAPE FROM MR. LEMONCELLO'S LIBRARY,
YOU'LL LOVE

AVAILABLE NOW!
Read on
to discover what happens next!

Excerpt copyright © 2016 by Chris Grabenstein.
Published by Random House Children's Books, a division of Penguin Random House LLC, New York.

Early in the second week of January, each member of Team Kyle received a thick envelope in the mail.

When they opened it, they found an engraved invitation:

SPLENDIFEROUS GREETINGS AND SALUTATIONS!

YOU AND YOUR FAMILY ARE HEREBY
CHERRY CORDIALLY INVITED TO THE
ANNOUNCEMENT OF MY STUPENDOUS NEW NEWS.

FRIDAY NIGHT
SHALL WE SAY 7-ISH?

THE ROTUNDA READING ROOM OF
THE LEMONCELLO LIBRARY

REFRESHMENTS SHALL BE SERVED,
INCLUDING CHERRY CORDIALS.

AND THERE *WILL* BE BALLOONS.

REGARDS,
LUIGI L. LEMONCELLO

* * *

Friday evening, Kyle and his family piled into their mini-van and drove downtown to the library.

"Isn't this exciting?" said Kyle's mother. "I should've baked a cake."

"Any idea what the big announcement is?" asked his dad.

"Not a clue," said Kyle. "But we're hoping Mr. Lemoncello is going to ask us to star in more TV commercials."

"Please, no," moaned Kyle's brother Mike. "Your head's big enough already."

Snowflakes swirled in the misty beams of light flooding the front of the domed building that used to be a bank until Mr. Lemoncello turned it into a library. Kyle noticed several TV news satellite trucks taking up the parking spaces along the curb.

"You better get in there, Kyle," said his dad. "We'll go find a place to park."

"Have fun!" added his mom.

Kyle dashed up the marble steps and into the library's lobby.

Miguel and Sierra were waiting for him near the life-size statue of Mr. Lemoncello perched atop a lily pad in a reflecting pool. The statue's head was tilted back so the bronze Mr. Lemoncello could squirt an arc of water out of his mouth like he was a human drinking fountain. His motto was chiseled into the statue's pedestal:

KNOWLEDGE NOT SHARED REMAINS UNKNOWN.
—LUIGI L. LEMONCELLO

"Hey, Kyle!" exclaimed Miguel. "The place is packed. Everybody was invited! All twelve of the original players."

"Including Charles Chiltington?" asked Kyle.

"He's a no-show."

"I hope Andrew Peckleman doesn't show up, either," said Sierra with a slight shiver. Peckleman had been Chiltington's ally in the escape game and had tricked Sierra out of her library card so he could spy on Team Kyle.

"He was definitely invited," said Miguel. "But he won't be coming. Ever since he got kicked out of the game, Andrew doesn't really like libraries. He even quit being a library aide at school."

"That's sad," said Sierra.

"You guys," said Akimi, coming in from the Rotunda Reading Room, "there's all sorts of TV news crews inside. Including that reporter from CNN."

"Which one?"

"The guy with the hair."

"And there's food in the Book Nook Café," said Miguel. "Tons of it."

"So why are we hanging out here?" said Kyle. "Let's go."

The four friends hurried under the arch that led into the vast Rotunda Reading Room. The rotunda was packed. Clusters of brightly colored balloons were tethered to the green-shaded lamps on the reading desks. Hidden surround-sound speakers blasted a brassy, heroic fanfare.

Overhead, the Wonder Dome was a fluttering display of fifty state flags flapping against a cloudless blue sky, where, for whatever reason, a very muscular couple in ancient robes rode a chariot back and forth across the curved ceiling like it was a horse-drawn comet. They reminded Kyle of a Greek god and goddess straight out of the Percy Jackson books.

"Wow," said Miguel. "Do you think Rick Riordan's going to be here? That would be so awesome!"

All the animated action was displayed on ten wedge-shaped high-definition video screens—as luminous as any sports arena's scoreboard. They lined the underbelly of the building's colossal cathedral ceiling like glowing slices of pie. Each screen could showcase individual images or join with the other nine to create one spectacular presentation.

"Whoa," said Akimi. "Check out the statues. They're hardly wearing any clothes."

"And," Sierra said, "they look like they're made out of marble."

"Right," said Akimi. "*See-through* marble."

Tucked beneath the ten Wonder Dome screens in arched niches were ten 3-D statues glowing a ghostly green. Holograms.

"They all remind me of Hercules," said Kyle, taking in the dizzying array of muscular wrestlers, javelin throwers, discus flingers, and runners. "Except for the lady with the horse."

"I think that's a Spartan princess named Cynisca," said Sierra, who read a ton of history books, too. "She won the four-horse chariot race in 396 BC and again in 392 BC in what we call the ancient Olympic Games."

Akimi arched an eyebrow. "You sure she isn't that girl from *The Girl Who Loved Wild Horses*?"

Sierra laughed. "Positive!"

"Splendiferous greetings and salutations to one and all!" boomed Mr. Lemoncello's voice from the loudspeakers as the trumpets blared their final fanfare. "Thank you for joining us this evening. It is now time for my big, colossal, and jumbo-sized announcement!"

Kyle held his breath and crossed his fingers.

He really hoped he and his friends were going to star in more commercials.

Being famous was fun.

And kind of easy, too.

Blazing circles of bright light swung across the second-floor balcony to shine on Mr. Lemoncello.

Spotlights following him, he scampered to the nearest spiral staircase, slid down the banister, and dismounted with an impressive backflip. When his boot heels hit the ground, they squawked like a chicken, then mooed like a cow.

"Dr. Zinchenko? Kindly remind me never to borrow boots from Old MacDonald again."

Mr. Lemoncello wore a bright red and blue Revolutionary War outfit with a ruffled collar and a cape. A plumed tricorne hat completed the costume. He pulled out a brass handbell and rang it. Loudly.

"Welcome, boys and girls, families and friends, esteemed members of the press."

Mr. Lemoncello smiled for all the television cameras aimed at him.

"Clarence? Clement?" He clanged his bell a few more times. "Please bring in today's mail."

Clarence and Clement, the beefy twins who headed up security for the Lemoncello Library, marched into the Rotunda Reading Room flanked by six robotic carts loaded down with United States Postal Service mail bins.

"Dr. Zinchenko? How many e-mails have we received on this same subject?"

Dr. Zinchenko consulted the very advanced smartphone clipped to the waistband of her bright red pantsuit. "Close to one million, sir."

"One million?" Mr. Lemoncello shuddered. "And that's just the bad beginning. But, not to worry, I have come up with the happy ending! You see, fellow library lovers, kids all across this wondermous country are eager to prove that *they* are bibliophilic champions, too. Therefore, oyez, oyez, and hear ye, hear ye."

Kyle covered his ears. Mr. Lemoncello was clanging his bell like crazy.

"Let the word go forth from Alexandriaville to all fifty states. I, Mr. Luigi L. Lemoncello, master game maker extraordinaire, am proud to announce a series of games that will rekindle the spirit and glory of the ancient Olympic Games held, once upon a time, in Olympia—the one in Greece, not the capital of Washington State. Therefore, I hereby proclaim the commencement of the first-ever Library Olympics! A competition that will discover, once and for all, who are this sweet land of liberty's true library champions. Dr. Zinchenko?"

"Yes, Mr. Lemoncello?"

"Kindly invite your network of crackerjack librarians all across this country to organize regional competitions."

"Immediately, sir."

"Oh, it can wait until tomorrow. I, of course, will pay for everything, including the Cracker Jacks."

"Of course, sir."

"Bring me your best and brightest bookworms, research hounds, and gamers. Our first Library Olympiad shall commence on March twentieth. The ancient Greeks had their summer games, so we'll take the first day of spring."

"How many members should be on each team?" asked Dr. Zinchenko, who was furiously tapping notes into her tablet computer.

"Five," said Mr. Lemoncello, "the same number as on Team Kyle. Our hometown heroes are hereby officially invited to these Library Olympics, where they will defend their crown—which, to keep things Greek and chic, will be made out of olive branches."

Kyle gulped.

Another competition?

Against the top library nerds in the country?

He didn't like the sound of that. He liked being a champion and staying a champion.

"Um, sir?" said Miguel, raising his hand.

"Yes, Miguel?"

"Haley Daley moved to Hollywood. We're down to four."

"What about Andrew Peckleman?" asked Mr. Lemoncello. "He only cheated in the first game because someone who shall remain nameless bullied him into doing it."

Mr. Lemoncello pretended to cough, but his cough sounded a lot like *"Ch-arles Ch-iltington."*

"Andrew won't play," said Miguel. "He says he hates libraries."

"Oh, my. Well, we must certainly work on changing that. For now, we will stick with *four* members on every team. Just like the four horses pulling that Spartan lady Cynisca's chariot."

Yep, thought Kyle. *Sierra was right. Again.*

"Once we find our other Library Olympians," said Mr. Lemoncello, "we'll fly them here to Alexandriaville and commence our duodecimalthon."

"Your what?" asked Akimi.

"Duodecimalthon. It's like a decathlon, only with *twelve* games instead of ten."

"Why twelve?" asked Kyle, who was already trying to figure out how many games his team would need to win to keep its title.

"Because 'duodecimalthon' sounds a lot like 'Dewey decimal system' if you say it real fast with a mouthful of malted milk balls, don't you agree?"

"Yes, sir."

"Good," said Mr. Lemoncello, raising his bell and striking a heroic pose. "The four members of the winning team shall each receive a full scholarship to the college of their choice."

The audience applauded. Some parents even whistled.

"That's right. It's very whistle-worthy. The winners will receive four years of paid tuition plus free room, board, and books. Lots and lots of books. Now go find me my champions!"

On your mark. Get set.
Lemon. Cello. Go!

The race is on in the third splendiferous adventure!

#1 *New York Times* bestselling author of
Escape from Mr. Lemoncello's Library

MR. LEMONCELLO'S
GREAT LIBRARY
RACE

"Discover the coolest library in the world."
—James Patterson

CHRIS GRABENSTEIN

COMING SOON!

AND DON'T MISS

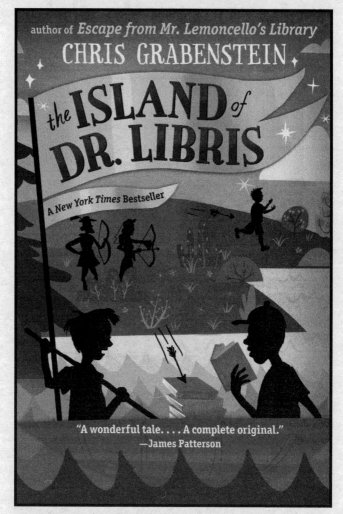

author of *Escape from Mr. Lemoncello's Library*

CHRIS GRABENSTEIN

the ISLAND of DR. LIBRIS

A New York *Times* Bestseller

"A wonderful tale. . . . A complete original."
—James Patterson

Where stories come to life . . .
Keep reading for a preview!

AVAILABLE NOW!

THE THETA PROJECT

Lab Note #316
Prepared by
Dr. Xiang Libris, PsyD, DLit

I am thrilled to report that after an exhaustive search, I have found the ideal subject for our first field test, which will commence as soon as Billy G., a twelve-year-old male with a very vivid imagination, arrives on-site.

His mother will be busy. His father will be away. He will be bored.

In short, Billy G. will be perfect.

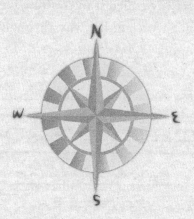

Just behind the brass keyhole, which looked like a yawning lion, Billy saw a small slip of paper the size of a fortune cookie fortune.

It was under a strip of clear plastic tape that had turned brown around the edges. The fortune itself was so tiny Billy wished he had a magnifying glass.

He looked around the room.

Some of the shelves were decorated with trinkets—like a miniature Gandalf figurine in front of a copy of *The Hobbit* and a whaling ship in a bottle near *Moby-Dick*.

But no magnifying glass.

What about Sherlock Holmes? thought Billy. *He always has that magnifying glass.*

There was a library ladder attached to the longest

wall of books. Billy rolled it over a few feet, climbed up two rungs, and, working his way through the alphabet of authors, found *The Adventures of Sherlock Holmes* by Sir Arthur Conan Doyle. *Score!* Right in front of the book was a toy magnifying glass—the kind you might get with a Happy Meal. Billy wiped the layer of dust off the lens, climbed down the ladder, and went back to the bookcase.

Holding the miniature magnifier right up against the glass doors in front of the slip of paper, he squinted to read letters so small they might've been typed by a mouse:

I am an odd number.

Take away one and I become even.

What number am I?

Okay. This was pretty cool. A riddle. Billy loved solving puzzles.

He did some quick math. "Three, five, seven, and nine are odd numbers. Take away one, and you get two, four, six, and eight."

This riddle wasn't very good.

Any odd number you subtracted one from automatically turned into an even number. You didn't need to be an assistant math professor like his mom to know you could do that kind of subtraction to infinity and never end up with a decent answer.

He reread the riddle. In school, whenever he was stumped on a quiz, he found it helped to reread the question, see what it was really asking.

I am an odd number.

Take away one and I become even.

What number am I?

Billy smiled.

The riddle didn't say "subtract one." It said "take away one." *One what?* It wasn't specific.

He snapped his fingers. "The answer is seven," he said aloud. "Because if you take away one *letter*—the 's'—you end up with the word 'even.'"

Of course, knowing the answer to the riddle didn't put the bookcase key in Billy's hand.

So he climbed the library ladder again, gave himself a sideways shove, and started looking for a book with "seven" in the title.

When he reached the far end of the shelves, he stepped up a rung and gave himself a shove back the other way.

Halfway across the room, he found what he was looking for.

The Seven Voyages of Sinbad the Sailor.

Billy pulled out the book and flipped it open.

No key tumbled out.

He ruffled the pages.

They weren't bookmarked with a skinny skeleton key.

He put the book back, climbed down the ladder, and stared at the locked bookcase.

Seven *had* to be the answer to the riddle. But was it the secret to finding the key?

Billy noticed something: The brass keyhole wasn't just a yawning lion. It was the *Cowardly* Lion.

Duh!

The Wizard of Oz cuckoo clock.

The hands were frozen at seven and twelve. *Seven* o'clock.

Billy stood on the chair and examined the cuckoo clock more closely.

Were the clock hands actually keys?

Was he supposed to snap one off?

Then he had another idea.

He pried open the little door above the twelve. Something popped out.

It wasn't a cuckoo bird or even a barking Toto.

It was an antique skeleton key with the Wonderful Wizard of Oz's moon-shaped face inscribed on its head.

And it fit the bookcase's keyhole—perfectly.

THE THETA PROJECT

LAB NOTE #318
Prepared by
Dr. Xiang Libris, PsyD, DLit

My instincts proved correct.

Billy G. passed the final aptitude test. Following scant clues and using his imagination, he found the key much more quickly than I had anticipated.

Now, more than ever, I am confident that this boy will be the "key" to our extraordinary future.

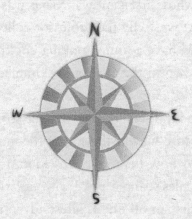

Since the Hercules book was the only one in the case propped open and displayed on a book stand, Billy grabbed it first.

Inside the red, dark-as-ketchup cover, Billy found a bookplate:

Ex Libris
X. Libris

"Ex Libris X. Libris" made him smile.

His dad, who liked to play with words and had two unfinished novels and a screenplay tucked away in his desk, once told Billy that "ex libris" is Latin for "from the books of."

Dr. Libris, whose first name was Xiang, was also X. Libris.

Maybe that was why the professor collected books—just so he could have a funny-looking bookplate.

Billy sat down in the chair and skimmed a few pages of *The Labors of Hercules*.

He read about how Hercules was the strongest man in the world because he was the son of the immortal Greek god Zeus. And how his uncle, Poseidon, the god of the sea, gave Hercules's ship a poke with his trident spear to send the muscleman off on his latest adventure.

"Where's the rock dude?" Billy flipped forward past a chunk of pages.

Found him.

Hercules was in a garden where he'd just plucked three magic apples. On his way out, the big rock dude, whose name was Antaeus, challenged him to a wrestling match.

> *"You would challenge me?" said Hercules. "Do you not know who I am?"*
>
> *"I care not, you feeble fool!" roared Antaeus. "I am the mightiest wrestler who has ever lived. None can defeat me!"*
>
> *In a blind rage, Hercules grabbed Antaeus firmly around the waist, raised him high above his head, and hurled the brute to the ground.*
>
> *But Antaeus bounced back up, his strength fully restored.*

Hercules was astonished. "I do not believe my eyes. Not only are you not injured, your muscles have doubled in size."

"So have my skin and bones!" Antaeus flexed his rocky physique. When he stood, he was even taller than he had been when Hercules threw him to the ground.

Awesome superpower, thought Billy. He was totally getting into the story. In his mind, he could see the rocky guy growing every time Hercules knocked him down.

He could hear Antaeus roar, "You feeble fool!"

Antaeus's voice was so loud in Billy's head it made the glass in the bookcase rattle.

Wait a second.

That was impossible.

Billy looked around the room.

Nothing happened.

And then, from somewhere *outside,* far off in the distance, Billy heard Antaeus again.

"Beware, Hercules! For I shall surely crush you!"

"So funny I fell off the bed." —Izzy B., 4th grader

Ready for OUTRAGEOUS fun in the sun?

Dive into Chris Grabenstein's HILARIOUS new series!

Welcome to Wonderland . . . the world's wackiest motel!

Keep reading for a preview of book one!

Gator Tales

Like I told my friends at school, living in a motel is always exciting—especially during an alligator attack.

"To this day, nobody knows how that giant alligator made it up to the second-floor balcony of my family's motel on St. Pete Beach," I told my audience.

The cafeteria was so quiet you could've heard a taco shell snap.

"Maybe it took the steps. Maybe it just stood up, locked its teeth on a porch railing, and flipped itself up and over in a mighty somersault swoop. The thing was strong, people. Very, very strong.

"I heard Clara, my favorite housekeeper, scream, '¡Monstruo, Señor Wilkie! ¡Monstruo!'

"'Run!' I shouted, because Clara's always been like a second mom to me and I wanted her to be alive enough to see her daughter graduate from med school.

"Well, she didn't need me to shout it twice. Clara abandoned her laundry cart while that alligator raced toward the room at the far end of the balcony. And I knew why: the chicken.

"See, the family in room 233—a mom, a dad, two kids, and a baby—had just gone upstairs with a whole bucket of the stuff. Heck, I could smell it twenty doors down. The giant alligator? He smelled that secret blend of eleven herbs and spices all the way back at his little lake on the Bayside Golf Course, where, legend has it, he's chomped off a few ball divers' arms.

"Thinking fast and running faster, I made it to Clara's deserted laundry cart. I grabbed a few rolls of toilet paper and lobbed them like hand grenades. The T.P. conked the gator on his head just as he was about to chomp through the terrified family's door.

"That's when the giant lizard whipped around.

He looked at me with those big bowling-ball eyes. Forget the chicken. He wanted *me*! He roared like smelly thunder and sprinted down the balcony.

"I just grinned. Because the gator was doing exactly what I wanted him to do. While he barreled ahead on stubby legs, I braced my feet on the bumper of the laundry cart. I lashed several towels together to create a long terry-cloth lasso. I twirled it over my head. I waited for my moment.

"When the gator was five, maybe six, feet away, I flung out my towel rope, aiming for his wide-open mouth. He clamped down. I tugged back. My lasso locked on a jagged tooth. 'Hee-yah!' I shouted. 'Giddyup!' The monster took off.

"What happened next, you wonder? Well, I rode that laundry cart all the way back to the crazy alligator's golf course, where I sent the gator scurrying down into its water hazard. 'And stay away from our motel,' I hollered, and I guess that gator listened, because he's never dared return."

When I finished, everyone applauded, even Ms. Nagler, the teacher on cafeteria duty. She raised her hand to ask a question.

"Yes, ma'am?"

"How'd you and the alligator get down from the second floor?"

I winked. "One step at a time, Ms. Nagler. One step at a time."

She, and everybody else, laughed.

Yep, everybody at Ponce de León Middle School loves a good P. T. Wilkie story.

Except, of course, Mr. Frumpkes.

He came into the cafeteria just in time to hear my big finish.

And like always, he wasn't smiling.

Truth and Consequences

"**M**r. Wilkie?" Mr. Frumpkes had his hands on his hips and his eyes on me. "Lunch is over."

Right on cue, the bell signaling the end of lunch period started clanging.

Fact: Alligators cannot run fast for long distances. They are cold-blooded and therefore quickly deplete their energy reserves. The alligator in your story could NOT have transported you to a golf course two miles away.

Between you and me, I sometimes think Mr. Frumpkes has telepathic powers. He can make the class-change bell ring just by thinking about it.

"Ah," he said, clearly enjoying the earsplitting rattle and clanks. "Now we don't have to listen to any more of Mr. Wilkie's outrageously ridiculous tales!"

My first class right after lunch?

History with Mr. Frumpkes, of course.

He paced back and forth at the front of the room with his hands clasped behind his back.

"Facts are important, boys and girls," he said. "They lead us to the truth. Here at the Ponce de León Middle School, we have a motto: *'Vincit omnia veritas!'*"

I couldn't resist making a wisecrack. "I thought our school motto was 'Go, Conquistadors!'"

Mr. Frumpkes stopped pacing so he could glare at me some more.

"*'Vincit omnia veritas'* is Latin, Mr. Wilkie. It means 'The truth conquers all.'"

"So it *is* like 'Go, Conquistadors!' because conquistadors conquered stuff and—"

"I'm beginning to understand why your father never shows up at parent-teacher conferences, Mr. Wilkie."

Okay. That hurt. My ears were burning.

"But since Mr. Wilkie seems fixated on conquistadors," said Mr. Frumpkes, "here is every-body's brand-new homework assignment."

"Awww," groaned the whole classroom.

"Don't groan at me. Groan at your immature classmate! Thanks to Mr. Wilkie, you are all required to write a one-thousand-word essay filled with cold, hard facts about the man whom this middle school is named after: the famous Spanish conquistador Ponce de León. Your papers are due on Monday."

"Whoa," said my friend Pinky Nelligan. "Monday is the start of Spring Break."

"Fine," said Mr. Frumpkes. "Your papers are due tomorrow. Friday."

More groans.

"Let this be a lesson to you all: facts are more important than fiction."

I was about to disagree and tell Mr. Frumpkes that I think some stories have more power than all the facts you can find on Google.

But I didn't.

Because *everybody* in the classroom was making stink faces at me.

I Scream, You Scream

I refused to let Mr. Frumpkes win.

"Oh, before I forget—quick announcement: you guys are all invited to the Wonderland Motel after school today. My grandpa wants to try out his new outdoor ice-cream dispenser. The ice cream is free, limit one per guest."

The groans and moans of my classmates turned into whoops of joy. Mr. Frumpkes tried to restore order by banging on his desk with a tape dispenser.

"We're here to discuss history, Mr. Wilkie! Not free ice cream!"

But everybody loves free ice cream.

That's just a cold, hard fact.

Unless it's soft-serve.

Then it's kind of custardy.

To

THE ADVENTURES OF
WALTER THE WEREMOUSE

Best wishes,

BY
JOHN DASHNEY

John Dashney

ILLUSTRATED BY SHEILA SOMERVILLE

Children's Writing Festival

SEATTLE, WASHINGTON

1996

STORM PEAK PRESS

157 YESLER WAY, SUITE 413

SEATTLE, WASHINGTON 98104

This book is for
Braden Dashney,
who always wanted one,
and for
Karen & Sarah Robertson,
who helped get it started.

CONTENTS

CHAPTER ONE

The Old Woman

The moon hung in the sky like a big ball of cheese. Or that's how it looked to Walter Wampler as he trudged slowly home from work. It was a pale yellow moon and nearly full, making it look like some-one had been nibbling at its edges.

Walter, who liked cheese very much, sighed and kept on walking. He was young, short and underweight; that's what everyone noticed at first. But if you looked at him closely, you saw that it wasn't quite so. Another inch or two and he wouldn't really be short. Another four or five pounds and he wouldn't really be skinny.

The trouble was that nobody ever looked at Walter Wampler very closely. Or if they did, they put him down as a Just Too. That's just too young and small to be a man and just too big and old to be a boy.

Walter was hungry. For as long as he could remember, he had always been a bit hungry. Never starving, but al-ways in the foster homes where he grew up, at the schools he had attended, at the job where he now worked, he felt a bit hungry. He always had enough to get by, but he had never once pushed his chair back from the table, patted his stomach and said, "I'm stuffed!"

This was odd because Walter worked in a restaurant. In fact, he worked in one of the biggest restaurants in one of the largest hotels in the city, though not as a chef. Not even as a waiter. Walter cleaned the tables, scraped the plates and helped wash the dishes. Then at night, after everything was closed, he swept and mopped the floor.

The job was boring and monotonous. "Someone has to do it," everyone said. "So, Walter, it's up to you."

That's what the owner and manager said. That's what Chef Maxim-Rene said. That's what all the waiters said. That's what they told him in foster care and in the schools he had attended before he finally quit. Whenever a messy, boring or unpleasant job came up, somebody somewhere would decide that it was up to Walter to do it.

Sometimes he wondered just who that somebody was and why he or she had decided that all the messy, boring and unpleasant jobs had to go to Walter Wampler. But on this one night he was too tired to wonder, and he was still just a bit hungry. He could do nothing about the hunger just then, though he could at least look forward to getting home and going to bed.

Home was a tiny room on the top floor of a big old rooming house run by Pomona Mona, the former roller derby skater. Walter avoided her as much as he could. She was nearly the size of a football player, and her appearance was enough to give him nightmares. But at least she believed he existed.

Walter had left school and his last foster home nearly a year ago, after someone in the Department of Human Services entered the wrong data in a computer bank and wiped out his identity. "Sorry, Walter," everyone had told him, "but we can find no record of your existence."

"I exist!" he told himself for the thousandth time. "I'm real and I want a life! A life with some adventure in it!"

Suddenly Walter noticed that he was not alone. Half a block ahead, an old woman struggled with two heavy packages. When she tried to walk, one started to slip. When she stopped to adjust it, the other started to slip.

Walter stopped to watch her. Two steps, stop and adjust the first package. Two more steps, stop and adjust the second package. Two more steps, the first package was slipping again. At this rate it would take her half an hour just to walk a block.

Walter was very kindhearted, and the sight of anyone, especially an old woman, in any kind of difficulty always made him want to help. So he ran up to her and asked, "Can I help you with those packages, Ma'am?"

The old woman looked up at him for a second or two. She was even shorter than he, and a shawl covered her face so that he could only see her eyes. Then she said, "Once, twice, that would be nice."

I guess she means yes, Walter decided, though it seemed like a strange way of saying it. He took the packages, one under each arm, and followed the old woman.

He followed the old woman as she turned into a side street. "This way! This way! No time to delay!" she cried out.

Walter stopped, amazed. He had walked this way to work and back again for almost a year and had never before noticed this little side street. It was just an alleyway, dimly lit and gloomy. The old woman urged him to hurry, so he trotted after her as best he could.

He began noticing strange things. First, the street, if it could be called that, seemed to run on and on without getting any wider or brighter. Second, the packages, which were light enough at the outset, seemed to grow heavier and heavier. Third, the old woman seemed to get livelier and quicker. Walter soon had to run just to stay even with her.

"How much farther?" he gasped.

"It's not far, but we have no car!" the old woman replied.

Why does she talk in rhyme, Walter wondered. Of course, we don't have a car. This place, whatever it is, wouldn't be wide enough even if we did. It goes on and on, and yet I can't see anything but shadows. What is happening here?

Abruptly the street ended. A building loomed up in front of Walter so immediately that he nearly ran into it. The old woman threw open a door and darted into a dim hallway.

"Well, here we are! I said it wasn't very far!" she cried.

Walter now felt very tired. He was tired of strange alleys that ran smack into strange buildings. He was tired of strange packages that seemed to grow heavier with every step. And he was tired of strange old women who spoke in riddles and rhymes.

"Up the stair and then we're there!" she called out from the first landing.

Walter took a firmer grip on the packages and started up the stairway. At the landing he turned and saw another flight leading to another landing. At that landing, he saw another flight, and after that, another.

Something is wrong here, he thought as he climbed. I see steps and landings and walls, but never any doors. Where is she taking me?

He hesitated, but the old woman called out from somewhere up ahead, "Just a few steps more and you'll be at my door!"

I'm sick of rhymes, he decided. I'm also sick of stairs and old ladies who can run up them like mountain goats. I'll go one more flight. Then she can take her packages the rest of the way herself.

But at the next landing the old woman called out, "No more stairs! Save your prayers!" and pushed open what seemed to be just a part of the wall.

Walter found himself in a room as dark and as dim as the alley. He could see the outline of furniture and other objects, but nothing in any detail. The old woman was still just a shadow. If there was a light, she did not turn it on.

"Now I can talk to you without making rhymes," she said.

Walter stood awkwardly in the middle of the dark room with the packages under his arm while questions raced through his mind. Who was this old woman? What was this place? Why was there no light? But all he could say was, "What do you want me to do with these packages, Ma'am?"

"Put them anywhere," she answered. "They don't matter. What is important, my boy, is that you have passed the test!"

"What test?" Walter asked.

"My test!" she replied. "You were kind enough to help, and you didn't ask a bunch of foolish questions. Oh, you asked one or two, and you thought a lot of them. You're full of questions. But you seem to know when to ask and when to keep quiet. So you have passed, and you're entitled to the reward!"

"A reward?" Walter asked. This was something completely new to him. In all his life he could not remember getting a reward. Pay and salary, yes. Thank-yous and even an occasional tip, yes. But a real, honest-to-goodness reward? Never.

"A reward!" the old woman repeated and handed him a paper bag. "I believe you like cheese, Walter," she added.

"How did you know that?" Walter asked. "And how do you know my name? I don't think I told you," he added.

"It is my business to know things," the old woman answered. "Let me give you one thing more." She placed something in Walter's hand. It felt like a plastic card, yet it was somehow different.

"You can use it to phone me," she explained.

"I don't have a phone," Walter objected.

"I know that too, Walter," the old woman said. "Use any pay phone that takes a card. But you must shut your eyes when you put the card in, and don't open them until you hear a click. Shut them again when you remove it, and whatever you do, don't let anyone else use this card or even see it!"

"All right," Walter said, a little doubtful. "But I can't imagine why I would ever be calling you."

"I know that too, Walter," the old woman sighed. "You can't imagine. That's your one big fault, and that's about to change. I know that your life so far has been boring and uneventful. Well, that's about to change too. I can't promise that you'll always be happy. No one can promise that. I can promise, though, that from now on your life will not be boring!"

By now Walter was really full of questions. Before he could ask any, he heard a phone ring and an answering machine click on.

"Hello, George," the machine said. "This is the old woman and I can't come to the phone right now. Try to remember what I told you and stop wearing those yellow socks! Don't let them push you around and avoid eating lasagna on Thursdays." The machine clicked off.

"George is such a pest!" the old woman sighed. "He only just barely passed the test. But you will do better, Walter. I'm sure of that!"

Walter wasn't so sure. "How did the machine know who called?" he asked.

"That's the machine's job," the old woman replied. "Now it's time for you to leave. You're going to have a very interesting day tomorrow, and you'll need to be ready for it!"

Walter, bag in hand and card in pocket, started down the stairs. "Oh Walter," she called out as he reached the landing. "I must give you a warning about that cheese!"

Walter stopped and listened as she spoke this rhyme:

"This is a mystical, magical cheese.

Eat as much of it as you please.

Just make sure your eating is done

Before the setting of the sun.

Don't take even the smallest bite

When the moon and stars come out at night!

And never sell it, no matter how driven!

It must be a gift that is freely given!"

She stepped back through the wall and it closed behind her. Walter walked back to where she had vanished. There was no sign of a door. The wall was solid and smooth. He shrugged and started back down the stairs.

He could not remember how many dozens of steps he had climbed, but to his surprise it was only two quick flights back down to the alley. And in less than half a minute he could see the lights of the main street up ahead. He was still shaking his head when he turned for home.

I can't have dreamed it, he decided, because I still have the bag and the card. But what kind of a place was that, and how did that old woman know so much about me? He shook his head helplessly. He suddenly felt tired again, too tired to figure things out.

He wondered if he could find the alley again if he retraced his steps, but decided not to try. Home and bed suddenly mattered more than anything to him. He was yawning long before he reached the big old rooming house where he lived.

As he let himself in the front door, he heard a meow from his landlady's cat. Walter called the cat Rancid, since its breath smelled of long-dead mice. His landlady, Pomona Mona, the ex-roller derby star, had named it Jammer. By whichever name, Walter despised it, and the cat felt the same way about him.

"Is that you, Walter?" Pomona Mona called out from behind her door. "You're late tonight."

"I was delayed," Walter replied and climbed the steps to his room on the top floor. He put the bag with the cheese into what he was certain was the world's smallest refrigerator, switched off the light and then collapsed on the bed without even bothering to take his shoes off.

Tomorrow I'll realize I dreamed all this, he decided, and then fell asleep.

CHAPTER TWO

Genuine Bulgarian Bagels

I t must have been a dream, Walter decided when he
awoke the next morning. Nothing like that ever happened in real life. Or, at least, nothing like that had
ever happened in *his* life. Just to convince himself, he
patted the pocket which would not contain the old
woman's card.

But the card was there.

He took it out and examined it closely. It was the size of a credit card, felt like plastic, and yet it wasn't. Its color flickered from off-white to pale yellow to very light grey, depending on how the light struck it. Printed in raised letters was the following message:

THE OLD WOMAN, INC.

On The Street That Really Isn't

Answers To Anything, Anytime

Phone 777-11,11,11,11

Walter shrugged and stuck the card back in his pocket. He was now very hungry, and if the card was real, then the sack with the cheese must be real too. He opened the mini-refrigerator and there it was. He smiled. Riddles and answers could wait. Breakfast couldn't.

The cheese was the shape of a small melon and weighed about three pounds. Enough to last for several days, Walter decided, if he was careful and if he liked it. He cut off a piece with his pocketknife and the smell was sweet and strange, like smoky fruit.

It was the best cheese he had ever eaten. The taste of smoky fruit was there, along with a rich cream flavor. And there was something else, something more, something old and very precious. If gold had a taste, he thought, this would be it.

Not only did the cheese itself taste great, but it improved other things as well. An old apple suddenly tasted like it had just been picked. A piece of stale bread might just have come fresh from the oven. A cup of instant coffee tasted just like fresh-brewed. It was the best breakfast Walter had eaten in years; maybe the best ever.

11

For the first time Walter whistled and took the stairs two at a time as he left for work. Pomona Mona, had she been there to see it, would have been amazed. But Pomona Mona was already out skating, as Walter knew only too well.

Every morning his landlady roared through the neighborhood on her skates for an hour or more. "Gotta keep myself in shape," she told anyone who cared to listen (and many who didn't care to, as well). "Never know when the Bombers might need me again!"

Walter always dreaded those first few blocks. He never knew when Pomona Mona might sweep around a corner or roar up behind him. Apparently, her goal was to see how close she could come to him without actually colliding.

To her credit, Pomona Mona herself never touched him. But Rancid rode along on her shoulder, and Rancid had a nasty habit of sticking out a paw and nicking Walter's ear as they swept past.

On this morning an overpowering sense of confidence seemed to settle on Walter as he saw Pomona Mona sweep around the corner and charge straight for him. She was a formidable sight in her red Bombers jersey with a white 13 on the front, her hair done up in bright green rollers and blue knee pads over a pair of orange stretch pants, stretched about as far as pants could be stretched. It was a bit like being charged by an out-of-control rainbow.

This time Walter only smiled and waited until the very last instant before jerking his head (and his ear) just out of Rancid's reach. The cat overbalanced and dug in its remaining claws to keep from falling.

"Yeowf!" cried Pomona Mona. Without breaking stride, she grabbed Rancid's ear between her finger and thumb and pinched. "See how you like it!" she muttered as the cat yowled and leaped from her shoulder onto a branch as Pomona Mona shot beneath it. Walter laughed and kept walking. The day was starting out well.

As he walked he pondered, if the card is real and the cheese is real, then is The Street That Really Isn't real too? He pulled out the card and read the name again. "I've been on it," he muttered, "so it has to be real. I wonder if I can find it again."

He knew it was no more than four or five blocks from the hotel where he worked. He was sure that the old woman had not crossed a street before she ducked into the alley, and he remembered the block he was on when he first saw her. So it should be easy for him to find it again.

But it wasn't. There was no side street, no alley, nothing at all. The buildings were set so closely together that even Rancid would have had a hard time squeezing between them.

He knew he had the right block. He was sure he could pinpoint the exact spot where the old woman had ducked into the alley. But there was no alley, just a shop, a very old, very solid shop with a sign over the door announcing:

Normally, Walter would have assumed that he had been wrong and would give up without checking further. But on this day he felt different. Maybe it was the cheese. Whatever it was, he took a deep breath and stepped into the shop.

Smells bombarded him from all directions. First came the smell of things baking and things just baked. Then there was the scent of old wood and polish, pipe smoke and coffee, and aromas of soups and spices. No street had passed through here. For a moment he felt foolish.

"*Zdravei!* Can I help you?" The voice, loud and deep, should have come from a giant. The man behind the counter, though, was hardly bigger than Walter himself.

"I. . . I'm looking for an address," Walter stammered.

"Indeed?" replied the small man with the big voice. A bit of a smile played around the corners of his mouth. "There are a great many addresses in this city, Young Man. Did you have a particular one in mind?"

Walter looked at him more closely. Ivon (if it was he) had a face that seemed too large for his head. His mouth, his nose and a huge mustache took almost the entire bottom half. His eyes and eyebrows seemed to leave no room for his forehead, and his ears were extra large in a space that called for medium. There was a look of kindness about him, so Walter decided to chance it.

"I am looking for a place called The Street That Really Isn't," he announced as matter-of-factly as he could.

"A street that really isn't?" Ivon repeated, and then his oversized face broke into a huge grin. "My friend, I can tell you all about streets that are. But streets that are not? Well, they are not. Are they not?" he added with a flourish.

Walter nodded. It did sound rather silly. But he had noticed something. Just between Ivon's puzzlement and his grin — for no more than the quickness of an eyeblink — he had seen another look, and that look told him that Ivon knew something.

"I just thought you might have heard of it," Walter said.

"Alas, no," Ivon replied, "although it does sound fascinating. A street that really isn't? Tell me, my friend, where did *you* hear of it?"

Walter was about to show him the card when he remembered the old woman's warning: "Don't let anyone else use this card or even see it!" So he simply smiled and said, "An old woman told me about it. She said I had passed a test."

"A *staritsa?*" Ivon asked. "My friend, you must not believe everything that old women tell you." He gave Walter a wink and another grin. "And you must believe even less of what the *young* women tell you!" he added.

"Thank you for the advice," Walter replied.

"Advice, alas, costs nothing," Ivon complained. "If all I had to sell was advice, I would soon be broke. How about a Genuine Bulgarian Bagel? Nothing makes the morning better!"

"How do I know it's a Genuine Bulgarian Bagel?" Walter asked.

"Because it is made by me, and I am a Genuine Bulgarian!" Ivon replied with another flourish. "Ten dozen I sold this morning for breakfast. In another hour I'll sell six dozen more for coffee breaks. Now I'm alone, so I'll sell you one cheap."

Walter shook his head sadly. "Even cheap would be too much," he said. "It's the end of the month. I won't have much more than air to live on until payday."

"Who knows?" Ivon insisted. "This may be your lucky day. By tonight you may have enough for one, or two, or three!"

"I doubt it," Walter said. But then he remembered that look he had seen for the space of an eyeblink. "Will you be open tonight?" he asked.

"Of course! By day I sell, by night I bake! My *sladkarnitsa* never closes!"

"All right," Walter agreed. "If my luck does change, I'll stop by for one on my way home tonight."

"They go well with cheese!" Ivon called after him, and again Walter wondered just how much he knew.

Walter decided he would call the old woman after work. There was a pay phone that took cards just outside the hotel dining room. He would wait until the restaurant closed and he was alone and then make the call.

That morning Walter attacked the stack of dirty breakfast dishes with an energy he had never shown before. His hands, usually slow and a little clumsy, seemed to move with a life of their own. The dishes were done in half the usual time, so Walter began scrubbing some of Chef Maxim-Rene's pans.

He had already cleaned two when the chef happened to notice him. Maxim-Rene was jealous of his equipment and usually objected to Walter even touching his pots and pans. This time he took a just-washed pan, examined it carefully, and gave Walter a nod of approval.

"It will do," he said, which was about the highest praise he ever gave to anyone.

Walter thought no more about it until lunchtime. He had just finished clearing tables when Maxim-Rene beckoned to him from the kitchen. At first Walter thought something was wrong. Then he noticed that the chef was actually smiling.

"We had an extra plate at the luncheon today," he said. "One of the guests had to leave before we could serve. It's already been paid for. Why don't you take it?"

Walter gaped. Things like that occasionally happened, since it was a big restaurant in a large hotel, and there were luncheons and banquets nearly every day. But always, the senior waiters were the ones to get the extras. Walter had to make do with leftovers and scraps.

"Why me?" he asked as he took the plate.

"I liked the way you cleaned my pans today," Maxim-Rene replied. "Keep it up and I will find other things for you."

That was all the hint Walter needed. The chef's pans glowed that afternoon, and an unclaimed banquet for Walter mysteriously appeared that night. For the first time in his life, Walter pushed back his chair, patted his stomach and muttered, "I'm stuffed!"

Then he went back to work.

Later, when he was alone, Walter took the old woman's card and went to the phone. This is ridiculous, he thought. How do you dial elevens? But he remembered the old woman's words, inserted the card, closed his eyes and waited for the click. After all, he decided, the worst that can happen is that I'll lose a card I have no use for anyway.

He heard the click. And when he opened his eyes, there on the bottom row, next to the zero, was an eleven. So many strange things had happened to Walter that day that he wasn't even surprised. He simply punched the number.

The machine came on the line after one ring. "Hello, Walter," it said. "This is the old woman, and I can't come to the phone right now. But I'm glad you're following my instructions. Would you believe that half my clients don't even have the gumption to use my card? And yes, you are a client, since you passed my test. I'm glad your day has gone so well. Remember to close your eyes when you hang up and don't open them until you hear another click and have the card. Stop in at Ivon's on your way home tonight, and call me again some time. I enjoy hearing from you." The machine switched off.

Walter closed his eyes, felt for the card and heard a click. He also heard the chonk of coins falling into the return slot. He opened his eyes and saw an ordinary phone once again. He opened the return slot and was surprised to find four quarters.

He would stop for a Genuine Bulgarian Bagel after all.

CHAPTER THREE

Surprises and Temptation

Walter got another surprise when he opened the refrigerator the next morning. The cheese was still there, in fact, *all* of it. There was no sign that he had cut a piece to eat.

"A cheese that grows back?" he asked himself. "Well, why not?" So many odd things had happened during the past thirty-six hours that the idea of a renewable cheese seemed perfectly logical. This time Walter cut a piece twice the size of yesterday's, ate part of it with some instant coffee and stuck the rest into his pocket.

He whistled and took the stairs two at a time again. The morning was clear and cool, with a promise of warming up later on. He walked quickly and confidently, without fear of Pomona Mona or Rancid. He found himself eager to try his luck with them again.

Walter had covered two blocks when he heard the skates behind him. Again he jerked his head at just the right moment, and again Rancid missed him. This time the cat did not try to stay on Pomona Mona's shoulder, but jumped, hit the ground running and disappeared into the shrubs with a yowl of rage. Walter watched his landlady take the corner. From behind she looked like a small, psychedelic rhinoceros.

There was still no sign of The Street That Really Isn't, though Ivon's was open. Walter still had two of his four quarters, so he walked in and laid them on the counter.

"Ah! You liked what you had last night!" Ivon beamed. A fresh supply of bagels and other goods filled several bins. Ivon must have been working for several hours already. Walter wondered when or if he ever slept.

"It was very good," Walter agreed. He had been tempted to try some of the old woman's cheese with it, but remembered her warning about not eating any when the moon and stars were out.

Ivon split a bagel and scooped up some cream cheese. "Don't bother with that cream cheese; I brought something else," Walter said and took the piece of cheese from his pocket.

"What kind of cheese is that?" Ivon asked.

Walter broke off a piece and handed it to him. "Try it," he urged. "It's like nothing you've ever had before."

Ivon bit into it carefully, and the look Walter had seen for the span of an eyeblink came over his face once again. It remained there for several seconds as Ivon chewed thoughtfully. Then he poured two cups of coffee and handed one to Walter.

"I thought as much," he finally said. "My friend, someday I may be able to tell you many things. But right now I can say only this. You will always be welcome here, whether you have money or not."

Strange, Walter thought. I came in to find answers, and I leave with more questions. What did he mean by that?

Walter's morning passed quickly. The work was still boring, but his hands seemed to move with a life of their own. He found that he could let them work by themselves, while his mind concentrated on other things.

Who was the old woman and how much did Ivon know about her and The Street That Really Isn't? And what would happen to him today? She had told him that his life would never again be boring, but just how many strange adventures did he want?

Nothing happened right away. Walter finished the breakfast dishes and set the tables for lunch even faster than he had the day before. Maxim-Rene came up with another spare lunch and Walter went back to work. He still had a feeling, though, that something was about to happen.

It did. The lunch rush was over and only two or three groups lingered at their tables. Walter was clearing away dirty dishes when he heard a crash and a thump behind him. His first thought was that he had knocked something over. Then he heard a second crash. He spun around and saw one of the diners staggering back from the table, one hand clutching at his throat and the other waving wildly.

The man's companions sat as if glued to their chairs. Walter realized instantly what was wrong. "The man is choking!" he said to himself.

Before he was even aware of it, Walter dropped his plastic tub of dirty dishes and rushed to the choking man. He stepped behind him, wrapped his arms around the man's middle and joined his hands in a big fist just below the breastbone. He pressed swiftly inward and upward as hard as he could. The man made a sound that was part gasp and part cough, then something shot out of his mouth.

The man then staggered to a table and leaned there gasping for nearly a minute. "Piece of steak," he finally managed to say. "Got caught in my throat. Young Man, I believe you saved my life!"

By this time, Maxim-Rene and several waiters had come running. Walter shook his head. "Any of us could have done the same thing," he said.

"Perhaps," the man agreed, "but you were the one who did it." Walter seemed confused and slightly embarrassed. The diners, the waiters and the chef were all staring.

"I did not realize that you knew how to apply the Heimlich Maneuver, Walter," said Maxim-Rene.

"I didn't either," Walter admitted. "It just kind of happened!"

"Lucky for me!" put in the diner. He was a big man with a balding head and very sharp eyes. Those eyes now looked Walter over carefully. "I see you do not own a watch," he commented.

Walter glanced at his wrist. Of course, there was no watch. Nor was there a pale strip on his lightly tanned skin to show that he had ever worn one.

"Now you do," the man said. He took a heavy gold watch from his own wrist and handed it to Walter, who could only stare. Never in his life had he ever received a present of any real value. Slowly, he put it on.

"Thank you!" he managed to whisper. "It's beautiful!"

"So is the rest of my life, which I now have back," the man replied. "I trust that this young man will soon be promoted," he added to Maxim-Rene. "If not, I'll be happy to hire him myself!"

The rest of the day drifted by like a dream. Walter was so caught up in the wonder that he even forgot to eat dinner. But he did not forget to stop at Ivon's.

"I can't explain how it happened," he told Ivon over coffee. "I didn't think I could do things like that. I must have read about it somewhere. I just grabbed and squeezed and out it popped."

"Perhaps," Ivon answered, "it was another test."

"What do you mean?"

"You told me last night that the old woman said you had passed a test," Ivon explained. "Maybe she was giving you another. If so, I'd say you passed again."

Walter couldn't sleep that night. He lay awake and listened to his new watch tick away the minutes and the hours. The dial glowed like a miniature moon.

His forgotten dinner was making its absence felt. Walter could feel the old hunger returning, sharper than ever. There was nothing to eat. Nothing, except the cheese.

Again the old woman's words returned. "Don't take even the smallest bite, when the moon and stars come out at night!" Walter got up and walked to the window. The stars were out and the moon was big and round and full. And he was so hungry!

Walter Wampler had gone hungry many times before, when he had no choice in the matter. This time he had a big, luscious cheese in his refrigerator, and just a silly rhyme warning him to wait until morning. Still, the old woman had been right on other things. Hadn't he better trust her here too?

He sighed and went back to bed, though sleep still wouldn't come. He went to the refrigerator, took the cheese from the paper bag and held it. One little piece, the size of the one he had broken off for Ivon, had not grown back. He sniffed it and caught the scent of smoky fruit.

"No!" he told himself. "Go back to bed! You can wait until morning!"

But morning was still hours away. Walter hesitated, then picked up the knife.

"Just one little piece!" his stomach said.

"Don't do it!" his mind warned.

"Do it! Do it!" his stomach pleaded.

Walter was caught in a tug-of-war. He couldn't put the cheese down. He wouldn't cut it either. His stomach seemed to grow bigger and emptier by the moment. He lifted the cheese and smelled it again. The scent of smoky fruit and cream shattered his resistance.

"Just one little piece for tonight," he decided. "I won't make a habit of it. But after a day like today, I need to celebrate."

He cut into the cheese, then withdrew the knife and listened, half-expecting to hear some kind of protest. There was no sound, nothing but the gentle ticking of his new watch.

"It's all right," he told himself. "One little piece can't hurt. It will just help me get to sleep."

He cut out a wedge and put the cheese away. The piece was bigger than he intended, but not all that big. He went back to bed and began to nibble.

A warm drowsiness spread over him as he ate. He seemed to drift away. His bed was now a boat, floating down a broad, silent river. At first, he could hear nothing at all, then came the faintest of whispers from far up ahead. He could not understand them. Perhaps if he raised his head. . . .

He was far too content and comfortable to move.

The whispers became murmurs, louder now, and with a note of menace. The bed drifted faster. The murmurs became growls and the growls became a roar. The bed began to spin.

Rapids! he thought. How did I get here? What do I do?

The bed spun, bucked and rocked as if it were alive. Walter hung on and shut his eyes. There was nothing else he could do. The roar grew louder. Something terrible was approaching, and he did not dare raise his head to look! Then the roar suddenly stopped and he was falling. The fall seemed to go on and on.

Suddenly he was awake, totally disoriented. He knew only that the fall had stopped and his bed was still again. He realized that he must have had a dream, and that he was safe again, and he still held the cheese in his paw.

The old woman was right, he decided. This stuff should definitely *not* be eaten at night. Well, live and learn and no harm done. He would wait for morning before. . .

Hold it! Wait! He looked again at the cheese and what was holding it. He blinked twice and looked again.

It was a paw, no doubt about that! Pale and hairless, with claws instead of nails. It still gripped what was left of the cheese, but the grasp felt clumsy and strange.

He tried to sit up, but couldn't get his balance. He rolled to the edge of the bed, then dropped to the floor. That was better, he thought. Why try to stand up? It's easier down here on the floor on all four. . .

What was happening to him? The room was still dark. He could see well, though only in blacks and greys. He scurried over to the light switch and stood erect, but his paws were too clumsy to flip it. He poked at the switch with his nose and, on the third try, flicked it on.

Light flooded the room, hurting his eyes and leaving him unable to move for several seconds. When his eyes finally adjusted, he scurried over to the dresser, pulled himself erect and gazed into the mirror.

GASP!

Staring back at him was a mouse, the largest mouse he had ever seen! And it was wearing his pajamas!

CHAPTER FOUR

A Mouse in Pajamas

Walter dropped to the floor and shivered uncontrollably. This is not happening, he thought. This is only a bad dream. I will shake myself awake, stand up, look in the mirror and I will *not* see a very large mouse wearing my pajamas!

He shut his eyes and shook himself. He rolled onto his back, kicked at the air and bumped his head rather hard on the floor. That should do it, he decided. He stood erect and blinked at the mirror.

Walter Wampler did not blink back. A very large mouse, complete with a shiny black nose, large whiskers, small dark eyes and Walter's old faded pajamas, was still there.

It was not a dream after all. Walter Wampler had been transformed into the largest mouse the world had ever known. He fell back onto the floor and tried to cry, but no sound came out. He could not bear to look into the mirror again.

What can I do now? What will happen to me? How can I live as a mouse? Why did I eat that cheese? Why did I ever help that old woman? Why?

After a few minutes of shivering and asking why, he calmed himself. All right, he decided, I look like a mouse. I can still think like a human. I wonder if I can still talk like a human?

He moved his mouth and nothing happened. He tried again, concentrating, using all his will, trying to make himself say his name. The result was a low-pitched, drawn-out, baritone "Squeak!" Exactly what you might expect to hear from the world's largest mouse.

What can I do now, he wondered again. I can't stay here! I've got to get help! Where?

The old woman, he decided. She will know what to do. I've got to find The Street That Really Isn't! I found it once; I can do it again!

First he had to get out of the house without being seen. Pomona Mona was probably asleep, but Rancid was probably awake. I wonder, he thought. I look like a mouse. I sound like a mouse. Do I smell like a mouse? Can I move like a mouse? He remembered the phrase, "As quiet as a mouse." That was what he would have to be, and he would have to learn fast.

His door was shut, but not locked. He used his forepaws, nose and finally his mouth to open it. Then he entered the hall and saw the stairs.

Moving four feet instead of two was tricky at first, and he nearly tumbled down the steps. Walter was a quick learner, and he soon moved quietly and confidently.

His nose worked better than it ever had. Smells he had never known before flooded in. He stopped at the foot of the stairs and tried to sort them. Polish and cleaners were familiar, but now much sharper. He detected a strong scent behind a door, a human, one of the other lodgers. He moved away and down the flight of steps to the main floor.

A new scent froze him on the stairs. This one seemed to scream "Danger!" It had to be Rancid, prowling the house and looking, for what? He had never before given much thought about what cats did at night. Now he realized they hunted.

And more than likely, they hunted mice! If he could smell Rancid, could Rancid smell him?

This is silly, he tried to tell himself. I'm still more than twelve times the size of that cat. What could he possibly do to me?

He could wake Pomona Mona, he answered. And you are *not* twelve times the size of your landlady! What if she comes after you? How do mice defend themselves?

They don't, he realized. All they can do is run and hide.

You can still think, he reminded himself. Walter sat on the steps and forced himself to think. Should he go back to his room or try to get out?

Out, he decided.

Very well, he had to get through the front door. While it was locked, he knew it could be opened from the inside without a key. Was he agile enough to do it?

Only one way to find out: try it.

The Rancid smell grew fainter. The cat must be moving to the back of the house. Walter crept down the stairs and over to the front door. He stood on his hind legs and grasped the lock with both paws.

Paws, he soon realized, do not have thumbs. It was like trying to work a lock with his feet. With a great deal of practice, it might be done. But there was no time for practice. If he was going to get out at all, it would have to be quickly.

He tried using his nose, but it wasn't much help. It could push the catch up, but it needed to go down. He opened his mouth and jabbed at the catch knob with his teeth. He missed the lock entirely and sunk his incisors deep into the wood paneling.

Instinctively, he pulled down and peeled away a long shaving of wood. His front teeth worked just like a carpenter's plane.

Gnawing! That's what mice do! That's what rodent teeth are for, and he was a rodent now! He remembered that a beaver could gnaw down a tree, and he was five or six times the size of a beaver. He probably had the most powerful gnawing teeth in the country. In an hour or so he could chew his way right through that door!

Only he didn't have an hour to spare. He didn't even have a minute. Rancid's scent filled his nose again!

He jabbed at the catch once more. This time his teeth caught it and forced it down. He heard a click and knew that the door was unlocked. Now to get it open!

His paws were so clumsy. By pushing with one and pulling with the other he slowly forced the doorknob to turn. When he thought he had it far enough, he carefully stuck his front teeth over the knob and pulled. The door opened.

Rancid snarled from somewhere in the darkness behind him. Walter spun and dropped to all fours. He saw two eyes glowing like points of fire. The cat, crouched just a few feet away, was studying him.

Walter's mouse feelings told him to run, and Rancid's cat instincts told him to attack. Walter's thoughts overcame his feelings and he stood his ground. Rancid, far from being the world's smartest cat, was still not stupid enough to attack something the size of a human, even if his sense of smell told him it was merely a mouse.

Rancid twitched his tail and Walter wriggled his whiskers. Neither of them backed away. It was a stand-off. This can't go on, Walter thought. I can't sit here all night!

He squeaked the harshest, nastiest squeak he could come up with, reared up on his hind legs and lunged forward. Rancid yowled and ran, and Walter let himself out the front door.

Suddenly everything was different. The wind blew the scents of many animals past his nose. The sounds of the night, sounds he had never heard or noticed as a human, pounded at his ears. He pulled the door shut, crouched on the porch and stared into the darkness.

No colors. He knew that mice were colorblind. So were cats and dogs. He had never seen as many shades of grey, thousands of them!

As he crept down the front steps, he heard the roar of an engine. A pair of brilliant lights swept around a corner and stabbed into the darkness. A car! As a person, he thought nothing of cars. As a mouse he now realized, they are enemies! He scurried back up the steps and cowered behind a post. He must not be seen!

As the car passed down the street, Walter realized the difficulty of his mission. Everything and everyone would be against him. Until he found The Street That Really Isn't, he could expect to meet only enemies.

Cautiously, he crept back down the steps and scurried over to a tree. He rose on his hind legs and sniffed. Strong, pungent odors, dozens of them, different, yet somehow the same! Dogs! A whole pack of them! He felt a surge of panic.

Then he remembered, it's a tree! The dogs have left their marks. Some of the scents could be days, even weeks old.

The pavement felt rough and hard on his paws, so he kept to the grass, moving silently from lawn to lawn. Staying in the shadows he stopped every few seconds to sniff. He was getting better at distinguishing scents: cats, dogs, birds, humans and other rodents.

Cats would be no problem. None would be foolish enough to attack him, and their yowls wouldn't raise enough alarm. Birds and other rodents were also safe. But dogs? They were another matter! Some were nearly as big as Walter, and even the little ones could make enough noise to rouse humans.

Walter stopped and sniffed again. The wind was blowing toward him, and he could smell two cats prowling up ahead. His whiskers, he realized, could also sense things. He was not sure just how to use them yet, but realized they could be helpful.

His tail bothered him, all scrunched up inside his pajama pants and beginning to ache. There was nothing, however, he could do about that now.

He reached the end of the block and smelled dog scent on the telephone pole at the corner. The street was a stinking mess of oil and exhaust fumes, but he had to cross it.

Stop! Look! Listen and smell! All clear! Go for it!

Walter had never done a flat-out sprint on four legs before. He shot across the street so quickly that he nearly tripped on the far curb. At the last instant he jumped, and the leap carried him over the curb, beyond the sidewalk and halfway up somebody's lawn.

I jumped over twenty feet! he realized. Maybe twenty-five! And I must have been at least six feet up in the air!

A dog barked furiously from inside the house. Walter dashed for the safety of a hedge. He found an opening and squeezed in just as a porch light snapped on and a man's voice said, "What's the matter, Cruncher? Is there something out there?"

Walter crouched motionless as the door opened and the man stepped out. Cruncher continued to bark. "Oh no!" the man said. "I'm not letting you out to run around all night. Wait till I get the leash!"

Walter did not wait. He was off and running as soon as the door slammed. He crossed a lawn, cleared another hedge with a leap that took him nearly thirty feet, dodged around two trees, hurdled a fence, crossed three more lawns and came to another street.

Dogs began barking behind him. First there were two, then four, then eight, then too many to count. Walter crossed the street in two bounds without slowing or looking, but he could not outrun the speed of sound. The barking swept up behind him and then passed him. Nearly every house seemed to have a dog, and they were all suddenly awake and alert!

Fortunately, almost all the dogs were inside or tied up. One small terrier rushed out at him, but Walter spun, reared up on his hind legs and bared his teeth. The dog skidded, lost its footing and rolled right up to him. Walter still had enough of his human nature to give it a kick, though not very hard, and the dog ran off yelping.

Another block, and he reached the edge of the downtown area. Houses and lawns gave way to buildings and parking lots. Walter dodged behind a pile of crates next to a loading dock and paused to catch his breath. Just two more blocks to The Street That Really Isn't. Behind him the barking grew fainter and finally stopped.

In the sudden silence he heard a rustling from behind. He whirled and saw three small mice staring at him, too frightened to move. He sniffed and could smell their fear. Don't worry, he tried to tell them. I won't hurt you. What came out when he tried to reassure them was a

35

low, threatening rumble, like a badly played French horn. Two of the mice fled and the third stood frozen to the spot. Walter nudged it with his nose and it fell over, paralyzed with fright.

Walter had no time to worry about a petrified mouse. He rolled it behind a crate and prepared for the last two blocks ahead. Should he try to sneak through them or sprint them?

He crept along the wall past the loading dock until he reached the street. He saw doorways and lampposts, but not much else. I'll sneak, he decided. Doorway to doorway. Cautiously, he crept around the corner.

Right into the beam of a flashlight!

"Hold it!" cried a voice that meant business. "Stand up and put your hands against the wall!"

Walter crouched, frozen in the light. Then the beam shifted and he could see the outline of a policeman behind it. One hand held the flashlight, though Walter was more concerned with the other hand.

It held a gun!

"I said, stand up and put your hands on the wall!" the officer repeated. The light swept over Walter again. "Hey! What is this? A great big mouse in blue pajamas? Are you coming back from a costume party or are you some kinda weirdo?"

Even if he could argue or explain, Walter knew that this was neither the time nor the place for it. He leaped straight up and over the policeman, knocking the flashlight from his hand. The cop went down, the gun went off and the bullet broke a window across the street.

That settled the question of sneaking or sprinting. Walter was at the far end of the block and running with all the speed he had when something incredibly fast buzzed past his ear and he heard the roar of the gun once again.

He tried to zigzag. Just half a block more! The policeman did not fire again. Thirty yards more! Look for the alley!

But there was no alley!

Ivon's Genuine Bulgarian Bagel Shop stood right where it always had. Walter slid to a stop and looked back. The policeman was a block behind, but still coming; and he still had the gun!

Walter didn't hesitate. He ran straight for Ivon's door!

CHAPTER FIVE

Being Tailed

Ivon was not easily shocked, but the sight of a man-sized mouse sprinting into his shop in faded blue pajamas amazed even him. He dropped a pan of bagels he was removing from the oven and yelled something in Bulgarian. It did not sound nice.

What was worse was that he dropped the pan to grab a knife, a very large knife that looked capable of slicing things bigger than bagels!

Again there was no time to explain. Walter had a man with a gun behind him and a man with a knife in front of him, and neither of them in a mood to listen to squeaks. He looked quickly around and then leaped for the counter.

Ivon had left a large marking pen with its cap off lying beside his cash register. Walter grabbed the pen in his mouth as Ivon approached and made four quick slash marks on the counter, joining them to form a crude W. Then two quick down marks and a cross-stroke A. Then down and across, L. By this time Ivon had stopped to watch.

The T was as easy as the L, and the E took only four quick strokes. The R was going to be a problem, but by now Ivon understood.

"Walter, is that you?" he asked.

Walter nodded. At least, he could communicate that way.

"Can you talk?" Ivon asked.

Walter shook his head, then glanced at the door. He could hear footsteps.

"Are you in trouble? Is someone after you?" Ivon asked.

Walter nodded again.

"Behind the counter, quick!" Ivon said.

Walter jumped down behind the counter and squeezed between two cartons as the footsteps grew louder and the policeman charged into the shop.

"Can I help you with something?" Walter heard Ivon ask.

"Officer Mulholand," the policeman replied. "I'm looking for a suspect who may have fled this way on foot."

"What sort of suspect?" Ivon asked.

"Well, it looked like a mouse."

"Indeed?" Ivon said. "I don't have time to notice mice, Officer, unless they happen to live in my shop, in which case I set traps for them."

"You'd notice this one!" said Mulholand. "He stood a good five feet tall and musta weighed at least 125 pounds!"

Walter had to admit that Mulholand had his height correct, though the weight guess was a bit too high.

"And he was wearing what looked like a pair of blue pajamas," the officer added.

"Blue pajamas?" Ivon asked.

"*Faded* blue pajamas," Mulholand said.

"Does that make a difference?" Ivon asked. "Let me see if I understand this. You want to know if I have seen a gigantic mouse in a pair of faded blue pajamas? Were they his own pajamas or someone else's?"

"Don't know for sure," Mulholand said. "But they looked suspicious."

"I suppose they would," Ivon agreed. "May I ask what crime this mouse is suspected of?"

"I don't know," Mulholand admitted. "But he's a suspicious character and I wanna ask him some questions!"

"How do you expect him to answer them?" Ivon asked. "I have never heard mice utter anything but an occasional squeak."

"I'll figure that out when I catch him," Mulholand answered. "Mind if I take a look around?"

"Yes," said Ivon, "I think I would mind. I'm a busy man, Officer, and I don't need people poking around my shop looking for mice, no matter what their size."

"I can come back with a warrant," Mulholand threatened.

"Do that," Ivon urged. "Go back to your station and tell your sergeant that you want to wake up a judge in the middle of the night to have him sign a warrant giving you permission to search my shop for a five- — or was it a six-foot? — mouse in faded blue pajamas. You must also explain that you have no reason to charge this mouse with anything, except being unusually large. Can you guess what the sergeant is going to say?"

Mulholand did not answer, so Ivon continued.

"He will probably ask if you have all your shorts in your suitcase, which is what I am wondering too!"

"I know what I saw!" Mulholand growled.

"And I know what I see," Ivon replied. "I do *not* see any mice, at least, not at the moment. And even if I did, is that against the law?"

41

"I can go to the Board of Health," Mulholand threatened once again, but this time not so boldly.

"They were here last week," Ivon said. " My *sladkarnitsa* got their highest rating. The certificate is in the window. Do you think that would have happened if they had found six- or seven-foot mice hanging around the place?"

"There was only one and he was only about five feet!" Mulholand objected.

"Officer, I think you are overstressed," Ivon remarked as calmly as he could. "Let me get you a Genuine Bulgarian Bagel. Nothing better for soothing the mind and easing the tension."

Mulholand apparently knew when he was beaten. "Okay," he said. "Put lotsa cream cheese on it. But remember this! I know what I saw, and I'm gonna track this mouse down and catch it, or my name's not Herbert J. Mulholand!"

Walter heard the sound of footsteps again. He waited until Ivon whispered, "All clear! He's gone!" before he crept out from behind the counter.

Ivon offered him a bagel. Walter stood on his hind legs and grasped it awkwardly with his front paws and tried to nibble it. This was difficult, and he dropped it several times.

"So?" Ivon asked. "You have not been a mouse for long?"

Walter nodded, nibbled and dropped the bagel again.

"Did this just happen tonight?"

Walter nodded. The bagel slipped again, but this time he managed to hang on to it.

"And there is a full moon tonight," Ivon added. Then he seemed to think very hard for several seconds. Walter nibbled at the bagel. He was getting better at it.

"Walter!" Ivon said so suddenly that the bagel dropped again. "Have you ever heard of lycanthropy?"

He spelled it, but Walter shook his head.

"It means the study of werewolves," Ivon explained. "I realize you are not a wolf, but you are a very large mouse. Is it possible that you are, a weremouse?"

Walter answered with an un-mouselike shrug.

"If you're a weremouse, and if weremice are anything like werewolves," Ivon continued, "then you will return to your human shape with the coming of daylight. I suggest you return home and see if this happens."

Walter finished the bagel and nodded in agreement. His tail was beginning to throb again. He hopped back up on the counter, took the pen in his mouth and scrawled T-A-I-L on the counter.

"Ah!" said Ivon, "let me help you with that!" He pulled off Walter's pajama pants and straightened out the tail. "Does that feel better?"

Walter nodded again and tried to show his thanks.

"*Nyama zashto,*" Ivon said. "You're welcome. I could keep these for you, but it might be better for you to have them, in case you don't make it back to your house by dawn. Let me put them on you backwards!"

He did so and helped Walter get his tail through the fly, now in the back. "It looks a little strange," he admitted, "but not nearly as strange as you would look if you became human and found yourself out on the street with no britches!"

Walter nodded. Ivon went to the door and peered carefully up and down the street. "All clear," he announced. "Stop in and see me on your way to work. If you're human, that is!"

Walter sneaked from lamppost to doorway to phone booth until he reached the loading dock again. There was no sign of the petrified mouse he had left behind the crate. Either it had come to its senses and left, or a cat had gotten it.

I'd better not go back the way I came, he thought. Every dog along the way will be awake and alert. I'll go down one or two blocks and then take a shortcut.

Walter's whiskers seemed to tingle. He brushed them against the side of the building and felt the smoothness of the bricks and the grainy texture of the mortar between them. That's what whiskers are for! They're as sensitive as fingers, like having extra hands on the side of my face!

Walter was becoming more and more aware of his abilities as a mouse. His eyes, though colorblind, functioned well at night. His hearing was very good. His sense of smell was amazing, and now he understood whiskers. His paws were still clumsy, but he would get better with them. But what was he going to do with his tail?

He'd figure that out later. Just then he had to decide whether to go left or right, north or south. He could remember walking to the north as a human. It seemed like there were plenty of trees, bushes and shrubs.

Okay! he decided. North it is. He turned left and began creeping from shadow to shadow.

Walter had covered two blocks and was ready to turn for home again when his ears caught the sound of footsteps and his nose picked up the scent of a human. He ducked behind a trash can as the footsteps drew closer. They were unsteady. He caught yet another smell, something strong.

Alcohol! his memory told him.

BLAANG! The can rocked and nearly tipped over as something heavy struck it. A startled Walter jumped from behind it, right into the path of a man who looked down at him and smiled! For a second they stared at each other. Then the man spoke.

"Hullo, Moushie!" he said in a slurred and unthreatening voice.

Walter continued to stare. The man was drunk, but not afraid. The other two men he had met as a mouse had been sober. One tried to shoot him and the other pulled a knife on him.

"You're the biggesht little moushie I ever sheen!" the man continued. "Hope I didn't schare ya. Didn't mean t'bump inta yer moushie houshie there! Did I wake ya up? I shee ya got yer pajamash on, never sheen a moushie in pajamash afore." He giggled, then hiccuped. "Fraid I had a teeny weeny bit too much t'night!"

I can believe that, Walter thought. I'm glad you're on foot and not behind the wheel of a car. This was neither the time nor place for conversation, even if he could talk. He tried to edge away, but the man blocked his path.

"Shay, Moushie," he said. "Mebee you could help me get home. I don't sheem very shteady on m'feet."

Walter did not see how he could do that, but the man had it all figured out. With a surprisingly quick move, he reached down and seized the end of Walter's tail!

"Now," he continued, "you just walk shtraight down the shtreet, 'n I'll tell ya when t'turn!"

This is not going to be a good night, Walter concluded. To be a mouse was bad enough, but now he had a drunk using his tail as a tow rope. Unfortunately, there was nothing he could do about it. The man may have been too unsteady to walk straight, but his grip was like iron.

"Thash a good moushie!" the man encouraged him. "Jush a block 'r two down thish way!"

Please! Don't let us meet anyone! Walter prayed as he towed the man along, his tail throbbing. The man's grip would not loosen, and whenever Walter tried to quicken the pace, the man pulled back. Walter soon discovered an old animal truth: it hurts to have your tail pulled.

A car crossed the intersection just ahead of them. At least the street was dark enough that a driver catching a glimpse of them from a distance might think it was a man walking his dog.

"Turn left, Moushie. Down thish way." Walter obediently turned left. "Shmart Moushie!" the man complimented him. "Jusht up the shidewalk here." He fumbled for his keys and dropped them. "Can't shee 'em," he complained. "Where'd they go? Can you get 'em fer me, Moushie?"

Walter scooped up the keys with his front paws, rose on his hind legs and held them out. "Good Moushie!" the man mumbled gratefully. "Want ya t'meet my wife. Bet she's never sheen a moushie like you afore!"

That was exactly what Walter did *not* want. As the man dropped his tail to take the keys, he whirled and ran. Dogs and cars no longer mattered. This was sheer, blind panic!

Dogs began to bark again before he had covered three blocks. A whole pack ran howling and yelping in pursuit. Walter hurdled two chain-link fences and soon left them far behind.

His feet seemed to have eyes of their own. He dodged over, under and around everything in his path without even thinking and put nine blocks between himself and the drunk's house before he slowed down and stopped.

I can't do it this way, he told himself. I have to think like a human and work my way back yard by yard.

There had been something wonderful, as well as terrifying, in his headlong dash. Running full out and bounding over fences! Sprinting faster than any human had ever been able to run! All right, he promised himself, I'll be careful now, though someday, sometime, I've got to run like that again!

47

Walter took nearly an hour to sneak his way back home. The door was still unlocked, and he opened it much more easily than the first time. He stopped and sniffed. Rancid's scent was old and faint. The cat was not around.

He crept quietly back up to his room and looked out the window. The sun would be up in less than an hour, and he would know then if the transformation was permanent or not. For now he could do nothing but wait. He curled back up on the bed and went to sleep.

CHAPTER SIX

The Bagshott Collection

When Walter awoke, he was Walter again. The face that stared back from the mirror was whiskerless, human, ordinary and, in a word, Walterish.

Was it all a dream? he wondered. Everything had seemed so real at the time. Now, with the early morning sun shining through his window, he had trouble believing that the past night's adventures had really happened.

Well, there was one easy way to find out. If he really had turned into a gigantic mouse, then the mark he had made with his teeth on the door would still be there. He dressed quickly. The thought of cheese for breakfast did not appeal to him. He ran downstairs without eating anything.

By the time he reached the bottom floor, Walter had just about convinced himself that it had all been a bad dream. He could *not* have turned into a giant mouse. Many strange things had happened since he met the old woman, but that was impossible. He smiled confidently as he bent down to check for the mark that, of course, would not be there.

The mark was there!

Walter's knees trembled as he realized that it had *not* been a dream. Then another terrible thought struck him. Would it happen again tonight? I've got to see Ivon, he decided. Then, first chance I get, I'll phone the old woman. He felt for the card in his pocket and sighed with relief. He still had it.

Walter ran down the front steps, then checked his stride and forced himself to walk. Ivon's was always open, and he would be unable to phone until much later. He had covered a block, and his breathing was nearly back to normal, when he heard Pomona Mona's skates behind him.

This time she did not swoop past. "Walter?" she asked as she drew even and slowed to keep pace with him. "Did you notice anything, well, *weird* last night?"

"Not really," Walter answered as innocently as he could and with his fingers tightly crossed. "What do you mean by weird?"

"I woke up this morning and found ol' Jammer hiding under the covers at the foot of the bed. He wouldn't come out, not even to skate with me, and you know how much he likes to wave at you when we go by."

Walter remembered how painful those little waves could be. "Do you think something frightened him?" he asked.

"Nothing scares Jammer!" Pomona Mona said. "That's what's so weird. That ol' cat doesn't know the meaning of fear!"

Right! Walter agreed silently. Old Rancid is too dumb to know the meaning of fear, or anything else. But he sure found out what fear was last night!

Aloud he asked, "Do you think you ought to take Ran—, I mean, Jammer to the vet?" And he smiled as he thought of needles the length of railroad spikes and pills the size of marbles.

"Maybe," Pomona Mona replied. "I'll see if he's any better tonight. I've still got a feeling that something weird is going on!"

"What do you. . ." Walter began, but his landlady flashed away on her skates before he could finish.

Ivon's was open, as always, and the breakfast crowd still lingered. Walter had to wait nearly half an hour over a cup of coffee before Ivon and he were alone.

"Back to your old self again," the Genuine Bulgarian Bagel Maker said as he poured a refill. "I'm glad to see it!"

"What am I going to do?" Walter asked. "You saw what happened last night. Is it going to happen again?"

Ivon shrugged. "I can tell you all about bagels," he replied. "But of weremice I know next to nothing. How do you feel this morning?" he added with some concern.

"Really, not bad," Walter admitted. "I should be all tired out, but I'm not. It was all so scary last night, and yet, at times, it was fun! Running and jumping faster and farther than anyone ever has! I mean, I felt like I could go on and on and never stop!"

"Do you want to become a mouse again tonight?" Ivon asked.

"No!" Walter answered quickly. Then he gave Ivon a sheepish smile. "But deep down inside, there's a tiny little part of me that says 'yes'!"

"Then listen to that tiny little part of you," Ivon urged. "Tiny little parts are usually the most interesting. I myself will promise you this. If you ever need help, whether you are a man or a mouse, my shop will always be open for you."

For some reason, Walter felt better when he left Ivon's *sladkarnitsa,* although once again Ivon had only hinted and not really told him anything.

Strangely, he did not feel tired at all, even though he had only slept for an hour or two. The work flew by as quickly as the day before, and, at the first opportunity, Walter used his card to call the old woman.

"Hello, Walter," the answering machine said. "I can't come to the phone right now, but I do have a few things to tell you. First of all, you have just proved that you are human. You didn't follow directions, did you? So now you find yourself in a mess, or is it a mess?"

What does she mean by that, Walter thought. Of course I'm in a mess! In fact, I'd call it first-class, Grade-A trouble!

"Remember how you felt last night?" the machine continued. "How much fun it was to run and jump? How well you could hear and smell and see? How strange and wonderful it felt to be a wild animal? If you want to learn more, Walter, take the afternoon off, go to the library and look up a book on musanthropy by Professor Homer Bagshott. That's B-a-g-s-h-o-t-t. Now, hang up carefully and wait for the click."

This time Walter followed directions. He shut his eyes, waited for the click and heard the chonk of coins falling into the return tray. He pulled out eight quarters, enough for bus fare to the library and another bagel or two.

Walter had never before had the nerve to ask Maxim-Rene for time off, but the chef only smiled. "You've worked so fast that you have some time coming. I think we can spare you for an hour or two."

The city library seemed huge to Walter, who had never been there before and did not know what to do. A clerk sat him at a computer and showed him how to code in his requests for information. "Just type in the author, title or subject," the clerk said. "Then push this key, and it will give you all the data you need."

Walter did not know how to spell "musanthropy," so he typed in "Bagshott, Homer" and pressed the entry key. The following data came up on the screen:

"Bagshott, Homer Noble (18??—19??), America's greatest procrastinator. Developed ideas for 107 great books, but never got around to writing any of them. Thus, thirty-four major universities never got around to honoring him. Dates of birth and death not known, nobody ever got around to recording them. All titles available in the Bagshott Collection. Access limited to cardholders. Walter, this is how you spell 'musanthropy'."

Walter blinked in surprise, but cleared the screen and entered "musanthropy". The following information appeared immediately:

"*Musanthropy: The History, Legends, Lore, Behaviors, Customs and Feeding Habits of the Weremouse.* An unwritten book by Professor Homer Noble Bagshott. Dewey Classification: 1000.1 (Bagshott Collection of Unwritten Books). Access limited to cardholders. Don't waste time gaping at this, Walter. You'll be late."

Walter did not gape. He was getting used to surprises by now. He sensed that no clerk or librarian would show him the Bagshott Collection. He would have to find it himself. Perhaps, he thought, this was another test.

He was pretty sure that the Dewey Decimal System only went up to the 900's, but he decided to begin his search there. The 900's were history, and the very last book on the very last bottom shelf was numbered 999. It was a book on the exploration of Antarctica.

That was it. Beyond was nothing but blank wall. No shelves, no books, nothing. Walter picked up the Antarctica book and leafed through it. The very last page was loose and came out in his hand. Curious now, he examined it more closely. It was not a part of the book, but instead a sheet of paper with instructions printed on it.

"To go on to the 1000's, insert card in slot in wall and push gently."

What slot? Walter scanned with his eyes and then felt with his hands. His eyes missed it, but his fingers, feeling along the bottom of a strip of molding, found an opening just large enough to admit a card.

No question about which card, Walter only had one. He looked around to make sure no one was watching, slipped the old woman's card into the slot, and pushed gently on the wall.

Slowly, a section began to fold inward. When it was open enough to admit him, Walter slipped through and found himself in a tiny room. It was hardly bigger than a closet and lit by a single overhead bulb. Two walls were lined with shelves of books. A third contained a small table and chair. Just above them a sign announced, in very large letters:

BOOKS ARE NEVER TO LEAVE THIS ROOM!

Walter pulled his card out of the slot, and the wall closed gently behind him. Okay then, where was the book he wanted?

It was, in fact, the very first volume. Walter pulled a thin book bound in faded red leather from the shelf and blew the dust from the cover. He opened it to the title page and read the same information he had seen on the computer screen. He also read that the book would have been written about 1910 and that it would have contained several illustrations if the author had gotten around to drawing them.

Very interesting, Walter thought. But where is the information I need? I don't have time to read it cover to cover.

He turned to the first chapter, titled "What Everyone Needs To Know." Good place to begin, he decided.

"For those who need to get back to work," Professor Bagshott had written (or would have, if he had gotten around to it), "a few basic facts about the weremouse can be explained at once.

"The weremouse is a man transformed into a mouse, usually a very large mouse, as the result of some spell. The most common cause is the eating of enchanted cheese at night."

Just my luck, Walter thought.

"Unlike its deadly cousin the werewolf (or *loup-garou* in French), the weremouse is harmless and sometimes even helpful to men and other animals. However, it is greatly feared by men and most animals."

This was news to Walter, who had not yet known anyone to be afraid of him. He read on.

"The transformation takes place at the stroke of midnight and lasts until dawn. How often the person under the spell becomes a weremouse depends upon how many times he or she eats the cheese at night."

Now we're getting somewhere! Walter thought. This is what I need to know!

"If the victim stops after only one such mistake, he will, from that time on, become a weremouse on each night of a full moon, and each night immediately before and after. If he continues to eat by night, however, he will be transformed more often."

Okay, Walter thought. But is it safe to eat it by day, and can the spell ever be reversed or broken?

"The enchanted cheese may still be eaten safely during the day," Professor Bagshott continued (or would have if he had gotten around to it), "but any part consumed by night will never be renewed, as is the case with any part given away. And once the cheese is completely consumed. . ."

Here Walter came to the end of the page. He tried to turn, but the pages stuck together. He turned clear to the back of the book and read the following notation:

"Musanthropes (weremice) may only read this book one page at a time. Otherwise they will lose track of time and stay too long. Weremice and other cardholders who finish this book might be interested in my works on werecattle and the making and tasting of enchanted cheeses."

Walter glanced at his watch, shook his head in disbelief and looked again. His two hours were nearly gone, though he did not believe he had been in the room for more than five minutes. Time ran under different rules in the Bagshott Collection.

Walter quickly used his card to exit the room. He pulled the wall shut behind him, left the library and then caught a bus back to work.

The rest of the day passed almost as quickly. Walter hurried home without stopping at Ivon's. He could see the moon climbing up into the night sky.

According to his calculations, this was the night after the full moon, which meant that he was due to become a mouse again!

Walter raced up to his room, put his pajamas on (with the pants backwards) and climbed into bed. He watched the luminous hand on his watch creep slowly toward midnight. What should he do? He felt tired, but too excited to sleep. Should he stay in the room or venture out again? Going out was dangerous, very dangerous! Staying put would be safe. He would be himself again in the morning and no one would ever know. . . .

Then he remembered how it felt to run by moonlight, to jump higher and farther than any human had ever dreamed and to smell and hear the wild things of the night.

Walter would go out again. He had to.

He got up, crept downstairs, unlocked the front door and left it slightly ajar, so that he could open it quickly with his nose or a paw. Then he returned to his room, took off his pajamas and watch and stretched out on his bed to wait for the transformation.

The hands on his watch crept closer and closer to midnight.

CHAPTER SEVEN

A Weremouse in the Suburbs

The transformation was much easier this time. As the hands on his watch touched midnight, Walter rolled to the edge of the bed and dropped to the floor. He lit on four paws and was a very large mouse again.

He scurried down the hall and paused at the head of the stairs to sniff. No sign of Rancid. Down the stairs and then another pause to sniff. Nothing. On to the first floor and yet another sniff. This time he picked up Rancid's scent, but it was very faint. The cat was probably hiding in Pomona Mona's bed.

The front door was still ajar. He slipped through and pulled it shut behind him. As long as it was not locked, he knew he could open it easily enough with his paws. Then Walter the Weremouse slipped out into the night.

He thought about making for Ivon's again, then changed his mind. All the dogs along the way would be alert, and Officer Mulholand might be waiting for him too. He would try the other way, out into the suburbs.

Walter began a mouselike creep from yard to yard. He had no idea what he expected to find. He had no idea what he was even looking for. A voice inside him asked, "Why am I doing this? People in the suburbs keep guns in their houses. I could get shot!"

"Not if you are careful," another voice inside him answered. "As for what you might find, who knows? Whatever happens, at least this night will *not* be boring!"

After he had crept several blocks, Walter noticed that the houses began to change. They were newer, lower, spread farther apart, with wide, carefully-tended lawns. The occasional smell of cat still reached him, but the scent of dog was very rare. Suburban dogs, it seemed, were either kept inside or penned up in back yards.

Walter began to move more quickly. He ran two blocks without pausing and bounded across two streets. Now the houses became fancier, and here and there lights shown from behind curtains and drapes. He picked up the sounds and scents of people still awake and moving in their homes.

Mouselike fear surfaced again and he realized it was a warm night. Windows were open and most of the sounds came from television sets.

Walter shook his whiskers and moved on. The streets no longer ran straight and divided into blocks. They twisted, looped and snaked their way up and down hills. The houses became even longer and bigger, and now large, elaborate fences began to appear.

The street he had been following came to a dead end near the top of a large hill. Before him stood a big fence and a sign that read: "Private Property! Keep Out!"

As a human, Walter Wampler was about as law-abiding as a citizen could be. But as a weremouse? Laws don't apply to weremice, he decided. I can go anywhere I want. I'm going in there!

Walter crept all the way around the fence, looking for a break or a weak spot where he might slip through. But the fence was solid and well-maintained, with spear-tipped iron poles set too closely for him to slip between them.

The house and grounds covered more than an acre. Walter could see the house, huge and dark, in the center of the grounds. He could not get through the fence.

He doubted very much if he could get over it. Very well, he would go under it!

Rodents are natural burrowers, so Walter simply let his instincts take over and began to dig with his forepaws. The earth had been softened by recent rains, and in less than a minute he was squeezing through his makeshift tunnel and popping up on the other side of the fence.

I'm a trespasser now, he realized, though he did not feel at all like a criminal. He was an explorer, an adventurer, a discoverer! What strange and terrible things would he find in the wilds of this unexplored estate? It was a child's game, but Walter Wampler had never had the chance to play such a game as a child.

Now, as a mouse, he could.

Walter had a human imagination to go along with his animal abilities. He dodged from one carefully tended shrub to another, looking, listening, sniffing for signs of life, signs of enemies. He found none. The whole estate seemed deserted.

There must be someone around, his human reasoning told him. They wouldn't all go away and leave a place like this totally unprotected. Maybe there's a caretaker or an alarm system.

Walter crept clear up to the house, but still found nothing. The house itself was tightly locked, and Walter had no desire to break in. In back, by a patio, something caught his interest.

It was a swimming pool, and it was full. Walter Wampler had never learned to swim. He had always been afraid of water. But now he was drawn to it. Mice knew how to swim by instinct, or did they?

Well, there was one way to find out!

Walter jumped in and mouse-paddled across to the other side. He could swim! It was easy! He had no trouble keeping his head above water, and he even used his tail to steer while he paddled with his paws. The water felt cool, not too cold. His fur, he realized, acted as insulation.

He swam for several minutes, enjoying the feeling of sliding through the water. I've got to try this as a human, he decided. It can't be all that hard to learn. Well, I suppose it's time to get out. Let's see, where's the ladder?

There was no ladder.

Walter swam all the way around the pool looking for a way out. He found nothing except a couple of holes where a ladder and rail had once been bolted. He swam to the shallow end and tried to stand on his hind legs, but even at its shallowest point, the pool was more than three feet deep. Walter's head and neck stuck out above the surface, but the rim of the pool was almost two feet above the water, and he couldn't reach it with his forepaws.

He was trapped!

Sheer blind animal panic seized him. He swam wildly in circles and clawed at the side of the pool, but his paws found nothing to grasp.

Stop! he commanded himself. Think! You've got a human mind. Use it!

He quickly realized that, if he could stay afloat until daybreak, he could climb out easily enough as a human. But then what would he do, naked, wet and miles from home?

No, he concluded. I've got to try to jump for it. If I crouch all the way down and then come straight up from the shallowest point, I just might make it!

Walter forced his head under water and curled himself into a ball. Then he pushed off as hard as he could and rose straight from the pool like some mousy missile. His forepaws scrabbled for the rim, found it, and he flipped himself forward. Walter the Weremouse did a somersault and landed on the patio. Safe!

He shook himself and then completed the drying process by rolling in the grass. Wow! he thought. A whole lawn for a towel! He started back for his tunnel, walking in the open, certain that he was alone.

Halfway to the tunnel he froze. His ears caught the sound of an engine, still far away, but coming closer. Then he saw lights swing around the corner at the bottom of the hill.

Walter raced to his tunnel and squeezed himself through. He dodged behind a tree as the car approached the dead end. The driver cut the lights and stopped the engine, but no one got out. This made Walter curious, and he crept out from behind the tree and sneaked over beside the car.

He heard voices, a boy and a girl, arguing. "C'mon! Take a hit," the boy said. "It's not gonna hurt you."

"I'm scared!" the girl answered. "I've never tried a joint before."

"It's only pot! What do you think it's gonna do?"

"I. . . I don't know. That's why I'm scared."

"C'mon!" the boy urged. "Don't believe that stuff they tell you. All it does is make you feel good."

"Well. . ."

"Look! Just try it! It's okay! I use it all the time!"

"You do?"

"Sure! And I don't see pink elephants or giant mice either!"

Walter had almost decided to leave them alone and sneak on down the hill, but that last remark was too much for him to pass up. "So," he said to himself. "You've never seen a giant mouse before? Well, my young friends, you are about to!"

The boy had just handed the joint to his girlfriend when Walter the Weremouse leaped from the bushes and landed squarely on the hood of the car. He reared up on his hind legs, beat on his chest with his forepaws and let out his loudest and most warlike squeak.

The girl went into hysterics. The boy went into hysterics. They screamed and hugged each other in sheer terror as Walter danced and capered on the hood. Then the boy grabbed at the keys and the engine roared to life again.

Walter jumped for the bushes as the car shot forward and sped down the hill. He watched the taillights grow smaller and smaller. Then, just before they disappeared, he saw another set of lights, flashing lights! There were police in this neighborhood as well!

Somebody is going to have some explaining to do, Walter thought as he watched the flashing lights and heard the siren. But why was that policeman cruising up this way? Did I set off a silent alarm? I don't think I'll wait around to find out.

Walter remained in darkness and shadows as he made his way back down the hill. He kept away from the street that the boy and the police cruiser had taken and chose another route through another neighborhood.

The suburbs, he soon decided, were dull. People and dogs stayed inside. Walter did encounter a few cats and treed a couple of them, just for fun. But he soon grew bored.

Might as well go on back home, he decided. It will be daylight soon, and. . .

Daylight! Yikes! I've got to get back now!

Walter ran as only a terrified mouse could run. The neighborhood was strange, though he knew the general direction he should go. He kept to the lawns whenever he could, as grass was easier on his feet than pavement. The yards flew past. He bounded over fences and hedges with leaps that even a steeplechase horse would have envied.

How much time did he have? He was suddenly aware that he wore no pajamas — not even a stitch — and that a naked human would attract almost as much attention as a pajama-clad mouse.

Two blocks, three, four! "Pace yourself!" his mind screamed to his legs. "You still have nearly three miles to go. You'll never make it at this pace!"

Walter slowed himself to a lope, which was still fast enough to outdistance any human sprinter. He ran eastward and looked up at the night sky. Was it his imagination? Or was the horizon already growing paler and brighter?

Seven blocks, eight, nine! He looked straight ahead and counted the blocks. Another quick glance up at the sky; it *was* lighter now, no question about it. Dawn was only minutes away!

Twelve blocks, thirteen, fourteen! The suburbs blended back into the city again. The houses were older and closer together. He was back in familiar territory!

Sixteen blocks, seventeen, eighteen! His lungs seemed to be on fire and his legs grew heavier and heavier. He had to keep going. The sun would break over the horizon any minute!

Twenty-one blocks, twenty-two, twenty-three! Walter's tongue hung so far out of the side of his mouth that he thought it would drag on the ground. He could feel little flecks of foam on his jaws. He now knew where he was. Just a few more blocks to go!

Twenty-six blocks, twenty-seven, twenty-eight! He could see Pomona Mona's house ahead! The horizon was now a soft, creamy shade of grey that he knew would look pink to a human. Could he make it in time?

Twenty-nine blocks, thirty! He broke into a final, exhausting sprint and bounded onto Pomona Mona's front yard just as the sun topped the eastern rim of the sky. The first ray of sunlight caught Walter in mid-spring. He felt its warmth shoot through him like an arrow.

He froze in mid-leap and dropped onto the lawn like a wounded animal, which was just what he was. He rolled over and over. When he stopped he was Walter again. He lay gasping and naked in the middle of the yard.

And just at that moment, Pomona Mona opened the front door to go skating.

CHAPTER EIGHT

Promotion and a Discovery

S trangely enough, it was Rancid who saved Walter. As Pomona Mona opened the door, the cat caught the last whiff of weremouse scent. Rancid yowled and shot straight up the still-closed living room drapes.

Pomona Mona turned back to swat Rancid down and open the drapes, and in those few seconds Walter was able to scramble into the bushes beside the front porch. He huddled next to a flowering Camellia as the ex-roller derby star laced up her skates and charged off into the morning, leaving in her wake a string of rather nasty remarks about the cat.

In fact, Rancid had done Walter two favors. Pomona Mona had been so mad that she had slammed the door, but forgotten to lock it. Walter glanced around to make sure all was clear. Then he leaped onto the porch and slipped inside.

Rancid gave another yowl and shot back up the drapes. Walter just grinned and said, "Thanks, Buddy! I owe you one!"

Walter took the stairs two at a time, ducked into his room and threw on some clothes. Then he cut a large piece from the cheese, grabbed a leftover Bulgarian Bagel, made a cup of instant coffee and sat down on his bed for a quick breakfast.

Once again he did not feel tired, even though he had been up all night and had just run three miles in world-record time. The cheese seemed to taste even better, although the slice he had cut by moonlight, along with the bit he had given to Ivon, had not grown back.

That was okay, he thought. As long as I'm careful, there's still plenty for me. I won't give any more away, and I sure won't eat any more after sundown!

A happy, whistling Walter ran back down the steps. He might not have been quite so happy if he had known what was happening a few miles away.

Officer Mulholand was getting ready to go off duty. He had spent the night behind a desk, rewriting and filing reports. Officer Mulholand hated desk work, but he was stuck there for the next two weeks. The owner of the broken window had been very upset, and Mulholand's explanation of having been startled by a giant mouse in faded blue pajamas had not gone over very well.

Mulholand had just yawned and glanced at the clock for the twenty-fifth time when one of the patrolmen came in chuckling and scratching his head.

"Man, did I get a strange one tonight!" he said.

"What happened?" Mulholand asked without much interest.

"Got a call from the caretaker at the Griffiths place up on Larkspur Hill," the patrolman said. "Claimed he heard some suspicious noises. I was just starting up the hill when a car shot past me like a bat outa you-know-where!

"So I chased it down and pulled it over. Turned out to be a couple of kids who'd gone up there to park and smoke weed. I found the joint right on the floormat between 'em, still lit!"

"Happens a lot," Mulholand shrugged.

"Yeah, but get this! They both claimed that a giant mouse jumped outa the bushes and attacked their car! A giant mouse! What's going in to the wacky-baccy these days?"

Officer Mulholand, no longer bored, suddenly sat straight and fumbled for a pen. "This *is* kind of interesting," he said. "Tell me more about it."

He began to make notes.

As Officer Mulholand wrote, Walter arrived for work. Chef Maxim-Rene immediately introduced him to another young man.

"Walter," he said, "this is Miguel. I've hired him to do your job!" He smiled a wolfish smile.

"*My* job?" Walter gasped. "But why? How? What have I done?"

"You've been promoted!" Maxim-Rene replied. "One of our waiters quit, and I want you to have the job. It will mean a raise in pay, and a bigger share of the tips!"

Walter was dumbfounded. He had never been promoted before, except at school, and even that, he sometimes thought, was only because the school believed in promoting everyone. He tried to think of something to say. A half-muffled "Wow!" was the best he could do.

"We won't need you for another hour," the chef continued. "Go find a store and get yourself some good shoes and slacks and a white shirt. We'll furnish the tie." He handed Walter some money. "This ought to cover it," he said. "Consider it a bonus."

As Walter left the restaurant, Officer Mulholand left the station. Officer Mulholand did not go home. Instead, he checked out a squad car and drove toward Larkspur Hill.

Walter's day passed like a dream. At first he was nervous, but he soon realized that he could handle the job easily enough. His normal shyness vanished, and he laughed and joked with the customers. He even made suggestions when they were not sure what to order.

I do this! he realized as the lunch rush subsided. I am actually good at something! I wonder if I could ever learn to cook like Maxim-Rene? I bet I could!

For the first time in his life, Walter Wampler felt excited and ambitious.

Officer Mulholand also felt excited and ambitious as he squatted by the side of the road and studied the ground. He had examined the hole that Walter had dug and the tire marks in the soft earth.

But he had also found pawprints, pawprints like none he had ever seen before!

"They laughed at me," Mulholand muttered as he got to his feet and walked back to the squad car. "But they won't be laughing much longer!"

He spoke into the radio mike. "Headquarters, this is Mulholand. I'm up at the end of Larkspur Road."

"Mulholand, what are you doing up there?" the dispatcher asked. "You're supposed to be off duty."

"Never mind that!" Mulholand replied. "I need Patrolman Rizzo and the tracking dog up here pronto! I'm on to something, and it could be big!"

"It had better be!" the dispatcher warned. "Ten-four!"

As Mulholand waited for Rizzo and the dog, Walter waited for the dinner crowd to arrive. His new shoes pinched his feet a bit, but he had never felt happier. He had been promoted!

Officer Mulholand also felt happy as he watched Patrolman Rizzo examine the pawprints and shake his head in wonder.

"It's the print of a mouse, all right," Rizzo said. "But it *can't* be a mouse print. Not unless you believe in mice the size of cougars!"

"Can your dog track it?" Mulholand asked.

"Finigan can track anything," Rizzo replied. The dog, a large, sad-eyed bloodhound, seemed to nod in agreement. "But what are you going to do when we find it?"

"Shoot it," Mulholand responded.

"No way!" Rizzo said as he shook his head, which was large and sad-eyed like the bloodhound's. "A mouse this size is bound to be on the endangered species list. We'd catch it from the environmentalists if you shot it."

"All right then," said Mulholand. "We'll capture it alive."

"Think we need a permit for that," Rizzo responded, "and I'm not sure where we can get one."

"Okay then, we'll *study* it."

"Think we need a biologist for that," Rizzo answered, "and I'm not sure. . ."

"Where we can get one!" Mulholand finished the phrase. "Okay, we'll *observe* it. I guess police are allowed to do that!"

"First we gotta find it," Rizzo said. "C'mon Finigan! Time to go to work!"

Finigan sniffed at the pawprint, then stared up at Rizzo with a questioning look and an uncertain "Woof!"

"He's a people-tracker, not a mouse-tracker," Rizzo explained. "I don't think this is part of his job description."

"Tell him to make an exception," Mulholand urged. "I'm gonna find this thing, whatever it is, and prove to some people downtown that I am not overstressed and in need of counseling!"

Finigan led them down the hill, across lawns, through bushes and around trees. "These people aren't gonna like us tramping over their yards," Rizzo warned. His face, sad and wrinkled, looked even more like the bloodhound's.

One angry lady did threaten to call the police after Finigan led Mulholand and Rizzo through her flower bed. "We *are* the police!" Mulholand informed her. "What do you want us to do? Arrest ourselves?" The lady flounced back into her house.

"Told you they wouldn't like it," Rizzo said.

After a few more blocks the trail straightened out and Finigan began to pick up the pace. "What do you make of this?" Mulholand asked.

"It's either running from something, chasing something or making for some spot," Rizzo guessed. "Maybe it's got a den around here somewhere. I think mice live in dens, don't they?"

Mulholand wondered. They were heading back into the city, not far from the spot where he had encountered the mouse in pajamas two nights before. Neither of the youngsters had mentioned pajamas, but it had to be the same mouse. There couldn't be more than one of them.

Or could there?

The trail ended right in the middle of Pomona Mona's front lawn. Finigan sat down on the grass and howled. "That means the scent stops here," Rizzo explained.

"Then here's where we start the investigation," Mulholand replied. He walked up the steps and rapped briskly on the front door.

Pomona Mona was not in the best of moods when she opened it, since the knock had come right in the middle of her favorite soap opera. "What is it?" she growled in a voice that had terrorized skaters from Los Angeles to Houston.

Officer Mulholland stood his ground. "Police, Ma'am," he said. "We're trying to track down a suspicious character."

"Well, you've sure come to the right neighborhood for that!" Pomona Mona replied. "I don't know anyone around here who isn't suspicious, 'cept for Jammer and me."

"Jammer?" Mulholland asked.

"My cat," Pomona Mona explained. "Hey! Something's been spooking him real bad the past coupla days. Think it might be your suspicious character?"

"I don't know," Mulholland replied thoughtfully. "Is your cat scared of mice?"

"You trying to be some kinda comic?" Pomona Mona growled. Her eyes narrowed as she thought of what she could do to Officer Mulholland if they were both on skates.

"I mean big mice!" Mulholland added hastily. "*Very* big mice!" He stopped and looked at her more closely. "Say, haven't I seen you somewhere before?" he asked.

"I sure ain't never seen you before!" Pomona Mona replied.

"No, but I'm sure. . ." Suddenly he snapped his fingers. "You were on TV once! You used to skate!"

Pomona Mona's frown melted away. "Right!" she said. "Derby Days and The Rockin' Rollers! I was a jammer for the Bombers back in the old days!"

"I remember!" Mulholand cried and dropped his voice to imitate an announcer. *"Nobody* gets past Pomona Mona!"

"Right again!" Pomona Mona agreed. "I laid out more breakers than any other gal on the circuit! Did you ever get a chance to see me in person?"

"Never had the chance," Mulholand answered sadly.

"I got some of my best games on tape. You wanna come in and watch a few?" Pomona Mona was beaming now. Here was someone who remembered her glory days. "I've even got an old program or two I could autograph for you!"

"Great!" Mulholand said and stepped inside, while a sad-eyed Rizzo sighed at the sad-eyed bloodhound. Finigan sighed back.

"Might as well go back and get the car," Rizzo told Finigan. "It's gonna be a long afternoon!"

It was a short afternoon and evening for Walter. He helped serve a banquet and waited on regular tables as well. Then, after work, he called the old woman again.

"Congratulations on the new job!" the answering machine said. "You will not be transformed for another four weeks, but you may be in for another surprise tonight."

Walter, somewhat puzzled, hung up and collected a dollar's worth of change from the return slot. He bought a couple of bagels and walked back to the rooming house.

He was surprised to see a police cruiser, with a sad-eyed man and a sad-eyed dog inside, parked at the curb. He heard voices as he opened the front door. Pomona Mona had company.

A curious Walter looked into the front room. Pomona Mona and a policeman were sitting on a couch, eating potato chips and watching old roller derby tapes.

"Hi, Walter!" she cried, catching sight of him. "Come on in and meet Officer Mulholand! He was one of my biggest fans!"

But Officer Mulholand stared long and hard at Walter. "Haven't I seen you somewhere before?" he asked.

CHAPTER NINE

A Night in the Woods

F or a moment, and just for a moment, Walter froze. Mulholand had never seen his human form, so he couldn't know anything about Walter being a weremouse. And even if he could, was it illegal to turn into a giant mouse every now and then?

No! Walter thought, and answered, "I don't think so," as casually as he could. Mulholand had seen Walter's moment of fear, and he could sense that Walter was hiding something.

That's what *you* say, the policeman thought. But I'm gonna keep an eye on you, Fella, because you're trying to hide something. And I *have* seen you before, somewhere, sometime.

"Do you say that to everyone, Herbert?" Pomona Mona asked.

"I was right about you, Mona," Mulholand replied.

Herbert? Mona? Walter was not thrilled with the idea of his landlady and Mulholand getting to know each other. He left as quickly as he could and ran back up to his room. Perhaps it was time to think about moving. He would soon be able to afford a better place anyway.

Despite the scare from Mulholand, Walter slept peacefully through the night. He had dreams which were forgotten as soon as he woke up. The cheese still furnished an excellent breakfast, and he whistled on his way to work.

I'll stop at Ivon's, he decided. I've got plenty of time.

Ivon greeted Walter with a smile, then his huge eyebrows rose straight up his forehead, and his eyes made quick, darting movements over Walter's shoulder.

Walter turned and saw Officer Mulholand standing on the sidewalk and peering through the window at him.

The next morning, when Walter arrived at work, he found Mulholand sitting in the hotel coffee shop. The following day, Mulholand came into the dining room for lunch and sat in Walter's section.

He's trying to rattle me, Walter realized. Two weeks ago it would have worked. But not now. I can play that game too!

Walter smiled and waited on him, making sure to recommend the most expensive items on the menu. Mulholand took a look at the prices and ordered a bowl of soup.

This went on for nearly a week. Walter worked; Mulholand watched. Walter smiled; Mulholand frowned. Walter recommended expensive things; Mulholand ordered soup. Walter never panicked; Mulholand never left a tip.

Finally Mulholand gave up. His stomach demanded more than a bowl of soup for lunch, and he couldn't afford the rest of the menu. But he did drop by to see Pomona Mona two or three times a week. She fixed chili dogs, and they watched the soaps or tapes of her old roller derby days until he had to go on duty.

Whenever Walter walked through the front door and smelled chili dogs, he knew that Mulholand was on the watch for him.

His search for other lodgings had not gone well. He had found several nice places, but they all wanted large deposits in advance. Any move would have to wait until he had saved enough to pay the deposits, and that would take at least a couple of months.

Meanwhile, the moon had waned to nothing and was growing back to full again. Transformation time was just a few days away, and Officer Mulholand was still hanging around Pomona Mona and her chili dogs.

He is not going to disappear, Walter realized. So I guess I have to. But where should I go?

Out into the woods, he decided. If I am going to be an animal, then why not go where other animals are? I'll take some camping equipment with me, and no one will ever suspect anything.

So Walter took part of his next paycheck to an outdoor store and checked out the camping equipment. After a look at prices, he limited himself to a backpack and a pair of boots.

"How about a tent or a sleeping bag?" the clerk suggested.

"No thanks," Walter said. "I don't think I'll sleep much."

That much he knew for sure, but where were the woods and how would he get there? Walter Wampler had been a city boy all his life. None of his foster parents had ever taken him camping. In fact, he had never been on a vacation.

I'll take a bus, he decided. I'll ride clear to the end of the line, then get off and walk until I find the woods. Or until I find something.

So the next evening Walter left work early, caught a bus, and rode far out into the suburbs. One by one, the other passengers dropped off. Finally, Walter and the driver were alone.

"How far are you going, Buddy?" the driver asked.

"As far as you can take me," Walter answered.

"First time in a week I had somebody ride clear to the end of the line," the driver commented. "Nobody out here uses the bus. Everyone has two or three cars."

"Uh, are there any woods out this way?" Walter asked.

"Nah, not really," the driver said. "Oh, there's a little stretch over by the country club, but it's just a few acres. They left it because it looks nice for the golf course. The rest is all housing developments and farmland."

Perfect! Walter thought. A place that's big enough to hide in, but not big enough to get lost in. "You can let me off by the country club," he said. "What time is the first run back in the morning?"

"Seven o'clock," the driver replied as he slowed to let Walter off. "Pick it up right over there. Good luck with whatever you're doing," he added while shaking his head.

But I *don't* know what I'm doing, Walter thought as he stepped off the bus and looked across the golf course to the line of trees. The sun was already down, and only a faint glow remained along the western horizon. All Walter did know was that he had to cross the course and get into the trees without being seen.

There were lights in the clubhouse, but no golfers out on the course. Walter slipped across the fairways and dodged around the sand traps and greens until he reached the edge of the miniature forest. He slipped inside and felt the darkness and the trees close around him.

"Now what do I do?" he asked himself.

He checked his watch. The hands, glowing in the dark, indicated that he still had nearly three hours to wait.

"Might as well explore a bit and find a place to hide my stuff," he announced to the night and the woods.

So, like a clumsy pioneer, Walter Wampler pushed into the miniature wilderness. He found a trail and followed it through to the other side. Another trail crossed it, so he backtracked and explored it too.

His eyes grew more accustomed to the darkness, but they were not as sharp as a mouse's. He sniffed, and his human nose could only pick up the faintest scent of trees and something moldy.

This is totally, totally boring! he thought. Other guys my age are having fun dating girls, while I'm sitting out here in the woods waiting to turn into a giant mouse!

Walter had never had a girlfriend. He thought about how nice it would be to have one. Then he thought about what she might do when she saw her boyfriend turn into a giant mouse, and he shuddered. It would take a very, very special girl to deal with something like that!

He poked around in the woods until he found a hole near the base of a tree with some large rocks beside it. Strange, he thought. It looks like someone dug that. But why?

Slowly, the time for the transformation approached. At five minutes to midnight Walter took off all his clothes, stuffed them into the pack and hid it in the hole at the foot of the tree. He set two of the large rocks over the pack to keep it safe from other curious animals.

Although the night was not all that cold, Walter shivered. What is this going to be like in January? he asked himself. I can't be out here like this in the snow!

The transformation took only seconds. Walter felt a weight on his shoulders, pressing him forward and down. His hands were paws before they touched the ground.

The sudden change in his sense of smell hit first and hardest. A moment before, he could smell only two faint odors. Now there seemed to be dozens, all pungent and sharp. Walter the Weremouse stood on his hind legs, wriggled his whiskers, and tried to sort them all out.

Trees! Bushes! Shrubs! Animals! Birds! He forced himself to concentrate on animals. Mice, squirrels, rabbits, a prowling cat, and others he could not identify.

Walter picked one of the strange scents and followed it to the edge of the trees, then out onto the golf course. The trail, whatever it was, headed for a small pond that formed one of the hazards. The scent grew stronger.

Walter had no idea what he was tracking, or what he would do when he caught up with it. He saw a lumpy object at the water's edge. His whiskers tingled and he moved closer. The object turned and the moonlight reflected points of light from a pair of eyes.

Walter stopped and stared. The animal was still just a dark smudge against the water, but now the moonlight reflected from a row of teeth bared in a mocking grin. Walter hesitated, then took a step forward. The grin vanished, the eyes closed and the strange animal flopped over on its side. Slowly, carefully, Walter approached and stared down at, a possum!

So that's what it is, he thought. Gad, they're ugly!

He could see other tracks and smell other scents in the mud at the water's edge, and he realized that he was thirsty too. Should he chance taking a drink from the pond? Why not?

Walter stuck his snout (for that was what it was) into the pond and lapped greedily. The water tasted strange, yet somehow good. Mice have a different sense of taste, he realized, and the water here has no chlorine or fluorides.

He was also careful to smudge out his tracks before he returned to the forest. He wondered, is there anything in the woods I can eat? What do mice eat, besides cheese? Seeds? Grains? Grass? Yuck!

His eyes and ears were also much sharper now. He could hear scurrying and see shapes as the population of the miniature forest went about its nightly business of feeding and, he observed, being fed upon.

An owl swooped low over the grass at the edge of the trees, then flapped away with something clutched in its talons. Probably a mouse. Owls have to eat, and mice have to take their chances.

He tried to convince himself that he was safe. Nothing short of a cougar would take him on. Well, maybe a lynx or a wildcat. But there can't be any this close to town.

He picked up another strange scent and trailed it back into the forest. What could it be? This was better than a guessing game! The scent grew stronger and Walter's whiskers began to tingle again.

There it was up ahead! Something very dark, with a big, fluffy tail. Dark and, oh! Dark with a very white stripe!

Walter quickly backed away as the skunk turned around and stamped its feet in warning.

That was a little too close, Walter thought as he watched the skunk amble away. Maybe I'd better not push my luck any more. But there was still one more strange scent. Should he follow it? Why not?

Again the scent trail led down to the pond. Walter followed it cautiously. He heard a splash and then a thrashing sound in the shallow water. He crept closer until he saw the silhouette of an animal. He recognized it at once, a raccoon!

It had caught a frog or a fish and was washing it off before making a meal of it. That's strange, Walter thought. Why wash something that has just come out of the water?

Walter crept still closer. He knew the raccoon must have smelled him by now, but the scent of a mouse would cause no alarm. Better not get too close, though. They do have big teeth and claws. Man, is he ever going to be surprised when he does turn around!

Suddenly the raccoon spun around and raced back into the woods. He never even saw me, Walter realized. What spooked him?

Walter stood on his hind legs, sniffed, and caught the one scent that scared him more than any other. It was the one animal he really had to fear: man!

Walter raced for the shelter of the trees. Once he reached them, he stopped and sniffed again. Two men, coming his way. He could see them now in the moonlight. Two dark shapes making their way carefully across the golf course, like men who did not want to be seen.

What were they up to?

Walter edged farther back into the woods as the two men approached, talking in voices too low for humans to hear. Walter's mouse ears picked up the conversation easily.

"Why leave the stuff in the woods?" one of them asked. "Be a lot easier just to hand it over."

"Safer," the other replied. "We're never seen together this way. We just leave the stuff in the hole by the tree. Tomorrow a golfer hooks a shot into the woods and goes in to hunt for it. He picks up the stuff, leaves the cash, and we come back tomorrow night and get it!"

"Yeah, but I don't like this place. Gives me the creeps!"

"Afraid of the mice and rabbits?" his companion taunted him. "Don't go shooting any of 'em. We can't have any noise!"

"Okay! Okay! Let's find the hole!"

Oh no! Walter thought. The hole! I bet it's the one where I hid my stuff!

Walter raced back down the trail. Which tree was it? It was off this way somewhere, but how. . . .

Stop! his mind ordered. Use your nose! Backtrack yourself!

Walter stopped, sniffed, found his own trail and followed it back to the tree. He scrabbled furiously at the rocks with his forepaws. "Move!" he pleaded silently. "Please move!"

Slowly, grudgingly, the rocks gave way. Walter jammed his snout into the hole, seized the pack strap with his teeth and pulled. The pack came free and Walter ducked back into the bushes just as the beam of a flashlight swept across the tree.

"Here it is!" one of the men said. "Hey! Look at those tracks! Some animal's been nosing around here!"

"Yeah!" the other agreed. "Funny-looking track. Wonder what it is? Find me some more rocks. We sure don't want this stuff dug up!"

"That golfer's gonna be mad when he sees this pile," the first man said, and Walter heard the thump and clack of rocks being piled on top of something.

"I don't care about that," the second man replied. "We'd better find some cash here tomorrow night, or that golfer will find out what mad really is!"

Walter heard the footsteps again, growing fainter this time as the men left the forest. Just to be safe, he remained hidden until he had slowly counted to one thousand in his head. Then, very cautiously, he crept out from the bushes. The men were gone, and the hole had been filled in and covered with rocks.

Filled in with what? Why had they come at this hour to do it? Should he dig and find out?

Leave it! a part of him urged. It's no business of yours! Don't get involved!

If it's what you think it is, another part of him replied, then it *is* your business. Yours and everyone else's in the community. You can't walk away from it!

So Walter the Weremouse pushed, pulled, scrabbled and dug until the hole revealed a package wrapped in heavy plastic. He carefully pulled it out with his mouth and forepaws. The package, he guessed, weighed between two and three pounds. Walter would have whistled, if he had been able to.

Instead, he held it in his teeth by one corner and made his way back to the pond. At the water's edge he ripped it open with his claws. The package was full of a white, powdery substance, just as he had guessed.

Walter spilled as much of the contents as he could into the pond. Then he swam with the rest out to the center, let go, and watched the package sink.

I don't think I'll come back here tomorrow night, he decided as he swam back to the bank. It might not be healthy. Somebody *is* going to be very unhappy!

As the sun poked over the horizon, Walter stood on his hind legs and stretched. His body grew longer and leaner, and, as he yawned, he covered a human mouth with a human hand.

"I'd better get back across the course," he said as he dressed. "That bus may come early."

The bus was actually right on time. But Walter hurried across the course so fast that he forgot to make sure that all his tracks were wiped out.

He would regret that later.

90

CHAPTER TEN

Shashki and Cinderella

Tonight, Walter decided, he would go back to Ivon's. But he would go before midnight, as a human, and let the transformation take place at the shop, where he could be safe with the one person he trusted with his secret.

The idea made him feel better, and the day passed quickly enough. Just before the dinner rush began, one of the other waiters beckoned to him.

"Hey, Walter!" he said in a voice just above a whisper. "There's gonna be a party tomorrow night after work. Can you come?"

This was another first. Walter had never been invited to a party, or anything else, in his life. He had been ordered, commanded and told to take part in things, but he had never been asked or invited.

"Really?" he asked. "What kind? Where? For what?"

"Here," the waiter replied. "You want to come or not?"

"Well, sure! But. . ."

"Relax!" the waiter urged. "It's for Cindy, that cute little blonde waitress. It's her birthday. We're gonna surprise her with a cake and a party."

This too was new to Walter. He had been surprised many times himself, usually unpleasantly, but — not counting the time he had jumped on the hood of the car — he had never been part of a surprise for anyone else.

"I'll be there!" he said.

A large banquet kept Walter busy until late that evening. It was well past ten by the time he finished work and was able to leave. He decided not to go home at all and headed straight for Ivon's. The shop was empty of customers, but the lights were on and the door unlocked.

Walter found Ivon in the back. He was tending a large pot of boiling water and singing to no one in particular as he dropped raw bagels into the pot:

"First we boil and then we bake.

Out of the oven and give 'em a shake!

On we toil, and make no mistake,

The life of a bagel is hard-o;

The life of a bagel is hard!"

"Nice song!" Walter applauded. "Is it traditional?"

"It will be," Ivon replied. "You see, I am writing it, and I am as traditional as they come!"

"How much have you written?" Walter asked.

"So far, only this verse," Ivon admitted. "But it's a start. Think about it, Walter, Ivon's Genuine *Traditional* Bulgarian Bagels! Prepared and served by a Genuine Traditional Bulgarian Bagel Maker! My new image; think it will work?"

"I don't know," Walter answered. "Do you think you'll be able to fit a sign that long across the front of your shop?"

"One worry at a time, Walter," Ivon said. "Why did you drop by? Are you perhaps looking for a safe place to assume your, shall we say, other identity?"

"Yes," Walter responded. He had decided to say nothing to anyone about last night in the woods. Somebody might tell somebody else, who might tell somebody else, until some very unpleasant people might finally hear about what Walter had dug up and destroyed.

"Well," Ivon said, "it would be nice to have some company tonight. Stay here in the back, though. Your friend Officer Mulholand sometimes drops by."

"I wouldn't exactly call him a friend," Walter said with a little bitterness.

"Ah! but who knows?" Ivon argued. "Things may turn out differently than you think. The wise man, Walter, is slow to judge. Only fools and baseball umpires make snap decisions. And only baseball umpires are paid to make them."

"I like that," Walter said. He liked Ivon as well. The man was a teacher, a real one, a natural one.

As if reading his mind, Ivon asked, "Do you know how to play checkers or chess?"

"No one ever bothered to teach me," Walter replied.

"Then I will teach you," Ivon said. "Tonight. We'll start with checkers. It's easier to learn. The British call it draughts. In my own native language it is *shashki*."

"I won't be much competition," Walter remarked as he watched Ivon set up the board.

"Who knows?" Ivon said once again. "I like the game, but I'm really not very good at it. You may have a knack for it, in which case you could be winning before the night is over. Now, here is how the pieces move. . . ."

Even with Ivon's coaching, Walter lost the first game in a matter of minutes. The second game ended almost as quickly. But by the third game, Walter had begun to catch on. He lost, but he did manage to get one of his men crowned and jumped several of Ivon's pieces. The fourth game lasted a quarter of an hour, and Walter nearly won it.

"Doggone!" he said as he looked at the clock. "Five minutes to midnight. We don't have time for another game."

"Why not continue?" Ivon replied. "I've never played against a mouse before. Let's try it! We have most of the night, and you can still think and reason. You could become the first mouse in history to win a game of *shashki.*'

Walter shook his head. "Don't you ever sleep?" he asked.

"Indeed I do!" Ivon answered proudly. "That is one thing I am very good at. I am a sprint sleeper!"

"What is a sprint sleeper?" Walter asked.

"Let me explain with an example," Ivon replied. "Suppose you were running, trying to get somewhere. Now, how quickly you got there would depend upon how fast you ran. If you doubled your speed, you would get there in half the time, right?"

"Right," Walter agreed.

"Well," Ivon continued, "I can sleep more than twice as hard as the average person. So I need less than half as much."

"That could be useful," Walter said after some thought. "Could you teach me how to do it?"

Ivon shook his head. "No, it is not something that can be taught. It is a gift, like. . . like your ability to become a mouse. By the way, Walter. It's nearly midnight. I suggest you go into the men's room and get ready."

95

Walter walked into the restroom as a human and came out two minutes later as a weremouse. Ivon had moved a bench up to the table with the checkerboard, and Walter was grateful. Chairs were not designed for four-legged creatures.

Walter hopped up on the bench and pondered his first move. His mind was full of questions, but he couldn't ask them now. If Ivon's ability was a gift, then where had it come from? Ivon knew more than he was telling, but how much more?

He touched one of his men with his paw and slid it onto another square. Paws, he soon realized, were not designed for checkers. Making jumps and crowning kings would be a real challenge.

But the game ended in a draw. Man and mouse played each other down to one king each, and neither of them could maneuver the other into a trap. Ivon closed the game board with a rueful smile.

"Walter," he said, "you just made history, sort of. You're the first mouse ever to play a human at *shashki* and not lose. Now I think I will sleep for a couple of hours. Will you watch the shop for me?"

Walter nodded. "Good!" Ivon said. "Just remember to keep away from the front windows." He threw himself down on a cot, shut his eyes and instantly began to snore.

So the night passed. Ivon slept, woke, boiled and baked. Walter prowled, watched, scurried and sampled. He tried to take a nap, but that was impossible. At last the sun came up, and Walter the Weremouse became

Walter Wampler again. He dressed, drank some coffee, and then hurried home to shower and change.

"Walter, have you been out all night?" Pomona Mona asked. She was sitting on the steps tying her skates as he came up the walk.

Walter nodded and gave her a grin and a wink. Might as well let her believe I'm a party animal, he thought. She'd sure never believe the truth!

"Didn't think you were that kinda guy," Pomona Mona tittered, and then she skated off into the morning.

Walter looked forward to the party, but dreaded it at the same time. Tonight was another weremouse night, and he would have to make sure that he was home, at Ivon's or some other safe place when midnight came. He could not let the transformation take place at the party. Weremice were not party animals.

But Walter soon discovered that he was a party animal, or that he could be with a little more practice. It was a good party, and Walter was enjoying every minute of it.

Maxim-Rene had baked a special cake for the event, and there was plenty of singing and dancing and games. Walter had never learned to dance, but Cindy and another waitress volunteered to teach him.

That night Walter discovered something else about himself. He was a naturally good dancer. The steps came easily, and he moved with a grace that surprised him and everyone else. Perhaps it was his experience as a weremouse.

"Oh Wow!" Cindy said as they danced slowly together. "You're a great dancer! You can move just like a. . . a. . ." She seemed stuck trying to think of a good comparison.

"A mouse?" Walter suggested.

"Ecch!" Cindy exclaimed. "How can you say such a thing?"

"It just popped into my mind," Walter replied.

"I can't bear to think of them!" she said. "They're so. . . creepy!"

"Oh Cindy!" Walter said to himself. "Would you ever be in for a surprise if we were still dancing at midnight!"

The thought gave Walter a jolt of alarm. He glanced at his watch. It was past eleven-thirty.

"Hey!" shouted one of the other party animals. "Turn down the lights a bit!" Cindy seemed to think this was a good idea and snuggled closer to him.

"I. . . I'm sorry!" Walter stammered. "I've. . . I've got to go!"

"Go?" Cindy asked. "Where? Walter, it's not even midnight!"

"I know! But. . . but. . ."

"What's the matter, Walter?" asked a suddenly irritated Cindy. "Are you Cinderella or something? Are you going to turn into a pumpkin at midnight?"

"Not *exactly* that," Walter replied truthfully. "But I do have to go! Believe me! I'm sorry!"

Walter left the hotel quickly and ran out into the night. He made straight for Ivon's, but pulled up a block short. A police cruiser was parked in front, and Walter didn't need three guesses to know who was in it. He ducked quickly around a corner and headed for home.

He looked at his watch and broke into a run. It would be close, but he would just make it. With less than two minutes to spare, Walter dashed up the stairs to his room and quickly flung off his clothes. He threw himself down on his bed just as the hands on his watch touched midnight.

Suddenly, he was a weremouse again!

He stayed on the bed for nearly an hour, but sleep would not come. I've got to go out and prowl before I can sleep, he realized. It worked the first time for me. If I stay close around the house, nothing will happen.

He crept down the stairs and opened the front door with his paws. He was getting better at using them, and the latch was no problem this time. He could not smell Rancid in the house. So what? The outside is big enough for both of us, he decided.

Walter confined his prowling to the back yard and stayed well away from the street. There was not much excitement or adventure to be found in Pomona Mona's back yard. Walter felt relieved, but also just a little bored.

He thought about Cindy and what kind of excuse he could make for running out on her. I think she actually likes me, he realized. Or at least she did. But if I tried to dance with her now, what would she say?

He did not want to think about it.

Even if he did soothe her feelings about tonight, in four weeks it would all happen again. . . and again. . . and again.

A strange sound cut in on his train of thought. It was not a purr, not a moan, not a hum, but something close to all three. It was coming from outside stairs leading down to a cellar door. Walter crept over to investigate.

It was Rancid. The cat had cornered a mouse at the bottom of the steps and was toying with it. The mouse wasn't dead, or even badly hurt, but it was trapped. Rancid crouched on the step just above it and batted at it with his paws. The mouse ran frantically back and forth.

Walter had no great love for other mice, but he cared for Rancid a whole lot less. As the cat poked at the terrified mouse with one extended claw, Walter reared up on the steps behind him and roared out his war squeak.

Two things happened very quickly. Rancid shot straight into the air, over the railing and up the nearest tree. The mouse fell over in a dead faint.

That was fun, Walter thought. But now what do I do?

He considered the problem. If he left the mouse, Rancid would soon return and make short work and a quick meal of it. If he stuck around until it came to, dawn might catch him out in the yard. If he took it up to his room, Pomona Mona would have sixteen different kinds of fits.

If she found out about it, that is. But how could she find out about a mouse?

He carefully picked up the still-unconscious mouse in one paw and made his way back around the house. He crept cautiously back up to his room and laid the mouse on his bed.

No, he thought. That won't work. I've got to find a safe, secure place for it. . . .

Aha! He remembered an old shoebox somewhere in his closet. He dug it out, bit two holes in the top for air, then gently put the mouse inside and replaced the lid.

"Not the best place in the world to recover in, Little Fella," he said to himself. "But it's a lot better than what you were facing outside!"

This time when he curled up on the bed, Walter was able to go to sleep.

CHAPTER ELEVEN

Little Fella

Walter knew he was human again as soon as he woke up. He knew it because he was in a bad mood, a foul mood, a nasty mood. It was an everyone's-against-me, the-whole-world-is-rotten, why-can't-anyone-understand case of the blues; and only a boy who has just lost a girl — or a girl who has just lost a boy — can ever relate to it.

To make matters worse, he couldn't even say that his romance with Cindy was over. The fact was: it had never begun.

Walter looked at his face in the mirror like a critic all set to write a bad review. He picked out every possible flaw, and a few impossible ones, as well, then sat down on the bed. He spent five minutes feeling sorry for himself. All he wanted was a girlfriend. Life wasn't fair!

He was saved from his despair by his stomach, which reminded him that he was hungry. Automatically he began fixing breakfast. Then a scratching sound caught his attention. At first he was puzzled, then he remembered the shoebox, opened the lid and peered inside.

The mouse stared right back at him, seemingly un-afraid. Perhaps it had given itself up for dead and was simply waiting to see how it would all end.

Walter calculated the cost of last night's adventures in his head. The total came out this way:

Lost: one girl

Gained: one mouse

Not a very good bargain, he decided.

Still, it was unfair to blame the mouse for his prob-lems. He had saved it. Now he had it. What was he going to do with it?

"You hungry, Little Fella?" he asked. He did not expect an answer, but the mouse sat up and looked at him and seemed to nod as though it understood.

Seems to be intelligent, Walter thought. Cute too, as mice go. Let's see now, what and how do I feed it?

Cheese, of course! And it has to have a little water. Walter grabbed an old ash tray left by a previous lodger. As Walter did not smoke, he used it for pennies, paper clips and rubber bands.

He emptied the dish and rinsed it out in the bathroom across the hall. This is silly, he thought. Mice don't care that much about hygiene. He made sure it was clean anyway. Then he cut a small piece of the cheese. He knew it would not be replaced, but it was just a small sliver.

"Gotta go now, Little Fella," he told the mouse as he placed the water and cheese in the shoebox and shut the lid. "I'll be back tonight. I'm going to keep you in here for a couple of days, until you're stronger. Then I'll let you go."

Again the mouse looked back at him as if it understood.

For the first time since he had met the old woman, Walter Wampler dreaded going to work. Cindy would demand and deserve an explanation for his snub, and what could he tell her? The truth was totally unbelievable, and Walter knew he was no good at lying.

Pomona Mona also looked upset and depressed as she sat on the front steps tying her skates. "Something's wrong with Jammer again," she complained. "I thought he was getting better, but last night he jumped right under the covers with me. He won't even come out to go skating this morning!"

That should have cheered Walter up, but he could only shake his head and say how sorry he was to hear it.

"And I even got myself some new skates!" she continued. "What do you think of these little beauties, Walter?"

Walter saw that they were Rollerblades, four wheels set in a single row, looking nearly as sleek as ice skates. The thought of Pomona Mona ripping though the neighborhood on them made him uneasy.

"You really cover the ground on these babies!" she said. "Wish I'd had 'em in the old days when I skated the circuit with the Bombers. Nobody in the league could have touched me if I'd worn these!"

For someone her size and age, Pomona Mona was still very quick and sure on her feet. Before Walter could comment on the new skates, she was off down the sidewalk, grey hair in bright green rollers bouncing behind like little tin cans tied to the bumper of a newlyweds' car.

But Walter was too depressed to laugh.

He stopped at Ivon's for coffee, courage and advice. The breakfast crowd was leaving, and Ivon soon joined him at a table in the corner.

"Why the sad face?" Ivon asked. "You have no more transformations for another four weeks."

Walter told him about the party and how he had been forced to run just as Cindy was beginning to snuggle up to him. "To top it all off," he added, "it was her birthday and I messed it all up for her. So what can I say to her?"

"Do you want to tell her the truth?" Ivon asked.

"How can I?" Walter protested. "She'd think I was crazy!"

"Then do you want to lie?" Ivon asked again.

"I can't," Walter admitted. "She's too nice for that."

Ivon stroked his chin thoughtfully. "Then you must be mysterious," he said at length. "Apologize, yes. She deserves at least that much. Take her a flower, just one, and not very expensive. But say nothing more."

"What if she asks me why?"

"Look sad," Ivon urged. "You can do that easily enough. Tell her it's a secret you have sworn never to let out. Then say no more."

"How is that going to help?" Walter asked.

"It will make her curious," Ivon replied. "And curiosity is the one thing that will overcome anger in a girl. Or at least this was true in Bulgaria," he added.

"Do you think it will work here?" Walter asked hopefully.

"If she is human, and I assume she is, though I sometimes wonder about Americans," Ivon answered.

So that morning produced another first in Walter Wampler's life. He had never been in a flower shop before. He selected a single white rose and flinched at the price. Liking Cindy could turn out to be expensive.

But the rose worked. Cindy wasn't exactly thrilled, but her anger cooled. She no longer seemed miffed. "I only wish you'd tell me why you ran out like that," she complained.

"I'm sorry," Walter answered as sadly as he could. "It's something I can't tell you, or anyone else!"

"Really?" She now sounded more curious than angry.

"Believe me," Walter said, "if I could tell anyone, it would be you."

"Tell me what?" Cindy was all curiosity now.

"What I can't tell you," was Walter's reply, and he gave her a quick half smile while keeping the sad look in his eyes.

"Well, if you're *really* sorry," Cindy said, "then you can at least walk me home tonight."

"Sure!" Walter agreed. "We can stop for coffee and bagels."

"*Zdravei*, Walter!" Ivon cried as they entered his shop late that night. "Who is the *gotino momiche*, that is, the pretty girl, you have with you?"

"This," Walter answered with some pride, "is Cindy." He had never had a date to show off before this. Ivon joined them at their table. The rest of the shop was empty.

"Your good friend Mulholand no longer drops by," Ivon complained as he gazed at the empty tables. "Apparently he prefers your landlady's chili dogs to my bagels."

Walter shrugged. "It's his life, and his stomach lining," he said. He was much too interested in Cindy to worry about Officer Mulholand's eating habits.

Cindy was growing more curious by the moment. "I've never heard of this place before," she said. "Don't you advertise?"

"There is no need," Ivon replied. "If someone wants a Genuine, Traditional Bulgarian Bagel, this is the only place to come. If one does not want a Genuine, Traditional Bulgarian Bagel, then there is no reason to come."

"But what if someone isn't sure?"

"You can always be sure about bagels," Ivon answered. "A bagel is like love. Once you have felt it, once you have experienced it, you know when it is real. And a Genuine, Traditional Bulgarian Bagel is like the truest of all loves. It can never be doubted and never be replaced."

"I never thought of a bagel that way," Cindy admitted.

Nor had Walter. To him a bagel was something to eat, and love was something about which he had only read. He had often wondered what it was like to be loved, really loved. He had been cared for, fed, clothed and sent to school, but never really loved. People had provided for him. Some had even been very kind to him.

But no one had ever said they loved him.

Would Cindy ever say that? He took a bite from the bagel and thought about how he loved the crunchy, chewy taste. What a curious word! It could mean so many things.

All this time Ivon was watching them. "Walter has much to learn," he remarked to Cindy. "But in a way he is much like one of my bagels. Once you have met him, you do not forget him."

Walter blinked. Nobody had ever said *that* about him before either. He had always thought of himself as one of the most forgettable people on earth. Was Ivon serious or simply trying to help him impress Cindy?

Cindy was impressed, no doubt about that. Walter walked her home, kissed her goodnight — another first, and a very pleasant one — and whistled to himself all the way back to Pomona Mona's.

He saw Officer Mulholand's squad car parked at the curb and could smell the chili dogs all the way from the front porch. Officer Mulholand seemed to have found a second home, or at least a free lunch.

Walter sat on the steps and tried to make sense of the day. He heard a rustle in the bushes and saw Rancid prowling through the shrubbery. He whistled softly and crooked a finger at the cat as a peace offering, or at least a truce, but Rancid hissed and scrambled up a tree.

Walter climbed the stairs to his room and got ready for bed. He heard a scratching from the shoebox again. Little Fella, at least, would be glad to see him.

He opened the lid. The cheese and the water were gone. "Hungry, Little Fella?" he asked, and once again the mouse seemed to nod.

Walter felt in his pockets. He had intended to bring back a piece of bagel, but being with Cindy had made him forget. The water was no problem, but what could he feed the mouse?

It would have to be cheese. Another little sliver would never be renewed, but he still would have all the rest for himself. I know what happens when a human eats this by moonlight, he thought. But what happens to a mouse? He did not wish to harm Little Fella. The mouse seemed eager for the cheese, standing on its hind legs, sniffing and making little nodding motions with its head.

"I suppose one little sliver won't hurt you much," Walter said as he put the cheese and the ashtray full of water back in the shoebox. Then he went to bed. Just before he closed his eyes, he glanced at his watch. Midnight.

Walter had strange dreams that night, almost like those he had dreamed on the night he had first eaten the cheese. When he awoke, the sun was streaming in through the window, and he could hear a bird singing in a tree outside.

He could also hear sounds from the shoebox. Little Fella was apparently much better or at least much stronger. "I'd better let him go today," Walter thought out loud, and for some reason, the thought made him sad.

As he became fully awake and alert, Walter noticed something strange about the sounds from the shoebox. They were different and un-mouselike, but determined and persistent.

"Hungry again, Little Fella?" Walter asked as he opened the lid. "I suppose . . ."

Walter stared, frozen in amazement. There was no mouse in the box. Looking up at him was a human being, no more than five inches tall!

It took several seconds for Walter to realize that the cheese had worked its magic again, and that Little Fella was no longer a mouse.

Walter stared, blinked, stared again, and became aware of yet another fact.

Little Fella was not a fella either!

CHAPTER TWELVE

A Sacrifice of Socks

Wh12at can you do with a girl who is five inches tall? Walter considered the problem. Shutting her back in the shoebox was out. You could do that to mice, perhaps, but not to humans.

Should he simply leave her in the room while he went to work? No, she might get out or Rancid might get in. And Rancid was a cat in whose kindness and mercy Walter was extremely unwilling to trust.

So she would have to come with him. But how? She could not simply be folded and stuck in a pocket along with keys and spare change. And how could he keep track of her at work?

First things first, he decided. After all, she was completely naked. He must find her something to wear.

Walter dug through his dresser and closet looking for something, anything, that might fit her. A handkerchief, maybe? But he knew he didn't have any. . .

Aha!

He found an old sock at the bottom of a drawer. Its mate had been lost in the wash long ago, and Walter had stuck it away in the hope that its missing mate might turn up someday. If he could fix the sock somehow, it just might work.

He held the sock up beside her to get a rough idea of the proper length. It was, of course, way too long, which could be remedied with a pair of scissors. The miniature girl stared first at Walter, then at the sock. She seemed curious, but quite unafraid.

Walter cut through the sock midway between the toe and heel. Then he snipped off the end of the toe and cut slits for her arms just below the hole he had made for her head. He held it out to her and she looked at it, then at him, and then she shook her head as if to say, "What's that?"

"That," Walter replied to her unasked question, "is what you are going to have to put on if you want to come with me. Mice can run around without any clothes on, but people can't. Here, I'll show you what to do."

He took a t-shirt from his drawer, removed his pajama top and pulled the t-shirt on over his head. Then once again he offered her the sock.

The miniature girl stuck her head through the hole in the toe, and then her arms appeared through the slits on the side. The dress, if you could call it that, fell halfway between her knees and feet and fit her about as well as a small tent. She accepted it with a shrug, but did not look very pleased.

Okay, Walter thought as he got dressed himself. That's one problem out of the way. Now, what am I going to do with her?

"I'll take you to Ivon's," he told her. The Genuine, Traditional Bulgarian Bagel Maker would know what to do. "You can stay in his shop while I go to work."

After all, he added to himself, Ivon and the old woman got me into this. They can doggone well help me get out.

That made two problems down and one to go. Walter was beginning to feel better. Now, how was he going to carry her?

He decided to let her ride in his shirt pocket. The former mouse did not object, in fact, she looked almost happy. Walter put on a jacket, which he could use to cover her if people got too close. But she would be all right as far as Ivon's.

He remembered again the old woman's words: "From now on, your life will never be boring."

She had certainly been right about that!

Walter Wampler set off down the street as nonchalantly as could be expected of a young man with a live miniature girl riding in his shirt pocket. Pomona Mona flashed by on her new Rollerblades, but she was so upset by Rancid's sudden relapse that she didn't notice Walter's passenger.

Ivon's was still crowded with breakfast customers. Walter sat at a small table in a dark corner and waited for the crowd to leave. The girl in his pocket began to wriggle. I hope she's housebroken, he thought with some alarm.

Ivon joined them as soon as the last breakfast customer left. His large, dark eyes grew even larger and darker as Walter took a five-inch girl wearing the toe end of an old sock from his pocket and set her on the table.

"A *kukla!*" Ivon wondered. "No!" he answered himself. "It is not a doll! It's alive, a tiny *gotino momiche!*"

"If that means a pretty girl, I agree," Walter said. "But what am I going to do? I can't take her to work with me, and I don't dare leave her at home with Rancid around!"

"I can keep her while you are at work," Ivon reassured him. "But how did this happen? Where did you find her?"

As quickly as he could, Walter told the story of rescuing the mouse from Rancid, feeding it some of the cheese by moonlight and then about his surprise when he opened the shoebox.

"Can she speak?" Ivon wondered.

"I don't know," Walter admitted. "I haven't asked her anything."

"Then do so," Ivon urged. "Be a gentleman. Offer her some coffee. Better sweeten it first."

"Uh, would you like some coffee, Little Fel. . ." I can't call her that, he realized. He began again. "Let me get you some coffee, uh, Girl, No, Miss." The girl nodded, but said nothing.

Walter poured sugar and cream into his cup, stirred, blew on it to cool it, then dipped out a teaspoonful and offered it to the miniature girl. She looked at it curiously, but made no move to taste it.

"It's okay," Walter reassured her and took a drink from the mug to prove it. "Try it. I think you'll like it."

The former mouse sniffed at the creamy coffee in the spoon. Then she lapped it with her tongue, jumped back, spat it out and made a noise that sounded like "Aah!"

"She doesn't like it," said a disappointed Walter.

"She's probably not used to anything hot," Ivon remarked. "Blow on it some more."

Walter dipped out another teaspoonful and blew on it until he was sure it was cool. The girl first tasted it carefully. Then she stuck her face into the spoon and lapped away greedily.

"Her table manners could use some work," Ivon commented, "but I'm glad my coffee passes the test."

"We ought to come up with a name for her," Walter suggested. "We can't keep calling her 'Girl' or 'Mouse' or 'Little Fella'."

"Indeed not!" Ivon agreed and thought for a moment. "How about *Mishka?* It means *mouse* in Bulgarian. We should also try to teach her to speak, since she can make sounds. If you don't mind, I'll work on that today, whenever I have time."

"Okay," Walter said, "but make sure it's English. Bulgarian won't do her much good in this country."

He picked the girl up and stroked her hair with his little finger. "Goodbye, Mishka," he told her. "I'll see you again this afternoon or tonight."

The girl blinked back and, for the first time, smiled.

Walter used his card to call the old woman from work. He heard the familiar ring and click, and then the machine came on.

"Hello, Walter," it said. "I can't come to the phone right now, but I'm certainly glad you called. You have another complication in your life now, but will it be good or bad? I suggest you go to the library and see what Professor Bagshott has to say about mouseweres. You'll find it most interesting."

Walter hung up and again heard the chonk of coins falling into the return tray. He wondered if the phone company suspected what the old woman was doing to them. They would not be very happy about her cards, he decided as he retrieved a handful of quarters.

116

After the lunch rush, Walter asked for and got some time off. He hurried to the library, stuck his card in the secret slot, and once more found himself in the little room that housed the Bagshott Collection of Unwritten Books. He took down the volume on weremice and glanced at the table of contents.

Chapter Five was titled "Mouseweres and Other Strange Variations." Sometime, Walter decided, I've got to take a few days and read the whole book. This page-at-a-time stuff is just not very efficient.

"Just as a human can become a weremouse by night," Professor Bagshott had written (or would have if he had gotten around to it), "so a mouse can become a mousewere by day. But this can only happen if the mouse is given the cheese by a human."

Now he tells me! Walter thought, and regretted that he had not taken the time to read the whole book. But he had not gotten around to it, which made him a bit like the professor.

"The mousewere is very small to begin with, and keeps its human form only between dawn and midday. However, with every feeding of the cheese, it will become larger and retain its human form longer. Unfortunately, it will also become a larger and larger mouse. This can lead to problems, since enchanted cheese is very hard to find and cannot be replaced."

"So what am I going to do with her?" Walter thought aloud. "I can't just abandon her. If she has to be human, then she ought to be full-size and full-time. But how much time and cheese will that take?"

He read on.

"The mousewere, according to the data I might have collected, continues to think and act like a human even after it returns to its mouse form. This becomes more noticeable as it continues to grow. However, it must be given the cheese every day, or else. . ."

And here Walter came to the end of the page. A glance at his watch told him it was time to get back to work. The "or else" — whatever it was — would have to wait for another day.

Meanwhile, the phone company was not going to wait for another day. "We've got trouble with one of our units at the big hotel," a supervisor told his crew. "It's making calls to a number that does not exist, it's losing cash, and yet it shows absolutely no signs of being tampered with. We've got to do some detective work and find out what's going on."

Officer Mulholand also thought about doing some detective work when he stopped off at Pomona Mona's for chili dogs later that night.

And in another part of town some very unpleasant people were doing some detective work, as well. Someone or something had destroyed very valuable property belonging to them, and they were not about to forget it!

It was late when Walter finally returned to Ivon's. "Your Mishka has become a mouse again," Ivon told him sadly. "It must have happened during the lunch hour."

"I know," Walter replied. "Where is she now?"

"Safe in the back watching television," Ivon said. "What do you want to do now?"

"Take her back home, give her some more cheese and see what happens," Walter decided.

"Just so," Ivon agreed and produced a cloth bag. "Put her in this. You might not want to carry a live mouse in your shirt. I've added some bagel crumbs she can munch on the way."

Mishka showed no sign of fear and jumped into the bag without any coaxing. Even so, Walter carried her very carefully, and opened the bag every few minutes to give her fresh air.

Officer Mulholand's squad car was parked in front of the boarding house again, and Walter caught the smell of chili dogs from the front porch. Pomona Mona had company again.

He crept quietly up to his room and let the mouse out of the bag. "There's no need to shut you up in the shoebox, Mishka," he said, "but stay here in the room. Rancid is prowling around out there somewhere, and you remember what he is like!"

The mouse shivered and nodded in agreement.

"I'll rinse out your sock and it'll be dry by morning," Walter added. "Uh, would you like some more cheese?"

The mouse nodded again and her tail twitched eagerly. Walter took the cheese from the refrigerator and studied it.

The sliver he had cut the night before was gone. He knew it would never be replaced. But the rest was as soft and as fresh as on the night when the old woman had given it to him.

He suddenly felt that he did not want to cut another slice, even though Mishka had to have it if she was to become more human. This was *his* cheese. Walter Wampler had never before been aware that he could be selfish, probably because he had never really had anything to be selfish about.

But now he had.

He knew that he could simply put the cheese back, and there was nothing the mouse could do about it. Mishka had no grounds for complaint. After all, if it hadn't been for him, she'd be well-digested cat food by now.

Then he felt ashamed. What had *he* done to deserve the cheese in the first place? Not very much. He took the knife and cut the cheese in half.

"This part's for me and that part's for you," he told Mishka. "But I have to give it to you just a bit at a time, because once you eat it, it's gone. Understand?"

Mishka sat up on her hind legs and nodded again.

He cut a slightly bigger sliver for Mishka out of her half, then put the cheese away. He felt a sudden tiredness creeping over him. "Time for humans like me to hit the sack," he told her. "Sleep or stay awake, but don't leave the room. Okay?"

Mishka nodded and began to nibble at the cheese.

Again Walter had strange dreams, though not as frightening as before. He awoke with a start as the early morning sun fell upon his face.

Mishka was awake and human again. Walter blinked and stared. She had doubled in size and was now about ten inches tall. She had put on the sock, but it was now nothing more than a shirt.

Walter sighed and reached for the scissors. He would have to sacrifice another sock. He took one from his least favorite pair and cut it close to the heel. He added slits for Mishka's arms and head and handed it over.

Mishka took off the old sock and put on the new one, which covered her down to the knees. She looked at it and frowned.

Walter sensed that she was unhappy and knew she was trying to think of something. But what?

Suddenly Mishka picked up the old sock and put it on over the new one. "That's right!" Walter thought aloud. "She can see colors now!" The two socks blended nicely, but Mishka looked at the ragged edges and frowned.

Walter took the scissors and trimmed the old sock even with Mishka's waist. Then he evened the edge on the new sock as best he could. Mishka smiled and looked pleased.

"Wait a minute!" Walter cried. "If I can find it. . ."

He began pawing through his closet again. Someone, sometime had left an old piece of ribbon among the junk that naturally gathers at the bottom of a closet. He had always meant to clean it out, but now he was glad he hadn't.

He found it and cut off a small piece. It was bright red and, when he wound it twice around Mishka's waist and tied it in a bow, it made her outfit look almost pretty.

"That's the best I can do for now," he told her. "When you get bigger, I can get you some real clothes."

Mishka smiled and held out her arms to be picked up. As Walter placed her in the bag — for she was now too big for his pocket — she pointed to the sock dress and very carefully said, "Good!"

Or at least, that's what it sounded like.

CHAPTER THIRTEEN

Something Fishy

"But this is amazing!" cried Ivon as he stared at the newer and larger edition of Mishka. "Why, at this rate she could be a full-size young lady in about a week!"

"And in two weeks she could start at center for the Boston Celtics!" Walter added. "But what do I do with her now?"

Mishka seemed to enjoy being the center of attention. She stood before a mirror Ivon had propped on one of his back tables, studying her new outfit and muttering "Good!" over and over.

"Very good!" Walter agreed.

"Very good!" Mishka repeated carefully.

"She has a fine ear for language," Ivon observed. "In another day or two, she will be speaking in sentences."

Walter nodded. He was happy at Mishka's progress, yet at the same time he worried over the problems it caused. How was he going to keep her hidden as she got bigger and bigger? It might be several days before she could grow large enough to be safe from Rancid. What could he do with her in the meantime? And what was she going to wear? Another day's growth like today's and she would be too big for any of his socks, yet still way too small for regular clothes.

And what was going to happen at night? Would she become a bigger and bigger mouse as well? How would he keep her hidden then?

This was all very new to Walter. He had never had to worry about anyone else before. He had never been responsible for anyone besides himself. He wasn't sure if he liked it or not.

"Ah! You see the problems ahead," said Ivon, reading his mind. "But look at the good points too. She might become just the girl for you, Walter. After all, you would be the only couple in the world who knew what it was like to be mice!"

"I hadn't thought of it that way," Walter admitted.

"Well, do think about it," Ivon urged. "You have shown yourself able to solve problems before. Put your mind to this one and see what you can do. You really are a remarkable person, Walter, as well as a remarkable mouse!"

Walter thought about that on his way to work. A remarkable person? He had always considered himself the most unremarkable person in the world. But yes, he did feel bolder now, more confident and able to cope with things. What was causing it? Could it be the cheese he was now eating every morning at breakfast?

The cheese reminded him of Mishka again. At the rate she was growing, she would need bigger and bigger slices from her half. What would he do when her half was gone?

Maxim-Rene was having a fit at the restaurant. By mistake two big luncheons had been scheduled for the same time. Both dining rooms were packed. Walter and the other waiters were kept on the run, while Maxim-Rene and his assistants prepared and set out plates like a squad of hyperactive robots.

Walter had just started for the banquet rooms with a large tray full of plates, when he suddenly stopped. Something did not seem right. He wrinkled his nose and sniffed like he had as a mouse. Yes, something was wrong. Not terribly wrong — hardly noticeable — but wrong. He put down the tray and checked each plate. They all looked identical, but one smelled just a bit different.

Walter quickly served out the others, then took the suspect plate back to the kitchen. "I may be imagining things," he told Maxim-Rene, "but I don't think we ought to serve this one."

Maxim-Rene took the plate, sniffed once, and then exclaimed, "*Mille Tonnerres! C'est terrible!*" Walter knew then he was right. The chef only spoke French when something was very, very good or very, very bad.

"Walter, how did you notice this?" Maxim-Rene demanded.

"The smell, I think," Walter replied. "Somehow, it wasn't quite right." He hesitated. "Did I make a mistake?"

"No! You were correct!" the chef answered. "This fish has spoiled. Not much, perhaps, but enough to make someone very sick. The *sauce aux oignon* almost masks it. We have two luncheons and four different main courses. There was no time for me to check everything personally."

Maxim-Rene clapped his hands and shouted, "*Attendez!*" Everyone — cooks, waiters, waitresses, busboys — snapped to attention. "Serve no more of the fish!" the chef ordered. "Bring all the plates to me. I will inspect each one. Walter, I have a special job for you!"

The old Walter would have trembled at being singled out by the great Maxim-Rene, but this morning he listened calmly as the chef said, "Go through the dining room and check every one of the fish plates. Be as quick and as quiet as possible. But if you smell one that seems wrong, remove it! No matter what!"

Walter saluted and grabbed a pitcher of water. It was a sudden inspiration, something else he was not used to. "I'll use this as an excuse to get close," he said.

Maxim-Rene nodded his approval and Walter was off. He circulated through the dining room, pretending to fill water glasses while he checked for the smell of fish that was not quite right. He found only one. It had just been served and the customer, busily talking with his friends, had not yet touched it. He was just about to start when Walter, leaning over to fill his glass, appeared to slip and sloshed water all over the plate.

"Oh! I'm terribly sorry!" Walter cried as he whisked the plate right out from under the diner's fork. "I'll bring you another one immediately!"

He hurried back to the kitchen. "What about this one?" he asked Maxim-Rene. "I didn't notice any others."

The great chef checked the plate and swore softly in French. "Right again, Walter!" he said. "I myself found two more. I hope that is all. *Juste ciel!* Thank heaven we had just begun to serve when you noticed it!"

"How bad are they?" Walter asked. "How could it happen?"

"It would not be fatal," said Maxim-Rene, "but four people would have been very sick!" His eyes narrowed. "Walter, this could not have happened by accident. Something is, indeed, wrong here!"

Walter did not have time to worry about it. The two groups kept him and the other waiters busy for more than an hour. Finally, after the last dirty plate had been removed, Maxim-Rene summoned Walter to his office.

"Do not tell the others," the chef said, "but what happened today was deliberate. Someone mixed four spoiled fish in with the fresh ones. It was one of my assistants who betrayed us."

"But why?" Walter asked. "Why would someone want to make people sick in a place where he worked?"

"To discredit the restaurant and me," said Maxim-Rene. "I discovered who it was. He had been bribed by one of my rivals. I have fired him, of course." He shuffled some papers, then suddenly looked up at Walter. "So now there is an opening for an assistant chef. Do you want the job?"

"Me? A chef?" asked a dumbfounded Walter.

"Pourquoi pas?" answered Maxim-Rene. "Why not? You have shown me that you have the instincts. The rest I can teach you. We can start tomorrow, if you are willing. Of course, it will mean another raise."

Walter the chef, a pupil of the great Maxim-Rene! It was an honor he had not even dared dream about, and now it was his for the taking! All because he had been sharp enough to notice something wrong with the fish beneath the onion sauce. What had given him that ability? His experience as a mouse? Perhaps the cheese?

The cheese made him think of Mishka again, and for some reason that made him nervous. So he took time on his break to call the old woman once more.

"Hello, Walter," said the familiar voice. "I can't come to the phone right now, but I'm glad you called. Congratulations on your new job! You'll do well at it. As for your other problem, check out some of the stores around where you work, and I think you'll find an answer. Better find another phone to call me on in the future. The telephone company is beginning to get suspicious!"

Walter hung up and heard a whole series of chonks as quarters tumbled into the tray. He was tempted to call again just to see how many coins he could gather, but this time he heeded the old woman's warning. Someone from the phone company was bound to start checking.

Walter knew very little about the downtown area, except that it was full of big stores and malls that sold things that were far too expensive for him to buy. Or at least, they had been up to now. So, with an hour to spare and a pocket full of quarters, Walter Wampler went exploring.

He found what he needed in one of the malls, in a shop called Dolls 'N You. It carried all types and sizes of dolls and a large selection of doll clothes. A large woman with grey hair — looking a bit like an overgrown, elderly doll herself — asked if she could help him.

"I'm, uh, looking for some doll clothes," Walter explained. "It's, uh, for my niece. A. . . a birthday present."

"Why don't you get her another doll?" the doll woman asked. "We have some very nice ones on sale."

"Uh, no," Walter replied. "She, uh, has a whole bunch of them already. I. . . I mean. . . she doesn't need any more. She just wants some new things for them."

"Well, we can certainly fix you up with that," the doll woman replied. "How large are her dolls?"

Walter was stumped. How big would Mishka be tomorrow morning? And how much bigger still on the morning after that? He ought to get several different sizes. He hoped his supply of quarters would be enough to cover it.

Walter finally settled on three outfits that looked like they would fit someone ranging from a bit over one foot to a bit over two feet in height. It took all his quarters, and Walter hoped that Mishka would cooperate by growing at the proper rate.

The doll lady was puzzled. "Are you sure you have the right sizes?" she asked. "I can't give you a refund on these. Could you have your niece bring the dolls in and we could measure them to be sure?"

"I, uh, don't think that would work very well," Walter said.

It was late by the time Walter finished that evening. Two large banquets had been scheduled, and the staff was one man short after Maxim-Rene had fired the employee who had sabotaged the fish. Walter scarcely had time to think about his promotion or Mishka or what size or form she might be by now.

But the evening finally ended, and Walter saw Cindy just as he was getting ready to leave. "Congratulations on your new job!" she told him.

"How did you know about it?" Walter asked.

"Nobody can keep a secret around here," Cindy replied. "We all know how you saved the day. Hey, we could have been closed down if those people had gotten sick!"

She sounded relieved and genuinely grateful, but Walter was a little disturbed about her claim that nobody in the building could keep a secret. He would have to be very careful.

"Let me walk you home," he said. "We'll stop in at Ivon's for a bagel."

Cindy smiled but shook her head. "Can't. I'm meeting someone later on. Maybe some other time."

"Okay," Walter replied. He was surprised that the turn-down did not bother him that much. He hurried to Ivon's and got there just as his last customer was leaving.

"How is she?" he asked.

"She is a mouse once again, but this time a much bigger mouse," Ivon replied. "And her transformation came about two hours later today."

Mishka was indeed bigger, close to the size of a rat now. She sat up on her hind legs and wriggled her snout as if to say, "Glad to see you again!"

"I had her watch television all morning," Ivon said. "I kept it on the educational channel. I don't think we want her learning English from commercials. She kept watching after she became a mouse again. It will be interesting to see tomorrow how far she has progressed."

"And how much she has grown," Walter added, and told Ivon about the doll clothes and his promotion.

"I am not surprised," Ivon remarked. "I said you were a remarkable person, Walter. And I think Mishka will be a remarkable person too."

Mishka rode home in the bag once again, nibbling on bagel crumbs. Officer Mulholand's squad car was parked in front of Pomona Mona's house again, and Walter could smell the chili dogs as he climbed the stairs to his room.

Another thought troubled him. Was Mulholand really interested in his landlady? Or was he using her as an excuse to investigate the house and the people who lived there? If so, then neither Walter nor Mishka could ever be safe.

It was definitely time to move. With the raise and his new job, he could afford something better.

"I'll give notice and start looking for another place tomorrow," he told Mishka as he cut her a larger slice of cheese. Her half would soon be gone at this rate. "We'll find a place with no snoopy policemen, and no cats! Does that sound good?"

The mouse nodded and began to nibble the cheese.

CHAPTER FOURTEEN

The Library Smuggler

Mishka grew at a steady rate of about four inches per day. Each set of doll clothes fit her, but only once. By the end of the week, Walter was back at Dolls 'N You, searching for larger sizes. The doll lady looked at him suspiciously.

"Didn't your niece like the others?" she asked.

"Yes, but she's bigger now," Walter replied. "I mean, they're bigger now. That is, she's gone in for bigger dolls. Never mind, it's rather complicated."

But Walter could find only two larger sizes. After Mishka passed three feet, he would have to look elsewhere.

Mishka's human phase now lasted from dawn through late afternoon, but Walter's new job kept him busy all day. He would drop off a small human at Ivon's in the morning and collect a very large mouse at night. She was slowly learning to speak.

At least she was reaching a size where she would be safe from Rancid. She was also getting harder and harder to transport. Walter carried her in his backpack now, though even that wouldn't work much longer.

Walter also knew that he was asking a lot of Ivon. How much longer would the Genuine, Traditional Bulgarian Bagel Maker be willing to run a day care center for mouseweres? Hopefully, Mishka would soon be large enough to pass as an ordinary girl, and she would keep her human form all day.

If the cheese lasted, that is.

Walter searched through the hotel and found another phone to use to call the old woman. He needed both advice and change. Mishka had to have new clothes again, and her half of the cheese would run out that very night.

"Hello, Walter," said the familiar voice. "I can't come to the phone right now, but I'm glad you called. You need to go farther to find a safe phone, but never mind that for now. Go to a department store and check out children's clothing. Get her something she can grow into."

Walter thought, how much growing? The machine picked up on his thought, as if it had read his mind.

"Remember, she will continue to grow as long as she gets the cheese, but only for as long as she gets the cheese. Once you stop giving it to her, that's it. Oh yes, her ability to use the language could improve if you take her to the library and let her study a book the professor might have written. It would have been called *English for Non Humans*, a very helpful book for mice and other creatures."

The machine clicked off. Walter drew out his card and listened to the coins and they chonked into the return tray.

That night he walked home with a twenty-pound mouse in his backpack. Rancid was nowhere to be seen. Neither was Officer Mulholand. But Pomona Mona met him at the front door.

"What are you carrying around with you these days?" she asked him.

"Why, a twenty-pound mouse that I'm training to hunt down your cat," Walter answered with an innocent smile.

"Walter, don't joke about such things!" Pomona Mona complained. "Old Jammer's got the whim-whams something awful! Do you really think there's something after him?"

Walter shrugged, smiled and hurried on up to his room. Sometimes the truth was just as effective as a lie, and even more unbelievable.

But Pomona Mona remembered his words, and they started her thinking.

The next morning Walter found that a three-foot Mishka would no longer fit in his backpack. So he emptied out his laundry bag and Mishka, dressed in the last and largest doll clothes he had been able to find, climbed in.

"Gotta do the wash this morning," he explained to Pomona Mona as he strolled out the front door.

"Awful lumpy laundry," his landlady observed. "Why, I could swear I saw it wriggle! Must need washing *real* bad! Walter?" she added, "are you sure you want to move out?" Her voice sounded almost sad. "You've changed so much in the last couple of months. You're not a little pup anymore."

Walter looked embarrassed and muttered something about his new job and new responsibilities. Pomona Mona had terrified him until he had met the old woman. Now he could see her as a comic, lonely and almost likable older lady. He found himself hoping that Officer Mulholand liked her for more than her chili dogs.

"You've grown too," Pomona Mona observed.

It was true. Walter was an inch or so taller and a good ten pounds heavier. He was still small, but no one would mistake him for a boy anymore.

He dropped Mishka off with Ivon and said, "I'll pick her up again right after lunch. We need to go to the library."

"Good!" Ivon agreed. Walter sensed that he understood.

Walter knew he faced some problems, but he felt he could handle them. The first was how to smuggle Mishka into and then out of the library. The bold way is the best way, he decided.

He took a large empty carton from the hotel kitchen, wrote Special Delivery on the side in bold letters, then asked for an hour off and hurried back to Ivon's. Mishka, still human, climbed into the carton and they went to the library.

The library had a security system, but only people coming out were checked. Walter made his way in with no trouble, used his card to get into the Bagshott Room, and then wondered what to do next.

He couldn't take the time to read to her, especially if the book was like the professor's other unwritten works. Mishka was a remarkable girl, as well as a remarkable mouse. But could she learn to read all by herself?

He quickly found the book and scanned the table of contents. One chapter was headed, "A Mouse-English Dictionary" and took up more than fifty pages. He turned to that chapter and saw columns of words on one side of the page and scratches that looked like they had been made by mouse paws on the other.

Mishka could handle this by herself, he realized, but it would take her all day and all night. Could he leave her alone that long? And what about the cheese?

Walter did have some cheese he had cut for himself as an afternoon snack. He checked the carton and discovered that Ivon had slipped in some bagels. That took care of food, but what about her other needs?

He leaned against one wall to think. The wall moved. Walter pushed harder and saw that the wall opened into a tiny bathroom, complete with a sink and running water. A glass and a bowl were set out on the sink, and Walter filled them both.

"You should be all right until tomorrow," he said. "Study hard and don't eat the cheese until you become a mouse." He hesitated. Some things were embarrassing, but they had to be said. Walter took a deep breath and continued.

"Better take all your clothes off as soon as I leave," he said. "They might still fit in the morning, but not if you transform in them. I'll bring some others when I come back, just in case. Uh, one more thing. . ."

Mishka looked at him expectantly. Walter blushed.

"Use that," he said, pointing to the toilet, "whether you're human or mouse. People have this thing about getting rid of their messes, and whoever comes in here next will appreciate it."

Mishka nodded understanding, and Walter felt relieved. "I'll knock three times before I use my card," he said, and demonstrated. "Do you think you'll be all right?"

Mishka carefully answered, "Yes," and then began to read.

Walter got out of the library with no trouble. People leaving empty-handed were not even noticed. Tomorrow would be another matter.

Again he regretted the loss of the cheese. Yes, he could cut himself some more, but that one piece was gone for good. His half was no longer a half, and it would keep getting smaller as Mishka kept getting bigger.

"Unless you stop giving it to her," a part of him said.

Walter tried to shake the thought out of his head, but it would not quite go away.

Maxim-Rene kept him busy all afternoon to make up for the lost hour, but as soon as the evening banquet was prepared, he was free. He quickly ran over to the mall, which included a large department store. Walter made his way to children's clothing and pondered his choices.

This again was something new.

He selected a pair of blue pants with an elastic waistband, a white pullover shirt with long sleeves and a pair of heavy socks that could double as moccasins. He looked at the price tags and realized that underwear and shoes would have to wait.

While Walter was buying clothes, Officer Mulholand was having chili dogs with Pomona Mona. "Y'know, I just can't figure that Walter out," Pomona Mona said as she dished him up a plate.

"How so?" Mulholand asked.

"Last night he came home with his backpack full to busting," she said. "When I asked what was in it, he told me it was a twenty-pound mouse he was training to hunt down ol' Jammer. Then this morning he left with a big laundry bag. He *said* it was his wash, but I could swear it was something alive!"

Mulholland was suddenly very interested. "Is the backpack still up in his room?" he asked. "Would you just happen to have a key?"

When Walter returned, his room was just as he had left it. The backpack hung on the back of his chair, exactly where he had placed it the night before. He had no way of knowing that the inside had been carefully cleaned, and that certain crumbs and hairs were being analyzed down at the police lab.

Walter also had no way of knowing why Cindy felt sad. "Poor Walter," she sighed as she sat at a table. "I hope he's not feeling too bad because I won't go out with him. He's a wonderful person, but not quite as wonderful as you," she added. "Do you think he'll be all right?"

"I think he may be recovering already," Ivon replied, and sliced another bagel for her. And as he sliced, he sang her the second verse of his new traditional bagel folk song:

"Serve 'em hot with lots of cream cheese!

Don't let 'em cool and don't let 'em freeze!

They're always guaranteed to please, But!

The life of a bagel is short-o,

The life of a bagel is short!"

"What a poet!" Cindy sighed.

The next morning was Walter's day off. He slept in and waited until midmorning before walking to the library with the package of clothes. Once again he had no trouble getting in, and he suddenly saw how he could get Mishka out.

He knocked three times, then used his card to open the wall. Mishka was human again, and had added another four inches to her height. The doll dress was now way too short and way too tight. How she had ever managed to get it back on was a mystery.

"Walter!" she cried as soon as he closed the wall. "It's so good to see you again! I'm afraid I've grown some more," she said. "I don't think this dress is going to work."

"Try these," Walter said, and handed her the package. He was amazed at how well she could speak. The professor might have written a very good book, if he had ever gotten around to it.

The pants were far too long, and the shirt was almost a dress in itself. But that was what Walter wanted. At least they might last a few days that way. He helped her into them, then folded up the sleeves and pant legs until her hands and feet were visible. Mishka did not like the socks.

"Can't I just go barefoot?" she asked. "It doesn't feel right having things on my feet!"

"Not til we get out of here," Walter told her.

"How are we getting out?" Mishka asked. "I don't think I'll fit in that carton anymore."

"We won't have to use it," Walter explained. "There's a story hour for small children going on now. It ends in a few minutes. You're about the right size, although you have a grownup's face. I'll carry you out on my shoulder, and we'll be part of the group."

"Why do you want to carry me?" Mishka asked.

"You don't really look or walk or sound like someone who is four or five," Walter explained. "And if you seem to be asleep, no one will talk to you, and it won't seem strange that you don't have shoes on. And we can drape your hair over your face to hide it too."

"Don't I look nice?" Mishka protested. She was learning human feelings very fast.

"You look great!" Walter assured her. "But little girls are cute and you're, well, beautiful! Believe me, there is a difference!"

"I can see being a human won't be easy," Mishka sighed.

"Hey!" Walter said. "I still have trouble with it, and I've been one all my life."

So Walter draped Mishka over his shoulder and prepared to leave the Bagshott Room. "Close your eyes, make a fist, put your thumb in your mouth and suck on it," he advised. "That's what sleepy little kids do."

"You humans are strange!" Mishka commented.

"*We* humans," Walter corrected. "You're one of us now, at least for the moment."

Walter and Mishka mingled with the crowd leaving the story session. Several small children were also being carried, so Mishka didn't really stand out. Walter had not counted on being about the only *man* present.

"You look so young to be a daddy!" exclaimed an older woman with three grandchildren in tow. "It's so nice to see daddies come to our programs! Did your little girl enjoy it?"

Walter smiled, nodded and hurried on.

He decided to head straight for Ivon's and to carry Mishka all the way. He suddenly realized he was happy about it. He had never really held anyone, protected anyone or been responsible for anyone before. He liked it.

Mishka really was asleep. She still had her thumb in her mouth, but that was fine with him. It felt good to carry someone. He could not remember being carried himself. Mishka seemed to like it. He did not want to put her down.

Walter was so happy that he did not notice three people watching him. One wore the uniform of the telephone company and was sitting in an official telephone company truck. He looked serious, but not really mean.

The other two looked mean. Their names were Honky and Tonk, and they watched through smoked glasses behind tinted windows in a big black car. Officer Mulholand was not the only person to discover large tracks and to hear stories about a giant mouse that seemed to disappear at dawn.

Ever since that night in the woods by the golf course, some very unpleasant people had been very angry. And Honky and Tonk happened to work for them.

CHAPTER FIFTEEN

So Much to Learn

"What's it like to be a mouse?" Walter asked Mishka a couple of hours later. "I mean, a real mouse, all the way from birth. I'm just learning, and there's still so much I don't know."

"It's not what you humans call fun," Mishka answered.

"*We* humans," Walter reminded her again. "You're human for more than half the day now, and you'll soon be full-size." A sudden thought troubled him. "Do you like being human?" he asked. "Are you sorry I gave you the cheese?"

"If it wasn't for you, I'd be gone," she replied.

"That's not what I mean." Walter began.

"Walter," she interrupted. "How long do humans live?"

"Seventy years. Sometimes eighty. Sometimes more. Sometimes less," Walter answered. "It sort of depends on a lot of things."

"I think I understand what a year is," Mishka said. "It was in one of the professor's books. If I've got it right, then mice are lucky to live more than two. Most of us don't get much more than one. Some of us not even that."

"Why is that?" Walter asked.

"Because we are meant to be food," Mishka answered simply.

They sat at one of Ivon's back tables and sipped coffee while they talked. Mishka had developed a liking for coffee, as long as it contained plenty of sugar and cream. In the background they could hear Ivon humming and whistling as he prepared a fresh batch of bagels. Otherwise, the shop was empty.

"I don't think you realize how many enemies a mouse — I mean, a real mouse — has," Mishka continued. "Dogs, cats, hawks, owls, snakes, even rats will kill us whenever they can. And humans can be the worst of all!"

"Then why do you stay around us?" Walter asked.

"Because we need food and shelter too," Mishka answered. "Your houses are warm, and there are always crumbs and bits of this and that. We take the chance that we'll live long enough to have at least one litter. If you're a female, that's all you want out of life, to live long enough to have a litter or two."

"Did you?" Walter asked, and then was embarrassed and angry with himself for asking her.

But the question didn't seem to bother Mishka. She simply shook her head, "No. In another one or two of your weeks, I would have been ready, if I could have found a mate. But I was the last of my litter, and my mother was gone too."

"What happened to them?" Walter asked.

"There were five of us," Mishka replied. "The cat got two. An owl got one. A trap got one and my mother was poisoned."

There was no sign of grief on her face.

"What about your father?" Walter asked.

"I never saw him. I think the cat got him too. But mouse fathers don't care for their babies. Sometimes they kill them."

Walter shuddered. Maybe being an orphan raised in foster care wasn't so bad after all.

"It's a short, tough, mean life," Mishka told him. "You want to eat before you get eaten and have others before something gets you. That's about all there is to it. Do you think I should be sorry to leave it?"

"I guess not," Walter admitted.

"But I need to know more about being human," Mishka said. "Can you take me back to that room again? I feel safe in there, and there is still so much for me to learn."

Great idea, Walter decided. If she stayed in the Bagshott Room for two or three days, she would grow to almost full human size and keep her human form until late evening. It would also give him time to find another place to live.

"I'll take you there tomorrow night after work," he said. "By then you'll be human until early evening. Ivon can supply you with bagels and I'll. . . give you some more cheese."

Those last words came out with difficulty. Two or three more days would take just about all of the cheese. And once it was gone, there would be no more.

Ivon gave Walter a sympathetic look and promised to supply the bagels. "It is nothing," he said. "Far better she should spend her time reading good books, even ones that were never written, than watching the tube all day."

And again Walter wondered how much Ivon knew.

Mishka stood up on her chair, leaned over and kissed Walter on the cheek. "The professor says this is what people do when they care for each other," she remarked. "It feels strange. On the television, they do this all the time. They must all care a great deal for each other."

"That's one way to look at it," Walter admitted.

By the next afternoon Mishka had grown another four inches. Her clothes were still big, but not by much. In one more day they would fit her just right. In two more days they would be small, but they still might fit. In three more days. . . .

In three more days, Walter suddenly realized, he would be completely out of cheese.

It was early evening when they walked into the library. Mishka, still human, wore a pair of beat-up children's shoes that Walter had scrounged at a Salvation Army store. She still hated to wear anything on her feet, but had promised to keep the shoes on until they reached the Bagshott Room.

The evening was warm and the library nearly deserted. They made their way past the 900's, and Walter used his card to open the wall. Mishka kept her head turned and did not look at the card. Walter had to admit that she followed instructions better than anyone he knew, including himself.

Walter left her in the Bagshott Room with cheese and bagels and a collection of books that had never been written. His cheek tingled where she had kissed him goodbye. Once again he did not notice the man in the official telephone company truck.

But two other men did.

The black car with the tinted windows followed the truck that followed Walter back to Ivon's. The truck turned onto another street one block from the *sladkarnitsa,* but the car did not.

"Want to take him now?" Honky asked.

"Why not?" Tonk answered.

The car began to speed up, then suddenly slowed. Officer Mulholand had just parked in front of Ivon's, and was watching Walter approach.

Honky swore under his breath. "The whole world must be watching this guy!" he complained.

"Never mind," said Tonk. "He's the one we want. We'll hit him tomorrow or the next day."

From the look in his eye and the tone of his voice, he had more in mind than a tap on the shoulder.

Walter was unaware that Officer Mulholand had probably just saved his life. So was Officer Mulholand. They met right at Ivon's front door and eyed each other cautiously, like two boxers, each waiting for the other to make a move. Finally Mulholand said, "Walter, I need your help."

"How?" Walter asked.

"Something strange is going on, and you know something about it. I'm not sure what it is, but you are."

"What am I supposed to be sure of?" Walter asked. He hated to lie, but answering a question with another question wasn't exactly lying, not quite.

"What do you know about mice?" Mulholand asked.

"What is there to know?" Walter again answered with another question.

"Cut the comedy, Walter. I'm talking about big mice, *real* big mice! Mice that can terrorize cats. Mice that can dig great big tunnels under fences and dance on the hoods of cars. Mice that leave huge pawprints in odd places. Mice that seem to disappear into thin air. Mice that sometimes wear blue pajamas."

"Blue pajamas?" Walter asked again.

"*Faded* blue pajamas," Mulholand added. Mice that also leave hairs in backpacks. *Your* backpack, Walter!"

"Are you accusing me of carrying mice in my backpack?" Walter asked. "I didn't even know it was against the law."

"It isn't," Mulholand admitted. "But the hair samples we found would have to come from a mouse the size of. . ." Mulholand paused to check his notes ". . . a woodchuck or even a beaver."

"That would be a pretty big mouse," Walter agreed.

"But I think there's an even bigger mouse," Mulholland replied. "One that's almost your size, Walter. And the problem for you is that I'm not the only one who thinks so."

"What do you mean?" Walter asked as innocently as he could. "Who else believes in this mouse, or mice?"

"Organized crime," Mulholland answered. "Two kids who saw it have been talking. So have some people who found its pawprints. Apparently this mouse dug up and destroyed a stash of illegal drugs, but it forgot to wipe out all its tracks. I understand there's a contract out on it, and I'm not talking about a personal appearance contract either!"

"But what does that have to do with me?" Walter asked. "As you can see, I'm not a mouse."

"No," Mulholland said, "but you know something about it. I know that much. And if I know that much, others probably do too. Are you sure you don't want to talk about it?"

For one instant Walter was ready to spill everything. He would tell Mulholand all about the old woman, the cheese, the card, the Bagshott Room, Mishka and everything.

But then, he realized, what would happen to her? She still needed a couple more days to grow to full size. If something happened and he wasn't there to give her the cheese, she would never become fully human.

"I can't tell you anything now," Walter said with real sadness in his voice. "Maybe in a few days. . . ."

"I figured as much," Mulholand replied. "I'll try to watch out for you the best I can. Don't make it too hard for me."

He left and Walter was alone with Ivon. *"Jivotut ne e lessen,* Walter," the Genuine, Traditional Bulgarian Bagel Maker said. "Believe me, life is never easy!"

When Walter let himself into the Bagshott Room after work the next day, Mishka had grown another four inches. She was now the size of a large ten-year-old, and the clothes, except for the shoes, fit her perfectly.

"How are you coming with your studies?" Walter asked.

Mishka shook her head. "There is so much to learn about being a human," she said. "I never realized you spoke different languages. Doesn't that confuse things?"

"Sometimes," Walter admitted.

"And all these things you invent to hurt each other! Why don't you just use claws and teeth like. . ." She paused and shook her head again. "I was about to say 'us'. But I guess I'm one of you now."

She did not seem all that happy about it.

"Mishka," Walter said as gently as he could, "I know we humans can do bad things. But we can be good too. You'll see."

"That's another thing for me to learn," Mishka replied. "Animals aren't good or bad, they just *are*. The cat tried to kill me because he was a cat and that's what cats do. I don't hate him for it."

It was Walter's turn to shake his head. Mishka was going to need protection, even after she became fully human. He took the cheese from his pocket and handed it to her.

"Is that the last piece?" she asked.

"No," he said, "there's still one more. Ivon sent some more bagels too. Will you be all right for another day?"

"I think so," she said. "I have all I need, but could you leave your watch with me?"

"Sure," Walter answered, "but why?"

"I want to see just how long I remain human," she replied.

Again Walter felt a twinge of selfishness. The watch was the first real present he had ever received. It hurt to hand it over, even for just one day. But he knew he would do just about anything for Mishka.

As Walter left the library, the man from the Telephone Company stopped him on the steps. "Can you come with me?" he said. "I'll drive you back to that bagel shop, but I need to talk with you."

Walter tried his best to look puzzled. "What's all this about?" he asked, hoping that he sounded genuine.

"Someone has been using unauthorized credit cards to rip off the telephone company," he said. "Cheating the telephone company is like cheating the government. It's cheating everybody!"

"But why are you telling me this?" Walter asked. He had a bit of trouble with the comparison.

"Because many of the calls have been coming from the hotel where you work, and your boss says you're his sharpest employee. Will you help us get to the bottom of this? There could be a medal in it for you!"

The telephone company giving medals? Walter sat back, puzzled but relieved. "I'll do what I can," he said.

But if Walter was relieved, Honky and Tonk were not. "That guy leads a charmed life!" Honky murmured from behind the tinted windows in the black car. "We missed him again!"

"Never mind," said Tonk. "He comes to this library almost every day. We'll get him next time!"

"Why not tonight at his house?" Honky asked.

"No," Tonk answered. "That cop hangs around there too much. We can afford to wait one more day."

"Wonder what he does in there?" Honky muttered. "Whatever it is, he'd better finish it up tomorrow, 'cause that's about all the time he's got!"

Early the next morning, Walter put the last piece of cheese in his pocket and started for work. He had not slept well. Part of him kept coming up with reasons for keeping the cheese for himself, and then another part of him would come up with reasons for giving it to Mishka.

Finally the giving side won out. That last piece would bring Mishka right up to his own height, and then. . . .

He was not sure what he would do then.

It was late when Walter got off that night. Two banquets and a sick waiter had forced him to work overtime. Luckily, this was also the night that the library stayed open late. If he ran all the way, he just might make it.

Walter ducked out of the back of the hotel and ran. He was nearly out of breath when he took the library steps two at a time and shot through the main door before Honky and Tonk could react.

"Follow him!" Honky hissed. "He's not gonna get away from us this time!"

The two hit men just caught a glimpse of Walter as he ducked down one of the aisles. "Relax!" Tonk said. "We've got him now. There's no exit that way. Take your time and remember, we gotta make him talk before we hit him!"

Honky and Tonk slowed to a walk, pretending to look at book titles as they closed in on their quarry. But by the time they reached the 900's, Walter had disappeared into the Bagshott Room.

"Where did he go?" Honky fumed. "That guy vanishes like a spook! I don't like this one, Tonk. Something's wrong!"

Tonk scratched his head. "There's no way he could double back past us," he decided, "and there's no way out up ahead. He must have ducked into some kinda hiding place. We'll wait. He's gonna hafta come out sometime. And when he does. . . ."

Mishka was now five feet tall. The top of her head was level with Walter's nose, and her clothes barely fit. One last piece of cheese and they would be the same height. Walter fought down his selfishness and handed it over.

Mishka shook her head and handed it back.

"Don't you want it?" Walter asked. Mishka shook her head again.

"No," she said. "You keep it."

"But. . ."

"I was human til midnight last night. I'm almost your size now. That's enough. I can't take the last piece from you. It wouldn't be what you call right. Let's go!"

Walter took his watch back and pocketed the cheese. "That was an even better present than the watch," he said as he opened the wall and closed it behind them. "Now all I need to do is find a new place for us to live. Then nothing will ever be able to bother us!"

"I wouldn't bet on it!" Honky said as he pointed a very large pistol straight at Walter's heart.

CHAPTER SIXTEEN

A Gift Freely Given

"Who are you?" Walter asked, his voice barely more than a whisper. He had never stared down the muzzle of a gun before, at least never as a human. But what could he do? He felt utterly helpless. It was worse than the first time he had transformed into a mouse.

"No," said Honky. "That's not the way it works. *We* ask the questions. *You* answer them!"

"What questions? I've never seen you before!" Walter protested, though he had a sudden, sinking feeling that maybe he had, in a grove of trees on a golf course one night!

"We want to know about a mouse," Tonk informed him.

"A mouse?" Walter asked again. "Why ask me that? You're in the library. Look it up. I think it's under natural history."

"Nice try, but it won't work," Honky replied with a smile that Walter found even more frightening than a scowl. This place is closed and we're the only ones here. Tonk and I can take all night, but you won't last that long. They never do!"

"Suppose I can't answer you?" Walter persisted.

"Then we'll shoot you," Tonk told him.

"And if I do answer them? Or at least, if I try?"

"We'll still shoot you," Honky replied. "But we'll be a lot nicer about it!"

Walter made a decision. "I'll tell you anything you want to know, *if* you'll let her go," he said, indicating Mishka.

"Nope," said Tonk. "She's in it with you. She's seen us. She gets it too. That's the way it works. Sorry."

He did not sound sorry at all.

Walter realized that they were trapped. There was no way to run and no place to hide. Their only hope lay in his ability to outthink and outwit these two hoods. He thought as hard as he could and, beneath and behind his fear, he saw the glimmering of an idea.

"The answer is in there," he said, pointing to the wall they had just come through. "But you'll have to come in with us."

"Lead the way," said Honky. "But don't try anything cute. I get very angry when people try things. And when I'm angry, I'm not a very nice person!"

I can believe that, Walter thought as he took the card from his pocket. He knew that he had sacrificed the card by letting them see it. But if he could lure them into the Bagshott Room, then perhaps Mishka and he stood a chance of escaping.

He inserted the card in the slot and pushed. The wall opened, but the card did not return. We'll never be able to enter this room again, Walter realized without regret. If he could not outwit these two, Mishka and he would never enter any room again.

"Hey! What kinda place is this?" Tonk asked.

"The mouse's den," Walter answered, thinking even as he spoke. What advantage did the room give him? If he only had time. . . .

Time! That's it! It moved quickly in here. An hour compressed itself into just a few minutes. If he could stall until midnight or so.

Then he remembered. At midnight Mishka would become a mouse, and they would shoot her instantly.

And then they would shoot him. Unless. . .

"So where is this mouse?" Honky asked. The gun in his hand did not waver.

"It, it usually comes right after midnight," Walter replied. Another idea began to glimmer.

"Don't try to con us," Tonk warned. "You sure of that?"

"Yes," Walter answered. The plan was taking shape now. "It's, it's my birthday tomorrow. It promised to bring me a present."

"Well, Happy Birthday!" said Honky. "We'll give you a present too, the last one you'll ever get!"

Walter ignored the remark and hurried on. "Actually, he gave me part of it last night, to see if I would like it. It's cheese!"

"Cheese?" Tonk asked.

"Cheese!" Walter repeated. "And I do like it. He said he'd be back tonight with some more. You can't buy it in stores. It's kinda special!"

"A mouse bringing cheese?" Honky wondered. "Ain't that supposed to work the other way? The mouse we're looking for takes things!"

"Yeah!" Tonk added. "Things that ain't his. Things that ain't been paid for, if you get the idea!"

Walter understood, but he kept talking. "This mouse is special too, as I'm sure you know by now. For some reason, he likes me. We've become very close. In fact, I think I know him better than anyone does."

"Bad luck for you!" Tonk replied. He too held a gun, and he held it very aggressively.

Again Walter shivered inwardly, but ignored the remark and hurried on. "It's a wonderful present though! The best cheese ever made! My girlfriend and I ate all but the last piece. We came back to get more, but he hasn't come back yet. He'll be here by midnight! He wouldn't miss my birthday!"

"Bad luck for him too!" said Honky as he glanced at his watch. "It's nearly midnight. We can wait."

Ivon could not wait, not any longer. Something was wrong. He could feel it. Walter and Mishka were in danger! He reached for his phone and punched out a number.

"Miss Pomona Mona?" he asked. "Is Officer Mulholand there?"

"Didn't realize it was so late," Honky remarked as he looked at his watch again. "Don't time just fly when you're having fun? We might let you celebrate your birthday, for maybe ten seconds!"

He grinned. It was not a very nice grin.

Walter ignored it. "Can we eat the cheese too?" he asked.

"You're looking at just a few minutes to live, and all you can think about is having a snack?" Tonk asked. "You're either the coolest or the craziest guy we've ever hit!"

Walter slowly took the cheese from his pocket. "If you ever tasted this, you'd understand," he said.

"I don't understand!" Mulholand complained in the meantime. "First you hide this guy from me, and now you insist that I find him! What's going on here?"

"Just drive!" Ivon urged as the squad car sped toward the library. He could not explain his feeling that Walter and Mishka were in danger, but he knew that at least one *prestupnik,* one criminal, was after them. Why else had they not returned?

"Get there, Herbert!" Pomona Mona urged. She sat between them, holding her skates in one hand and her cat in the other. "If anything happened to Walter, I think poor old Jammer'd just pine away and die of sorrow! Wouldn't you, Jammer?"

The look in Rancid's eyes suggested otherwise, but the cat made no comment.

But Honky and Tonk had plenty to say. "You're trying to pull something on us, but it ain't gonna work!" Tonk exclaimed. "Nobody pulls anything on us! Right, Honky?"

"Right!" Honky agreed. "I'll bet you're trying to con us into taking that cheese from you and eating it. Well, forget it! We're not suckers! It's probably poison!"

Walter broke off a small piece, and the aroma of smoky fruit filled the Bagshott Room. "No," he said. "I don't want you to take it. I want it for myself."

"It does smell kinda good," Tonk admitted. The gun in his hand wavered ever so slightly. Honky licked his lips.

"And it tastes even better!" Walter replied, popping the piece into his mouth. If this works, I'm in for trouble, he thought. But if it doesn't work, then nothing is going to matter any more. He broke off another piece and gave it to Mishka.

"I might poison myself," he said, "but do you think I could poison my girlfriend? Of course, it doesn't matter, since you're not going to eat any of it!"

"Not so fast," cried Honky. "I might try just a bit!"

"Why should I give you any?" Walter asked as innocently as he could. It must be a gift freely given, he remembered. I can't just let them take it.

"You give us the cheese," Honky replied, "and we'll be real nice when we, um, take care of you. Otherwise, we could be very nasty and messy!"

Walter tried his best to sound reluctant. "Well, okay."

He held out the cheese to Honky. "No fair!" Tonk objected. "He always keeps the biggest piece for himself. You divide it."

So Walter divided the last piece as evenly as he could, and the two hit men gobbled it down. "You're right," Honky admitted. "That was the best cheese I ever ate!" He glanced at his watch again. "Midnight already! Happy Birthday, Walter! Time for your present! I'm counting to ten. One. . ."

"Locked!" Mulholland exclaimed as he rattled the library door. "Doesn't look like anyone's in there."

"If you will allow me," Ivon said, and took something from his pocket. Mulholland heard a click, and the door opened.

"How did you do that?" he asked.

"Doesn't matter. I won't be able to do it again. Better have Miss Mona wait in the car. We have to hurry!"

"Four. . . five. . . Hey, Tonk! I feel kinda funny!" The gun in Honky's hand wavered more noticeably.

"So do I!" Tonk answered. "What was in that stuff?"

Walter could feel it too, that same rushing, whirling sensation he had felt on the night he first ate the cheese. This would be no easy transformation for him.

And Mishka, what would happen to her?

"He tricked us, Tonk!" Honky cried as he tried to stand upright. "Shoot him!"

"I can't!" Tonk answered. "Something's happened to my hand! Something's happened, all over me!" His gun also dropped.

Walter felt the weight pressing him down. His own hands were becoming paws again. He dropped on all fours, kicked off his shoes and wriggled his whiskers. Just before he lost his voice, he cried, "Now, Mishka! Get 'em!"

Mishka leaped at Tonk while Walter jumped on Honky. The two hit men were bigger mice, though Walter and Mishka had the advantage of experience. For the moment it was an even fight.

Honky tried to grab for his gun, but Walter pushed him away and then bit down on the outstretched fore-leg as hard as he could. He felt his teeth go through coat, shirt and hide, and then he tasted blood in his mouth for the first time.

A squeak of pain from Tonk told him that Mishka had scored as well. He knew that the two hit-mice were larger, and that eventually their size would make the difference, so he had to end the fight quickly, before Honky and Tonk learned how to handle their new bodies.

"Listen!" Ivon exclaimed. "I hear something! Over there, behind that wall!"

Walter grabbed Honky's gun and held it with both paws. Honky cowered against the wall and tried his best to snarl. Mishka and Tonk were still rolling on the floor. Walter pointed the gun high over everyone's head and pulled the trigger.

BLAMM!

The explosion nearly deafened all four of them. The recoil sent the gun spinning across the room and knocked Walter down. The door to the Bagshott Room flew open and a voice from the outside yelled, "Police! Freeze!"

But none of them did.

Officer Mulholand was prepared for one giant mouse. He might have handled two. But four gigantic mice, each of them completely dressed, were too much. He stared, mouth wide open in amazement. So did Ivon. Then things happened even faster.

Walter and Mishka bolted past Mulholand and Ivon before they could react. Honky also made it by. But as Tonk sprinted past, Mulholand smacked him one behind the ear with his nightstick and laid him out cold on the floor.

"Get after the others!" Mulholand cried. "I'll take care of this one!" He reached for his handcuffs, wondering as he did if they would work on paws.

Ivon reached the main door just as Walter, Mishka and Honky bolted down the front steps. Walter and Mishka raced up the street, while Honky ran the other way. He could not run as fast as Walter and Mishka, but he was too fast for Ivon.

Pomona Mona too had sensed trouble and had her in-line Rollerblades laced on. "Get that one!" Ivon yelled, pointing at Honky. "I'll take the others!"

Pomona Mona needed no urging and Honky was no match. She shot down the street in hot pursuit of the fleeing mouse. At last, she thought, another chance to nail someone and really lay him out! Little sparks flew from the pavement wherever her wheels touched down.

A desperate Honky tried to zigzag as the ex-roller derby star steadily gained on him, but his coat, pants and shoes kept tripping him up. He dodged into an alley, looking for a fire escape, some stairs, something to hide behind, any place where he could be safe for a moment! Pomona Mona swept right in behind him!

He whirled and tried to spring to one side, but she was ready. She dropped a shoulder which caught him in mid-spring, right in the pit of his mousy stomach! Honky slammed into a brick wall, bounced off a garbage can and sprawled unconscious on the pavement.

Pomona Mona picked him up by the scruff of his neck, draped him over her shoulder and skated back up the street. "Too bad nobody has a camcorder," she muttered. "That hit would have made Plays of the Week!"

Meanwhile, Officer Mulholand had handcuffed Tonk's left hind paw to his right front paw and dragged him back to the squad car. "Mulholand to headquarters," he wheezed into the transmitter. "I am investigating four, I repeat, four, giant mice in suspicious clothing."

"Four giant mice? Mulholand, you need to come in for counseling now!" headquarters responded.

"I have one in custody," Mulholand replied triumphantly. "Check that!" he added as he saw Pomona Mona returning with Honky. "We have *two* giant mice in custody!"

"Two giant mice? Mulholand, what is going on there?"

"*Nobody* gets past Pomona Mona!" Mulholand replied.

Ivon was only too happy to let Walter and Mishka escape. He knew they would head for his shop, and he wished them good luck.

The shop was the only safe place Walter knew. What would happen later didn't concern him. Now they had to hide, quickly!

Walter and Mishka rounded the last corner and sprinted for the shop. Then they skidded to a stop and stared.

Ivon's *sladkarnitsa* was gone.

The Street That Really Isn't was there once again.

CHAPTER SEVENTEEN

The Old Woman Again

It was just as Walter had remembered from that night nearly two months before. A narrow alleyway, dimly lit and yet full of shadows, where Ivon's bagel shop had stood just a few hours before. The buildings on either side crowded in on it, as if trying to squeeze it shut.

Mishka was paralyzed by the sight of it. She made tiny, squeaking sounds, and Walter guessed she was asking him how this could happen. He wasn't sure himself. He knew only that the Street had appeared for them, and that they had to enter it.

He gave her a nudge with his nose and she followed him. Once again the buildings crowded closer; and even with his mouse vision, the way ahead was dim and uncertain. Something like a fog seemed to settle over everything, and he did not want to look behind him.

"Keep moving! Keep moving!" he said silently to both Mishka and himself. Like the night when he carried the old woman's packages, the way seemed to stretch on and on. They must have walked several blocks by now.

Or were time and distance measured differently here too?

Once again the building at the end loomed up so suddenly that they nearly ran into it. There was no sign of the old woman, but Walter knew she must be inside, waiting for them. He found the front door and pushed it open.

Mishka was still with him. Walter found himself admiring her courage more than ever. She had only been a full-size human for one day, and already she had been forced to fight for her life against two criminals and then follow him down The Street That Really Isn't, a place that not even a long-term human could explain.

He found the stairs and they began to climb. Walter could not remember how many flights there had been that first time when he had the packages and the old woman had bounded on ahead of him. But he knew they seemed to go on and on forever.

How would he know the right landing? He could see nothing but smooth blank walls and stairs that led from one landing to another to another.

"You'll know when you get there," a voice inside him said. "Just keep on climbing!"

At last he heard a familiar voice call out, "Just one flight more and you'll be at my door!"

Then the stairs ended at a wall that opened inward, much like the door to the Bagshott Room. With his keen mouse eyes, Walter could see someone or something moving in the shadows behind it. He knew it must be the old woman.

"Come in! Come in!" she called. "You must be tired, and there is still so much you need to know!"

Walter stared, but the old woman was still no more than a shadow, just a lighter piece of the darkness in the room. He strained his eyes trying to see better, but everything remained somehow shapeless, like the setting of a dream.

"It's time you know who I really am," the old woman said. "I'm really not anybody, but my name might have been Agnes Bagshott."

Walter looked as surprised as it is possible for a mouse to look. He wanted to speak, to ask her all kinds of questions, but he knew only squeaks would come out. The old woman continued.

"I know you can't speak, Walter," she said, "but you can listen. You can understand. The important thing is that you have passed another test, the most important test of all!"

Walter could listen, all right, but he did not understand. What sort of test had he passed? And what did it mean?

"Let me begin at the beginning," the old woman decided. "That's always a good place to start. You know who my father was, or who he might have been?"

Walter nodded, although he still wasn't sure.

"The professor was a great man who never got around to doing great things," the old woman explained. "I should have been his daughter and carried on all his great work, but he never got around to getting married and having me. That's why I'm not really anybody. I never had the chance."

Walter tried to look puzzled. This was all very strange.

"My brother would have built this building, but he never got the chance to be either. It's on The Street That Really Isn't. Perhaps a better name would be The Street That Might Have Been. There are lots of streets like this one, Walter, but no one gets a chance to see them. No one but you and a very small, select group of others."

A faint glimmer of understanding began to glow in Walter's mind. But why had he been one of the few?

"So I have a job," the old woman continued. "I can't call it my life's work, because I don't really have a life. But I can give these select few a chance at a life, a rewarding life, an exciting life!"

170

Walter wanted to say, "You've certainly done that with me!"

"But, of course," the old woman went on, "you have to earn it. Once a month, no more than that, just before the full moon, I can leave this place and make contact with real people like you."

"But why people like me?" Walter asked silently.

"Why people like you?" the old woman answered as she read his mind. "Because the only people who can see me are those who are like me. People like you, Walter. I give them a chance, if they want to take it."

Walter looked puzzled again.

"They can help me or they can ignore me," the old woman explained. "Most of them ignore me. So many times they ignore me! They live, but they don't have any life in them. A few of them do help. You were one, Walter. So was a penniless Bulgarian immigrant named Ivon."

So that's why he seemed to know so much, Walter thought.

"Ivon had a card like yours, and he helped you as much as I would let him. He wanted to do even more, but I was firm with him. It was up to you to make your own choices, and you did very well."

Walter wrinkled his nose as he tried to think of the choices he had made.

"I gave you two gifts. You gave them both up to help someone else. Yes, you were selfish at times, and you didn't have much choice last night. But you managed to stumble through to success, and that's all we can expect from a human."

The old woman paused and then said, "It may interest you to know that Ivon gave up his card to get into the library to help you. His other gift was an ability to go without sleep."

Aha! Walter thought. So that's how he could do it!

"He is losing that too, but he will soon have a partner to help him. I think you know her, Walter. Her name is Cindy."

So that's why she wouldn't go out with me, Walter realized. But he felt happy for both of them.

"Walter, you gave up your cheese to give Mishka a chance to become human. She will be, and so will you, most of the time. You chose well when you chose the Bagshott Room."

Walter wanted to reply that he didn't have much of a choice.

"You gave out and ate the last of the cheese in there to save Mishka and to bring two criminals to justice."

Walter shivered again. He had forgotten about Honky and Tonk. Had they managed to escape as well?

"They did not get away," the old woman reassured him. "Officer Mulholand captured one of them, and your landlady caught the other. Did quite a number on him, in fact!"

She paused. Walter tried to catch a glimpse of her in the dimness, but shadows were all he could see.

"Enchanted cheese has powerful effects when it's eaten out of spite and meanness," she continued. "Those two will remain as they are for the rest of their lives. They did some terrible things as humans. Maybe as mice they'll be better."

I doubt it, Walter thought. But what's going to happen to us? We both ate the cheese in there too.

"You'll be human again when the night is over," the old woman said. "You'll still become a mouse on the three nights of the full moon, but you'll have someone to share the experience."

Walter felt Mishka nuzzle up against him. He wanted to put an arm around her, but all he had were paws.

"Mishka will also be human, except for those three nights. The rest of your lives will be up to you. But remember the professor and live them! Don't put things off. Someday you will run out of tomorrows and have only yesterdays."

Walter and Mishka both nodded.

"You might begin by thanking Officer Mulholand and Pomona Mona," the old woman suggested. "They both did a lot for you."

Well yes, they caught the two hit-mice, Walter thought. But what else did they do?

"If Mulholand had not parked his car in front of Ivon's that night, you would not have been in that yard to save Mishka. And if Pomona Mona had not kept a cat, you would never have met her. And if Rancid, as you call him, had simply pounced and gobbled, instead of toying with Mishka. . ."

Walter got the idea.

"Sometimes those who seem to be your enemies don't turn out that way. Remember that!"

Walter nodded. He would buy a catnip toy for Rancid. Maybe even some breath mints.

"It will be morning soon, and Ivon will want to open his shop again. You'll need to leave The Street That Really Isn't before daybreak. You've lost the cheese and your card, but you have something better now."

Walter wasn't quite sure what she meant by that.

"You have your future," the old woman told him. "You don't need my help anymore. Mishka, so do you."

Walter knew the interview was over. He nodded and started for the door. "You've been a very satisfactory client," the old woman called after him. "Very satisfactory indeed!"

Once again it was only two or three quick flights back down to the alley, and they soon saw the lights of the main street up ahead. As they neared the end of The Street That Really Isn't, Walter felt his forepaws come up off the pavement. Soon he was standing erect.

He glanced at a front paw and saw that it was now a hand. Mishka was human too. They were both barefoot, and their clothes were rumpled and torn from last night's fight. Walter's cheek was badly scratched, and Mishka was badly mauled.

They walked out of the narrow alley just as the sun broke over the eastern rim of the sky. Sparrows called to each other from telephone lines and building awnings.

A very nice day was beginning, a very nice day for both of them.

When they looked behind them, The Street That Really Isn't had vanished in the morning light. Ivon's shop stood where it always had, and the smell of things baking reached their mouse-keen noses. Mishka took Walter's hand and squeezed it.

"I'm hungry," she said. "Let's go get a bagel!"

The End

Grateful acknowledgment is hereby given to the Oregon State Library, Talking Book & Braille Services, and especially Nancy Stewart, David Hyde and Brian McBee, for their help in the preparation of this book. I also want to thank the Oregon Arts Commission, and especially Nancy Lindburg, for their faith in me; and Eugenia Marinova, of the Embassy of the Republic of Bulgaria, for giving Ivon a voice. And, of course, to Mom, who always said I could do it.